A WARLOCK IN WHITBY

Book Two of
THE WHITBY SERIES

Also by Robin Jarvis

THE DEPTFORD MICE trilogy
   The Dark Portal
   The Crystal Prison
   The Final Reckoning

THE DEPTFORD HISTORIES series
   The Alchymist's Cat

THE WHITBY series
   The Whitby Witches

A WARLOCK
IN WHITBY

Book Two of
THE WHITBY SERIES

Written and Illustrated
by Robin Jarvis

E R

First published in Great Britain in 1992
by Simon & Schuster Young Books

Reprinted in 1992, 1993 and 1994

Photoset in Palatino in North Wales by
Derek Doyle & Associates, Mold, Clwyd.
Printed and bound in Great Britain by
The Guernsey Press Co. Ltd, Guernsey, Channel Islands.

Simon & Schuster Young Books
Campus 400
Maylands Avenue
Hemel Hempstead HP2 7EZ

British Library Cataloguing in Publication Data available

ISBN 0 7500 1202 1
ISBN 0 7500 1203 X (Pbk)

CONTENTS

Whitby slept: the autumn darkness in which it cosily huddled was calm and still. Not a Christian soul ventured outside the snug caverns of bedclothes and the only shadows that roamed the dim narrow lanes were those of cats who prowled into the blackest recesses of night in search of prey and passion. A solemn and contented peace lay heavily over all.

A mild breeze stirred the midnight waters of the harbour into wave after gentle wave that rolled lazily up the shore only to return languid, sighing and spent. Save for the drugged, murmuring voice of the sea, Whitby was silent.

Upon the East Cliff, the silhouette of the abbey challenged the domain of the frosty moon, spearing the night with the jags of its ruin, more beautiful in its crumbling decay than ever it had been at the height of its glory.

Between broken pillars and gaping windows, the soft breeze moved, touching and stroking the weathered walls whose stones had withstood war and winter and become charged with the power that dwells in all ancient things.

But further along the abbey plain, just clear of the ragged shadows, the quiet calm was about to be broken.

Before the breeze, wild grasses bowed, slowly sweeping into a dry expanse which mimicked the rippling water of the harbour. Yet beneath the swaying, seeding heads the sleep of uncounted years was finally coming to an end.

Presently the soil began to pulse, bulging upwards as if it were alive. Then the grass parted as its thick, knotted tangle of roots stretched and ripped apart.

There came a frantic and urgent scrabbling in the hole that had appeared and then it was through!

Into the cold night a hideous claw emerged. The silver moonlight glistened on the barbed hooks as they tore away the soil to widen the fissure. Soon a pale, scale-covered arm reached up and thrashed wildly at the ground. The promise of release was the force which drove it. To be out in the wide world once more was its sole intention, away from the cloying chains of slumber and oblivion. Up, up out of the suffocating earth it came – worming and pushing until at last it was able to haul itself from the pit.

A vile, misshapen creature threw its hump-backed body upon the grass, gargling a mixture of phlegm and soil. The exertions of its escape were almost too much. For a while it lay wheezing and choking, its gills jerked open and shut, waiting for the old instincts to re-establish themselves. The underbelly heaved violently, gulping the sweet air down into forgotten lungs – filling them once more. Only when the breaths became less laboured did it think to look at its surroundings.

At once it sprang to its deformed and webbed feet, the stumpy legs trembling unsteadily at the effort. If there had ever been a demon to plague the fishes of the sea then surely this was it. A more repellent creature there never was. Two large round eyes stared out from the head, glowing with the sickly luminescence of those who dwell in the deepmost regions of the ocean where sunlight never penetrates. Up at the ageless stars these eyes glared, before swivelling round to fix on the abbey. The shining eyes blinked and three rows of needle-like teeth were bared and ground together.

The fish demon whirled about and beheld for the first time in over a thousand years the estuary of the river Esk. The world had changed much since those baleful eyes had last lit upon the settlement of Whitebi. Now, instead of the few huts that had sheltered under the protection of the cliff and the monastery, the banks of the river were crammed with buildings, and harsh orange lights blazed in the streets.

A horrible gurgle issued from the creature's throat as it pattered forward for a better view. The reeking species of mankind had smothered the land it had known and the fin on the top of its head fanned open as it hissed its hatred. The stale memories were flooding back now and the confusion was slowly clearing.

The years peeled away and before its luminous eyes the fish demon – last of the savage Mallykin race – remembered it all.

The strings of lights round the harbour blurred and flickered, becoming the blazing torches that had pursued it to the cliff back then. And there *she* stood, the veiled woman-beast. How boldly she had cornered it and how fearsome were the cries of the villagers who gathered behind her. The flames of their burning brands were painful to look on, yet even more deadly was the sound of her cold, ringing voice. Cringing to the ground, the creature dropped the limp remains of its meal; somewhere it heard another of the wretches cry out and then the staff was raised and came crashing down. After that it knew only the black emptiness of the earth as it gaped open to swallow it.

How many years had passed until the term of its imprisonment had come to an end? How many centuries had painfully stretched by?

The breeze that ruffled its fins was chill and the fish demon slowly returned to the present. With narrowing eyes, it backed slowly from the bitter lights of Whitby. All was lost now, how could it survive in a world that was so filled with enemies? Miserably and with a waddling hop, it hurried from the grievous sight.

Suddenly it froze – it was not alone upon the abbey plain. Amongst the grasses some other creature was prowling; a small, warm blooded creature.

A growl came from the Mallykin's stomach as it realized how ravenous it was. No food had passed into its gullet for longer than it could imagine and now the desire for fresh meat overwhelmed it, brushing aside all other concerns. The mouth lolled open and a pink, pointed tongue drooled over the chin. With nostrils questing the air, it searched for the animal in the grass. There – it could sense the rapid beating of a tiny heart.

With a frightful yell, the fish demon leapt forward. A horrific squeal rang out, then the creature disappeared into the night to devour the still wriggling meal in some darker, less open place.

1

AFTER THE WITCH

Whitby mornings are a constant. Nothing changes. Each one begins with the shriek of gulls and the return of fishing boats to the harbour, followed by the auction of the catch on the quayside. Today was no exception.

The hours moved slowly on. Bed-and-Breakfasts sizzled with eggs and bacon whilst shopkeepers lifted shutters to await the first customers of the day. Gradually the traffic on the small roads increased and the autumn holiday makers braved the keen November wind muffled in anoraks and tightly wound scarves.

With a gentle shudder, the morning train slid into the town. Out poured the children commuting to school from Ruswarp and Sleights. Along the platform they jostled one another, tugging at bags and duffle hoods, testing themselves on French vocabulary for the lesson later that day and hastily swapping answers to maths homework. After the children had barged and hurried out of the train the other passengers alighted and set off towards the barrier. There were those late for work, several day-trippers, a well-groomed young woman carrying a briefcase, a pair of rucksack-laden walkers who staggered under the weight of their canvas burdens, grumbling at one another for forgetting something vital and, lastly, a short, plump woman carrying a large sketchpad, a box of watercolours and a fold-up seat.

This colourful stampede surged away from the train, eager to be out of the confines of the station. Each one of them filled with wildly differing thoughts, from the antiquities of New Zealand contained in the museum, to the best place to get a cup of tea. But no, not all hurried down the platform; there, in one of the carriages, a single figure remained.

With deliberate slowness the man collected his luggage together; one battered suitcase and a small travelling bag. He stepped from the train and the morning sun fell upon his face.

He was a dark-haired man with a wiry, unkempt beard that framed his sunburned face. He wore no overcoat to keep out the wind, only a short tweed jacket that had seen better days. The elbows had at one time been patched with ovals of brown leather but one of these now wagged in the wind like a rude tongue. On most people this, combined with the slightly old-fashioned shirt, the collar of which was frayed and rather grubby, would have aroused feelings of sympathy or good-natured humour – but not on this particular gentleman; no one would have dared to laugh at him.

His eyes were like pieces of midnight, jewels of darkness in which no glint of day ever shone. Casually he put down his luggage and gazed after the last of his fellow passengers as they struggled to leave the station. Those deep dark eyes roamed from one person to another until at last they came to rest on the retreating figure of the smart young woman with the briefcase.

Just as light can vary from a dim glow to a blinding intensity, the same is true of darkness. For now those eyes blazed blacker than ever before as they lingered over the woman's finely sculpted form, following the outline of her slim shape and drinking in the gold of her hair.

Emma Hitchin, late for her job at the solicitor's office, shivered unconsciously, shuddering with a feeling that was more than mere cold. All thoughts of the apology she was carefully constructing for that miserable old Mr Hardcorn and his sour-faced son flew from her mind. At her shoulder blades that chill came stabbing in, tugging and searching. Curious, she turned her blonde head and her own hazel eyes caught sight of the bearded man standing by the train.

A look of amusement formed on her lips, but this quickly melted. There was something unusual about the man – he was certainly by no stretch of the imagination handsome, but he possessed a certain powerful charm and she found herself holding her breath under his continual gaze. Those impenetrable shadows beneath his brows beat out at her and the colour rose in her cheeks. Her lips curled into a girlish smile and the blood thumped in her temples.

The man returned the smile, then followed it up with a polite and formal bow. But all the time his eyes held her prisoner. For a few moments more he kept her bound to him and then she was released.

Emma reeled backwards as he dismissed her and the chains of his will left her. Flustered and sweating, she clutched at the collar of her blouse then, with one final, fearful glance at the stranger, she fled from the station.

Alone on the platform, the man grinned. Delving into the pocket of his tatty jacket he brought out a slim gold case. Taking a cigarette he struck a match and cupped his hands round his mouth. The sheltered flame, brought so close to his face, made no reflection in those raven-black eyes.

3

Deep he drew on the cigarette, inhaling the smoke and hissing it out through his lips until a thick, ethereal cloud had gathered about him. A difficult and dangerous trial lay ahead. He knew that the next few days were to be the greatest test of his cunning and endurance. He had prepared for every eventuality, however, and when this ordeal was over all the risks he had chanced would prove to have been worthwhile. Silently he reprimanded himself for indulging his ego back then. For the moment he must not attract attention – his enemies were everywhere. If they knew he had returned to England all would be lost. For that reason secrecy was paramount, but if his researches and suspicions were correct, then it would not be for long.

The nicotine fog stirred when he threw the cigarette to the ground and crushed it beneath his patent leather shoe. He was ready.

As the smoke billowed and dispersed around him, he moved to return the cigarette case to his pocket. In the bright, morning sunshine the words engraved on the gold flashed and glowed up into his bearded face.

> To my darling Nathaniel,
> *obediently* yours
> – ROSELYN.

The man's thin mouth twisted suddenly and the shimmering gold shone upon his teeth, discolouring and staining them. For a fraction of a second his face was a distorted vision of evil and cruelty and a cold chuckle resounded in his throat.

Nathaniel Crozier: historian, philanderer, warlock, high priest of the Black Sceptre, and the unseen hand behind countless unsolved burglaries of religious relics from all round the world. So infamous was he that some had dedicated their lives to tracking him down and putting an end to "the most evil man on

Earth". Yet here he was, he who always worked through others, he who never risked himself had hazarded much just to step on British soil once more. The widower of the late Rowena Cooper had arrived in Whitby at last.

* * *

"Missing Cats Mystery" read the headline of the *Gazette*. Since the beginning of October many pets had disappeared. At first, when rabbits had been wrenched from their hutches, the culprit was believed to be a fox – or perhaps that large dog which had been heard roaming the streets in the dead of night. But no one had heard that hollow, baying voice for some time now and when the number of missing animals continued to rise, suspicions were turned elsewhere. The popular theory of the moment was that an unscrupulous furrier was to blame – it was not unusual for cat skins to be used in the fur trade and as most of the vanished Tiddles and Toms had been fine specimens with luxuriant coats this seemed most likely. Cat owners had become extremely careful when they put their loved ones out at night. Some even tied them to long pieces of string to prevent them straying too far. The indignant cat-calls could be heard all over town when the time came for the poor pusses to be yanked back indoors.

Perhaps it was this concern for the well-being of the family pet that first started it all. One thing was certainly true however – Whitby had changed. For whatever reason, the seaside town was not the same place. Whereas, only a month ago, the inhabitants would greet each other with a friendly wave or stop in the street for a chat, now they merely nodded a terse acknowledgement. Over both the West Cliff and the East there was a brooding tension and a general sense of anxiety filled the hearts of everyone.

Norman Gregson lay slumped, stuffed in the only armchair capable of accommodating him. Over the bass drum of his stomach a pair of black braces strained, circumnavigating a bulk greater than they had been made for. Mr Gregson had gobbled enough breakfast to fill a giant walrus and that was precisely what he looked like. This most unpleasant and laziest of the Black Horse regulars had washed the four rounds of toast, two fried eggs, frazzled rashers of bacon and gristly sausages down with a bottle of stout. This was then followed by two pieces of bread which his wife, Joan, in a rare moment of domesticity, had fried in the same fat as everything else. Now he snorted and wheezed in his sleep, grease still dribbling from his open mouth and congealing on his pink, fleshy chin.

This contented, snoring oaf had only two passions in life, namely the aforementioned Black Horse, where the old joke was that he ran from one nag to another, and the vegetable patch in the back garden. Between rows of onions and cabbages Norman was a different person. All the tenderness he denied his wife and the world was lavished upon his darling, uncritical vegetables. Within the well-weeded confines of his very own realm, and safely screened by the lattice of runner beans, his heavy bulk could rest, away from the tart tongue of Mrs Gregson and the unfinished jobs in the house.

But that morning the armchair had his undivided attention because his harpy of a wife was pegging out the washing. On such days it was impossible to seek sanctuary outdoors. With sheets and nightgowns flapping and that carping voice screeching like fingernails down a blackboard it was better to pass the time unconscious. In his dreams his onions were the size of footballs and rosettes smothered the

garden like a forest of sunflowers.

A large, wet smile creased his round face and he uttered whimpers of pleasure when one of his cabbages was so huge that he actually hollowed it out and turned it into another potting shed. People came from miles around just to look at this marvel and there were rumours of a knighthood in the offing. All over Whitby the church bells were ringing in his honour and he swelled with paternal pride.

The doorbell rang again. Norman shifted uneasily, the empty bottle in his hand escaped from his plump fingers, rolled down the hillside of his belly and dropped on to the floor.

"NORMAN!" came a voice from the garden loud enough to alert ships at sea. "Norman! Answer the flaming door!"

The giant cabbage suddenly sprouted wheels, became a caravan and trundled far away. Mr Gregson grunted then woke up.

Once more the doorbell jingled angrily. He drew his fingers over the high, polished dome of his head, yawned and blinked.

"Get that! You big dollop of lard!" shrieked the klaxon from the garden.

Norman pulled a face and swore under his breath. "Shut up, you silly old mare," he mumbled drowsily. "I'm getting it."

Stretching, and imperilling the braces even further, he hauled himself from the chair. However, before he went to the front door, he did exactly what his wife would have done – he peered through the net curtain.

"Who's that then?" he grumbled, staring at the bearded man on the step. "What's in them cases? If it's brushes he's after sellin' he's had that!"

Unfortunately Norman was not as deft a lace-twitcher as Mrs Gregson for the stranger saw him.

Two dark eyes turned to stare at the round face in the window and for a moment Norman felt an inexplicable twinge of fear. Hastily he withdrew and shuffled to the door to see what the nuisance wanted.

"Well?" he demanded throwing the door open wide to intimidate the man by the size of his stomach. "What does yer want? I ain't gonna buy nowt, an' if'n it's charity yer after I don't hold wi' it!"

"My name is Crozier, Mr Gregson," came the soft reply, "Nathaniel Crozier. And there's no need to worry, I don't believe in charity either."

" 'Ere," Norman put in, "how comes yer knowed my name? From the Social Security, are yer? Wastin' my time snoopin' round askin' questions – it's me back an' me heart, Doctor says. Unfit for work I am, I told 'em before – now get out of it!"

But the stranger remained on the step and when he next spoke his voice was calm yet insistent. "Mr Gregson," he said, "why don't you invite me in – just for a moment?"

"Invite you in?" Norman repeated with a sharp laugh. "Beggar off!"

Still the man did not move, he stared fixedly at the huge bulk in the doorway and took a step closer. "Ask me inside," he said again.

Mr Gregson had had enough. He didn't like the look of this weird bloke. That was the trouble with living in a holiday resort, it attracted all manner of peculiar characters, especially in the off-peak season. He made to shut the door in the man's face but at that moment his wife emerged from the garden to see what all the fuss was about and pounded up the hallway.

"Who is it?" she squawked, unable to see beyond her husband.

"No one," Norman replied.

"Shift yerself and let me see!" Joan Gregson

growled, grabbing two handfuls of her husband's girth and pushing him aside. When she had managed to squeeze by, she looked at Nathaniel Crozier blankly. "Who did yer say it were?" she hissed back at Norman.

"Nobody, just some feller who won't clear off."

Joan assumed her natural stance of folded arms with eyebrows raised. "Well what does he want?"

"God knows!"

"Ruddy hopeless you are!" she snorted, clipping Norman round the ear with the back of her hand. "Couldn't yer be bothered to find out? My God but you're idle!"

A faint smile flickered over Nathaniel's face as the pair of them squabbled. This was more like it – he could easily manage Mrs Gregson.

"Dear lady," he began, "I was only trying to tell your husband ..."

"And you can keep yer flamin' nose out!" she snapped back. "Who the 'ell do you think ..." Mrs Gregson's voice faltered, the eyes of the man were so dark – she had never seen anything like them before. A curious tingling sensation caused her to shiver under the scrutiny of those lovely eyes and she found it quite impossible to remember what she had been about to say. "I ... I'm sorry," was all she could manage.

Nathaniel smiled more broadly and the woman felt her face flush. "Good morning to you," he went on. "I am afraid you must forgive me if I stare, dear, dear lady."

Joan suppressed a girlish giggle and fidgeted with the clothes-peg she still clutched in one hand. Whoever the gentleman might be, he was certainly charming.

"May I come in?" he asked her, and to the beguiled Mrs Gregson it seemed the most natural thing in the world to invite this wonderful stranger into her house. To deny him entry would be unthinkably rude and impolite. Her face lit up, glad beyond measure to think that someone as fascinating as this would want to spend time with her.

"No you can't!" came the gurgling response from her husband, who was still lurking behind her.

Joan whirled round and cracked him on the head once more. "In yer chair!" she spat. "If I want to have visitors, I flamin' will!"

Norman rubbed his head, glaring at her murderously. He was amazed that she had fallen for that load of corny rubbish, but when his wife wanted something there was nothing he could do to stop her. "Please yerself!" he growled, making for the armchair.

Mrs Gregson turned back to the man on the doorstep – her doorstep. "You'll have to excuse my husband," she apologized in the voice she reserved for the telephone and the hairdresser. "He were never brought up proper and don't know how to behave with company."

"I understand," beamed Nathaniel, "now where were we?"

"You were coming in."

"Ah yes," he said and there was a touch of uncertainty in his voice. He glanced quickly down to where the step met the doorframe then cleared his throat and began more brightly, "So, am I invited?"

"Course you are."

"Then say it."

"Please, come in."

The smile on Nathaniel's face faded and was replaced by a repugnant expression of triumph and scorn. He stepped arrogantly over the threshold of the Gregson house and put his luggage down in the hallway as if claiming the dwelling for his own.

It was a dingy place, the last lick of paint having been reluctantly daubed over the walls nine years ago and that was a drab biscuit colour. Cheap prints in even cheaper frames were the only decoration in the dreary hall, apart from a gaudy brass clock set in a picture of Big Ben, and Nathaniel allowed a sneer to cross his face. The pretence was over now, he had achieved what he wanted.

Mrs Gregson, however was still oblivious to the drastic change that had come over her charming guest. She sailed into the parlour eager to show off her home.

"In here," she called encouragingly, this was quickly followed by a whispered, "and you'd better behave!" to her husband.

With his hands in his pockets Nathaniel strolled into the room. He glanced round at the China dogs that cluttered the mantelpiece and smirked.

"What about a nice cup of tea?" Joan asked, straightening the pile of gardening magazines by her husband's chair.

"Nice?" echoed Nathaniel ironically. "And how do you measure whether anything is 'nice'?"

"It's a new packet," she answered, mystified at his remark. "If you don't want tea, we've coffee – there's some Garibaldis too if you like."

"No there ain't," her husband chipped in, "them's all gone."

"Pig!" she mouthed at him before turning back to Nathaniel. "Well what about some nice fig rolls – I know we've some of those, Norman don't like them."

Nathaniel Crozier threw back his head and laughed – his contempt now plain to see. "There's that word again!" he roared. "Do you realize how ridiculous you are, you stupid hag? 'Nice'! Is that the only way you can describe anything? What about 'desirable', 'tantalizing', 'insatiable'?"

Both Joan and Norman looked at him in astonishment.

"No," he continued with a shake of his head, "they're too passionate for your pallid tastes aren't they?" He gestured to the tacky ornaments around the fireplace, the coasters on the coffee table that depicted London landmarks and the striped, beige curtains. "Is this hideous litter really what you term 'nice'? You pathetic, tiny minded creatures. I had forgotten how witless people like you could be."

"'Ere!" erupted Norman from the armchair. "Who are you callin' names? Get out!"

Nathaniel ignored him but said to his wife, "You have a spare room here I believe. Have it made ready and take my luggage up for me."

This was too much for Mr Gregson. He dragged himself out of the chair faster than he had moved in a long time shouting, "Right! Your feet ain't gonna touch the floor, sunshine!"

He caught hold of Nathaniel's coat but the man whirled round and the blackness of his eyes stabbed out at him. "Get back in your chair!" he commanded. "I am in control now – return to your sty, you swine, before I lose my patience! Sit!"

Norman swayed unsteadily, the force behind that voice was unbearable, it fell on him like a great wall collapsing and there was nothing he could do to withstand it. Before he realized what he was doing, Mr Gregson sank back into the armchair and did not move again.

"Norman!" wailed his wife running over to him. "What's the matter, is it your heart? Speak to me!"

"He cannot," Nathaniel told her coldly, "I have paralysed him – the idiot, almost as odious as yourself, who would have thought there would be such a matching pair as you two in such a small town as this."

Mrs Gregson was bewildered. What had happened to the man? She had thought ... but that foolishness was over now. She brushed the hair from her face and shook her husband one more time. He was like a rag doll, only the beating of his heart when she pressed her ear to his chest told her that he was alive.

"Who are you?" she asked looking up at Nathaniel. "Why have you done this? What is it you want?"

"My name is Crozier," he replied, "I told your husband but he was too stupid to listen. I have already made my requirements known to you – a spare room for a few days, that should be long enough."

"Long enough for what?"

He did not answer her but looked at his watch, "Come now Mrs Gregson, surely you don't want to irritate me like your husband did? You need to be seen around the town or people will grow suspicious. However, if you want to be difficult, a suitable arrangement can be contrived without much inconvenience to myself but with much pain and suffering for you, I'm afraid."

Joan glanced at her husband whose eyes were wide and staring. He looked dreadful, like one who stared death full in the face. "No," she murmured slowly, "I won't be difficult. The spare room's this way."

She led Nathaniel back to the hall where she picked up his luggage and toiled up the stairs with it. On the landing she pushed open a door and showed him into the bedroom beyond.

"This was our son Peter's," she explained nervously. "It's been empty since he married and moved to Huddersfield. I always keep it aired though."

Nathaniel brushed past her and strode to the window.

"Not a very good view, I'm afraid," she said

wringing her hands in case that mattered, "the cliff rises so steep at the back of the garden, you can't see a thing other than what next-door are doing in theirs."

The man stared down out of the window. Mrs Gregson was quite right, you could see into the garden next door. He grinned to himself. For there, with a trowel in her hand, busily digging the weeds from a herbaceous border was a white-haired old woman.

"Excellent," he whispered before turning back to his frightened hostess. "The room is most satisfactory – I shall be perfectly happy here."

2

CONFRONTATIONS

Midday had come and gone and when Nathaniel set out to climb the one hundred and ninety-nine steps which scaled the cliff it was getting on for two o'clock.

At the summit he paused, not to catch his breath for he was remarkably fit for his forty-two years. No, he wanted to survey the town as his wife had done. To try and imagine what was running through her twisted and treacherous mind when she had stood there. "Oh Roselyn," he said quietly, "why did you try to break free? Without me you were nothing, it was my skill which released your true nature, my fine, dark, death-hound."

He tutted at the bustling streets below, where ignorant and unimportant people went about their humdrum existences. How he loathed such places. He despised those tiny narrow lanes surrounded by all those twee cottages. The sight repelled him, Whitby seemed so small and insignificant, yet here his wife had met her end. She who had faced untold peril in the remotest regions of the world and had been priestess under him in all their sinister ventures. It was difficult to believe and he wondered at it. "How could anyone in this seedy backwater have vanquished you?" he breathed. "Were you so hungry for freedom that you were blind to all else? What was

16

it that caught you unawares – who was it?"

Silently he turned from the scene, the bleak November wind coursing through his hair and tugging at the loose leather patch at his elbow. Surely he wasn't feeling grief at Roselyn's demise? It was an unusual sensation and it surprised him, until of course he realized that what he felt was annoyance. She had been useful – and to find a suitable replacement would take valuable time.

Shrugging off this pensive mood, he took the lane that ran behind the abbey and made for the next target on his itinerary.

The derelict house was ugly and shabby, the large window at the front was boarded up and weeds choked the garden path. It looked as though no one had lived there for years. Nathaniel examined the rotting gate and read out the name. "The Hawes." This was the place.

Here his wife, under the alias Rowena Cooper, had lived but the spell she had woven over the fabric of the building had perished with her and it had fallen back into its grim slovenliness. Maybe here there would be a clue as to what had happened to her. He pushed open the gate and the hinges groaned a high-pitched protest.

Nathaniel hesitated. He had heard a noise above the squealing metal. The sound had come from the back of the house and he waited as the feverish clattering grew louder.

"You stay still, young lady!" came a stern voice. "I've had enough of this, it'll be a piece of string for you like every other cat round here. I'm not Tilly you know – I shan't put up with this rebellious behaviour! There, what a disagreeable hole to be sure. Why you keep on coming back is beyond me – just you behave from now on ... Oh! Good afternoon."

From around the corner of the house an old lady

appeared. A ghost of a smile twitched over Nathaniel's face – it was the Gregsons' neighbour. He had not expected to meet her quite so soon but there was nothing he could do to avoid it now.

Alice Boston, a blustering ninety-two year old, marched up the weed-throttled pathway. She was a comical sight; a sage-green tweed cloak was draped around her shoulders and upon her woolly head, perched at a precarious angle and covered in cobwebs, was a shapeless brown hat. When she blinked her eyes disappeared within the wrinkles that circled them and as she walked the spare flesh beneath her chin swung from side to side.

"Dear me," she called sheepishly, "it really is very dusty in there. Terrible neglect – disgraceful."

Nathaniel watched with some amusement as she drew near and then said, "Is this your house?"

Miss Boston looked horrified at the suggestion. "Heavens no!" she declared puckering her face up at the very idea. "I live just off Church Street." The man simply stared at her and she realized how it must look to him. "Forgive me," she cried, "I understand now, you must be wondering what I was doing in there."

"I have to confess to a certain amount of curiosity," he replied. "Why would anyone like you go crawling through the dirt in such a wretched place as this."

"Oh, Eurydice!" she said flatly as if that explained everything. "Look here she is, the confounded animal." From the folds of her cloak she brought out a disgruntled looking cat which only possessed three legs. "Always taking off and scuttling to this hideous ruin." Miss Boston rattled on. "Not the most amenable of felines I'm afraid, I really don't see how Tilly put up with her – Matilda Droon that is, or was. She used to own Eurydice you understand, until she passed on. Oh my dear chap, you look quite bemused

– am I making myself at all clear? It really is most confusing, I suppose. Well, suffice to say that I have now taken charge of this little madam and her three latest offspring, although the first action I felt duty-bound to undertake was a visit to the veterinarian. She didn't like that I can tell you – no more litters for her, thank the Lord."

"I can see you are kept on your toes," observed Nathaniel. "But what an awful place to have to search through."

Miss Boston nodded and the hat lurched a little further down the side of her head. "Oh most certainly," she agreed.

"I don't suppose anyone has lived here for many years," he put in.

"On the contrary," she fiercely corrected, her chins wobbling adamantly, "only two months ago it was inhabited. Why I even had afternoon tea there! It was most certainly cosy enough then, I can assure you."

"Then what could have happened in two months to bring it to this sorry state?"

"I doubt if you would believe me young man. You'd only think I was a dotty old woman imagining things – most people do you know."

Nathaniel turned the power of his smile on her. "I'm not that young," he began, "and you're not that old."

Miss Boston clucked like a happy chicken, tucked Eurydice back into her cloak, leaned forward and looked from right to left in case anyone else was listening. "Well," she said excited to have an audience for her story, "the last owner of the house was not all she pretended to be. Totally mad she was and wicked to the core. I could tell you a few tales about that one which would curl your hair! Never has Whitby been host to a more evil person and she almost destroyed everything."

CONFRONTATIONS

The old lady's face changed and an expression of fear and dread stole over her as she remembered that dark time.

"What became of this person?" asked Nathaniel softly.

"She ... she died."

"How?"

"The tower. It collapsed."

"Explain!"

Miss Boston stared up at the man, he was almost shouting. Why was he so interested in Rowena Cooper? A terrible drowsiness began to creep into the old lady's muscles and he demanded once more that she tell him.

"I tricked her, manoeuvred her backwards in time to a point when ..."

Suddenly the cat beneath the cloak began to struggle again and one of its claws snagged Miss Boston's skin. It was like a pin bursting a bubble. Nathaniel's control was banished from her mind as the sharp pain raked down her arm.

The old lady was free. She shook herself and shivered, wondering what it was she had been about to say. Then she recalled what had already been said – Miss Boston was appalled. Why had she been so careless? How could she have spoken to a total stranger about those matters? Taking a deep breath she reprimanded herself and stuck out one of her chins defiantly.

"I'm terribly sorry," she said, rubbing her arm and looking at her watch. "I must get back home – the children will be out of school soon and wanting their tea. Excuse me."

Nathaniel simply smiled at her, then opened the gate. "No doubt we shall meet again," he told her.

Miss Boston slipped by him. Her gabbling tongue had unsettled her and she had grown suspicious of this charming stranger. All she wanted to do was get smartly away from him in case she let anything else slip. "I'm afraid we probably shan't," she declared, "meet again – I mean. Not for a while anyway – Bother!"

A corner of her cloak had snagged on a nail and she fumbled with it in agitation. Nathaniel went to her assistance.

"It would seem the house is reluctant to let you leave," he laughed.

"Devil take the house!" fumed Miss Boston impatiently, "And Devil take this gate because I *am* leaving – leaving Whitby as a matter of fact! There! Oh blow, it's made a little hole."

"Leaving Whitby?" Nathaniel murmured. "For good?"

Miss Boston stared at him. What did she have to go and tell him that for? "No," she said with caution, "I shall only be gone for about a week. Tomorrow I leave for London." There was a pause, the man obviously wanted to know more – why should he, the nosey … "An old friend of mine is ill, you see," she found herself saying, "not expected to survive the week. Poor Patricia, such a waste."

She clicked her tongue as if switching the troublesome instrument off, then gave Nathaniel one last look. With a nod she bade him farewell and set off down the lane, hitching Eurydice under her arm.

The man turned back to the house and frowned.

* * *

The tide was on the turn and the afternoon drawing to a close when the bell finally rang and the primary school children poured out of the gates where mothers waited for the younger ones. In one quarter there was a flurry of paper as the results from the afternoon's art lesson were held aloft in triumph. There was laughter, a game of "Tick" spontaneously commenced, someone bounced a tennis ball along the playground and a group of girls spoke in hallowed whispers of ponies and expensive dolls.

Only one child was alone. Amongst all the cheerful, carefree crowd he had no one to meet or talk with. He was never invited back to anyone's house to play or have tea. Nobody ever kicked the football in his direction and when he walked by a group at break-time he would hear them snigger. In the playground he was always the solitary figure leaning against the wall, watching the others having fun and playing games. No one liked him, in fact there was something about the child that frightened them.

When he had first arrived at the beginning of term they had tried to make friends with him, but he said such odd, disturbing things that they soon learnt to leave him be. Lately, however, several of the older ones had started to pick on him and two in particular had begun to make his life a misery. It was the same wherever he went – he was a freak, the others knew and so did he.

"You've got the Laurenson touch!" shrieked a girl involved in the game of "Tick". "You're 'It' now!" she squealed to the child she had caught. "You're the loony – Ben, Ben can't catch me!"

"Ssshh!" someone hissed. "He's over there!"

Ben turned to look at them. They were eight years old, the same as him – the girl, Mandy Littleton, was in his class. She gaped at him for a second then giggled and pelted away, screaming his name in ridicule at the top of her shrill voice. Ben pushed through the crowd gathered at the gates, he cast one bitter look at the parents still waiting for their children and ran up the lane.

There was someone he could turn to, someone

who would understand – apart from his sister and Aunt Alice she was his only friend.

By the shore, the failing daylight glimmered over the moving waters and long shadows stretched down the sand. Upon one of the boulders, beneath the cliffs, a solitary figure sat gazing out to the darkening horizon where sea met sky.

Nelda's eyes remained fixed upon that distant rim of the world, straining through the gathering dusk until it was too dark to see, even for an aufwader. Eventually she covered her face with her hands and sighed.

She was a strange-looking creature, youngest of the sole surviving tribe of fisherfolk who dwelt in caves under the cliffs of Whitby. Her face was as wrinkled and weathered as any human of advanced years, yet to the rest of her people she was merely a child. She knew what it was like to be alone, for there were no others of the aufwader race her age and there never would be. The females of the tribe were cursed; they either died carrying the unborn child or perished with the infant at birth. Such was the terrible punishment of the mighty Lords of the Deep who reigned in the fathomless reaches of the ocean, and so the numbers of the aufwaders dwindled and decreased over long, barren years.

The evening chill deepened but it was some time before Nelda was aware of it. There were too many worries weighing on her mind, too many uncertainties to notice the numbness in her fingers.

"Hoy!" came a voice behind her. "Nelda!"

The aufwader stirred from her troubled thoughts and looked over her shoulder. A human boy was running across the sands towards her. She made room on the boulder and waited for him.

"I wasn't sure if you'd be here," Ben cried when he drew near, "I haven't seen you for weeks."

Conscious now of the cold, Nelda huddled into her gansey and pulled the sleeves of it over her fists. "There has been much to attend to," she replied averting her face from the boy's questioning eyes.

"I thought it was something like that," he said. "I expect with winter coming there's lots to do, storing up your food in the caves ..."

"We are not squirrels!" she told him sharply. "The sea knows no lack, there is no dearth in the waters – or there would not be if it were not for your kind." Nelda turned away and glared into the gloom. "What do you know of my life beyond what you see here?" she cried. "Of the caves you know nothing. You have only stood in the entrance chamber – within those tunnels there is much you would not understand. There are places where even I have never been and where I hope never to have to tread. Inside those caverns there is more than the sound of water dripping over stone. Jealousies fester there, dark eyes watch, biding their time, burning with hideous fires that would consume me utterly and which I could never quench. A hunger lives down there! A vile, creeping horror, and it frightens me!"

The boy said nothing, for her outburst startled him and he did not know what to say. As she gazed at the waves washing over the stones he waited in awkward silence but when she turned to him again there was almost a smile on her small, curved mouth.

"Forgive me," she sighed, "I am out of tempers this day. It is nothing – it will pass." Nelda swept the hat from her head and rubbed her tangled hair. "But take care, Ben," she began, adopting a false, light-hearted tone, "you must not hail me so loudly. What if another were to hear you? Unless they are blessed with the sight as you are – they would think you crazed."

"I don't care!" he said. "What if nobody else can

see you? I can and that's all that matters. Do you know I've been here every day after school looking for you?"

She lowered her large grey eyes and her face creased into a warm grin. "Have you truly?" she asked.

"Yes, I even thought of shouting your name outside the hidden entrance, but I didn't want to get you into any trouble with the elders."

Nelda shuddered. "Then I thank you for not doing so," she said quickly, "I have no wish to anger them at present. The less dealings I have with the Triad the better."

"What's wrong?"

"You asked me that once before, do you remember?"

He nodded, "Back then you were worried about your father. You were afraid your uncle had killed him."

"And did the truth not reveal itself to be even so?"

"Yes, but what is it now?"

"Me," she replied softly, "I fear for myself."

"Can't I help?"

"Not this time, no, I must face this alone."

A gull flew overhead and Nelda paused to watch it soar over the cliff. When it had disappeared from view she slid from the boulder and stood on the sand, a solemn expression on her face.

"It is said that an aufwader's heart is a sure guide," she told the boy, "and mine is full of despair and dread. Listen to me, Ben, hear me now lest I am unable to tell you in later times. You have been a true friend. In the short time I have known you, you have done nothing but try to aid both me and the tribe. Never shall I forget your bravery in the search for the moonkelp."

Ben shook his head. "What are you trying to tell me?" he interrupted.

Nelda took his hand. "This is what my heart

foretells," she answered, "there will be a parting of the ways – our meetings will end, the two races of man and aufwader will be sundered for ever. We shall not set eyes on each other again – not till the seas are lost and the bones of the land broken."

"I don't understand," he mumbled. "Why can't we go on meeting? Has someone forbidden it? Are you ill? You're not telling me everything."

But she was looking up at the sky. It had grown dark and she pulled the hat on to her head once more. "I must return," she said quietly, "back to whatever doom lies in wait. Look for me, Ben, here at this time, when the sun is low. If I am at liberty to come – I shall." And with that she hurried over the rocks and disappeared round the cliff.

Ben knew she had gone to one of the secret entrances which led to the aufwader tunnels. He felt miserable. "Nelda!" he feebly called after her. "Nelda."

Immediately his cry was taken up by two other voices. "NELDA!" they screeched. "NELDA!"

A sickening knot twisted in Ben's stomach as he spun round. There on the shore, where they had been spying on him, were Danny Turner and Mark Stribbit; the two boys who bullied him at school.

"Who yer talkin' to Laurenson?" hooted Danny.

"Nelda, Nelda!" crowed the other.

Danny swaggered forward, he was an ugly boy of ten years whose sole delight was in frightening those smaller and weaker than himself. He had the face of a thug with a skinhead haircut and the manners of a dung beetle – no, worse than that even. Throughout the school his name was a byword for terror and dismay. He was the one the other children dreaded and who the teachers talked about in the staff room.

He knew just about every swear-word that ever fouled the air and had made up a few of his own for

27

good measure. During assembly he would break wind during the Lord's Prayer, much to the distress of those unfortunate enough to be seated near him. His was the mouth which always cheeked the teachers and blew chewed-up pieces of paper through straws at them when their backs were turned. Then there was the infamous day when Susan Armitage took her coat from the cloakroom and discovered that someone had left "a present" in one of her pockets. No one knew how it had got there and although nothing could be proved, everyone suspected Danny. The coat had to be destroyed. Another of his favourite pastimes was travelling on buses and flinging eggs at pedestrians. Recently though he had mastered the dubious skill of spitting through his teeth and launching a thick yellow glob a full ten feet. He was one of the most unpleasant little yobs ever to have dreamt of having his knuckles tattooed.

The teachers despaired, for nothing they could do would change him. He steadfastly refused to be reformed. They had cajoled, bribed, even threatened, but the boy was out of control and in the past few weeks he had become worse.

Last Monday he punched little Mary Gibbons when she refused to hand over her dinner money, on Thursday he caught a seagull and wrung its neck, and now he and his stupid sidekick were concentrating their nastiness upon Ben.

"He's mad, ain'tcha, Pleb?" he said. "We thought yer was but now we know. Always talk to yersen, does yer?"

"Oooh Nelda, cooee!" tittered Mark.

Ben slithered off the rock and eyed the boys nervously. If he could only dash by them and make it over the sand to the pier steps.

"Yer frikened Laurenson?" Danny pouted mockingly. "Ain'tcha gonna tell us any more ghosty stories then?"

"Where's Old Bag Boston now?" sniped Mark. "She's as cracked as you are! Danny, tell 'im what we'll do to that three legged moggy o' theirs if we catch it."

"Tie it to a rocket on bommy night!"

"Or stick a banger up its bum!"

"Better still, build the bommie round it and roast the fleabag alive."

Ben darted forward, neatly sidestepping the first of his enemies, but Mark was ready for him and his quick fingers snatched his jumper.

"I've got him, Danny!" he yelled.

"Hold him!" snarled the other.

The two of them grabbed Ben's arms and pulled him round until his legs buckled and he tripped. Down on to the wet sand Ben went sprawling. In an instant he was struggling to his feet again but Danny was not finished with him yet.

"Stay down, yer goz-eyed loony!" he bawled, kicking his victim and pouncing on top of him.

Ben groaned as the full weight of the Turner boy flattened him against the sand. "Get off!" he shouted. "Let go!" squirming he managed to roll over until Danny was sitting on his chest and with his small fists tried to lay into him.

At once Mark seized his hands and pinned them down under his knees. Ben started to flail his legs in the air, trying to hit Danny in the back. One sharp punch to the ribs soon put a stop to that and Ben let out a hoarse grunt.

"Take off his shoes," Danny told Mark. In a trice it was done and the Stribbit boy flung them into the sea before returning to kneel on Ben's arms.

"That's better," hissed Danny. "Only donkeys kick, Laurenson, and yer not a donkey are yer?" He smirked and winked at his friend. "Us know what to call the likes of you – people what talk to thesselves are Cretins ain't they? What are you then? Yer a stinkin' little Cret – say it."

Ben said nothing so Danny slapped his face and Mark pressed down harder with his knees.

The boy cried out and in his suffering he wretchedly mumbled, "I ... I'm a Cret."

Both tormentors were overcome with laughter and Ben could feel every quaking cackle vibrate through his body. He closed his eyes and wished they were dead.

The vicious mirth subsided and the next stage of the bullying began. "Right then, Cret!" said Danny. "Time for yer to have a wash. But us all knows that Cretins don't use water – they're too gormless for that."

"What do they use then, Danny?" Mark asked in feigned innocence.

"Sand!" came the triumphant reply and the two of them scooped up great handfuls of the stuff then rubbed it into Ben's hair and pushed it into his face.

Ben spluttered and Danny shoved some into his mouth. The boy choked and retched whilst the other two fell about laughing hysterically.

"Look who's balkin'!" roared Danny.

"He's red as a tomato!" added Mark, "an' them's tears in his eyes. The Cret's cryin'!"

"So would I if I lived in a nuthouse like 'im. Here, Cret, let me help yer get the 'orrid old sand off." Danny brought his face close to Ben's and spat venomously. "That's fer bein' weird, yer snotty little weed! No wonder yer an orphan – yer mum an' dad prob'ly topped thesselves to get away from yer! AAAARRGGG!"

Suddenly Danny flew backwards, screeching at the top of his voice. Ben felt the weight disappear off his chest and he craned his neck to see what was happening.

"Danny!" wailed Mark in surprise.

"Let him go!" came a fierce voice.

"Jennet!" gasped Ben.

Danny rubbed his neck angrily. It was Ben's sister who had sneaked up behind them. The girl had yanked him violently by the collar and a livid red mark was already glowing across his throat. He glared at her, she was a couple of years older than him and Mark but she was still only a girl.

"Right!" he stormed. "You'll be sorry for that!" With a loud yell he hurled himself at her, but his attack was shortlived for Jennet swung her schoolbag by its strap and brought it crunching into his face.

The boy let out an awful howl and stumbled about blindly, cursing with his head in his hands.

Jennet stepped towards Mark but he took one fearful look at his friend and decided not to tackle the girl on his own.

Blood began trickling through Danny's fingers. "Me nodes!" he bawled. "You'b bust me nodes!"

"Clear off or I'll break something else!" she growled.

The two boys stared at her – this was too much, to be chased away and by a girl too! Danny's temper was boiling but the blood dribbling down his arm alarmed him. "You'll keep, Cret!" he said to Ben. "Ad' dex tibe you'll dot 'ave that dog of a sister to save yer."

Jennet rushed at them and the boys ran off.

Ben wiped his face and staggered to his feet. He felt ashamed. Silently he waded into the sea and retrieved his shoes.

"You all right?" his sister asked.

He nodded but said nothing to her.

"They're little hoodlums they are," she continued. "What did you get mixed up with them for? He's a baddun that Turner lad – everyone says so, even his

31

sister Rachel."

Ben poured the seawater out of his shoes and squeezed his feet into them. Jennet watched him and shook her head in disbelief.

"What are you doing?" she asked, "You'll catch a death putting them back on. Honestly, Ben, you're hopeless!"

"Shut up!" he shouted. "Just leave me alone!"

Jennet couldn't believe her ears. "Well excuse me!" she cried. "Who was it rescued you back then? God knows what would have happened if I hadn't stopped those two!"

Ben turned on her. "They would have got bored and stopped!" he screamed. "But now you've gone and made it worse! They'll never leave me be now! What did you have to go and hit Turner for? He won't be happy till he beats me up – or worse. If that's what you call helping me, Jen, then thanks, but don't bother doing it again!"

He stomped off up the shore, leaving Jennet to sigh – she hadn't stopped to think her brother might not want to be saved. He was right she had only made matters worse, Danny now had a score to settle.

"Ben," she called, "wait a minute – I'm sorry." Quickly she ran after her brother and put her arm around him. "I only did it because … because you're all I've got."

"You're not my mother!" he snapped, shaking her off.

"Ben!"

The boy looked at her – that had hurt. It had been a mean thing to say and he was already feeling guilty. "Sorry," he said.

Jennet took his hand. "Come on," she murmured, "let's go home."

Up the pier stairs they trailed, until they came to Church Street. It was empty. All the locals were indoors having tea and the shops were getting ready to close for the day. They met only one other person on their way back to Miss Boston's cottage; Mrs Rigby was one of the women who ran the wool shop and as the children passed her she stopped them.

She was a short, stocky woman with no neck to speak of. Her hair was blonde and curly and several moles peppered her face, although occasionally she tried to hide them under brush-loads of blusher. This was not one of those times and Mrs Rigby resembled someone who had been spattered with mud.

"Hello, Luvs," she hailed the children, "I don't suppose you've seen my Mokey have you?"

Jennet liked Mrs Rigby – or rather she liked to see what new knitted creation the woman was wearing. Today it was a white turtle-neck with patch pockets, covered in gold triangles and bizarre, bumpy lumps of wool. The girl stared at it for a moment. She had to admire the woman's courage for no one else would have dared to be seen dead in it, then she collected herself. Mokey was Mrs Rigby's cat.

"No," she replied, "we haven't. Has he gone missing?"

It was only then that she noticed how dreadful the woman looked. Her face was haggard and there was a desperate edge to her voice. Mokey meant a lot to her. Mrs Rigby twisted one of the fluffy bobbles on her turtle-neck. "He's been gone all afternoon," she said distractedly, "I just don't know what can have happened. He's usually such an obedient little character."

"Maybe he's been got at," put in Ben. Jennet groaned and squeezed his hand till he yelped and pulled away from her. "He might have, mightn't he?" the boy protested. "Loads of others have."

Mrs Rigby trembled. "Oh the poor creature," she wept. "Oh my poor Mokey!"

"Don't worry," Jennet tried to reassure her, "We'll

keep an eye out for him. He's a marmalade cat isn't he?''

''That's right, a lovely coat he's got – oh, good God, how awful! To think that could be why he's been taken. To be skinned!''

''You should have put him on a string,'' Ben told her.

Mrs Rigby took from her pocket a length of twine and held it up for them to see. One end of it had been chewed and bitten through. ''But I did,'' she whispered, ''I did.''

3

IN THE CHAMBER OF
THE TRIAD

The passage was dark and narrow; here and there the rough, rocky floor was covered in slimy weed and only those sure of the safe path had ever dared venture down it. This was one of the oldest of all routes to the aufwader caves – unlike the others, this natural entrance had never been widened and made completely secure. In places it was almost impassable, it had always been a tight squeeze even for the smallest of the fisherfolk.

Only Nelda now used this tunnel and because of that she considered it to be her very own – somewhere secluded to escape to when life in the main caves grew unbearable. During the last couple of months she had spent a lot of time just sitting in the quiet, cramped darkness, alone with her thoughts and fears.

Some distance along the path there was a low outcrop of moss-covered stone which she used as a seat, and it was on this she now sat. An hour had passed since she had said farewell to Ben on the shore, but she had not yet had the courage to return to the rest of the tribe.

Slowly she rocked back and forth, her head resting in her hands. A great burden lay heavily on her spirit and she was at a loss to know how to escape what must come.

"Peace," she eventually said aloud to dispel the black mood which was stealing upon her. "Can I not be free to choose my own destiny?" Her voice rang in the tunnel, echoing round until it faded on the last word. "Destiny, destiny ..." it repeated.

Nelda peered into the gloom, just to be certain that it was indeed an echo and not someone hiding and playing tricks. Anything was possible and she was wise to be suspicious.

"No," she told herself after a long silence, "'tis nothing. Have I then come down to this, where I jump at shadows and the slyness of my own mind?" She tried to laugh but the sound was artificial and forced. It was no use, she could not shrink from it any longer, it was time to join the others.

Nelda rose and moved further up the passage, stooping then crawling until it opened out into one of the main aufwader halls.

Standing upon the more even ground, Nelda stretched and looked about her. The place was deserted. At that time in the evening most of the other fisherfolk would be in their chambers mending nets or cooking a meal over the fire.

Through the empty tunnels which connected the main halls she slowly wound her way. The caves were lit by oil lamps, set into niches in the rocky wall or suspended from the ceiling on chains. The lamps themselves were diverse shapes and sizes: mostly plain bronze bowls, but some had been fashioned into the shapes of fish with the flame licking from the mouth, and in one crevice a dragon's head glared out with blazing eyes. The light they radiated was soft and it flickered before the slight draughts, rippling over the green walls, creating the illusion that all was submerged beneath the sea.

IN THE CHAMBER OF THE TRIAD

It was not long before Nelda realized that something was wrong. Although she could hear the usual sound of crackling fires, and the scent of steaming broth and roasting fish tantalized her nostrils, there was nothing else. No aufwader voices drifted through the salty air and by now she ought to have bumped into at least one of the other inhabitants. A frightening disquiet crept upon Nelda – what had happened to the rest of the tribe – where were they?

With mounting concern she hurried to the nearest cell. It was the home of Prawny Nusk, a friend of her grandfather. He was a good-natured soul who spent most of his time smoking his pipe and whittling pieces of driftwood. She ducked under the fishing nets which festooned the ceiling, but the cell was empty. The cooking fire had been left unattended and was gradually dying; above it the iron cauldron which contained Prawny's supper bubbled and seethed. The broth within was spoilt and it splashed over the edge, hissing as it trickled down the sides, forming a black, sticky goo that dripped and fizzed on the hot embers. Nelda gazed round at the deserted room. Prawny's knife lay by his stool, next to a heap of wood parings, even his pipe had been left behind to smoulder on the rush-matted floor.

"Mr Nusk," she called, knocking out the glowing tobacco and stamping on it. Only the spluttering cauldron answered her.

Nelda ran out and in a louder voice shouted, "HELLO!", but all she heard was the echo of her own voice ringing through the tunnels. Hastily Nelda ran the rest of the way to her family's quarters, anxious and afraid.

When she reached the low entrance she paused before pulling aside the dividing curtain – what if there was no one here either?

Taking a deep breath, she threw back the cloth and stepped inside.

It was horribly cold and the lamp was not lit. But, in spite of the darkness, Nelda could discern a figure seated by the heap of ashes in the centre of the chamber. The figure was hunched and still, staring into the charred remains of yesterday's fire – as if waiting for some oracle to speak from the cinders. When Nelda entered he lifted his head.

"Grandfather!" she cried. "What is it? Where is everyone?"

Tarr reached for the staff which lay at his side and hauled himself from the rushy floor. His eyes fixed on her and at once she saw they were filled with pain and despair. "Lass!" he uttered thickly. "Ah wish tha hadna come back." The old aufwader rushed towards his granddaughter and caught her in a desperate embrace, clinging to her for dear life.

And then Nelda knew; all those weeks of doubt and uncertainty were finally confirmed. As the coils of her doom wound tightly around her she felt nothing; of all reactions this was the last she had expected.

"The summons bell has been rung," she said flatly. "That is why they are all absent."

Tears were running down Tarr's ancient brown face and dripping from his wiry whiskers on to her cheek. 'Theer was nowt ah could do," he sobbed, "nowt! Deeps take me if'n ah didn't do all ah could. But theers nowt to be done, he'll nivver be gainsaid."

Slowly Nelda pulled away from him. "Strange," she said, "I did think I would be more upset than this. Why am I not weeping and tearing out my hair?" She pulled the hat from her head and let it fall to the floor. "Grandfather," she began in a wavering voice, "a part of me has died this night – inside I am numb."

"Then ah'll weep fer us both," he answered

huskily. "Come, lass." He held out his rough, calloused hand and she took it in her own. They left the chamber in silence, the only noise coming from Tarr's grief-ridden chest as it let loose all his sorrow.

Down the dim labyrinth of tunnels they made their way, hand in hand. Nelda knew where they were headed. She had been resigned to making this solemn journey for months now. It was, after all, her own rash words which had brought about this evil moment and there was no escape. Nothing could release her from the fate which was waiting – nothing except death.

Deeper under the cliff the two fisherfolk went, down the steep Ozul Stair to remote and seldom visited caverns. Only once before had Nelda been down there: when Hesper, her late aunt, brought her to see the fossilized bones of long-dead monsters. Again she walked the eerie gallery beneath them, that crowded host – like the hellish legions of a skeletal army.

Nelda and her grandfather left the fossils behind them and came to the Gibbering Road. This was a slender bridge of stone that stretched across a wide chasm. It was said that the gaping gulf it spanned was bottomless and contained the tormented souls of those drowned at sea. On stormy nights you could hear the hollow voices wailing in anguish. Occasionally the horrible shrieks had reached as far as the living quarters high above and all were forced to stop up their ears. Few of the aufwaders, even Old Parry, dared listen to those nightmare cries, for those who had were driven insane.

In single file they began to cross, with Tarr leading the way. As Nelda stepped on to the perilous bridge she happened to look down. It was a mistake; the world fell away and the blackness below was so impenetrable it seemed to have a substance all its own. Nelda pinched herself and concentrated on reaching her grandfather who was already on the other side. She wanted him to speak reassuring words but if the legends were true then any noise might arouse the souls of the dead. With her heart fluttering in her breast she hurried across and seized Tarr's hand once again.

They were getting close to the ancient heart of the aufwader realm. Through a series of dank grottos and evil-smelling tunnels they continued, whilst all the time the sound of running water grew in their ears. Nelda stared about her as they came to a huge cavern, larger than any she had ever seen.

It was filled with stalagmites that towered up to the dripping ceiling, forming immense, natural pillars of glistening rock. Underground springs foamed along deep channels worn into the floor and waterfalls cascaded over the emerald-coloured walls. It was a spectacular place, where land met sea in harmonious perfection, the joyous rush of water over stone was like music and it gave comfort to them both.

Since the time when the churning waters brought forth the land, this wondrous, subterranean cathedral had been sacred to the aufwaders. Even before man had driven them underground they had worshipped here and spoken of it with reverence. The Lords of the Deep were rumoured to have built it and some still clung to the belief that anything spoken here would be heard by them. A devoted few would still venture down at certain times of the year to plead for the aufwader cause and beg the mercy of the Deep Ones. If their prayers were ever hearkened to, however, they went unanswered – for the terrible curse was never lifted. Yet it remained a glorious, hallowed place.

Between the gurgling rivers of seawater, Tarr and Nelda walked until a great arch reared up before them. Huge columns of smooth rock supported the sweep of its curved roof which was encrusted with ammonites. An immense, heavy curtain of woven seaweed barred the way. It had been made in days long gone, by cunning hands whose skill had never been matched. Upon that intricate tapestry were symbols of the moon and sea and in nine panels it depicted the creation and destruction of the world, from its birth out of darkness to its return.

From behind the curtain they heard the buzz of many whispering voices. Tarr glanced at Nelda: was it too late to turn back? Could she bear the agony of living outside the tribe? For a second her breaths faltered and beads of sweat sprang from her forehead. No, she had already decided there was no way out. It took a while for her to compose herself but when she had, a slight nod to her grandfather told him she was ready for what lay beyond. Leaning on his staff he put out his hand but the curtain was drawn aside before he could touch it.

"Enter, Tarr," summoned a croaking but powerful voice, "and welcome, Nelda."

The cave was smaller than the one which preceded it, yet no less important. Here sat the Triad, those elders of the tribe who ruled all the others. Their word was law and woe betide any who disobeyed them.

Every member of the tribe was there and as the two figures entered they turned, their hushed whispers dying. All eyes were on Nelda and she gripped Tarr's hand more tightly. The assembled fisherfolk parted, clearing a path down the centre of the chamber. As Nelda passed by they hung their heads, too ashamed to meet her gaze. The atmosphere was electric and all shifted uncomfortably, for this was a black day in their history. Through this corridor Nelda and Tarr moved, coming finally to where the elders sat in judgement.

The Triad sat upon three grand thrones. The two

outer ones were decorated in patterns resembling the sea and stars but they paled in comparison to the one in the centre. The middle throne was magnificent, it dwarfed those beside it, rising grandly from the living rock, its broad back thrust upwards to the ceiling, where it clove in two to support a great silver lamp. Nelda stared up at it in wonder. The lamp was the shape of a boat riding waves of glittering crystal which absorbed the light from the tapering flame at the prow and scattered it throughout the chamber. It was dazzling, like the sun on the sea, and Nelda had to lower her eyes.

A hideous face was peeping up at her. It was only a carving beneath the seat of the main throne but above that crouched a figure that Nelda truly feared. He was more loathsome than any sculpted gargoyle, for he was the oldest of all the fisherfolk and leader of the Triad.

Esau had lived for eight centuries and each and every one of those years was etched on his face. He was a wizened, shrivelled creature, whose hands were more like claws. His matted forked beard was adorned with small shells and the long, unkempt hair which flowed down his humped back was tangled with seaweed and threaded with painted stones.

The talons of his fingers tapped the stone serpents that twisted around the arm of the throne. He was impatient and, as Nelda approached, leaned forward with undisguised anticipation. Though he was ancient his eyes were as sharp as ever they had been. They twinkled under the dancing light of the silver lamp and darted slyly round the chamber. He could see the expressions on all their faces – he knew what they were thinking. Well, let them, there was nothing they could do to stop him. He had waited a long time for this. Toying with the pearl that hung about his neck, he squinted at his fellow elders on either side –

they too were powerless to stop him and he could not prevent a gleeful cackle issuing from his cracked lips.

Tarr let go of Nelda's hand, it was the law that she must face this on her own. She stepped forward and stared defiantly at the hunched figure.

"I have been summoned," she said, managing a bold, fearless tone. "What is it the Triad want of me? I stand here guiltless and await your judgement." So ran the words of the trial and she waited for the response.

The elders who flanked Esau swallowed nervously. Neither of them could look at the young aufwader and they mumbled into their beards. Both hated what they must do and they struggled to pronounce what they had been instructed to say.

"Daughter of Abe," muttered one of them, "thou hast been brought to this chamber to answer." He stole a glance at Esau and shuddered. His name was Johab and he was only a little older than Nelda's grandfather. His sea-grey eyes closed and his pity went out to her – he could not continue.

Esau jabbed at the other elder to complete the condemnation, who reluctantly cleared his throat. He fidgeted for a time then said, "Dost thou remember what occurred two moons since? And dost thou recall the words thou didst speak?"

Nelda did not look at him but continued to glare at Esau. He was the one behind all this. It was time to draw him out, the charade had gone on long enough.

"I remember calling you an old fool!" she snapped.

A murmur ran round the rest of the tribe, but this time they were not angry with her, they agreed.

"Be silent!" Esau gripped the arms of the great stone chair and barked at everyone, his eyes gleaming with malice. Then he swung round and pointed an accusing, gnarled finger at Nelda. " 'Abide by my decision', I did tell thee!" he raged.

"And didst thou not answer?"

"I did."

Esau hugged his knees, panting eagerly. "And thine own words were?"

"So be it."

"So be it!" he screamed triumphantly. "So be it!" He crawled from the throne and put out his bony hands to the surrounding crowd. "From her own mouth she doth freely admit the bargain!" he cried. "If she did fail to return with the moonkelp, then unto me she would surrender her fate. And without that treasure came she back to these caves!"

He took a pace closer to her and lowered his ugly, withered head. "Now have I decided," he breathed into her face, "and thou must obey."

Here it came, the final pronouncement of doom, the jaws of her dreaded fate were closing and she could do nothing to save herself.

Esau raised an emaciated arm and all held their breath.

"Hear me!" he commanded. "Witness this – my judgement. For years beyond the span of many have I sat in council upon this throne and long and lonely have those years proven to be. My heart shrieks out at me! How often have I felt it bleed? I have hungered, I have craved – but no more! The gnawing solitude is come to an end at last. Nelda Shrimp, thou shalt be my bride!"

There, it had been said aloud. The fears of the whole tribe had been brought into the light and the truth of his lust reviled them all.

Nelda did not move; throughout all this she had been in the possession of an icy dignity but now hot tears streaked down her face.

Esau hobbled closer and reached out one of his filthy claws. She flinched as he stroked her hair. "Fear not, my beloved," he feverishly cooed, "I shall

never harm thee. For many years I have watched thee, many empty years – a soul cannot last alone. Be a companion to me in my dotage, that is all I ask of thee – nought else."

The leathery skin of his repulsive hand brushed against her cheek and Nelda drew quickly away. "Cease your pawing!" she demanded. "It's true you have the right to claim me, but I curse the day I uttered those foolish, ill-counselled words. Would that I could call them back!"

"I am fortunate thou canst not," he broke in. "Thou shalt be mine at the next full moon."

A horrified uproar erupted in the chamber. "The moon – she waxes even now!" the fisherfolk cried. "In only two days she will be at her zenith. Whither are your wits?"

"Tha canna intend to wed wi' me granddaughter two nights hence!" bellowed Tarr in outrage.

"I do indeed!" declared Esau clenching his crippled fists. "And there is nought you can do, Tarr. The law is with me on this. I have waited too long already – I shall not be kept from her another moon."

The clamouring continued and many vented their opinions on the lecherous elder. What he was doing was obscene. The only one who said nothing was Nelda herself. Through the turmoil her eyes met those of Esau and held them. In that brief instant, when the oldest of the fisherfolk stared at the youngest, their spirits strove for dominance. Each battled with the other and attempted to cast their snares, Nelda with the pure vigour of youth and Esau with the desperate tenacity of age. The air between their brows shimmered and once the elder took a step backwards, but he swiftly rallied and countered with such violence in his eyes that Nelda staggered and broke free.

"Enough," she gasped, "I submit. In two days I shall be yours."

The breath rattled in Esau's throat and he grasped the throne for support. She would be an excellent match for him and he gave a greedy, wheezing laugh.

Nelda, however, had not finished. "Yes, I shall marry you," she said, "but the ceremony must be attended by my human friend – the man child, Ben."

Esau snarled and he spun round like a whipped dog. "A human!" he cried. "Wouldst thou invite the entire accursed race into our halls?"

"I ask for one only," she replied. "If Ben is not here then there will be no wedding."

The elder licked his gums in annoyance, then he sneered and told her, "Verily thy friend shall attend. He is most welcome to witness our marriage – yet at that time say unto him all that thou wouldst, for in after days thou shalt never again see the human child. When thou art bound to me the upper world will be forbidden and thy friend shall be withered to death and rotting in his grave before the ban is lifted!" He turned his back on them all and returned to sit on the throne. The meeting was over.

The tribe glanced at Nelda uncertainly. One by one they gradually left the chamber and began the long trudge back to their homes, troubled in heart and mind.

Nelda shook her head sorrowfully. What she had feared was indeed coming to pass. Esau would keep her a prisoner down here, she would never see the daylight again and, after her wedding, Ben too would be a memory to be forgotten.

"Come, lass," Tarr softly spoke in her ear, "theer's plenty to see to."

With a final look at her future husband, Nelda followed her grandfather from the chamber.

Hunched on the throne, Esau fingered the pearl at his throat and wetted his dry lips at the thought of the forthcoming wedding.

4

THE CHARMING MAN

"Where is that confounded thing!" cried an exasperated Miss Boston. She heaved the large suitcase from her bed and peered underneath. "Well, what are you doing there?" she demanded of her nightdress. Wearily she dragged it out and stuffed it into the already bulging case.

Her friend, Edith Wethers, peered in through the bedroom door. "Hurry, Alice," she fussed. "The train to Darlington leaves in an hour. If you don't catch it then you won't make your connection."

Miss Boston puckered her lips and tried to control herself. Miss Wethers had been making useful comments like that all morning. "Haven't you got a post office to run, Edith dear?" she muttered through gritted teeth.

"I told you, Alice, I asked Mrs Simpson to open today. I knew you'd need all the help you could get."

So far as Miss Boston could see, Edith had been no help whatsoever. Still she could not criticize, for her friend had agreed to look after the children while she was away.

"There!" the old lady sat on the suitcase and fastened it before it could spring apart again. "I do believe I have everything."

Miss Wethers examined her watch and tutted. "Fifty minutes," she observed.

Alice took a firm hold of her luggage and hauled it from the bed. "Oh my word!" she exclaimed, staggering under the weight. "It feels as though I'm off to climb Everest."

"Do stop dawdling," urged Edith impatiently. "Why do you always have to leave everything to the last minute, Alice? It really is most irresponsible. What sort of an example are you setting for those children?" With her hands fluttering over the neck of her blouse she descended the stairs, blind to the rude faces Miss Boston was pulling behind her.

Jennet and Ben were waiting for them in the hall; they had said nothing to Aunt Alice about Danny and Mark for they didn't want to worry her.

"Here's your cloak," said Jennet, putting the tweed wrap around the old lady's shoulders.

"Thank you, my dear," smiled Miss Boston. "My my, I do believe I'm ready for the off."

"And not before time," remarked Edith.

Miss Boston ignored her and gave each of the children a hug. "I shan't bother to ask you to be good for Miss Wethers," she told them. "I know you're both sensible enough to behave when I'm away. Jennet, I'm relying on you – remember."

The girl nodded, she wanted to tell the old lady to have a good time, but as she was visiting someone on their deathbed it hardly seemed appropriate. Instead she said, "Have a safe journey – we'll miss you."

"Oh nonsense," chirped Aunt Alice. "It's only four days – why, I shall be back before you know it."

"Well, I hope so," said Miss Wethers.

"Now don't forget, Benjamin," Miss Boston continued, "it's your job to take care of Eurydice and her little ones. You know how much to feed them, don't you? And when Madam goes out, put her on a string. I'm not having you traipsing off to that horrible house after her when I'm not here."

Ben smiled, he was looking forward to having Miss Wethers staying with them. He knew she was allergic to cat fur and had been collecting some especially.

"Now, Edith," Miss Boston said turning to her friend. "I trust you'll be all right?"

Miss Wethers looked at her doubtfully. "Actually," she began, "there were one or two things." Her hand reached inside the sleeve of her cardigan and brought out a crumpled tissue with which she dabbed her nose. "I really don't feel at all prepared for this," she said, "you did rather spring it upon me. I'm just not qualified to look after two boisterous children. What will it do to my nerves? What am I to give them to eat?" She lowered her voice and in a delicate voice added, "And what about bathtime? What am I expected to do then? I tell you, Alice, I don't know if agreeing to this wasn't all a terrible mistake!" She buried her face in the tissue and blew hard.

Miss Boston rolled her eyes to the ceiling and spent the last of her dwindling patience. "Oh for heaven's sake, Edith!" she sighed. "Pull yourself together! It's too late now to back out of it. I'm depending on you – the letter from Patricia only arrived a few days ago and there just wasn't time to arrange anything else. As for bathtimes, Jennet can see to herself and so can Ben. So don't get yourself in a tiz, you won't have to acquaint yourself with the male anatomy at all."

Edith choked at that but Aunt Alice rattled on. "And what do you think they eat? They're not parakeets or a rare type of monkey – give them the same as you!"

Ben rather fancied being a monkey and he bared his teeth at Miss Wethers whilst scratching himself under the arms.

The postmistress stared at him in alarm and dragged Miss Boston into the parlour. "Did you see that?" she whined. "What sort of a boy is he? Alice,

I've only ever lived with my mother, and she was bedridden for thirty of those years. What if something horrendous happens – what am I to do? Never was good in a crisis. I'm not Prudence, you know. I won't be able to cope, I just won't!"

Miss Boston patted her on the shoulder. " 'Course you will, Edith. Besides, I shall ring you every day at the post office and if there is an emergency you have the telephone number of Patricia's house. But what could possibly happen in four days? Goodness me, look at the time, only twenty minutes to get to the station. Come along – do you want me to miss this train?"

At last Miss Boston managed to leave the cottage. The children and Miss Wethers were to accompany her to the train station and after five minutes of reassuring Edith about this and that, they were able to set off.

As they passed the Gregsons' house, the door opened and Nathaniel Crozier smiled at them. "Good morning," he greeted them amiably.

Miss Boston almost tripped over Edith in surprise. "Gracious me!" she exclaimed.

"We meet again," he said. "I told you we would. Off to London now, are you? I hope Mrs Gunning recovers."

"Er, thank you," murmured Aunt Alice, but she looked at the man strangely.

Nathaniel beamed more broadly and Miss Wethers blushed. "Mr Crozier, isn't it?" she twittered into her hand. "You met me in the post office yeserday. Are you settling in?"

"Most admirably," he replied, "and it's a great pleasure to see you again."

Edith turned bright pink, but she could find nothing else to say to the winning man and hung her head, feeling cross with herself.

Even Jennet found the man's smile pleasant and she too felt the colour rise in her cheeks. Quickly she looked away in embarrassment.

"Less than fifteen minutes!" declared Miss Boston. "Come along!" She bustled them out of the yard and through the narrow alley that led to Church Street.

Ben had been watching his sister with some amusement, he had never seen her be coy before. Hanging back from the others he turned to steal a final glance at the man who had caused Jennet to blush. Nathaniel was still standing on the Gregsons' doorstep but the expression on his face had changed. It was like a storm cloud passing over the sun and Ben grimaced at the ugliness of it. Shuddering, he fled back up the alley and joined the others.

"What did you say his name was?" Aunt Alice was asking the postmistress.

"Mr Crozier," Edith replied dreamily, "isn't it a lovely name?"

But Miss Boston was frowning at something and it was Jennet who answered, "Yes," she agreed, "it is lovely."

Aunt Alice was too lost in her own thoughts to notice – where had she heard that name before?

*   *   *

Young Mr Parks was the junior partner of Olive and Parks, the estate agents. Actually he was not that young but as he had succeeded his father it was easier for the locals to identify him as such in conversation. His nose was rather long and it ended sharply like a beak. The pale green eyes which sat on either side of this unfortunate protruberance were just that little bit too close together and they made him resemble a vulture. Sadly, from the first, his manner had also been against him, he was too flippant; when he showed prospective clients around desirable residences he had a habit of making jokes about the condition of the roof or the state of the floorboards. He thought he was putting them at their ease and jollying things along, but no one ever realized that he was trying to be funny and in his time had put off many an eager purchaser.

His lack of success over the years had taken its toll. Now the only jokes were sarcastic ones and he had grown tired of the business and wished he had done something else with his life.

While he fumbled with the large bunch of keys, he took time to consider his latest potential client. The man was standing some distance away from the property, no doubt admiring its grandeur. His clothes left a lot to be desired but, from the few brief words they had exchanged he was obviously well-educated. He must have a lot of money too, to be so interested in this property, for only the very wealthy could possibly hope to afford it. Mr Parks ignored the sense of uneasiness that he felt – how he hated going into this house.

"Here we are," he grinned, flourishing the correct set of keys, "I'll have the door open in a jiffy, Mr Crozier."

Nathaniel was too busy surveying the grand building to answer. It was one of the oldest properties in Whitby, some parts of it dated back to the tenth century and perhaps further still. Over the ages it had been extended and embellished; the chimneys were Elizabethan, as were the latticed windows, but in other parts you could glimpse Georgian craftsmanship and Victorian heavy-handedness.

"Impressive, isn't it?" said the estate agent. "Yes, we're very pleased to have this one on our books. Been in the Banbury-Scott family for – ooh, many years this has. A real showpiece it was. Do you know, architects and historians came from all over the country just to have a look at it? Unusual for such a treasure to be in private hands really, you'd have thought the National Trust would have snapped it up but they don't seem interested." The large oak door opened and he waved Nathaniel from the lawn. "Now, you do understand about the damage?" he asked.

"Your partner told me the last owner made some structural alterations."

The smile froze on Mr Parks's face. He hated it when Christopher Olive dropped him in it. "Actually," he explained slowly, "there's a little more to it than that. Now, don't misunderstand me, the damage is only superficial. There's nothing in here that can't be repaired." He sailed indoors, hoping the worst areas were still covered by dust sheets. The hallway wasn't too bad, though of course the panelling still had horrendous rents in it – why hadn't they hung up a few pictures as he had suggested?

Personally he found the entire place incredibly creepy, when he thought about what had happened to it. He clapped his hands together and tried to dispel the icy tingle that was prickling the hairs on his neck.

"Yes," he began, "as you can see, there is rather a lot of splintered wood and what a desecration to this divine parquet floor. I understand that all this vandalism took but a few hours to achieve." He did not mention how it had been done – the thought of a mad woman racing round the house, swinging an axe was enough to put anybody off. He turned to add something more but was perturbed to discover that his client was still standing on the doorstep. "Oh dear," he said crestfallen, "is it really so bad, Mr Crozier? One gets accustomed to the devastation. I suppose it must be quite a shock to you."

Nathaniel raised an eyebrow. "Actually I was waiting to be invited in," he replied.

Young Mr Parks gaped like a goldfish for a moment then was full of apologies. "Oh forgive me!" he pleaded. "I didn't think, one meets so few people with true manners these days. The barbarity of the great unwashed tends to rub off. Please, come in."

The bearded man entered and gazed around with interest at the dreadful state of the house.

Mr Parks followed him from room to room, always two steps behind. "You can see the furniture is all intact," he boasted. "Oh don't look at the fireplace, that really is too awful. What a mess."

Nathaniel prowled round like a hound after a scent. When they had reached the drawing room his agitation was plain to see. "Mr Olive told me that the last owner did all this," he said. "In your opinion, what would drive someone to such destruction?"

"Your guess is as good as mine," answered Mr Parks, but he saw that the man was not satisfied. It was time to tell him the whole truth – he would hear it from someone sooner or later. Drawing closer, he lowered his voice. "By all accounts, Mrs Cooper was rather peculiar. As soon as she got her hands on this place she sacked all the staff and went on the rampage. Gives me the abdabs it does. Totally unhinged, not a doubt of it. You only have to look at her other house, the one on Abbey Lane – we handled the sale of that one too. I understood she had the place totally redecorated, but it's worse than this. That's the trouble nowadays, you never quite know who it is you're dealing with. She was obviously a mental patient of some sort. Still, she didn't murder anyone so that's something to be thankful for."

Nathaniel allowed himself a private smile and asked dryly, "Do you know what happened to her?"

"Disappeared," said the estate agent, snapping his fingers. "Vanished without a trace. The police couldn't find her anywhere. I think she threw herself into the sea – people like that do all sorts of silly things, don't they? I had an uncle who kept guinea-pigs, not in hutches mind – let them have the run of the house. Towards the end he had over a hundred of the brutes, it was like a miniature cattle ranch in there. Do you know what he did when he finally realized he couldn't afford to feed them all? He just left the front door wide open – caused chaos on the road. The last I heard he had developed an unhealthy interest in hanging baskets. Other people's, naturally – remarkable."

Nathaniel had had enough. There was nothing more to discover here, not with this idiot trailing after him like an unshakeable shadow. He made a point of looking at his watch and said that he had seen enough.

"Oh, but you haven't seen half of the property yet!" exclaimed a disappointed Mr Parks. "There're the lovely rooms under the gables and such an impressive cellarage. Why you haven't even glimpsed the garden at the back – it was always immaculately kept."

"I'm not interested."

"Oh well," Mr Parks sighed, leading him back through the ruined hall, "I suppose you're busy. Would you look at that poor banister, solid oak you know and frightfully difficult to replace." He stared glumly at the splintered length of wood before returning to his client. "Do you know that after she ransacked the house the demented creature went outside and almost demolished the garden shed? As if all this hadn't satisfied her. Frightening, isn't it, how mad the human race can get?"

Nathaniel had reached the front door and was

about to pull it open, but he hesitated. "You know, Mr Parks," he said, turning and marching back through the wreckage, "I believe I *will* examine this garden of yours."

The garden of the Banbury-Scott residence was as grand as the building it surrounded. It had always been a source of tremendous admiration – and envy from those privileged to be invited to the garden fêtes held there. In summer the flower beds were awash with vibrant colour and the scent of the roses on an August evening was almost as strong as the cider the gardener used to drink. For decades, the sprawling lawns had been the pride of Grice. He had tended to the garden's needs through frost, drought and flood and its beauty was a testament to his care and innovation. But Grice had been dismissed along with the parlour maid and the cook, so for two months the garden had been neglected. The grass desperately needed cutting and dead leaves floated in the ornamental pond.

"We really ought to engage someone to see to this," commented Mr Parks, "before it gets totally out of control. Still, with winter coming I don't suppose we need worry too much. Come over here, Mr Crozier, there's a delightful secluded area, almost a secret garden and it gets all the sunlight in the summer. There's rather a nice statuette too, of ... oh."

Nathaniel had wandered away from the prattling man and was heading for an old stone hut situated against the garden wall.

Mr Parks came running after him. "There's nothing over here of much interest," he gabbled. "Wouldn't you rather see the path made entirely from terracotta tiles flown in from Mexico?"

"Is this where Mrs Cooper went after she had torn up the house?" Nathaniel asked striding up to the heavy door of the outbuilding.

The estate agent confirmed that it was but failed to see why he was so interested in a converted pig pen when there were so many other more interesting sights to view.

Nathaniel ignored him and pushed the door open. It looked like a whirlwind had visited the place. The high, stacked shelves had been thrown to the floor and all the nails and screws which had been carefully stored in tins were scattered everywhere.

"Dear, dear," tutted Mr Parks, "God knows what was going through her mind – sheer lunacy. Grice used to love sitting in here, he was so, well shed-proud, I suppose. Funny, he's never been back you know, won't come near the place. Poor man, it must be awful to have your private world violated in this manner. Would you look at that wall, hacked to pieces, plaster everywhere. Mind you don't get it on your clothes, Mr Crozier."

Nathaniel picked his way through the rubble. The near wall had certainly been ripped open. Most of the plaster that had covered it now lay at his feet and he ran his fingers across the bare stone it had revealed. There was a long trough cut into it. Nathaniel's eyes narrowed and he immediately stooped to search amongst the dusty heaps of broken plaster.

"Well, really!" sniffed Mr Parks, stepping back as Nathaniel stirred up a cloud of dirt. "What are you doing?"

The other man did not reply but continued to rake through the debris. Mr Parks stepped outside to escape from the dust, a handkerchief over his mouth.

And then Nathaniel found it. He knew there had to be something and there it was. From the piles of rubbish he brought out a fragment of plaster as large as his hand. One side was smooth, except for four strange symbols that had been gouged into it. A look of understanding passed over his face.

"Oh, Roselyn," he breathed. "how could you have made such a fatal blunder? Did you really give no heed to these?" He blew the remaining dirt off and inspected the fragment more closely. "The central sign is the mark of Hilda," he observed, "but what of the three which circle round it? Why were you so blind?" He could hardly contain his excitement. This confirmed all his researches and made every risk worthwhile. Quickly he slipped it into his pocket and stepped back outside.

Mr Parks was busy brushing stray flecks of dust off his suit. When his client rejoined him the estate agent eyed him uncertainly. "What were you searching for in there?" he inquired.

"Oh," Nathaniel shrugged, "I thought I saw a rat dart from the rubbish – I thought there might be a nest."

Mr Parks was appalled and pulled a horrified face. "A rat!" he repeated. "And you were scrabbling after it?" He shivered and covered his mouth with the handkerchief once more.

"I think I've seen all I need to for the moment," Nathaniel continued. "Thank you for your time, it has been a most instructive morning."

"Yes ... erm." Mr Parks had not quite recovered himself. "I'll show you out, then." His client, however, was already marching towards the house. "Rat nests," the estate agent muttered incredulously, "I ask you."

*　*　*

Jennet lay the book on her knee and ate a biscuit. It was blissfully quiet and peaceful as both Ben and Miss Wethers were out and she was alone in the cottage. Her brother had gone to see a friend of Aunt Alice's; not long ago Mr Roper had promised to help

59

make a guy for bonfire night and the boy was keeping him to his word. The postmistress, after spending the entire day fussing over one thing and another, had discovered that she had run out of tissues. She had dithered for a full half-hour before deciding whether to leave Jennet on her own or not and by the time she had left the girl was worn out.

Munching on the chocolate digestive, Jennet wondered if she could stand a full four days of Miss Wethers. The thought crossed her mind that it was the postmistress who needed looking after, not Ben and herself.

After some minutes she turned her attention back to the book. *Desert Amour* was a romantic novel that Miss Wethers had brought with her. Jennet usually had no time for that sort of literature, but today she made an exception and was surprised to find herself enjoying it. Mrs Rodice, the ghastly woman who ran the hostel that she and Ben had once stayed at, used to read books like this too and Jennet could understand why. It was just the sort of escapism she craved; the heroine, Veronica Forthgood, was a dark-eyed beauty who continually suffered from the machinations of her half-sister Sonia. It was Sonia, of course, who had tricked the hero, Maximilian Strong, into joining the Foreign Legion, and Jennet was just reaching the point where Veronica had finally found him, delirious under the desert sun, when a knock sounded at the front door.

Jennet considered letting whoever it was go away, but the thought occurred to her that it might be Ben back early from Mr Roper's. Reluctantly she put down the book and left the parlour to investigate.

"Good afternoon," said Nathaniel, once she had opened the door, "isn't it a glorious day for November?"

Jennet tried to conceal her pleasure at seeing him.

"Mr Crozier, isn't it? Can I help you?"

"Please," he grinned, "call me Nathaniel." His deep black eyes shone out at her and Jennet felt weak under their unwavering glare. "I seem to be locked out of the Gregsons'," he lied. "As you know, I'm lodging with them for a time. When I went out I left the spare key in my room and now it appears they have gone out also." He shrugged his shoulders like an apologetic child. "So," he mumbled shyly, "I wonder if you would be so kind as to invite me into your house for the time being – until they return."

"Oh," said Jennet uncertainly, "I shouldn't , you see there's only me here and Aunt Alice told me ..."

Nathaniel nodded, he knew all the time that she was alone, but said, "Then I wouldn't dream of bothering you any further. I quite understand and won't be in the least bit offended. I'll just sit on the Gregsons' step until they return."

He began walking back to the next door neighbours; but Jennet called after him, "No don't do that! I'm sure it's all right. You were talking to Aunt Alice this morning so she obviously knows you, it isn't as though you were a total stranger. Please, come in."

Nathaniel crossed the threshold into Miss Boston's cottage – that was boringly easy.

Jennet showed him into the parlour and the man looked about with interest. He was particularly taken with the books on the shelves and spent a few moments with his back to the girl, intently reading the spines. "Your aunt has an eccentric collection," he remarked, "an awful lot of mumbo jumbo here – does she really believe in this stuff? I hope such ridiculous faith doesn't run in the family. You seem far too intelligent for that supernatural nonsense."

Jennet shook her head. "She isn't really my aunt," she confided, "Ben and I just call her that, and no, I don't really believe in it – or I try not to. I don't even read the horoscopes in the paper."

"Very wise," he commented. "And what sort of thing *do* you read?"

"Oh, you know," she said airily, "all kinds. There are some history books up there I find quite interesting and..." Her voice faltered, for Nathaniel was glancing at the armchair where *Desert Amour* lay open in all its shameless glory.

Jennet felt herself blush. "That's Miss Wethers'," she blurted hastily. Nathaniel gave her a knowing look and she knew he guessed the truth – how embarrassing!

"I see," he said mildly, "so, the postmistress is a fan of Davina Montgomery. She is not alone in that, over half the women in Britain are addicted to such fiction. It is no crime to seek escape – how else could they cope with the drudge of their daily existence?"

"That's what I was thinking!" said Jennet.

"Were you indeed?" he asked. "Then you know there is no harm in dreams. Fantasies are as necessary to us as breathing – without them we should all perish. Each and every one of us must chase after our desires and embrace them. Do you not agree?"

"Yes."

He held her with his smile and Jennet found herself wanting to know all about this fascinating man. But his next question took her by surprise.

"Where are your parents?" he asked.

She looked down at the carpet before answering, "They ... they died two years ago."

"That must have been very difficult for you."

"It was – still is."

"You have been very brave, I see that a great weight has been put on your shoulders. Your eyes tell me this; a great deal can be learnt from the study of one's eyes – they are the mirrors of the soul. When you meet someone for the first time, what is it you look at – his nose, his hair, his mouth? When two lovers stare across a table at each other, what are they staring at? It is the eyes, those small windows that betray the inner self. Nothing can hide in them. Of all the separate, unreliable pieces of mankind they are the most honest. Tell me, Jennet, what do you see in mine?"

Jennet was nervous; she wanted to look and yet deep down some basic instinct was warning her not to. "Beware," it cautioned her, "beware."

"Look at me, Jennet," Nathaniel pressed.

Slowly she raised her head and stared into his eyes. "They ... they're so dark," she whispered, "black and cold, like splinters of black glass. I'll cut myself on them – oh!" she tried to wrench herself free but it was too late, Jennet was lost.

Nathaniel clicked his fingers in her face, the girl did not even flinch. "Sit down," he told her.

At once Jennet obeyed, she was completely in his power now and had no will of her own.

Nathaniel threw Miss Wethers' book on the floor and made himself comfortable on the armchair. "Tell me, child," he demanded, "tell me what you know of Rowena Cooper."

And so, Jennet told him everything. She spoke like an automaton, in a dead monotone and, with great detail, related the events that had occurred between Miss Boston and his late wife. How Rowena had searched for the magical staff of Hilda, murdering several of Aunt Alice's friends in the process and how she had at last found the staff, wielding it to the peril of everybody. When she had finished Nathaniel was not at all pleased.

"How could she have been such a fool?" he snapped. "Why did she not listen to me? The staff was not what I was after! How could she allow herself to be tricked – and by such a one as that senile amateur?" He rose from the chair and paced around the room, seething with fury until at last he turned back to Jennet. "And the staff of Hilda," he cried, "where is it now? Does Alice Boston possess it?"

"No," droned Jennet's reply, "it was taken from this world altogether."

The news seemed to be a great relief to Nathaniel and he relaxed. "Good," he said with a satisfied, unpleasant smile, "then that leaves the way clear. Thank you, my child, a most interesting little conversation, I can see you shall be very useful. It is perhaps unfortunate that your brother has the sight, even more worrying is the fact that it was he who discovered the moonkelp. Now he has the favour of the Lords of the Deep – that is a sobering circumstance. Still, I trust I can achieve my goal – one eight-year-old thorn in my side is something I can handle. There have been worse dangers. All will be well – for me at least."

Jennet rubbed her eyes, she had the most excruciating headache.

"Of course, when I was digging in Egypt, my group had the most awful case of jippy tummy I've ever experienced. Quite frightful it was. The location might have been exotic but all they saw for the first three days was the inside of the loo."

Dizzily, she stared across at the man in the armchair. He was mildy sipping a cup of tea and chatting away as if they had known each other for years. The pain was easing a little now, she had never sufferd from headaches before. Try as she might she could not recall what they had been talking about – she could not even remember making the tea.

"Are you all right?" asked Nathaniel with concern. "You look almost green. I've been rabbiting on, haven't I? Forgive me, one tends to forget how boring these anecdotes can be to other people. Dear me, here's me trotting on about Nairobi, Peru and Egypt without even noticing the effect it's having on you."

"I'm sorry," Jennet apologized, "it's just a headache, it's clearing now. Please – go on."

He smiled at her. "You are kind," he said, "but I've taken up too much of your time already. The Gregsons must be back by now. Thank you so much for inviting me in. You have been a most enchanting hostess." Rising from the chair he gave the girl a formal bow. Jennet felt the butterflies flutter inside – Mr Crozier had to be the politest man she had ever met.

"Let me see you out," she offered eagerly, running to the front door.

"Au revoir," he told her, taking hold of her hand and kissing it.

Jennet laughed with delight and opened the door.

Nathaniel stared past her at the yard beyond. "Hello there," he called.

The girl turned in time to see Miss Wethers give him an answering wave with her handbag. "Why, hello to you, Mr Crozier," she cried, "are you coming in for tea?"

"No, thank you," he replied, "this young lady has seen to that already. Now I must be getting back to the Gregsons', I have some important work to see to."

"But I thought you were on holiday!" exclaimed the postmistress.

"Alas no," he returned, "would that I were. Now excuse me, ladies." Flashing his beguiling smile, Nathaniel left them and rang the bell of the neighbour's house. The door opened and Mrs Gregson hurriedly let him in.

"Dear me," Miss Wethers tutted, "Joan Gregson

doesn't look very well. Did you see how pale she was? The fault of that layabout husband, no doubt. Come on, Jennet, Mr Crozier may have had a cup of tea but I haven't. I'm fair gasping for one."

They went indoors and Jennet put the kettle on the stove. "He's a nice man, isn't he?" she remarked happily.

Miss Wethers took some time before answering, as the cellophane on the packet of tissues refused to open. "Mr Crozier?" she eventually piped up from the hallway. "Yes, he is."

"He told me to call him Nathaniel."

Edith forgot about the tissues and wandered into the kitchen. "Did he?" she asked, a look of concern troubling her face. "Well, perhaps it would be better if you refrained from using his Christian name, Jennet dear."

"Why?"

"Well, it just isn't proper – and you shouldn't have invited him in like that. We hardly know the man."

"But he's so ... charming."

Miss Wethers let out a small gasp of surprise. That word had struck a chord in her somewhere.

"What is it?" asked Jennet puzzled.

"I don't know," Edith replied quietly, "I've just remembered something my mother once told me. I haven't thought about it for years, but ..."

The girl waited to be enlightened but the postmistress went searching for the tissues, flustered and feeling naked without one tucked in her sleeve to fiddle with. When she came back in the kitchen, Jennet was still waiting.

Edith dabbed her nose in distraction and relented. "A long time ago," she began haltingly, "when my father was alive and before I was born, times were bitterly hard. The only employment was fishing and my father would be at sea for days on end. Well, at

one such time my mother was alone in bed and there was a lot of noise coming from the yard below her window. You've seen where I live, it's pretty much the same as here with a yard around which all the other cottages are built."

Miss Wethers stared out of the window as she remembered the story the way her mother had told it to her. "There were two terrible men at that time in Whitby – awful troublemakers whom no captain wanted aboard. You can only guess how they made a living, but what money they did have they drank or gambled away. Unfortunately they lived in the same yard as my parents and every so often, on fine nights, would hold their revels out in the open – this was a particularly fine evening.

"A few other ruffians were also there, drinking heavily and getting soused. All evening my poor mother heard them get drunker and drunker. Imagine how afraid she must have been, a frail woman totally alone with no one to call to should she need help. And then the gambling began. A pack of cards was produced and a table hauled from somebody's kitchen. At the sound of it being dragged across the yard, my mother dared to peek through the curtain and saw them all stupid with drink. She put a chair against the door and crept back into bed, pulling the blankets up under her chin, wishing my father would return.

"The rabble below continued playing cards well into the night and their voices grew heated with vile curses. My mother never got a wink of sleep and then something happened which made her blood run cold.

"On the wall, above the bedhead, a red light began to glow. She was scared witless and couldn't move an inch. Well, this light grew larger until it reached the ceiling and then a man stepped right out of it."

Miss Wethers paused for breath, her eyes wide with some of the fear her mother had felt all those years ago. "He was strikingly handsome, I remember her telling me. Dressed beautifully – all in black, one of those old-fashioned dinner suits with the tails and a large, silk bow tie. Anyway off the bed he steps, tugging at his golden cufflinks.

"My mother could only stare at him and finally she stammers, 'Are you the Devil?' Well, this man he just gives her a little smile and says, 'Don't worry, it's not you I've come for.' Then he turns and walks towards the window where he melts into nothingness again.

"At that point my mother passed out and when she awoke the next morning discovered that a fight had broken out between those two men, one of them had pulled out a knife and stabbed the other to death." Her voice trailed off, lapsing into a soft whisper. "And that's why she always used to warn me about charming gentlemen – because the devil himself is a charming man."

Miss Wethers became silent as she recalled all the barriers the memory of this story had thrown in the way of any men friends she might have had in her life. When she drifted back to the present she found that Jennet was staring at her as though she had gone mad.

"Oh my," muttered Miss Wethers forlornly, "I don't really know what I mean by telling you all this. It was just a story my mother used to tell me that's all, probably wanted to keep me with her after father passed on and then when she was ill... and yet I can picture her even now, relating that tale, her face whiter than the pillows she was propped up on."

Jennet handed her the cup of tea she had poured out for her and Edith took it hurriedly, the crockery rattling in time with her jangled nerves.

"Well, I still think Mr Crozier's charming," Jennet told herself.

5

A SHOCK FOR MISS WETHERS

Ben lay before the coal fire, tackling a bowl of wallpaper paste and a pile of torn newspapers. He had already covered one half of a balloon with the grey porridge-like substance and was busily applying more to the other half.

Mr Roper's front room was the perfect cosy spot to spend a rainy afternoon. It was like one of those exhibits in a museum which demonstrates how people used to live. The rosepatterned wallpaper had not been changed for thirty years and neither had the lemon yellow curtains – even the light switches were the out-dated, round type. The old man's furniture also hailed from the time his wife had been alive to choose it and, over the years, the table, chairs and sideboard had steadfastly occupied their rightful places, so much so that they almost seemed part of the fabric of the house.

Jammed between the fading photographs that crowded the mantelpiece was an ugly clock that sombrely ticked the time away and gave rhythm to his days. Mr Roper possessed no television, such an intrusion into his home would have been unthinkable, instead a large wooden radio dominated one alcove and he spent many a pleasant evening

listening to the classical music programmes. The overall effect lent the room a warm, brown glow and when the fire crackled in the grate it was a delicious, snug nest that any tourist could peer in at and envy.

Mr Roper lived by himself on the West Cliff. For many years, since the death of his wife, he had become increasingly isolated from other people. Without his Margaret he found the world a bleak, confusing place and the struggle of existence a meaningless chore. When Miss Boston first met him he was in a lamentable state, unshaven and dirty, not caring how he looked or lived. It was she who shook him out of his despondency and snatched him back from the brink just in time.

Now he took pride in himself again and kept the house as Margaret would have wished. He had a lot to thank Miss Boston for and never forgot that fact, supporting her in all her endeavours – however bizarre.

When she had first mentioned that she was going to foster two unknown children, he was the only one in all her circle of friends who gave her encouragement and now he was glad that he had.

Ben and Mr Roper got on famously and once a week the boy would visit the old man. It was good to escape the female household of Aunt Alice and his sister once in a while. On fine days they would go fishing off one of the piers, but more frequently, when the rain kept them indoors, the old man would entertain Ben by recounting stories of his life and those of his family. All three of Mr Roper's elder brothers had been killed in the Great War and he himself had won a medal in the one that had followed. He kept this in the top drawer of the sideboard and only took it out on Remembrance Day and when Ben wanted to look at it. Although the stories he told about the war fascinated the boy, Mr

Roper never went into too much detail. He had survived some ghastly experiences and Ben was wise enough to understand; he never insisted on hearing a tale if he saw that it troubled his old friend. For Mr Roper, many memories were still too terrible to recall, as if the mere utterance of them would awaken the pain and horror once more.

Ben dunked another scrap of paper into the paste and plastered it over the shiny surface of the balloon. He hated the feel of papier mâché, it made his finger-tips pucker up and look like raisins, and if any splashed on to the backs of his hands or arms and dried, it became painfully glued to the hairs. The only good point about the messy process, as far as he could see, was that afterwards his flaking hands looked like the mummified remains of a grotesque zombie that had risen from a cold grave.

He wiggled his fingers menacingly before his eyes and gave a sepulchral moan – just as Mr Roper returned carrying a glass of lemonade.

"Ah, well done," said the old man setting the glass down by the boy, "you've nearly finished the first layer. I think two good'uns should be sufficient. He only has to last between here and the bonfire, remember." He eased himself into his favourite, battered armchair and watched as Ben slapped another layer all around.

"Did you manage to find any clothes?" the boy asked. "I've got an old jumper with holes in, but all my trousers are too good to burn."

Mr Roper nodded. "Don't you worry," he told him, "there's an old pair of pants in the wardrobe upstairs. I'll fish them out in a minute – there's a couple of odd gloves in a drawer somewhere too, they'd look right grand on him."

"He's going to be the best Guy Fawkes in Whitby!" said Ben proudly.

"In Yorkshire!" corrected Mr Roper, putting some more coal on the fire. "Did I tell you I got another addition to my collection the other day? Hang on then, I'll just fetch it."

Ben continued spreading the papier mâché over the balloon as the old man padded into the parlour. Since the death of his wife there had only been one love in his life and that was given wholly over to his beloved collection. Mr Roper collected cruet sets.

His parlour was a virtual shrine to salt and pepper pots of all shapes and sizes; there were china elephants, lighthouses, an entire pack of dogs, three cottages, a couple of penguins that wobbled when touched, an aeroplane, two cows, a glass camel, three people in a boat, a basket of fruit, comical bees set into a hive that contained marmalade, a Spanish flamenco dancer, spaceships, a miniature hatstand with the hats as the pots, a group of cartoon mice popping out of a Swiss cheese and many many more. Somehow he had managed to squeeze them all into his small parlour. They were displayed in glass-fronted cabinets, adorned the window-sills, huddled on shelves, jostled for position on the tops of cupboards and the areoplane had even been suspended on a wire from the ceiling.

He loved them all and much of his ample spare time was now devoted to scouring the local antique and bric-a-brac shops for anything new to add to them. It was his little haven of joy, where his sole delight was inspecting and dusting them. In a way they were the children he had never had and he treated them with the same amount of care and attention.

"Now then," he chuckled with pride as he gently took hold of his latest charge, "let's show you to a young friend of mine." He hurried back to the front room where Ben held the now heavy balloon between his slippery fingers. "Have you finished lad?" he asked. "Well, what do you think of this little beauty? Quite appropriate, isn't it?"

Upon his tender palm were a pair of china salt-and-pepper-pots, both in the shape of fireworks. They had been delicately made to look like rockets with yellow stars and scarlet lightnings painted on them; there was even a sculpted twist of blue touch-paper that came away to enable the salt and pepper to be poured inside.

Ben stared at them admiringly. "They're beautiful," he said.

Mr Roper nodded, too honest to disagree. "I think they're my favourites at the moment," he sighed, "I've put them pride of place next to the penguins."

"I wish I could have some fireworks," muttered Ben enviously, "real ones I mean. I bet Miss Wethers won't let me have any."

The old man smiled. "She might at that," he said kindly. "Now, I must put these fellows back with the others." He returned to the parlour and called over his shoulder. "As you've finished, you'd best go and give your hands a wash and leave that rascal's head there to dry."

"When will I be able to paint a face on him?" asked Ben. "He will be ready in two days' time won't he?"

In the parlour Mr Roper laughed and came back to the front room. "Aye, he'll be ready. If you come back tomorrow he should be dry enough and you can paint the bounder." He gave a little chuckle then added, "Mind you, we shouldn't really be doing this you know, old Fawkes was a fellow Yorkshireman and a soldier to boot. It's Bob Catesby who should be stuck on the bonfire – were his idea after all."

"But you've got to have a Guy Fawkes," Ben started to protest, "if I can't have any fireworks, at least..." then he saw that the old man was not being serious.

"I'm only pulling your leg," smiled Mr Roper. "Now, where are them old pants of mine?" He disappeared upstairs for a while and Ben could hear him pulling everything out of the wardrobe. The boy wandered into the kitchen where he washed his hands in the big square sink and thought about the face he would paint on the papier mâché head.

"Here we are," said Mr Roper brandishing a pair of grey trousers that smelled of mothballs. 'I'll tie some string round the legs and then we can start stuffing them with that newspaper you've got left.

Ben dried his hands and waited while the string was tightly fastened. Then they took great handfuls of paper, scrunched them up, and thrust them down the trouser legs.

"Tell me about the war again," Ben asked.

"You don't want to listen to my boring stories," chortled the old man, "it's time you told me one of your own."

"I don't know any," came the reply, "please."

"You don't know any?" cried Mr Roper in disbelief. "Why don't you go telling me that in the short time you've been in Whitby Alice Boston hasn't been filling your head full of tales. I've never known that lady resist the chance of entertaining someone who's willing to listen. A wealth of stories she's got!"

Ben grinned but as he glanced out of the window he saw that it was growing dark. He groaned inwardly. Miss Wethers had told him to be back before nightfall and he dreaded to think what fuss she would make if he stayed out one minute later than he ought to.

Mr Roper knew what the boy was thinking. "All right lad," he said, "you'd best get going. I know what it's like to be on the receiving end of one of Edith Wethers' mithering lectures." He went into the hall and brought Ben's duffle coat from the peg. The boy was staring thoughtfully at the stuffed trousers and the lumpy papier mâché head. "Don't you fret now," the old man told him, "Fawkes'll be dry by tomorrow – you come then and put as grim a face on him as possible."

Ben wriggled into his coat, fastening the toggles as he wandered from the cosy front room. "I'll bring that jumper of mine tomorrow as well," he said, "then he'll be totally finished."

Mr Roper opened the door and the chill November afternoon blew in as Ben wandered down the short path. When he reached the gate the old man called to him, "And make sure you remember a story to tell me – you'll not get out of it that easily."

Laughing, the boy waved and set off home.

Mr Roper closed the door and returned to the warmth of the fire. Switching on the radio, he sat in the chair once more and picked up a copy of *The Dalesman* to read. Presently he began to nod and slipped into a peaceful doze as the music of a bygone era swelled about him. To the sound of the big dance bands he held his Margaret in his arms once more and together they glided over the floor of his pepper-pot-scattered dreams.

Ben plunged his hands deep into his coat pockets, it was getting very cold. He quickened his pace, anxious to reach Aunt Alice's cottage in time. Gloom was gathering over Whitby, the narrow ginnel that ran down the side of Mr Roper's house was already filled with shadow. But for the crying of gulls it was eerily quiet. The boy hurried and was glad when he emerged into Bagdale, one of the main routes into the town. Past half-empty guest houses he went, only stopping to look up at the rising hill of Pannet Park where the museum was situated.

He thought about his sister and wondered what she had been doing all day – Jennet had been in a strange mood lately, always wanting to be on her own and refusing to play. When he had confided this to Miss Boston, she told him that Jennet was growing up. Ben did not like to dwell on this alarming fact too much, "growing up" meant that his sister would start having boyfriends, and he was afraid that sooner or later he would lose her. The pair of them had always been together and after the death of their parents it was she who protected and cared for him. Life without Jennet – even if she was a pain sometimes – was unthinkable. Ben pulled a glum face and hoped it would be a long time before he had to 'grow up'.

"CRET!" screeched a voice.

Ben spun round and there, to his dismay, he saw Danny Turner tearing towards him.

"I'm gonna kick you in!" the thug yelled.

Ben fled; after Jennet's attack on Danny yesterday there was no telling what he would do to get revenge. Breathlessly he ran as hard as he could, but knew there was no hope of escape, for Danny was faster than him. He cursed the awkwardness of his duffle coat – it was so heavy that it slowed him down. Soon he would feel rough fingers catch hold of the hood and he would become a punchbag for Danny's fists.

"Come 'ere, Cret!" his pursuer demanded.

Ben was terribly afraid, there was no way he could cross the bridge and reach Aunt Alice's cottage – he was done for. Desperately he glanced over his shoulder, Danny was closing on him.

"Coward!" accused the snarling voice. "Ain'tcha got yer sister to fight for yer?"

The pavement streaked beneath the two boys' feet as they pounded down the sloping road towards the harbour, but there was still a long way to go. This was no good, Ben told himself. He had only one chance and that was to hide.

Recklessly he leapt into the road. A car screamed

and the driver stamped on the brakes. Ben dodged aside as it skidded to a halt and then he was across. The man in the car leaned out of the window and bawled at him but the boy had scurried up into Pannet Park, up to where the shrubs and bushes screened him from the traffic below.

"Ruddy idiot!" the driver fumed. "Could've killed him!" He took hold of the steering wheel once more and gave a slight shudder at the thought. Then another boy darted out in front of him.

This one slapped the bonnet of the car as he passed and shouted, "Up yours Grandad!" then he too disappeared up the steps into the park.

Pressing close to the dense rhododendrons, Ben hurried from one side of the park to the other. Already he could see the exit to St Hilda's Terrace which led directly to the bridge – ought he to chance it he wondered? He waited indecisively, hiding beneath the drooping dark leaves of the shrubbery. Where was Danny? Ben held his breath and listened – he could hear nothing behind him, the Turner boy must have given up or gone the other way.

Stealthily he crept from the cover and peered back down the sweeping lawns he had just climbed.

"Oh no," he whispered.

Up came Danny, his face resolute and angry. "Laurenson!" he shrieked. "Yer for it now!"

Ben scrambled over the grass, hurtling towards the gateway. In a trice he was through, but instead of careering down the hill, he leapt over the wall of a nearby house and ducked quickly. With his face half-buried in a pile of damp, dead leaves he froze and waited.

Danny Turner shot from the park and glared about him. There was no trace of the Laurenson boy anywhere. "I'll get yer!" he shouted. "Ain't no use hidin'. Come out, yer whingin' Jessie!"

Ben remained exactly where he was, his chin submerged beneath the deep decay of autumn. He was extremely uncomfortable; the damp had soaked through his trousers and a repulsive, cloying smell of mould fouled his nostrils. A cloud of agitated flies buzzed around his head and his flesh crawled when one landed on his lip. If only Danny would give up and go home. "Go away," he mouthed, willing his enemy to retreat, "get lost."

Across the street, Danny snorted and spat with disgust. "Flamin' baby," he muttered, "next time I sees him – or that stinkin' sister, they'll be sorry."

He wandered along the terrace, kicking the gates of the houses as he passed by. In his cramped hiding place, Ben could hear the vicious 'clangs' growing fainter. He let out a sigh of relief. Now he could move. The dead leaves squelched as he stirred. Ben was glad to be free at last – he couldn't bear another minute with all those flies amid that putrid smell.

He raised his head from the wet pile, but what he discovered made his eyes bulge round and wide. Now he knew where the stench was coming from – and why there were so many flies. On the ground, just next to where he had been crouching, were the gutted remains of a cat.

Ben let out a cry of horror. The poor creature had been in a terrible fight. What meagre tatters of skin it had left were covered in vile rents and savage claw marks. He leapt to his feet and the flies zoomed back to their feast – Ben felt ill.

"What sort of animal would do that?" he murmured. "Not a dog surely?"

Then he noticed the colour of the bloodstained fur – it had been a marmalade cat. He thought of the woman he and Jennet had met yesterday and how frantic she had been. Here then was Mrs Rigby's Mokey, this awful carcass was all that was left of her little darling. It had been eaten. The back of Ben's throat burned as the bile bubbled up from his stomach and he turned away.

"Gotcha!" sniggered a voice.

Danny Turner jumped over the wall and grabbed Ben round the neck. It was too quick and sudden for the boy to resist and he felt his legs give way as Danny kicked them. Down he went and the Turner lad pushed him into the leaves a second time.

"Try to run, did yer, Cret?" hissed Danny, delivering a spiteful punch to Ben's ribs. "I'll show you and yer sister not to make a fool of me. Good job she never broke me nose or I'd have got me Dad's air pistol at the pair of yer. It puts eyes out it does – an' believe me I'd do it an' all!" He raised his fist to give Ben another punch but the blow never fell. His own eyes had lit upon Mokey's body.

Danny let out a long, admiring whistle. "Fwor!" he cooed. "Look at this!" He reached over and picked the corpse up without flinching. "This'd make a great mascot for the front of me bike," he drooled, "I could tie it to the handle bars – look at them eyes stickin' out on stalks!"

"Put it down!" shrieked Ben in outrage. "Leave it alone!"

A horrible smile flickered over Danny's thuggish face. "Put it down," he repeated in a whining imitation of Ben's voice. "Doesn't yer like it, Diddums? Does it scare yer?" He dangled the grisly body above the boy's head, bobbing it up and down like a yoyo. "Woooo," he taunted, "have a look at the big gash in its froat. Open yer peepers, soft lad! Look, I can make its tail twitch by pulling this bit."

Ben squirmed and screwed his face up. Danny was no better than an animal.

"Hur, hur," his tormentor chuckled, relishing the agony he was putting him through. "There's not much left of its innards, see – I can put my hand right up its ribcage and use it like a puppet." With his free hand he pinched his nose to produce a squeaky, nasal voice. "Ooh, Judy," he sang waving the cat in Ben's face, "that's the way to do it, that's the way to do it."

He laughed, then wiped the blood on Ben's coat. "Does yer not like me puppet show?" he asked. "I thought you crets went in for that sort of thing. I'll have to come up with summat else to keep yer happy."

"You're disgusting," Ben said angrily, "put it down."

At that, all traces of humour left Danny. "Don't you talk to me like that!" he growled. "I'm gonna teach you some manners I am. Feel sorry for this rancid moggy does yer? Well here! You can have it!" With a shout, he swung the cat round and pushed it into Ben's face.

The boy spluttered and tried to get free, shaking his head for the other to stop. But Danny was determined, he smeared the gory carcass all over Ben, then spat on him.

"Hoy, you two!" came a stern protest. "What the 'ell do you think you're playin' at?"

Danny glanced up. At the window of the house stood a gruff-looking man. The boy stuck his fingers up at him then hissed in Ben's ear. "This ain't over yet! Me an' my gang's gonna come after you. It won't be cat blood on yer then, but yer own!" With that he leapt over the wall and disappeared back into the park.

The owner of the house had left the window and was hastening to the door. Ben wiped his mouth with his sleeve and stared miserably at what was left of Mokey.

"Right!" roared the man, appearing from the

doorway with a stick in his hand. "Where are the beggars? I'll learn 'em to trespass and cheek me."

But the garden was empty and when he ran to the gate to glare down the street he could only see a duffle-coated figure hurrying towards the harbour. "Flamin' kids," he swore.

* * *

Miss Wethers threw up her hands and let out such a scream that Eurydice's kittens dashed upstairs and refused to venture out from beneath Miss Boston's bed for two whole days. Eurydice herself gave the remains a curious sniff, then sauntered away in a huff with her tail in the air.

"Take it away!" Edith squawked. "Get rid of it immediately! You horrid, dirty boy!"

Ben closed the front door behind him. All the way home he was hoping that the postmistress would not be the one to let him in. Unfortunately however, she had. At once she saw the stains on his face and that he was trying to hide something under his coat. When she had insisted on seeing whatever it was, he had reluctantly opened the duffle and shown her the newspaper parcel concealed within. Then of course she had to know what was inside it – he had tried to warn her but too late – Miss Wethers had confiscated it and opened the thing for herself.

Her shrieks were still shaking the plates on the draining-board in the kitchen when Ben knelt to pick the dead cat up again.

"Don't touch it!" she screeched, running up and down the hall as though she had sat on a wasp's nest. "You wicked, wicked child! How could you? Throw it away – Aaaagghhh!" She leant against the wall to steady herself and the tissue came flying from her cardigan to cover her eyes. "I must sit down," she whimpered, "I can feel one of my faints coming on – ooh, Jennet, help me."

Ben's sister was giving her brother deadly looks. How could he be so stupid? She shook her head at him then went to Miss Wethers' rescue. "Let me help you into a chair," she said taking hold of the spinster's arm. "I'll make you a strong cup of tea with lots of sugar in it."

Edith gagged. "Couldn't keep it down," she refused. "Where did the boy come by such a filthy thing? I'll have to fumigate the carpet." At that she looked down at her own hands and remembered that she too had touched the grisly parcel. "Eeeee!" she cried and dashed to the sink where she took the nail-brush and scrubbed herself with disinfectant.

"I found it," said Ben following them into the kitchen. "It's Mrs Rigby's, I couldn't leave it there could I?"

"Don't you dare bring that abomination into this kitchen, young man!" declared Miss Wethers adamantly. "What did you think you were doing? Just you wait till I tell Alice. I knew I wouldn't be able to manage. 'Children are nothing more than little monsters,' that's what my mother used to tell me, 'never have anything to do with them, Edith' she said. All these years I listened to her and now look how right she was!"

She ran into the hall, avoiding Ben as best she could then sped upstairs. "It's bath-time for you my lad!" she squeaked. "But goodness knows what I'm to do with your coat. I'll have to boil the thing and if it shrinks you've only yourself to blame."

Alone with Jennet, Ben crossed to the back door. "Ben," she said tersely.

"What?"

"Are you mad? What's the matter with you? Are you so stupid? Chuck that dead cat in the bin outside and tell Miss Wethers you're sorry. Honestly Ben you're such a child at times!"

The boy stared impassively at her. He did not want to mention his encounter with Danny Turner, she would only go and make matters worse again. "No," he said flatly, "I'm not going to put it in the bin – what would you think if someone did that to Eurydice or one of the kittens?"

"I'm sure I wouldn't care," she replied, "what else can you do with a dead cat?"

"I'm going to bury it in the garden," he told her pulling the door open. On the step he gave her one last, bitter look and added, "would you've cared if they'd put Mum and Dad in the bin too?"

Jennet slammed the door and Ben took the body to the far side of the garden then went in search of Aunt Alice's trowel.

6

THE FALL OF THE VEIL

The sleek, black taxi barged through the heavy traffic, like an impatient giant beetle. Through amber lights it roared, taking corners at an astonishing speed. In the back, Miss Boston slid along the seat one more time and blamed herself for not taking the Underground. It had been a break-neck, nerve-rattling journey all the way from Kings Cross, anyone would think the cabbie was driving the getaway car from a bank robbery. No, she was doing the poor man a disservice – perhaps he had been an ambulance driver before taking up this present career. She ventured to open one eye and peered at the back of the man's head. He was thick-set and had a cauliflower ear – maybe her first suspicion had been correct after all.

They raced over a zebra crossing, heedless of the people waiting on the pavement and Miss Boston covered her face with the hat that had been shaken off her head. "Ironic really," she told herself, "one of the reasons I decided to take a taxi was to see more of London." At that moment the cab hit a bump in the road, the old lady bounced off the seat and hit her head on the roof.

That was too much. She tapped on the glass that separated her from the driver and shouted, "Excuse me, would you care to drive a little more carefully? I'm not enjoying this at all!"

The cabbie shifted disagreeably and muttered something under his breath. "You wanna get there, missus, or don't yer?" he asked.

"Most certainly," she replied, "but preferably in one piece."

"Fifteen years I've been cabbin' it," he grumbled, "you out-of-townies come up 'ere for the day an' think you know it all. Just pipe down in the back an' lemme do my job."

Miss Boston stuck out her chins at his insolence but there seemed little else she could say. It had been a tiring day, most of it had been spent cooped up in a crowded, stuffy train and she was in no mood for an argument. "Unpleasant fellow," she merely mumbled, and left it at that, turning her attention to the blurred scenes that whipped by outside the windows.

From the little she had seen, London had changed dramatically since she had last visited – why that was over ten years ago now. There were many new buildings to admire, and criticize, even the shops had undergone startling transformations and on every side sheer towers of sparkling glass reached into the sky. The bustling city was a far cry from her more tranquil home.

"Such a mad dash everyone seems to be in," she observed. "Oh my!"

A car had pulled out in front of the taxi without warning and the cabbie pounded the horn whilst adding his own colourfully verbal abuse.

Miss Boston shook her head. How did people manage to live in this frantic place? She suddenly felt very small and insignificant compared to the sprawling old city that had engulfed her. Back in Whitby everyone knew her but here she was nobody.

It was a humbling thought and before she knew what she was doing she was feeling sorry for herself.

"Alice Boston!" she reprimanded quickly. "What do you think you're doing? This isn't like you – pull yourself together, woman. Remember why you're here and save your sympathy for those who really need it!" She tutted into her hat then held her head high. She wasn't going to let the capital city intimidate her!

At last, they arrived in Kensington and the taxi shot past the great museums before turning off into one of the quieter streets. With a jolt the vehicle skidded to a standstill and Miss Boston's hat sailed out of the window.

"'Ere we are, missus," the cabbie announced, "safe and sound."

The old lady gave him a frosty look and rummaged in her purse for the fare. "Outrageously expensive!" she remarked handing the money over.

"What – no tip?" the man protested.

"I'll give you a tip," she said brusquely, "learn some manners!"

"Stuff off."

Miss Boston alighted from the taxi with as much dignity as she could muster and dragged out her luggage. As soon as she shut the door the cab screeched and streaked away. The old lady put her case on the pavement and waddled into the road to retrieve her hat before she looked about her.

It was an impressive street. All the buildings were Georgian town houses, the kind that only embassies or film stars could now afford. They all had four floors, with two entrances at the front, the main doorway flanked by stout pillars and a flight of steps leading to the servants' quarters below.

Miss Boston pursed her lips and cast an eye over herself. Her clothes looked a wreck and she felt far too shabby to enter one of these grand houses. She spent a few moments smoothing the creases from her skirt and perching the hat back on her woolly head. Then, pulling her cape about her, she ascended the steps to number eleven and rang the bell.

The minutes ticked by, but nobody came to the door. Miss Boston pressed the bell again – perhaps there was no one at home, maybe she had come too late. She staggered down the steps and glanced up at the windows. The curtains were not drawn so her fears ebbed a little. Miss Boston decided to ring once more.

This time she kept her finger on the button for a full five minutes until she released it. "Most odd," she said aloud, "where is everybody?" She glared accusingly at the door as though it were to blame, then spied the letter-box. Cautiously, the old lady squinted up and down the street to make certain no one was watching before crouching down to lift the letter flap. Bringing her eyes close to the slot, Miss Boston peered inside.

"How peculiar," she muttered, "there appears to be something in the way, I can't see a blessed thing, it's all dark – no, why it seems to be material …"

Her voice failed her as the grey material moved behind the door, she saw a row of shiny black buttons, a white collar and then another eye loomed through the letter-box at her.

Miss Boston blinked and the other eye did the same before disappearing. Suddenly the door was pulled open and a superior voice demanded, "What have we here?"

The old lady looked up sheepishly. A tall, grey-haired man was studying her with the utmost solemnity. He was about fifty years old, possessing a long sharp nose which he could expertly look down. His eyes held no humour and the lids drooped over them in a weary, melancholy fashion. The right side of his thin mouth twitched as he waited for an explanation and his disparaging stare made Miss Boston feel about ten years old.

"I... I did ring," she stammered, rising to her feet, "but there was no answer, so I ..."

The man pulled a sour expression. "Whatever it is we don't want any," he said curtly. "Good day."

Miss Boston reached out her foot as he swung the door to. "I beg your pardon!" she declared, overcoming her embarrassment, "But I am Alice Boston. Patricia Gunning has invited me to stay for a few days."

The man regarded her through the half-closed door but made no attempt to let her in. "Mrs Gunning sees no one," he said.

"Well she'll see me!" she cried. "Stand aside and let me in!" Miss Boston gave the door a shove but he continued to hold it firm.

"The mistress is too ill for visitors," she was told, "if you leave your card I will see that it is brought to her attention."

Miss Boston was flabbergasted and was about to give the man a good telling off when he turned as though someone had spoken to him from inside the house. "Let her in?" he asked in surprise. "This is all very irregular."

Miss Boston craned her neck and tried to peer round him. "Patricia?" she called. "Is that you?"

The man gave her a reproachful look then opened the door. Miss Boston stuck out her tongue at him and pushed past.

The first thing that struck her as she walked inside was not the impressive oak staircase that swept up to the first floor landing, nor the gleaming marble beneath her feet, nor the sumptuously expensive oil paintings that hung on the walls all around – no, what Miss Boston noticed first was the piercing chill.

Shivering, she wrapped the cloak about her, all the time looking for the person the man had been speaking to. There she was. Descending the stairs was a hefty, bushy-browed woman. Miss Boston's shoulders sagged – this was not her old friend.

The stranger was dressed in a pristine white uniform, her dark, wiry hair scraped back into a bun. She was an uncommonly ugly woman; her face was ill-proportioned and square with a large jutting chin, when she spoke her words were clipped and precise like a sergeant-major's, but the eyes which fixed immovably upon Miss Boston were small and pig-like. Her bearing was masculine – and her frame one that any rugby player would have been proud of. Down the crimson-carpeted stairs she stomped, her heavy footfalls thumping a jarring rhythm throughout the house.

"Welcome, Miss Boston," she barked in a baritone. "We've been expecting you."

"I haven't," remarked the man acidly.

The woman ignored him and shook the old lady's hand vigorously in her own which were large and strong. "I am Judith Deacon," she said, "Mrs Gunning's private nurse."

Miss Boston flexed her squashed fingers thinking that there was more starch in this woman than in her uniform. "How is Patricia?" she asked.

Miss Deacon's face grew serious. "I'll be frank with you," she told her, "Mrs Gunning is most unwell, I'm afraid there isn't much hope for her. She is terribly weak and grows worse with each passing day. I confess that I tried to dissuade her from inviting you – I don't approve of anything that over-excites her."

"Most commendable," Miss Boston put in, "but I'm not exactly sure what ails her. The letter she sent was very brief and vague, could you enlighten me?"

The nurse nodded, stiffly clasping her spade-like hands in front of her. "My patient has a very delicate condition which needs constant attention. It began when she caught a bad cold and progressed from there – she is quite old you know."

Miss Boston reared her head. Patricia Gunning was nearly ten years younger than herself and had always shared the same vigorous health that she enjoyed. "Do you think I could see her now?" she asked politely.

Judith examined her watch and nodded, "Briefly," she said. "Since Mrs Gunning employed me I have kept her to a strict routine – I won't undermine all my efforts for anyone. You can have ten minutes with her, that's all." She spun on her heel and addressed the man who had opened the door. "Rook, take Miss Boston's luggage up to the guest-room on the second floor, it has been made ready for her."

The man raised his eyes to the high, decorated ceiling and breathed loudly through his long nose, rustling the bristling hairs which sprouted from it. "Very well," he said, greatly vexed at the inconvenience.

Miss Boston watched with amusement as he went sulkily out to fetch her case. "Don't mind Rook," the nurse told her, "he's only a butler with an inflated opinion of himself."

"Indeed?" said the old lady, privately thinking exactly the same about her.

"Yes," Judith continued, "when I took over there was a full complement of staff here but I ask you, with only one person to look after it was a scandal. Bone idle most of them were, I soon sent them packing. Rook I kept on to attend to those matters my work made impossible for me to see to myself."

"What do you mean you took over?" asked Miss Boston in surprise.

Miss Deacon strode to the foot of the majestic staircase and placed a hand on the carved oak banister, striking the pose of "Lady of the House". If she had not looked so ridiculous it would have been alarming. "I have complete authority here," she said, "I think I should make that perfectly clear straight away – I wouldn't have taken the position otherwise."

"But what about Patricia?"

The nurse managed an ugly smile, revealing her irregular tombstone-like teeth. "Oh she isn't well enough for that sort of responsibility. It is my duty to see to the smooth running of the household. No others are required here, we manage extraordinarily well on our own. Now, if you please." She began to climb the stairs and gestured for Miss Boston to follow.

Miss Boston did as she was bid. This was not at all the kind of reception she had been expecting. Were all private nurses as domineering and coldly efficient as this specimen, she found herself wondering.

Up the staircase they went and when they came to the landing Judith marched up to a dark panelled door. She waited for Miss Boston to catch up with her before turning the handle and entering.

It was the most unusual sickroom Miss Boston had ever seen. To get in she had to duck beneath a swinging bunch of dried herbs that had been pinned to the lintel. This was only the first of many, for countless arrangements of withered leaves and flowers covered the walls and hung from the ceiling. A pungent, aromatic scent laced the air, irritating the back of Miss Boston's throat and stinging her eyes till they watered. Strange pictures and symbols filled the spaces in between the dead plants, designs taken from old magical works, charms of protection and healing. Miss Boston recognized them instantly but thought nothing of it – it was no surprise to her that Patricia Gunning was a white witch, but then she always did have a tendency to go over the top with it all.

A magnificent four-poster bed took up most of the room and was covered in a fine canopy of creamy muslin. At its foot, from a silver incense burner, streamed a steady thread of green smoke, it was this that was responsible for the overpowering smell.

"Confounded contraption," Miss Boston chirped, blinking and wiping her eyes, "never did like the wretched things."

"You'll get used to it," assured Judith. "Come right in and close the door after you – I won't allow draughts of any kind."

Miss Boston obeyed then walked up to the bed. Through the fine muslin mist, she saw amid the great expanse of the covers a small figure lying on its side, its head turned from view. "Patricia?" Miss Boston began. "Is that you?"

Very slowly, and with the greatest of care, the figure moved. Patricia Gunning was a frail woman of eighty-three years. Her face was shrunken like an apple that had been kept too long and her limbs were brittle sticks. With difficulty she lifted her head and the long, silver hair which had been painstakingly arranged over the pillows floated about her shoulders. It had the same quality to it that is found in old mirrors, being a faded, tarnished glow and was more gossamer-like than the muslin which surrounded her.

"Alice!" came her sweet, tinkling voice. "Oh Alice, I'm so pleased to see you!" She reached out her thin arms in greeting and Miss Boston drew the material aside to hold her.

Judith Deacon watched icily as the two friends hugged one another and folded her arms.

"Dear Patricia!" exclaimed Miss Boston. "It really is good to see you again."

Her friend sank back on to the pillows and smiled. Her eyes were still the clearest and loveliest blue that Miss Boston had ever seen. "I was not sure if you would come," she sighed. "How is your enchanting Whitby? Do you still climb the abbey steps before breakfast? You look marvellous – a real tonic to me."

"Well it looks as though you could do with one," observed Miss Boston truthfully. "I think we could start by opening a window or two – the atmosphere really is thick in here, enough to make anyone feel poorly. I don't know how you can breathe."

Judith Deacon moved in front of the nearest window, barring it with her amazonian body. "No draughts!" she reiterated. "The temperature must be kept at a constant and the incense is vital to the regime I have instigated solely for Mrs Gunning's benefit."

Miss Boston raised her eyebrows, "Well I shall just have to take matters in hand now – won't I Patricia dear? Fresh air cures everything – there's nothing wrong with you a nice walk around the park wouldn't chase away."

The woman on the bed closed her eyes, "Oh Alice," she breathed, "please don't try to jolly me along. I know how ill I am – I'm dying, there's no escaping that fact. I haven't got much time left on this earth."

Miss Boston frowned. "Now that's enough of that talk," she said firmly. "Is this the same Patricia Gunning who climbed over the roof of the ladies' college for an illicit rendezvous with her future husband?"

Patricia gave a feeble laugh. "Oh what a night that was," she chuckled. "What a surprise my darling Walter had when he saw me shinny down the drain-pipe. 'Not the behaviour of a young lady' he said – oh he was so gloriously pompous in those days.'' She propped herself up on one elbow and gave Miss Boston's hand a slight squeeze. "How you've cheered me," she told her, "a good friend you've been to me, Alice – thank you for that."

"Keep your gratitude," replied her guest, "I don't want it yet. There'll be plenty of time still, you'll see."

Patricia said nothing, she lowered her eyes and let go of her hand.

At once, the ever-watchful Judith came forward. "Time for your medication, Mrs Gunning," she said taking a large glass bottle from the bedside table.

Miss Boston watched in silence as the nurse poured a small quantity of thick, brown liquid on to a spoon. "Surely that isn't one of your own brews, Patricia?" she asked in amazement.

"Mrs Gunning's potions are better than anything from the chemist," the nurse answered for her.

Miss Boston couldn't believe it. "But don't you think you ought to try conventional medicine?" she asked. "The old recipes are fine for headaches and rheumatism, but to rely on them now – isn't that being rather foolish? I always envied you your powers, Patricia, but this is madness."

"We know what we're doing!" rapped the nurse. "Now, open wide Mrs Gunning."

For an instant Miss Boston thought she caught a peculiar, almost frightened look on her friend's face as she opened her mouth.

"There's a good girl," said Miss Deacon inspecting the spoon, "all gone now."

"Thank you," muttered Patricia slowly.

The nurse screwed the top back on the bottle and replaced it on the table. Miss Boston was bewildered. "What sort of silliness is this?" she cried abruptly. "Patricia you must see a proper doctor – you're seriously ill!"

"The doctor has been to see Mrs Gunning," the nurse informed her. "Unfortunately he said there was nothing he could do. This at least gives her a certain amount of relief."

Miss Boston was appalled. "Nonsense!" she declared. "What kind of a nurse are you?"

"A caring one," came the reply.

"Alice," Patricia broke in, "tell me all your news. Did you really adopt those children you wrote to me about? I hope my influence helped. Did you have a good Hallowe'en? Did the children bob for apples and hollow out turnips – were there pomegranates and chestnuts? Are you still practising the craft or is it too much for you now? I haven't woven so much as a charm for warts in months." She spoke hurriedly, as if trying to defuse the situation and Miss Boston allowed herself to be drawn into the small talk for her friend's sake.

They exchanged a few, brief sentences then Miss Deacon checked her watch and announced that it was time for her patient's nap. "Now, you know the routine," she said in a no-nonsense voice best suited to a nursery, "four o'clock till six we have our rest." Reaching down she swiped the pillow from under the woman's head and tucked the bedclothes tightly round her.

Miss Boston's chins wobbled in surprise. "But I've only just arrived," she protested, "surely a few more minutes won't matter?"

The nurse threw her a vicious look and turned to her patient with her arms folded. "Mrs Gunning," she began crossly, "I cannot and will not have your routine disrupted in this manner. You employed me to look after you to the best of my abilities. Would you kindly tell your friend not to interfere in matters she is patently ignorant of? If she questions my authority once more I shall pack up and leave – is that what you want?"

"No!" Patricia cried, her whole body trembling. "Please Judith, I'm sure Alice meant no harm." She placed her shaking hand on Miss Boston's arm. "If you love me, do as she says," she implored, "do this for me I beg you."

Miss Boston patted the tiny hand, disturbed by the influence the nurse had over her friend. "Anything you say Patricia, dear," she said, not wishing to distress her any further.

"Promise, Alice," Mrs Gunning insisted, "that while you're here you'll follow Judith's instructions regarding me, however – unorthodox you might think them."

"I promise," Miss Boston relented. "I suppose you know what you're doing. I'm just happy to see you again."

Patricia smiled and glanced up at the nurse before sinking back in relief.

"Time to go," Miss Deacon told the visitor. "She needs to rest now."

Miss Boston rose from the bed where she had been sitting and Judith drew back the canopy. "When can I see her again?" she inquired.

The nurse ushered her to the door. "I will permit one more visit this evening," she told her. "Now, perhaps you would care to go to your room."

"Yes, I suppose I could unpack," said Miss Boston thoughtfully.

"If you really think that will be necessary. Your dinner will be in the dining-room at seven o' clock sharp."

Before the door was closed on her, Miss Boston took one final look at her friend. The figure on the bed seemed to be only a shadow and the muslin which enveloped her the first manifestation of that other, grimmer veil, which would soon fall between them.

The guest-room which had been made ready on the second floor was as comfortable a bedchamber as she could wish. The walls were a pale shade of lemon and the prints on the walls were pretty views of Italy. Fresh flowers had been arranged in a crystal vase and Miss Boston was grateful for their fragrance after the choking fumes of the sickroom. Her case lay on the bed where Rook had left it but on consideration she decided not to touch it just yet. Instead, she opened the window and let the last weak rays of sunlight shine on her face.

"Well, Alice," she told herself, "what are you going to do now?" The old lady drummed her fingers on the window-sill, her thoughts smouldering on the formidable nurse. She reminded her of several notorious landladies that she knew in Whitby – but her aggressive manner far exceeded anything they had been rumoured to display to their guests. "Judith Deacon is rather a mystery," she mused, "I wonder what possessed Patricia to employ her in the first place?"

When she eventually unpacked and placed all her things neatly in drawers or on hangers, she decided that it was time to explore the rest of the house. "After all," she told herself, "I can't be expected to sit here and do nothing until dinner surely?"

Patricia and her late husband had only bought the house eight years ago, so it was all new to Miss Boston. The last time she had visited they had a place in Knightsbridge. Mrs Gunning had certainly married well for Walter had been extremely wealthy.

The old lady left her room and descended to the first floor landing once again. At the top of the staircase she saw a telephone tucked into a niche which she had not noticed earlier. "Perhaps I should call Edith," she thought. "No, the post office will have closed long ago. You really must get a telephone installed at the cottage, Alice! I won't be able to get in touch until Monday morning now – botheration!"

As she passed the door of the sickroom Miss Boston was tempted to press an ear to it, but she resisted the urge and trotted down to the hall.

"I suppose there must be a library in here," she mumbled, "Walter was a prolific reader." For nearly an hour Miss Boston familiarized herself with the layout of the ground floor. There was an impressive dining-room that contained a long oak table which stretched from one end to the other and could easily seat at least twenty guests. Beyond that there were five other rooms but everything inside them was covered by dust sheets and this fact alone gave Miss Boston dreadful misgivings – it was as though her friend were already dead. There was something extremely wrong about the entire business and that frightening nurse was at the centre of it all.

Aimlessly, Miss Boston went from room to room but never wearied of peeping beneath the dust covers to see what was hidden beneath.

Patricia had exquisite taste and had furnished the house with her own individual style. Miss Boston often wondered what Walter had thought about "Patricia's little hobby" as she always used to call it. Did he mind the paintings of the moon and stars that covered the walls of the sitting-room? And what about the special carving Patricia had commissioned from one of Britain's finest sculptors? It was a lighthearted tribute to her particular interest and hung above the fireplace; wooden cats, toads and mice swirled about in a semi-circle that also contained other objects associated with the craft. There were cauldrons, pointed hats, magic wands, charmed plants, corn dollies, amulets and even a broomstick.

Miss Boston grinned wryly and draped the sheet back over the carving. "What a gaudy display," she muttered, "quite ostentatious – dear oh dear."

Eventually she found her way to the library, it was a lovely room, books of all shapes and sizes obscured the walls and the old lady spent some time poring over a few of them. When she glanced up at the small clock on the table it was half-past six and she slid the volume she had been reading back on to the shelf.

"Soon be time for dinner," she observed, "I must go and freshen up. What must I look like? A brisk wipe over with a flannel should invigorate me and chase the journey's grime away." And with that she returned to her room.

At seven o'clock Miss Boston was seated at the long dining table while the butler served her dinner. It was one of the most disheartening meals she had ever eaten. Sitting alone in the middle of that immense table was bad enough but the food itself was drab and barely palatable. First of all, Rook brought in the soup which was a watery thin liquid straight from a tin and had not even been heated properly. Miss Boston was at a loss to tell what flavour it was supposed to be, but she forced it down and gave the butler a gratified smile.

"I take it Miss Deacon will not be joining me?" she said.

"No," came the pert reply, "she always dines with the mistress in her bedchamber."

"Such devotion," the old lady commented, tentatively sipping the lukewarm soup. "And do you cook the meals for them as well?"

"Miss Deacon sees to both the mistress's and her own requirements, madam," he said. "I am left to fend for myself. We have had no outside company for many months now – not since Cook was dismissed."

"Don't you think that rather odd? I mean, what is

your opinion of this private nurse? Isn't she too efficient?"

His mouth twitched into what looked like a sneer but it was difficult to tell with him. "I'm sure I don't know what you mean, madam," he replied. "The mistress knows what she is doing – but I haven't seen her for God knows how long. What concern is it to me? I am here merely to serve – I know my place. She tells the nurse and the nurse tells me."

Miss Boston managed to finish the soup and laid her spoon down in relief. Unfortunately she could not stop herself grimacing as the last of the tepid substance slid slimily down her throat.

Rook eyed her suspiciously as he removed the bowl and went to fetch the main course. Miss Boston sniffed. Surely she detected a decidedly alcoholic smell? When the man returned she was even more certain of it.

After a full fifteen minutes, Rook came, staggering into the dining-room wheeling a trolley before him. His legs seemed unable to co-ordinate properly and he tripped more than once on the way.

The main course consisted of cold potted meat and a rather limp-looking salad. Rook dumped the plate unceremoniously before Miss Boston and hovered behind her while she picked through the sad lettuce leaves with her fork, thankful that there were no naked flames nearby – for Rook was definitely drunk! Walter Gunning always kept a good cellar and the butler, it seemed, was fond of sampling it – tonight he had settled on an excellent Napoleon brandy. The old lady wrinkled her nose – the atmosphere in the dining-room was becoming quite like Christmas.

Miss Boston ate as much as she could and leaned back in her chair. At once Rook snatched the plate away, muttering at what she had left, and sent the whole thing clattering back on the trolley. Lettuce leaves flew everywhere.

Swaying unsteadily, Rook glared at the carpet where they had fallen and bent down to retrieve them. After falling on his face he abandoned the attempt and stuck his long nose in the air.

"Would madam care for des...deshert?" he slurred, grabbing hold of the trolley for support.

Miss Boston blinked at him. "Er, no thank you," she answered.

Rook drew himself up and fixed her with one bleary eye. "And why not?" he demanded. "What'sh wrong with it I ... I should like to know?"

"Nothing I'm sure," said the old lady feeling rather awkward, "but if you insist, I will have some please."

He nodded his head and rattled the trolley towards the door. "Comesh down 'ere without telling no one then turns her nose up at me des...des... at me pudding."

Miss Boston sighed and wondered what the next course would prove to be. "I dare say it is very dull for the poor man, stuck in here with very little to do all day but to help himself to the cellar – tut, tut. Does he make this a regular occurrence? The racks must be very empty by now if he does."

Another fifteen minutes dragged by. Rook was undoubtedly fortifying himself with another generous helping of brandy. When he returned he was practically riding on the trolley and brought it to a thunderous halt right beside the old lady's chair.

"'Ere it is," he declared. "Get your false teeth round this madam."

On to the table he tossed a bowl of tinned peaches, seized a small jug and poured a quantity of cream carelessly over everywhere except where it was wanted. Miss Boston gritted her teeth as it splashed on to her skirt and blouse and her jowls quivered indignantly. That was too much! She jumped up and threw down her napkin.

"Strangely enough," she stormed, "I actually prefer the cream on the peaches – not on me. You can be sure I'll inform the mistress of the house about this atrocious behaviour. I have never seen such a disgraceful exhibition! You, sir, are drunk as a lord – I suggest you go and make yourself a strong cup of coffee forthwith! And I'll have you know that all my teeth are my own – goodnight!"

She raged out of the dining-room, leaving Rook gaping after her. "Good grashush," he burbled, smiling for the first time in weeks, "what a smashing temper the old crock has."

Miss Boston spent the next half-hour sponging her clothes and shaking her head. When a knock sounded at her door she almost missed it.

"Miss Boston!" came a gruff voice.

The old lady hurried to the door and opened it – Judith Deacon was standing there impatiently. "I trust you dined well," she said.

The old lady was about to tell the nurse what she thought of the butler but decided against it. Not even he deserved the kind of roasting this nightmare woman would dish out. Instead she asked, "May I see Patricia now?"

"Of course you can. She has asked to see you and is waiting. Follow me please."

Miss Boston was led once more to the sickroom, but as soon as she stepped inside she could see that her friend's condition had worsened in the space of only four hours.

Mrs Gunning was visibly weaker, it seemed a terrible effort to her just to keep awake. Miss Boston knelt by the bed, pulled the muslin curtain aside and tried to conceal her shock at the sight of her. The pale blue eyes were roving slowly round, not focusing on anything – it was as though she had been drugged.

"Patricia," Miss Boston said, "it's Alice."

The patient moved her head at the sound of the voice but did not seem to see her. "Alice," she croaked in a faint whisper, "where are you?"

"Here, dear, take my hand."

The eyes swivelled round, blinked drowsily and the mist cleared from them. "Oh Alice," she groaned, "you should see your face – do I look as terrible as all that?"

Miss Boston tried to be a bit more cheerful, pushing to the back of her mind the nagging doubts which had surfaced. "Certainly not," she rallied, "I was just thinking about home – I hope the children are all right with my friend Edith. She's the most awful ditherer you know – probably had umpteen upsets today already."

"Ah," murmured Patricia sadly, "children. How lucky you are. If only Walter and I had been so blessed. Perhaps if we had I wouldn't ..." The shadow of the nurse fell on her and Mrs Gunning began to tremble. She glanced nervously at Miss Boston and then her pale, worn face grew suddenly resolute.

"Alice," she began with a desperate urgency, "Alice listen to me. Please, you must remember that I didn't have a choice."

"Pardon, dear?" said Miss Boston. "I can't hear you, Patricia."

"You must ... you must not delay. I don't matter any more!"

The rustle of a starched uniform crackled behind them as Judith Deacon took a step closer.

"What are you trying to tell me?" said Miss Boston, concerned at the anxiety that had contorted her friend's face.

"Oh forgive me, Alice, say you forgive me – please!"

"I don't understand," Miss Boston told her. "Patricia do calm down, you're working yourself up for no reason."

"Evil!" she cried, gripping the old lady's hand as tightly as possible. "Great evil!"

"That will be all!" broke in Judith's commanding voice, "Really, Miss Boston, I must ask you to leave, can't you see you're upsetting my patient? I will not tolerate the distress you are putting her through."

"But she's trying to tell me something."

The nurse took Patricia's head in her large hands and stared into the eyes. "She's delirious," she said sternly, "these fits come over her from time to time, a remnant of the fever she had three weeks ago." She gave Miss Boston an angry look and said, "I asked you to leave, would you please do as I say?"

The old lady rose but Patricia was unwilling to let go of her hand. "No," came the pathetic, barely audible voice, "don't leave me."

"OUT!" ordered Judith furiously. "She is too ill for you to be present – I warned her this would happen."

Miss Boston walked uncertainly to the door. Should she leave? What was Patricia trying to tell her – was it really all a figment of her poor, fevered brain?

The patient began to convulse and the nurse roared, "I shall not tell you again – do I have to throw you out, Miss Boston?"

At that the old lady left. There was nothing she could do but it stung nonetheless, she felt as though she were betraying her friend. Gloomily, she waited outside as the commotion blazed in the sickroom. Finally silence fell, the door opened and Judith Deacon's square head peered round.

"She's settled now," the nurse informed her. "I think it would be best if you didn't see her again tonight – she might be more lucid in the morning, although this attack has drained her considerably.

She's far too frail for this excitement."

"Yes," Miss Boston murmured, "poor Patricia, tell her I'll see her first thing – I pray she'll be stronger then."

Judith watched as the old lady unhappily plodded upstairs before returning to the sickroom with a cruel glint in her small, dark eyes.

Mrs Gunning shuddered as the nurse approached the bed. Her mouth fell open and she stammered, "I … I never said anything, I wouldn't…wouldn't say anything."

"You've been a bad girl, Mrs Gunning," Judith snarled with menace. "That was very naughty, you know you're not allowed to tell her don't you? You deviated from what we rehearsed, you almost ruined everything."

"I didn't!"

The pig-like eyes flashed and the nurse growled, "Oh but you so very nearly did – well you won't have a second chance!" She raised one of her strong hands and clenched it into a fist. Mrs Gunning gave a terrified whimper and cringed into the pillows.

7

AT THE CHURCH OF ST MARY

Ben slept fitfully, most of the bedclothes lay in a crumpled heap where he had kicked them. Squirming, he rolled over once more and murmured unhappily. Ghastly images invaded his dreams, spectral shadows of Danny Turner rose from the frightened corners of his mind like a dark angel whose face was locked in an eternal laugh that pierced and cut right through him.

The bully's apparition wheeled overhead, screeching his doom and crying for blood. Ben tried to flee, vainly wading through the thick black smoke of his sleep. Down swooped the nightmare Danny, his hands now claws, reaching for Ben like an eagle pursuing a lamb.

"Go away," Ben moaned, turning and throwing the sheet from him as though it were the great wings which beat against his face. "No!" he yelled – and then awoke.

It took a few moments for him to get his bearings, the room was so dark that he suspected his dream was not yet over, but when his eyes had adjusted to the gloom he relaxed and wiped his forehead. He was covered in perspiration and his mouth was horribly dry. He sat up, groping with his toes amongst the discarded bedclothes for his slippers. A few moments later he was treading softly along the small landing.

The house was incredibly still and quiet. The well of darkness which filled the space at the foot of the stairs unsettled him. Ben almost reached for the light switch – but he did not want to wake his sister or Miss Wethers, whose gentle snoring he could faintly hear coming from Miss Boston's room. Instead he conquered his nerves and hurried down, passing quickly through the black hall, fumbling for the handle of the kitchen door. Once safely within, he ran the tap and filled a cup with water.

It took two of these brimming cupfuls to quench his thirst and when he had finished Ben stretched – ready for bed again. Just as he was about to climb back up the stairs, the boy paused and turned round. From the yard outside he had heard a noise. It was the sound of a front door closing, followed by determined footsteps ringing over the concrete. Curious, Ben quickly nipped into the front room and peered out from behind the curtains.

The dim glow of the street lamp came fanning in through the alleyway, bathing the yard in a pale wedge of orange light. Ben wiped the remaining drowse from his eyes and stared out.

Nearby stood Nathaniel Crozier. Fortunately his back was to Miss Boston's cottage or he would have seen the boy's face at once. He had just left the Gregsons' house and was carrying a large, heavy-looking bag that clinked when he swung it over his shoulder. He took a step into the slanting light and his shadow flew far behind him, falling across the window where Ben was spying. The boy ducked quickly; it was as if the shadow were aware of him, for Nathaniel immediately turned – but all he saw was the slight movement of the curtain as it fell back into place.

Crouching beneath the sill, Ben listened for the man's footsteps, half expecting him to come over and glare through the window. That thought alone prevented the boy from returning to see what was really happening and two long, uncomfortable minutes ticked by. Not a sound came from the yard – what was Nathaniel doing out there? Ben's heart thumped nervously. He could imagine the man's face pressed up against the glass, his dark eyes penetrating the curtains and searching for him. He wasn't sure why he was so afraid for he hardly knew Mr Crozier and in fact he seemed to have charmed both Jennet and Miss Wethers. Yet he recalled the ugly look on the man's face he had witnessed early that morning and knew he had reason to be frightened. Then, just as he was about to risk lifting the curtain, something touched his arm. Ben gave a squawk and fell backwards in surprise.

Eurydice gave a slight purr – it was unusual for anyone to come down here at this time of night. She pushed her head against him in the hope that he would let her out.

"Get lost," he whispered to the cat. "Go to your basket."

She gave a toss of her head and glided back into the darkness of the room as deftly as if she still had all four legs.

The sound of footsteps echoed from the yard outside. Nathaniel was leaving. Ben swallowed and dared to lift his head over the edge of the window-sill. The man's shadow sailed through the alley and disappeared into the street beyond.

"What's he up to then?" Ben asked. Going over to the mantelpiece he took down Aunt Alice's clock. It was half-past two in the morning. He scowled. Nathaniel was obviously up to no good and his thoughts returned to the heavy bag he had taken with him – what was in it?

Without pausing to think what might happen, Ben dashed into the hall, dragged his coat from the peg and hurried outside, only stopping to put the front door on the latch because he didn't have a key.

The cold November night bit into him, nipping the bare spaces between the top of his slippers and the bottom of his pyjama legs. As he wriggled into the duffle he gave no thought to his reckless actions, nor how stupid he was being – if he was caught out at that time he would be in enough hot water to fill the harbour. All Ben could think about was Nathaniel. There was something extremely dislikable and wrong about that man – no matter what Jennet thought of him. Into the alley the boy ran, his slippers making no sound whatsoever, but when he came to Church Street he pressed himself against the wall and gazed around.

The main thoroughfare of the East Cliff was still as the grave; not one window was lit in any of the houses and Ben thought enviously of the sleeping inhabitants tucked up with their dreams behind the dark curtains. The urgency of his rash impulse was dissipating rapidly, he would much rather go back to bed. All was quiet, only the buzzing of the lamp-posts disturbed the deep calm. In this tranquil scene the slightest sound was amplified and Nathaniel's distorted footsteps rang loud and clear off the cobbles some distance away.

Ben gazed after him. The man was heading towards either the abbey steps or Tate Hill Pier. The boy darted across the road and hid in the entrance to a shop, watching to see which direction he would choose.

"He's going up the steps," he breathed, "but there's nothing up there except the abbey and the church."

Nipping in and out of the gloomy doorways, which in the ghostly sodium light of the street lamps resembled cavernous mouths, Ben gradually followed Nathaniel.

At the foot of the one hundred and ninety-nine steps he halted uncertainly. The man was only half-way up, should he try and follow he would certainly be spotted. Along all that laborious flight there was nowhere to hide and if he waited until Nathaniel had reached the top before starting, the man would be out of sight long before he completed the climb.

Ben stared round him desperately – parallel to the steps rose the old donkey road. It was a painfully steep slope, little used by modern traffic but sufficiently screened from the steps for his purpose. Without wasting another second, Ben charged up.

The chill airs above Whitby moved silently over the town, ruffling the feathers of roosting gulls and stirring the strands of smoke which continued to rise from dying fires in neglected hearths. From that great height the buildings appeared as toys, their roofs mere lids to be removed and the contents idly examined.

Nathaniel gave no heed to the view. It was much colder at the top of the steps and pulling up the lapels on his tweed coat, he spun on his heel. The great, dark shape of St Mary's Church reared up before him, blotting out the frosty stars in the black sky. The arc lights had been switched off hours ago and the vast square bulk had an almost menacing feel about it. The building was immovable and solid; a squat fortress that clung to the clifftop, enduring the severe gales which lifted the lead from its roof, and the freezing winters which ate into its stones.

Down the narrow path which wound between ancient and weathered tombstones Nathaniel picked his way. The sheer, grassy slope of the cliff edge was close by and he could hear the gentle rush of the waves breaking on the shore far below. The meandering pathway curved round to the rear of the church and came to a large wooden door. This was rarely used owing to its exposure to the raw, salty wind which raged in off the sea. But here Nathaniel stopped and put the large bag on the ground. There followed a muffled clanking of metal against metal as he searched inside the hold-all until he found what he needed.

Flourishing a crowbar, he marched up to the great door and thrust one end deep into a slender crevice inches above the handle. Then, the man pushed against the iron bar with all his might. The wood let out a long, protracted groan as splinters flew and the metal teeth sank in – deep and brutal. The door quivered as though in pain and Nathaniel's hands tightened about the crowbar – his knuckles shining white and his face alive with impatience.

"Yield!" he snarled. "Open for me, the ordinary laws do not apply here. This is a public place where all are welcome – yes, even I. Allow my entry!"

At that the lock was torn from the wood and the door shook violently. Nathaniel gave it a contemptuous kick and it swung slowly inwards.

Stopping only to pick up the bag, the man entered – still brandishing the crowbar in his hand.

Within the church of St Mary all was shadow. Even in the daytime the interior, like most things in Whitby, was striking and unusual but now all was forbidding and severe. The odd arrangement of pew boxes were like square cages which penned in beasts of pitch and shade and the walls seemed carved from jet. A brooding atmosphere filled the place, as if it were alive and watching, inflamed at this irreverent intrusion. The very air was tense and so overpowering that Nathaniel had to lean against the wall before he could bear to venture any further.

"Settle yourself, Crozier," he murmured, "it's nothing you haven't encountered before. Ancient sites of worship develop a certain ... presence, you know that." He ran his hand over the stone and half-closed his eyes. "This is most holy ground," he whispered. "Even before the Christ was venerated here it was a sacred shrine. The land remembers and old stones are charged with that knowledge. You must tread with care this night."

He took a few, tentative steps towards the central aisle and the noise of his movement resounded throughout. At the far end, upon the altar the gold cross gleamed coldly and Nathaniel hesitated, but only for an instant.

"Enough," he spat, "I will pass." And with that he pushed deeper into the church. At the altar he gave a malicious sneer before turning aside and passing between a row of pews.

The crypt of St Mary's was simply a small area in one corner reached by a cramped flight of wooden stairs. It was perhaps the oldest part of the building and contained many artefacts, found during excavations, which dated from the original Saxon church. In a tiny box, mounted on the wall, there was even a piece of the actual wattle and daub used in that earlier building. All around there were irregular chunks of carved stone, sections of pillars and slabs of floor tiles – these had been pushed against the walls in a wonderfully haphazard jumble. From a large window the dim moonlight slanted in, touching the stonework and illuminating the descriptive labels pinned to the boards. Peculiar triangles of darkness were cast between the stones, angular slices of night that wove through the carvings and spiked over the floor.

Down into this crowded level Nathaniel came. Glancing briefly at the biblical extracts painted on panels that covered the walls, he put the bag and crowbar on the ground. He could sense the accumulated age of everything in there, the long silent centuries lay heavily over all and he breathed deeply, relishing their history.

Nathaniel delved into his pocket and brought out the plaster fragment he had taken from the Banbury-Scotts' house. Holding it in the shaft of moonlight, he studied the four strange signs inscribed there. All day long he had examined them, trying to decipher their meaning and apart from the mark of Hilda only one other was now clear to him.

"Somewhere here," he told himself, "somewhere in all this disorganized lumber. I must have read the sign correctly – it can be nowhere else." He spread out the fingers of his left hand and quickly ran them over the stones at the front of the pile. "Nothing," he cursed. "Come on, come on, Nathaniel has come for you my little beauty."

Irritated, he drew himself up and held the plaster fragment in both hands. "Must I jab you out of hiding?" he growled. "Then so be it." He closed his eyes and began to chant under his breath.

A strange stillness descended over the church and the moon disappeared behind a cloud. All outside noise was extinguished, the faint glare that the night absorbed from the lights of the town was snuffed out and an impenetrable blackness seeped in. Nathaniel continued to chant, his voice gradually rising.

A breeze began to stir, the brass chandelier which hung from the ceiling slowly began to swing and a hymn sheet fluttered from the three-tiered pulpit. Still Nathaniel chanted, and the air churned about him. The warlock's hair streamed in the growing gale, his coat flapping wildly and the rush of the wind filled his ears as it tore around the church. The chandelier was spinning madly now and hymn sheets flew through the air like flocks of rustling birds.

"Unveil yourself!" Nathaniel cried. "Show yourself to me! I, Nathaniel Crozier, High Priest of the Black Sceptre, command you!"

Suddenly there came a terrible crash as the cross on the altar was hurled to the ground. The gale screamed up the aisle and the broken door slammed shut with a tremendous, thundering bang.

The warlock opened his eyes, his face pulled taut with the raging storm he had summoned. He opened his hands, stared down at the plaster fragment and smiled.

One of the symbols inscribed there was glowing, a golden light beat out of it, pulsing with life and energy. He held it above his head and the magical rays poured down.

"Excellent," he laughed. "Now, where are you my little rabbit? Pop out of your bolthole."

From the depths of one of the many dark shadows, there came an answering throb of golden radiance.

Nathaniel threw back his head in triumph then began to haul the surrounding rubble aside. It was arduous work; the stones were heavy and he tore his fingernails in his eagerness to clear them. The ground trembled as each slab was thrown down but eventually the way was made and Nathaniel reached in to retrieve what he sought.

It was a life-size head of stone, most of the features had been worn away but the eyes and mouth could still be discerned. For years it had lain forgotten and disregarded against the wall, covered and hidden by the rest of the ancient carvings in the Saxon crypt – but now Nathaniel had it. He took the head in his hands and the beautiful light which emanated from it shone in his face.

"Now you are mine," he marvelled, "and now you shall answer me." The stone pulsated with magical force, its light reaching high into the church, spreading over the balcony of pews that ran along the walls, giving everything a beautiful, glistering glow. The unnatural gale that the warlock had created died down and a delicious warmth rippled out into the night. Nathaniel had awakened the power of the head and a desperate thought clutched at his heart – what if he were unable to control it? All his designs would go astray – all his hopes and desires would come to nothing.

"Be still!" he shouted in the midst of his panic. "Cease this at once!"

But the head continued to pour out its energy. The inside of the church blazed with glory and dazzling beams shot from the windows, piercing the night outside. The powerful forces blasted high over the cliff like one of the beacon fires of old.

"Stop!" commanded Nathaniel, trying to shield his eyes from the blinding light. "STOP!" Even at this time of night someone was bound to see what was happening. He had been relying on secrecy and the cover of darkness to achieve his goal but this was like having a neon sign flashing to the world. His plans were in jeopardy – he would be discovered and his enemies alerted. He had to put an end to it and, with clenched teeth, called on all his dark powers. "Aid me!" he demanded. "Come to me – help me in this desperate hour! Give me the strength to counter, conquer and rule."

For a moment nothing happened and the golden light continued to flood out of the church, cascading over the graves, in an ever-swelling stream and gilding them in its wake. But then, very slowly, another glow began to appear. It was a sickly, greenish hue and it flickered about Nathaniel's hands as he called for aid. When the two opposing forces met, they crackled and spat, flashes of lightning roaring through the church.

"Submit to me," the warlock cried as the green light flowed over him. "You will answer – you must answer."

And then the contest was finished. The power of the head began to dwindle, the golden energy faded, engulfed in Nathaniel's all-devouring hatred. The brilliance died down and it became dark – except for the putrid luminescence that wrapped itself about the evil man.

The last glowing rays danced around the stone eyes then disappeared. The carving was nothing more than a stone head and the power of the warlock surrounded it.

"That is better," he said, "now, it's time for you to hear me, oh ancient one, answer to Nathaniel." He grinned horribly and commanded, "Speak unto me!"

Deep within the stone there came a grinding and a creaking. Nathaniel's dark eyes gleamed and the evil forces wound more tightly about the head. The noise grew louder, until the carved mouth began to move – the weathered lips parted and a hollow voice rang out.

"Hath the time now come?" it asked. "Is the end of all things arrived? Is Ragnarok upon us?"

"The end is not yet here," replied Nathaniel, "but that hour may not be far away."

"The staff is gone!" called the disembodied, echoing voice. "She has taken it back – the walls are breached!"

"Peace," calmed the warlock, "all is not yet lost, there may still be hope."

The stone eyes rasped open to reveal two almond-shaped slivers of flint. They studied Nathaniel closely and the voice asked, "Who art thou? Why didst thou invoke me?"

"My name is Crozier. The world is in peril and I must do what I can to help. Many years have passed since you were laid down, the knowledge of the ancient ones is long forgotten – only a few now have the skill to do what must be done."

"Then hail to thee, master of stone," said the head. "What dost thou wish from me?"

"I am a seeker after that knowledge," replied Nathaniel excitedly. "There are many questions which only you can answer if I am to prevent the darkness creeping over the land – tell to me all your wisdom, how did you come to be here? Who made you?"

The eyes closed slowly, and when the voice began it was filled with melancholy. "I am the oracle of the stone," it intoned, "and long have I done my work. A torment of emptiness have those years been. Hadda the elder made me, although I have worn many shapes, and set me above the lintel of the church that was before this. When the land was green and the circling seas uncharted."

"What was your purpose?" pressed Nathaniel in fascination.

The head replied mournfully. "The third guardian am I," it said, "defender of the weak against the power that sleeps and must not stir."

"Power?" repeated the warlock. "Explain – what power do you speak of?"

"Thou canst not understand," lamented the head. "None now can know of the pain and horror which rests. The world has moved on, even legends fade and are forgotten."

Nathaniel lifted the carving close to his own face. "Please," he asked in a silky, persuasive voice, "I want to know. Tell me of that distant time."

The flints regarded him keenly before the head

answered. "Hear me, oh human," it proclaimed. "You wish to learn of those dark days? Then listen and I shall speak of deeds great and noble and woes beyond number. Of the time before the dragon ships set sail, before the stones of the abbey were laid, before Saxon kings were buried in this haven and before Hild blessed it with her footsteps."

The head then recounted the history of Whitby, events that occurred many ages ago and recorded by no one. While it spoke Nathaniel listened, concealing the greed and malice that boiled within him.

"It was a wild land then," the carving continued, "the five tribes of the aufwaders lived along all the coast and man was as yet a stranger in this sea-lashed place. Since the time of waking, evil has stalked the world in all its guises, yet here in Whitebi the dark one had indeed made its home. For aeons there was nothing but horror here, and terror was the lot of those who dwelt nearby. The hills were a desolate wasteland, and Death a constant wanderer of the shore. The aufwaders suffered much and prayed unceasingly to the Lords of the Deep who did hear their woe and take pity. In those early days they still had dealings with the upper world and had not withdrawn to their vast realm beneath the waves."

"So what did their Marine Majesties do to deliver them from this peril?" asked Nathaniel sarcastically.

"There came a fearful day when the sun shone red with war and they arose from the foaming deep surrounded by a host of tritons ready for battle. In a deadly encounter that threw down cliffs and forged new mountains they did attack, but the enemy was mighty and blew poisonous rain upon them. Their vast army was almost vanquished in the cruel onslaught and the sea became awash with blood, yet finally they won through and the Great Lord himself grappled with the evil, deposing it in bitter combat.

122

"Then did the golden horns of the Deep Ones sound and their joyous trumpeting was heard unto the furthest corners of the world. All rejoiced, but even as their lord prepared to deal the deathblow his heart forewarned that the battle would not be won that day. Though the enemy be slain and fed to the scavengers of the ocean, it could never be destroyed and would in time return and conquer, bringing about the ruin of all. Thus he stepped aside and though the clamour rose about him he refused to dispatch the enemy. So, to the dismay of all, the evil was spared but the Deep Ones would not suffer it to despoil the land once more. Using all their craft and skill, they bound it in chains of enchantment and it passed out of knowledge, entering the distant legends of the time.

"An interesting myth," interrupted Nathaniel with little enthusiasm. "Almost every culture can claim a similar tale. What has an archaic legend to do with your presence here?"

Ignoring his scepticism, the head began again. "Even the strongest chain shall weaken," it told him, "and fall into ruin under the relentless march of years. So did the bonds of enchantment wither and they who first felt the rumour of the returning evil did realize the truth of the old tales and were afraid. Irl, mightiest of all aufwaders in skill and cunning, sought to strengthen the enchantment of the Deep Ones and wrought a talisman, instilling it with all his power to keep the evil one at bay. For this undertaking he did steal the moonkelp and so was punished, but not till he completed his task and carried off the thing he made. There, hidden from the five tribes, this sacred artefact kept strong the enchanted bonds and the world was safe again."

Nathaniel's eyes gleamed as he began to understand and the lust which smouldered within him burst into flame.

"But power fades," sighed the head, "and a day came when Irl's guardian was not enough. Evil grows wherever it lies and so it was with this – another shield in the armour of Whitebi was required. This was fashioned by the first of the human settlers who learned of the danger from the five tribes before they were estranged. A wise man was he, steeped in the lore of a fallen civilization and he made a sign of the moon, calling on the goddess herself to guide his work – and so was his guardian added to the defences and all was well for a time."

"And then?"

"Who can measure the rate of a canker that spends itself not and, resting, grows mighty in repose? The time came when another guardian was needed and so was I brought into being. The first bishops hallowed me and called on the Lord to protect them. So have I guarded the town throughout the centuries, constantly challenging and striving with that which sleeps, binding the ancient enchantment about it and adding to the sum of the other guardians' power." The head fell silent and the eyes closed sadly.

Nathaniel nodded, assuming a gentle, wise countenance. "And in the time of Hild another guardian was needed," he added, "and so she surrendered her staff?"

"Verily," returned the head, "when Hild came, already my labours were too great and evil was beginning to escape. A Mallykin had evaded my vigilance and slithered into the waking world. It was she who drove it back into forgetfulness and sacrificed her power for the safety of the world. Yet the staff is no more. It has gone from this place and it was the strongest guardian of us all. Without it we are weakened and the walls are breached. Once more the evils which were bred in the youth of the world are stirring. The Mallykin walks abroad again and the old enchantment decays with each passing moon. Soon shall the evil waken and all will plunge into darkness and despair."

"Is there nothing that can be done to prevent this disaster?" asked Nathaniel.

The head groaned, "Who now can forge and craft a device to protect us all? What of the old skills remain in this modern world? Who now can stop the enemy awaking?"

The warlock gave a small, unpleasant laugh. "Perhaps I can," he said.

"You?" the head muttered. "Can you in truth do this? Are your talents a match for what is needed?"

"I believe so," came the arrogant and self-assured reply. "I have absolute faith in my abilities."

"Then waste no time," urged the carving, "begin at once. For pity's sake commence the work – *it* is rousing. Have I not felt the shackles of sleep fall away?"

Nathaniel rubbed his chin as though mulling the idea over. "Yes," he mused, "I suppose I could do something. What I must really achieve is some way of uniting all the existing guardians and building upon their proven strength. But where am I to find them? They have been hidden for thousands of years."

"I can help!" the head cried. "I know where they were bestowed."

"Oh good," smiled Nathaniel. "You know, I was rather hoping you'd say that."

Behind him, a shadowy figure crawled along the aisle, slipping silently behind the pew boxes. Ben had followed the man up to the cemetery, keeping well out of sight as Nathaniel strode round to the back of the church. When he saw the man break in, he nearly ran to fetch the police but was too intrigued to learn what he was doing in there. At first he had thought that Mr Crozier was a burglar and was after the church silver, but when the strange lights had begun to shine Ben drew closer. Now he crept towards the vile, spectral gleam which emanated from the crypt, straining to catch what the voices said, yet anxious not to be discovered.

From what he had already managed to overhear, the boy was extremely afraid. He wasn't sure who Nathaniel was talking to – he thought perhaps it was one of the fisherfolk and that alone disturbed him, but what was all this talk of evil? Carefully, Ben stole nearer, the phantom light falling on his young face. He stealthily came as far as he dared then curled into a ball, intent on the voices which drifted up from the crypt.

"The oldest of the guardians is with the aufwaders," the head was telling Nathaniel, "and from this shall the nature of the evil be known. Irl bore it to the deepmost regions of their realm before the Deep Ones punished him for his crime and hid it therein. Who now knows of its existence? No one perhaps, but in the caverns beneath the cliff it surely lies and this only would Irl reveal as he was dragged into the sea to answer for the theft of the moonkelp. The guardian is engulfed in sorrow – that is all he would say, even as the water poured into his mouth and filled his lungs."

Slowly, and with little pleasure, Nathaniel considered this information – so that one at least was out of his reach. "And the second guardian?" he demanded.

"Is a wooden tablet," the head told him, "inlaid with pearl. The irresistible force of the waxing moon is its strength and is mightiest when it is full in the sky. Many and dreadful were the incantations muttered over this, and terrible were the promises sworn to the goddess. The man who made it perished as soon as it was done, having poured his entire soul into his creation."

"Yes, yes!" stormed Nathaniel impatiently. "But where can I find it?"

"The second guardian was entrusted to a Whitebi family," the head replied, "and since pagan times they have kept it safe and secret from all others, passing it down through generation after generation."

"Their name!" the warlock cried. "What is their name?"

"In former times their house was called Hegenfrith, but the sands shift and names alter. What they may be called now I do not know. All I can sense is that the guardian is still safe. After all this time it continues to do its work, enriching and fortifying the might of the others, drawing on the power of the moon at its zenith."

"Hegenfrith," Nathaniel muttered, committing it to memory. "So, there we are," he licked his lips and sniggered. "Tell me, oh oracle, what would happen if all the guardians were destroyed?"

The flint eyes stared at him incredulously, the man's voice had altered and was no longer friendly. "Then darkness would reign!" the head cried. "Evil would waken and the land laid waste. Without our continued protection Ragnarok would come."

"Such melodrama," Nathaniel scoffed. "Do you really expect me to believe that? It may have kept the primitive peasants in check but it won't deter me. No, I am a master of control and domination – there is nothing on this earth I cannot make yield and bow before me. Whatever this force is, evil or not, it shall be mine to command."

"No!" shrieked the head. "You must not believe that! I tell you it is beyond your futile strength. If you awaken this thing then be assured you shall be the first to die – it cannot be controlled! No one has dominion over evil, it consumes all who try to master it."

"I think I've heard enough now, thank you,"

Nathaniel retorted. "You have done your duty – for far too long in my considered opinion."

"What are you doing?" the head shouted. "Are there such madmen loose in the world?" But it was too late, it realized how it had been tricked and there was nothing it could do.

"Bleat all you can," the warlock laughed, "for your time is over. Nathaniel has come to deliver you from your woe. This night I shall end your dreadful labour." With a deriding laugh he hurled the head to the ground and chips of stone sparked from the flagged floor.

"Hearken to me!" begged the guardian in fear as it saw Nathaniel open the large bag at his feet and bring out a sledgehammer. "This is madness!"

But the warlock paid no attention to its beseeching cries. "Into dust we all must depart," he chuckled. "Isn't it about time you did the same?"

With one swift swing of his arms he raised the sledgehammer over his head and brought it crashing down.

"NOOOOO!" came a heart-rending scream.

In his hiding place Ben covered his ears. He was terrified at what he had heard and, as the vicious blows fell, he sprang to his feet.

The scene in the crypt was screened by the pews and he was thankful that he could not see what was happening. Yet the eerie green light that still flickered about Nathaniel threw his shadow upon the wall and that was enough. Down came the hammer, dashing the head to smithereens. Its plaintive screeches rocked the church and Ben felt them thump inside his brain.

"A curse on thee, human!" howled the voice in its agony. "May the forces thou hast unlocked hound thy black soul unto the end of time!"

Nathaniel's laughter welled up and he roared,

bringing the sledgehammer down in yet another crushing blow. There came one last piercing scream that tore through the very foundations of the church, shaking the rafters and rifling up into the tower where the bells vibrated and sang out a dreadful, discordant chime. And just when Ben thought he could stand no more, the voice was finally silenced forever.

Like a thing possessed, Nathaniel continued. Relentlessly pounding the pieces to powder, leaving not a fragment on the floor and crowing with horrendous savagery.

Ben hurtled from the church as fast as he could. Everything he had heard flew round inside his mind in a confused whirl and, leaping over gravestones, he charged back down the path for all he was worth.

When he reached the top of the abbey steps the ground shook. Ben heard Nathaniel's laughter ring from the church as the last pieces of the head were pounded to dust. The entire cliff trembled and the boy spun round.

From the church of St Mary there came a deafening explosion. The leaded roof buckled as a gaping hole was blasted out of it and through this shot a stream of golden light. With a great rush of dazzling sparks, the searing bolt soared into the dark sky and was sucked high into the cold void. Ben could only stare as the force boiled ever upwards, towering over the sleeping town, raging furiously towards the stars. And then it vanished. As suddenly as it had erupted from the church, it disappeared into the heavens and all was calm as if nothing had happened. Only an ugly great rent remained in the leaded roof.

Ben gaped in stunned astonishment, his eyes straining to follow the course of that blinding light. But all was dark now and when he lowered his face and saw the damage to the church he remembered that Nathaniel was still in there, for the man's laughter had not ceased yet.

Sickened and horrified, the boy turned back to the town which lay below him. Whitby seemed darker than before, the street lamps were dimmer and the cold closed sharply in. Shaken, the boy threw the church of St Mary one final glance before he tore down the steps and fled home.

In the crypt, Nathaniel drew his finger across the grey powder which now covered the flagstones. From his pocket he took out the plaster fragment once more and examined it carefully. There were now only three symbols inscribed there, and one of those was the obsolete mark of Hilda. Because of him, the sign of the last guardian had been completely erased. He grinned and slipped it back into his pocket.

"One down, two to go," he quietly chortled.

8

TORN FROM THE DEEP

Whitby awoke to a fine November morning. It was one of those rare bright days of late autumn which the year occasionally indulges in to remind herself of the summer that has past. The sky was clear and, though weak, the sun valiantly did her best, dancing brightly over the water and bouncing off windows as they opened to receive her. Of course, as the morning unfolded and the townsfolk bestirred themselves, it being Sunday, a great commotion soon gathered around the church where all gazed in dismay at the yawning fissure which grinned at them from the roof.

When the police arrived, they found the vicar sitting desolately in a pew. After organizing a cup of tea for him, they began surveying the wanton destruction. Apparently vandals had broken in and, after scattering hymn sheets and knocking the cross from the altar, a condition which the vicar had at once rectified regardless of any concern for the disturbance of clues, they had somehow managed to punch a hole through the roof. It was a lamentable commentary on the youth of today and the reverend was so angered by the brutal exhibition that he forgot himself and uttered a few choice words normally alien to a man of his calling.

At least nothing was stolen and when he had pulled himself together, he set about trying to find a tarpaulin large enough to cover the offending hole. Once the police had dusted for fingerprints, they departed to interview those in the youth hostel nearby to see if they had heard or seen anything suspicious the previous night. Eventually the service commenced and the vicar abandoned his chosen sermon for an impromptu and impassioned speech on vandalism in the community. Tempers were extremely frayed that morning, and the congregation almost cheered him on. The desecration had hit the very heart of Whitby and all were grieved that anyone could have committed such an outrage. But perhaps it was more than that, for not once did the thought of forgiveness enter anyone's mind – the destruction of the third guardian had already wrought an unpleasant change in the townsfolk.

* * *

Ben lurched out of bed, his eyes ringed with dark circles. As soon as he had returned from the church last night he had gone into Jennet's room, but she was sleeping so peacefully that he could not bring himself to wake her. Besides, he wasn't exactly sure what Nathaniel's discourse with the stone head had meant. So, instead of disturbing his sister, he decided to let it wait until the morning – by then he might be less confused.

For the rest of the night he had lain awake as snatches of the strange conversation came back to him. One thing was certain, Nathaniel Crozier was not what he pretended to be – he was as dangerous as Rowena Cooper had been and Jennet should be told first thing. With his head full of questions and doubts, the boy, already exhausted by his nocturnal adventure, slipped into an uneasy sleep just as the dawn edged into the sky.

It was past ten o'clock when he dragged his clothes on and dashed on to the landing. "Jen!" he cried. "Jen, you'll never believe me!" He ran into his sister's room but it was empty. Ben made for the stairs. "Guess what I saw last night!" he shouted excitedly. "It was awful!"

An answering call floated up the staircase. "Down here," came his sister's voice, "we're in the kitchen."

Ben jumped the last two steps and hurried to tell her what he had witnessed. "I know I shouldn't have," he gabbled breathlessly, "but when I saw him leave with that great big bag I couldn't stop myself. He's bad Jen, I mean really bad. All the way to the church I followed him and heard everything!"

Suddenly the boy's stomach turned over and a violent knot twisted in his guts. Standing in the kitchen, chatting amiably to his sister, was Nathaniel Crozier.

Jennet looked away from the man for a moment as her brother slumped against the door and stared across in mute horror. "Ben?" she said, puzzled at his extraordinary expression. "Are you all right? You don't look well, what were you saying?"

Nathaniel's eyes slowly looked up from the coffee he was drinking and blazed out at the boy. Ben's heart quailed under their burning gaze. Mr Crozier now knew that he had not been alone in the church. Ben took a deep breath and shook his head to dispel the black fear which was creeping over him. "What's he doing here?" he asked bluntly.

Jennet was taken aback by this rudeness. "Ben!" she hissed.

Her brother only glared back at the man. "Well?" he demanded.

Nathaniel lowered his coffee cup. "Jennet," he said

smoothly, "it would seem your brother does not like me."

"I'm sorry," she hastily apologized, "he isn't usually as bad-mannered as this." She gave Ben a hateful glance that told him he would be sorry, then turned her attention back to her guest. "Another biscuit, Nathaniel?" she asked.

"Mmm, thank you," he took the proffered digestive and bit into it, his eyes holding Ben the whole while.

The boy did his best to ignore those flashes of malice which stabbed out at him. "Where's Miss Wethers?" he asked his sister.

"Gone to church," she replied. "Thought it best to leave you in bed. She'll be back soon. Your breakfast's already on the table."

"I'm not eating it with him here."

"Ben!"

"Tell him to go!" her brother insisted.

Mr Crozier finished his coffee and took a step towards Ben and the door. "Perhaps it would be better if I left," he murmured. "I seem to be distressing the little boy."

"Don't pay any attention to him!" Jennet stormed. "He's being a baby, that's all. Honestly, if Aunt Alice were here she wouldn't let him get away with that. You just stay here and have another coffee, Nathaniel."

"If you insist," the man relented but, as Jennet turned her back to rinse the cup, he gave Ben a venomous and deadly look.

"I'm off out!" the boy said abruptly. "See you later, Jen." In a trice he had nipped out of the kitchen and was through the front door.

"Ben!" she called after him. "Come back here and eat your breakfast this minute!"

"Unusual boy," observed Nathaniel.

Jennet apologized for his behaviour again. "I don't know what's come over him," she sighed. "He's not usually so rude."

"Perhaps he had a nightmare," the man suggested. "Actually, would you forgive me if I declined that second coffee? I really must get going, there seems to be more work in store for me today than I had at first realized. Good morning."

Jennet showed him to the door, to prove to Mr Crozier that she, at least, had manners. "Goodbye, Nathaniel," she said warmly. "Perhaps I'll see you this afternoon – if your work permits it, of course."

"But of course," he smiled, tenderly taking her hand and squeezing it tightly, "I shall make certain of that."

Jennet flushed, he really was charming. She watched him return to the Gregsons' before closing the door with a delighted and dreamy look on her face.

* * *

Miss Wethers trotted down Church Street feeling totally irritated and disgruntled towards her fellow man – or woman. The vandalism of St Mary's was a sight she thought she would never have seen and the vicar had whipped everybody up into such a state of agitation that for the first time in her life the postmistress was itching for a fight – a verbal one, of course.

"Disgraceful," she twittered like a deranged canary, "to think there are such wretches, and here in Whitby too! I never did, in all my days. May they rot! Hanging's too good for them!" This was strong stuff from Miss Wethers and her eyes darted to and fro, peering suspiciously at everyone who went by, as if they were the heinous culprits. Only when she had

135

vented her steaming temper in an unprovoked attack on a passing tourist, calling him an insidious interloper who was ruining the fabric of the community, did she return to her normal self. Everybody in the street gawped at her and the unfortunate man hurried away from what was obviously the local lunatic. Miss Wethers hastily collected herself and gave a forlorn chirp as she realized what she had done. Quickly she ran after the innocent tourist to beg his forgiveness, but he thought she was wanting to continue where she had left off and scurried away as fast as he could. This made her feel even more ridiculous and she scolded herself sharply.

"Edith!" she said. "What has come over you? My oh my, what a spectacle you've made of yourself." Sheepishly she recommenced her journey towards Miss Boston's cottage – her face, appropriately for a postmistress, as red as a pillar-box.

It was whilst slinking into the alley, glancing round to see if anyone was staring at her, as she was sure they must be doing, that she walked into Ben coming the other way.

"Miss Wethers!" he cried, pleased to see her.

"Oh," was all she could manage for the moment.

"That man," he continued, "he's with Jennet. You've got to listen to me ..."

"What man?" she said distractedly. "Really Ben, I've had a most disagreeable morning, I've just done the silliest thing, and you wouldn't believe how wicked somebody has been – the poor, poor church ..."

"Yes!" Ben interrupted. "That man! Mr Crozier!"

The postmistress fluttered her hands over the buttons of her cardigan. "Is he with Jennet now?" she asked. "Oh, I'm not sure I approve of this. Alice Boston why did you leave me in charge? What I need is a good lie-down!"

"But ..."

"Be a good boy," she yapped dismissively, "and have a nice play on the seashore, or whatever it is you do. Only keep yourself clean and no bringing back any more ... dead little friends, hmm? See you at dinner time."

With a nervous twitch of her hand she pattered off to the cottage leaving Ben just as anxious as before. Who would he tell? If only Aunt Alice were here, she would listen to him. Miss Wethers was useless, the last thing he wanted to do was go and play on the beach ...

At that Ben tore from the alley and raced up Church Street, turning down to Tate Hill Pier and charging on to the sands.

Nelda would help him, she would believe what he had to say. Over the rocks he scrambled, hurrying under the concrete supports of the bridge which joined the cliff to the pier. Luckily the tide was out and only two other people stood by the shallow pools at the foot of the cliff. Ben took no notice of them, cupped his hands round his mouth and shouted "Nelda! Nelda!"

The couple turned to look at him but thought he was calling for his dog.

"Nelda!" the boy shouted again. "It's me, Ben. Can you hear me?"

There was no reply; the steep cliff reared high and silent above him and though he knew where the secret entrance to the aufwader caves lay, there was no answering call and the doors did not open. His throat was sore by the time he gave up. "Please answer," he mumbled into the breeze. "It's very important, *please*."

But after half an hour it was plain that either none of the fisherfolk had heard him, or Nelda was refusing to come out. "Why won't you listen to me?" he breathed unhappily. "There's no one else I can tell. Something must be done about Mr Crozier." Dragging his feet, the boy left the beach, gave the cliff face one last, hopeful look then climbed the stairs back into Church Street.

Although the morning was nearly over and his stomach was growling, Ben had no desire to return home. He desperately needed to confide in somebody, but who? With a slow, dawdling gait, he made for the swing bridge that linked the two sides of Whitby.

It really was a beautiful day; the harbour seemed filled with diamonds that glinted in the sunlight and the fishing cobles lazily rode the sparkling waves. Ben gazed blankly at the lovely scene. The dredger was chugging slowly out to sea, laden with the silt and sludge which it had scooped from the estuary floor and he absently waved at the crew. One of them returned the greeting but it did little to please the boy that morning.

"If only there was someone else," he sighed, turning his gaze from the harbour and across the bridge at the West Cliff. For a moment he contemplated going to the police station, but he doubted they would believe him – he found it difficult enough himself. If he tried to tell them what he had heard they would either laugh or put him in the care of a doctor. Still, he could always tell them that he had seen the man break into the church and leave out the rest of it – that might be enough for them to arrest him. No, it was only the word of an eight-year-old boy and Mr Crozier would soon squirm out of it. Ben recalled that even Miss Boston had been disbelieved when she had spoken against Rowena. No, this sort of business was beyond the reach of the normal authorities – their strong arms were helpless against the likes of Nathaniel.

Then it came to him, "Of course," the boy said brightly, "he's sure to listen!"

* * *

Mr Roper tucked the yellow duster into the pocket of his apron and replaced the lid on the can of spray polish. Whereas some people went to church on Sundays, he always tended to his collection, dusting and making them sparkle. Now his house smelled of polish and he cast his eyes over the crowded parlour in case one of the cruet sets had escaped the stroke of his cloth.

"Everything as it should be," he said with a gratified smile, "all gleaming and on parade."

It had been a long morning; the job increased with each new addition and, if his enthusiasm continued unchecked, he foresaw a time when it might take up the whole afternoon as well. Leaving the room, he untied the strings of the apron and, along with the polish, placed it in the cupboard under the kitchen sink.

"Just time for a nice cup of tea," he murmured happily, "and as a reward after doing all that dustin', I'll treat myself to some jammy dodgers as well."

Some time later, Mr Roper carried a small tray into his front room and settled himself in the armchair. The radio was switched on, but the volume was turned quite low. It was only to provide a background noise as his favourite programmes were not due to begin till the afternoon. He had often felt that there was nothing worse than a silent house. So, with the radio's faint sounds burbling about him, he crunched into a biscuit and poured the tea.

"Oh who can that be?" he declared as the doorbell rang. "If it's that Pewitt woman come to invite me to the old-time dancing again she can go and jump. I wish she'd let me alone. All right, I can hear you!" Irked at this interruption, Mr Roper passed into the hall and opened the front door.

"Ben!" he exclaimed in surprise. "You're early, I wasn't expecting you till later this afternoon. Come in, come in." He led the boy inside, noticing that he was unusually quiet. " 'Fraid I thought you were somebody else," the old man explained. "That woman from two doors down came round again last night after you'd gone. What a nuisance she's becoming. Keeps wantin' to foxtrot and tango with me. A body can only be polite for so long – don't know how I'll keep putting it off the way she goes on."

Leading Ben to the front room the old man asked gently, "What's addled you then, lad? You're in a right sulk this morning and that's a fact! You haven't even asked about poor old Guido."

Ben fidgeted for a moment. He wasn't sure how to broach the subject, he couldn't just blurt it out. "Mr Roper," he began uncertainly, "have you seen the man who's staying with the Gregsons?"

"Can't say that I have, but who'd be gormless enough to bide with them? She's a nasty tongue on her that Joan has – and her husband's a lazy good fer nowt."

"There is a man staying there," confirmed Ben, "his name's Crozier and …"

"Don't you like him?" asked Mr Roper kindly.

Ben shook his head. "Jennet does," he said, "I'm not sure what Miss Wethers thinks of him though, but no, I don't."

"Why's that then?"

"He's bad," Ben said simply.

Mr Roper leaned forward in his chair and put his teacup down. "What do you mean?" he asked solemnly.

And so Ben began to tell him all that had happened last night. At first Mr Roper seemed nervous and grew stern when the boy told how he had followed Nathaniel into the night. But, as the story progressed, a different look came over the old man's face.

"And then he smashed the head to bits," Ben said, coming to the conclusion of his tale, "and a great light shot out of the church roof and vanished into the sky. I waited till this morning to tell Jennet but when I woke up she was already downstairs with *him*! And now he knows that I saw everything and know what he's going to do to the other guardians if he can find them. When he does, something absolutely terrible is going to happen – I know it."

Mr Roper let out a deep breath, an admiring smile was on his lips. "Well I never," he said, "I never did hear the like before."

"What are we going to do about it?" cried Ben.

Mr Roper gave a chuckle. "Well, lad," he admitted, "I never thought you'd come up with something so elaborate. Ten out of ten is what I say to you. You had me going for a minute there, mind – very good. When I told you to come back with a story I wasn't expecting anything as rivetin' as that one, and you had it all off pat too. Full marks indeed, ho, ho!"

"But it's all true," the boy whispered. "I promise."

"'Course it is," agreed the old man, "and soon as I get a chance I'll phone the head wizard and tell him what one of his dastardly pupils is up to. He'll be zapped into a toad quicker than you can blink and all the world's worries'll be over."

Ben said nothing. He had been wrong – Mr Roper didn't believe him either. Only Nelda and Aunt Alice would, but they were out of his reach.

"Now then," said Mr Roper becoming slightly more serious, "you'll be wanting to see old Fawkes. Hang on while I fetch the scoundrel. Guardians of

Whitby!" he chortled to himself. "Very good." Leaving Ben in the front room, he went upstairs.

Ben decided it was pointless trying to make the old man believe him. It was clearly too fantastic a tale for anyone. He waited for his return and, remembering his hunger, ate a biscuit. What would happen if Mr Crozier got his way? According to what he had heard, nothing would be safe; the finality of that was only just beginning to sink in and the boy felt as if the doom of the world was approaching.

"Here we are," said Mr Roper, bursting through the door bearing a large, floppy figure. "Here's the very man."

The papier mâché head was completely dry now and he had already attached it to the rest of the body. "As you can see," he went on, "I've used an old shirt o' mine for the top half, I don't suppose you brought that jumper o' yourn? Never mind, you can add it later. I've put an old pair o' socks on the end of the legs for feet and tucked the trousers into them. Looks mighty swanky, don't he? All he needs now is the face and I've got some paints left over from the last jumble sale posters I did for your aunt."

Ben wasn't really in the mood for painting that day – especially as the head reminded him of that other one last night. But Mr Roper had obviously worked extremely hard to bring the guy up to this state and he forced himself to take an interest. The shirt and socks were not old at all and Ben was touched by this display of generosity.

Presently a garish and angry face began to appear on the papier mâché; two streaks of black gave it a neat little moustache and another, directly below the bottom lip, served for a pointed beard.

"What about eyebrows?" suggested Mr Roper. "That's right – blimey he looks fierce, an' no mistake." Throughout the whole of the delicate operation the old man did nothing but encourage Ben, he also supplied him with more biscuits and told him the funniest of his stories. The boy could not remember ever having spent a more enjoyable couple of hours, at times he even forgot the dreadful knowledge that he was burdened with.

When the painting was all done they both surveyed the figure and were greatly pleased. It was an almost perfect Guy Fawkes, all it required now was Ben's old jumper and perhaps a hat.

"Well done, lad," congratulated the old man, "he's right smart he is. Can't wait to see him sat on top of your bonfire. Got all your wood yet?"

"Yes, I've been collecting it for weeks. Aunt Alice helped too. There's a great pile of stuff against the fence at home. I should really get started on it this afternoon." He stared at the Guy's striking face; it seemed a shame to burn him, but with that beard he now resembled Mr Crozier and Ben felt that perhaps he would be happy to set it atop the bonfire after all.

"Would you look at the time," tutted Mr Roper, "it's your dinner you'll be missing if you're not careful. I don't want Edith Wethers on at me. You'd best take this villain home with you today, lad. A right scare he'll cause through the streets, I'll be bound."

Ben lifted the figure and slung it over his shoulder. Carrying it all the way home would be no problem – it was very light, being stuffed only with newspaper. "If you want," he said, "you can come and help me build the bonfire after dinner. I don't suppose Jennet will care to."

Mr Roper gave him a quick smile but answered, "I'm sorry, I can't today – there's a few things I've got to be attending to. Thank you all the same. Believe you me, there's nothing I wouldn't like better."

"Well, I'll see you tomorrow night then," said Ben

hopefully, "you've got to come and watch it burn. Miss Wethers said she'd make toffee apples and baked potatoes – I might even get a sparkler out of her."

"Oh, lad," gasped Mr Roper unexpectedly. His voice trembled and before Ben knew what to think, the old man whisked away and returned carrying a large square tin. "These are for you," he said quietly, "I were going to save them for tomorrow as a surprise like, but you might as well have them now. I remember the best bit about fireworks was looking at them in the box – all them fancy wrappers wi' stars and flashes on 'em, wonderin' what sort of show they'd make."

"Fireworks!" cried Ben. "For me? Oh, thank you!" He threw his arms around the old man and gave him a great hug. Mr Roper uttered a startled cry, holding the boy as if it was the last time he would ever see him and when he next spoke his voice was thick with restrained emotion.

"Aye," he mumbled, "them's all yours. Wait till you gets home before peeking, mind, and enjoy 'em tomorrow, lad. Now come on, you'd best be off."

He led Ben to the front door, but when the boy turned back to wave the usual farewell he saw that his friend was crying.

"Mr Roper," he said, walking back along the path, "are you all right?"

The old man put a hand over his eyes. "I'm only tired lad," he replied, "don't you fret."

Ben wasn't sure what to do. Perhaps Mr Roper had been thinking about his late wife or the brothers killed in the First World War. Deciding it was best to leave him alone, Ben waved again. "See you tomorrow," he said.

The old man watched him turn down into the alleyway then closed the door. "Goodbye, lad," he wept.

* * *

The massive jaws of the dredger plunged into the water once more. It had already dumped the last load of silt out at sea and was beginning the unending process all over again. The chains rattled as the iron claw sank to the bottom and seized a great portion of sludge. Up it came, through the foaming water, dripping with thick mud and weed. A cloud of gulls hovered overhead, greedily watching for any fish that it may have disturbed rising to the surface. Round swung the crane arm, back over the open cargo hold, where the strong teeth parted and disgorged half a ton of muck and slime.

"Right," shouted Peter Knowles, one of the three crewmen, "she's all finished, Dunk her in again."

The crane jerked round till it was out over the water and the huge open grabber swung slowly on its chains.

Peter gave a signal to Bill Ornsley, the operator, who nodded and the jaws dropped back into the harbour. The dredger rocked gently, and Peter leaned against the deck rail while he waited for it to re-emerge. He was tired, and longed for his roast dinner which would be on the table by the time he finished this shift. At least this would be the last load of the day, he consoled himself, thinking of the Yorkshire pudding smothered in gravy which he would soon be devouring as efficiently as the jaws of the dredger itself. He glanced up, over the harbour bridge in the direction of his home and sighed wistfully.

A short figure wandered into his view, and he raised his hand to shield his eyes from the bright sunlight. "There's that kid again," he said as a child ran across the bridge, "the one that waved before. Lives with that barmy old woman, doesn't he? She's too old to be fostering kids at her age. Hello? What's he got there then – looks like a dead body."

"Pete!" Bill's voice broke into his thoughts and all traces of roast dinners, cracked old women and ghoulish children vanished from his mind. Ornsley sounded worried.

"What's up?" he called.

The man pointed at the crane and then Pete too realized that something was wrong. The chains were groaning and an unhealthy whine issued from the winching motor.

"She's caught on summat," Bill cursed.

Peter peered over the side to where the chains disappeared into the water. "Like what?" he asked.

The other shrugged and scratched his balding head beneath his battered black cap. "Beggared if I know," he said, "could be anything – never know what's down theer. Mebbe some old timbers from a coble what sank years ago."

"Wouldn't we have come across 'em before?" asked Peter doubtfully. "We're here day in, day out."

Mr Ornsley gazed at the shimmering surface of the water and slowly shook his head. "No," he muttered, "you can't never tell what it's like on the harbour bottom. There's fathomless depths of mud swirling round, constantly shifting with the tide, coverin' and uncoverin' all sorts of stuff. Horrible suckin' mud that pulls you under and seals you up for a year or more." He pulled on the winch lever but the awful whining increased.

"Doesn't want to come up," Peter said. "Whatever it is must be stuck pretty good."

"She'll manage it," assured Bill.

At that moment the dredger pitched alarmingly and the crane juddered under tremendous strain. The water slopped over the deck as the vessel lurched from side to side and Peter only caught hold of the rail in time to save himself from being thrown into the harbour.

From the cabin at the stern the other member of the crew stuck his head out and bawled at them. "What was that?" he cried, gripping the wheel tightly. "Felt as though somethin' pulled at us!"

Bill stared worriedly at the winch motor; wisps of smoke were now hissing from it and the taut chains looked close to snapping.

"Let it go!" shouted Peter. "Whatever it is, drop it!"

Mr Ornsley threw himself against the lever as another tremor rocked the dredger. "I can't," he yelled, "it's jammed!"

A high-pitched, painful noise of twisting metal screeched out from the crane – the arm was buckling. Peter ran forward and tried to help Bill release the jaws but the lever was locked solid.

"She's gonna break!" he cried. "The chains'll lash round like whips, take cover man!"

Suddenly the dredger catapulted backwards, the jaws were free and the chains rattled loudly as the motor wrenched them from the water.

Both men raised their heads as the grabber rose to the surface in a frenzy of boiling, seething water.

"Thought we were goners then, Bill," said Peter. "Good job it let go."

Mr Ornsley checked the controls. "No it ain't," he whispered, "whatever it were caught on is still in them teeth."

Up from the thick harbour mud it came, up into the bright sunlight that filtered down into the churning water in soft, slicing rays.

With an almighty splash, the jaws exploded from the waves and before the chains could wind them up, they struck the prow with a shuddering blow.

Peter held grimly to the rail as the dredger tipped violently to one side, its tilting hull clanging like a funeral bell. The angry spray stung his face and the vibrations of the collision stung his clenched fingers, jolting through his body. Yet he paid no attention to this. Though the man in the cabin struggled with the wheel for control, all Peter could do was stare at what was gripped in the great iron teeth of the grabber.

It was the most unusual thing he had ever seen, and from it rained a waterfall of sludge.

"What in heaven is that?" he breathed.

As the deluge of filthy mud diminished, the outline of the mysterious object became clearer. It seemed to be kite-shaped and twice the size of a man. Peter stared intently, although it appeared to be made of stone, it was difficult to be certain because, except for a clump of fibrous black seaweed that had attached itself to the base, it was totally encrusted with barnacles.

Mr Ornsley looked up from the controls "Beggar me!" he exclaimed. "What the 'ell?"

"P'raps it's some kinda shield," suggested Peter, "part of a massive coat of arms or summat."

"That ain't no shield," whispered Bill, "call yerself a man o' the sea, look at it, man!"

"I don't ..." Peter's voice failed him as he saw what the other meant. "Impossible!" he cried.

"Aye," said Bill "but mark that bit at the bottom theer, where it tapers down. What do that look like?"

Peter felt ill. A dark red substance was trickling from the tangled mass of what he had at first assumed to be seaweed. The thing was bleeding!

"I might be gettin' on in years," murmured Bill, "but that looks like flesh to me."

Peter couldn't believe it. "You're wrong," he denied flatly.

"Face it, man," the other muttered darkly, "like it or not, that theer is the scale of a fish!"

Peter gulped and in a small voice whispered, "My God!"

They stared a moment more at the huge black diamond, then the jaws loosened. The weight was too much, the teeth parted and the giant object fell from its grasp.

"Fetch it back!" shouted Peter. "Don't let it disappear down there again!" He ran for the controls but Mr Ornsley seized his arm and pulled him away.

"You leave that be!" he said firmly. "There's some things I'll not mess wi'. Leave what you don't understand well alone – leave it!"

Peter whirled round, just in time to see the immense scale fall into the water. It smacked the surface then vanished completely, twirling slowly down into the concealing darkness once more, spiralling back into the mud.

Bill Ornsley turned away from the ever-widening circle of ripples. "All right, Mike!" he called to the man in the cabin, "it's all right now. No harm done, but I think we ought to give her a rest for the day, I'd like to give the motor a seeing-to this afternoon."

The man at the wheel waved his agreement and the dredger began chugging towards the quayside.

"Now then," Bill said looking squarely at Peter, "if you don't want to be laughed at for the rest of your days I wouldn't mention any of what you just saw to no one."

The other man gazed back at the water where a shred of torn flesh still floated until a gull swooped down and snatched it away. "Yeah," he mumbled, "I didn't see nothing."

"Nor did I," affirmed Mr Ornsley and he manoeuvred the grabber into the water once more, to wash away any traces of what neither of them had just seen.

9

MISCHIEF NIGHT

Ben slid another long plank from the heap at the side of the fence and dragged it over the grass. The main skeleton of the bonfire had, after many frustrating attempts, finally been constructed and seemed to be holding together. Before she had gone to London, Miss Boston had prepared a section of her garden especially for this, having dug up a large square in the middle, carefully laying aside the turves to be replaced afterwards. In her usual manner, she had merely shrugged off Ben's gratitude and said that the ashes would be good for the soil.

"Put that piece over there," said Jennet, "it needs the support on that side."

The boy bit his lip, his sister was being a real pain. Since he had returned from Mr Roper's she had done nothing but scold him for being rude to "Nathaniel", and when he had tried to escape her she had followed him into the garden – only to criticize all his attempts at bonfire building. There was no getting away from her and he thought ruefully of the fireworks the old man had given him – he hadn't even had a chance to open the tin yet!

In spite of this, a smirk spread over his face, for before he had entered the cottage he had tapped on the parlour window and waggled the guy in front of it. Even outside he had heard Miss Wethers shriek and the memory of her shrill yelps was the only thing that kept his mind off Mr Crozier and blotted out his sister's reprimands – she hadn't found the joke with the guy very funny either.

"Not there, stupid!" Jennet repeated. "Over here!"

Determined to ignore her advice, he placed the plank on the opposite side to the one she directed. At once the entire framework collapsed like a house of cards.

"Told you," she said infuriatingly.

In his annoyance, Ben gave the scattered timbers a sharp kick, to which his sister tutted, "Temper, temper."

"Give me a hand," he appealed to her, "instead of barking your orders – who do you think you are?"

"I'm not getting my hands dirty on all that old wood," said Jennet in a superior tone. "I don't want to get splinters in them or snag myself on a rusty nail – you could get tetanus from that." She spread her hands in front of her and examined them carefully, trying to picture what they would one day look like. Jennet had become enamoured with the thought of having beautifully long fingernails. So far, they were all coming along nicely and the last thing she wanted was to tear them on her brother's childish bonfire.

Ben watched in disgust as she scrutinized herself – Jennet was really changing. With a resigned groan he began gathering up the wood again and tried to rebuild the framework. What it really needed was some string tied around the top of the main supports, but unfortunately he was too short to reach – perhaps he ought to fetch a stool from the kitchen.

"Nathaniel's gone to the museum today," Jennet murmured, giving voice to her thoughts.

Ben did not want to talk about that man with his sister. It was obvious she would not listen to a word against him. The best course of action was to ignore her.

"He's going to trace his family roots," she continued, "apparently he came from round here originally – or rather his ancestors did. He's going through all the old parish records as far back as he can. Isn't that interesting? I told him that I wished we could do that, but I wouldn't know where to start. Then he said that I was too pretty to waste my time in dusty old books – wasn't that nice?"

Her brother bit his lip, a week ago she would have been furious if someone had made such a sexist remark, but no – it seemed Mr Crozier could do no wrong. If only she knew ...

Jennet watched Ben's clumsy efforts with the wood and took pity on him. "Really Ben," she said, "you're not practical at all, are you? Here, let me do it!"

"I can manage!"

"No you can't!" she grabbed the three main timbers and pushed each of them deep into the soft earth until the tepee structure was quite sturdy. "There," she grinned, "that's what should have been done in the first place."

Ben said nothing but stared truculently at the bonfire before leaving to fetch more wood. Jennet folded her arms and raised her eyebrows in the manner of Mrs Gregson. "Don't bother to thank me then!" she called after him.

Her brother returned bearing a piece of old wardrobe and laid it against the framework. "Is that it?" he asked Jennet. "Aren't you going to do any more?"

The girl grunted in exasperation and decided that her dream of elegant fingernails would just have to wait. "All right," she sighed, "but I'm not touching any bits that have woodlice crawling on them."

For the next couple of hours they forgot all quarrels and resentments. Jennet's enthusiasm grew alongside the pyramid of sticks and planks and she quickly stopped moaning once she became absorbed in the work. At times, it was quite like the old days again. When their parents had been alive their father had always loved November the fifth and made sure it was a special occasion for them too.

When Miss Wethers popped her head out of the kichen to see how they were doing, she was pleased to see the children united at last. "Well, Edith," she squeaked to herself, "that *is* a pleasant sight – how industrious they've been. Why, it's nearly finished." A momentary spasm of concern seized her as she thought of the actual fire. "Oh dear," she wittered, "I'll have to make sure they stand well clear of the flames, and I suppose that means I shall have to light it – I do hope I shan't get smoke in my eyes."

Miss Wethers hated Guy Fawkes night; even as a child she had feared it, and now she was accustomed to remaining indoors like a timid pet – away from all the bangs and sulphurous flashes. The only part of it she was really looking forward to was the burning of that horrible effigy. Ben had almost frightened her to death with it earlier and she had forbidden him to leave it downstairs, for she had the disconcerting fancy that it would creep up behind and jump out at her.

"Don't be too much longer," she called out before returning to the delightfully soppy book she was reading in the parlour to soothe her strung-out nerves. "It's getting dark."

Jennet was busily stuffing the inside of the nearly complete bonfire with newspaper and she gave the postmistress a wave of acknowledgement. "Nearly done," she said, before standing back to admire her efforts.

"Is there enough paper in there, do you think?" Ben asked. "Perhaps we should put in some of Aunt Alice's fire lighters, just to make sure it'll burn well."

His sister gave him a warning glance. "You keep your hands off those," she said sternly. "You're not that dumb, are you? You'll be wanting to pour petrol on it next! Do you know how many people get horribly burned doing stupid stunts like that?"

"It was only a suggestion," he muttered.

"Well it was an idiotic one!"

Ben arranged the last of his sticks around the bonfire, only to find that his sister was still looking at him when he had finished. "All right," he cried, "I didn't mean it! There's no need to stare like that!"

But, when Jennet spoke, all her anger had gone, in its place her voice held a forced casualness. Ben had heard that tone many times before and knew that it meant she was after something – usually something of his.

"Ben," she drawled nonchalantly, "don't you think it would be nice if we had a big Guy Fawkes party? I mean instead of just you, me and Miss Wethers?"

"There's Mr Roper too," he butted in. "He's coming, don't forget."

Jennet idly twisted a lock of her hair. "Mmmm," she agreed, "but that's still quite a small number of people isn't it? And both he and Miss Wethers are very old. They haven't got much in common with us, have they? I think it'll be dull with just them here."

Ben wasn't sure where all this was leading. "I don't think Mr Roper's boring!" he declared loyally. "Besides, there isn't room for lots of others."

"I wasn't going to invite lots," she answered, "only one more."

"Who?" asked her brother, although by this time he had already guessed.

"Well, what about Nathaniel?" Jennet said. "He must be awfully lonely staying with the Gregsons, they're about as cheerful as a couple of undertakers. I'm sure he'd love it – not only that, but it would be

155

the perfect way to show him how sorry you were for being so rude this morning."

Ben was paying no attention to her and had walked off, back to the cottage.

"Well, I can ask him if I want to," she said to herself. "I don't need your permission, it's as much my garden as it is yours!"

The girl gazed up at the windows of the house next door; perhaps Nathaniel had finished at the museum and was back already. Maybe he was watching her from behind the net curtains. Jennet hugged herself and let out a great, devoted sigh. "I'll nip round after tea," she said, "and see if he's free tomorrow. I'm sure he'll want to come if I'm here."

For a while, she indulged in a delicious fantasy in which she and Nathaniel were standing close to one another. Orange firelight played over both their faces, dancing in their eyes and burning in their hearts as he took her hand in his and held it tenderly.

"Spare me! Spare me!"

Ben came out of the kitchen holding the guy before him as though leading it to a place of execution and, to help create the illusion, he was doing all the voices. "Spare him not!" he commanded, trying to speak in a deep voice. "To the stake with him! You must pay for your crimes." He shook the papier mâché head then yowled, "No, no, I'll confess!"

"What've you brought that out for?" Jennet asked, ignoring the painted face which was nodding wildly at her. "It'll only get damp if it rains tonight."

"I want to see what he'll look like tomorrow," he explained. "I'll take him back indoors afterwards. See, I've put my old jumper on him too. Looks good, doesn't he? Mr Roper'll be pleased. Give me a hand sticking him up there, Jen, I can't reach."

Jennet lifted the guy and placed him at the pinnacle of the bonfire. "You'll have to put a pole up his back," she said, "he keeps falling over."

"I hadn't thought of that," admitted Ben, "pass old Crozier down again then and I'll ..."

"Ben!" snapped his sister.

The boy gave an unrepentant laugh. "Well he looks a little bit like your boyfriend," he retorted.

Jennet gasped. "Nathaniel is not my boyfriend!" she shouted.

"Not yet!"

"Benjamin Laurenson!" she bawled, making a grab for him, "You come here!"

Afterwards, Ben could never remember if he heard the cries first, or saw the figures as they leapt into the garden. For, even as he darted aside to avoid his sister's hands, the air was filled by many voices and a series of jubilant whoops came clamouring all about them. The two children spun round and forgot everything else.

"Get them!" screeched a horribly familiar voice. "Get the Cret and his stinkin' sister!"

Over the back fence came Danny Turner, Mark Stribbit and a gang of four other boys. In a trice they vaulted over the raspberry bushes and flower borders, trampling the poor plants underfoot, and charged straight for the two children.

"What do you think you're doing?" cried Jennet in astonishment. "Get out of here!"

"Shut it, scabhead!" yelled Danny. "Mick, Terry – grab hold of her, Glen you take the Cret!"

Before they knew what was happening, both Jennet and Ben were seized by the wrists and had their arms twisted behind their backs until tears sprung from their eyes.

"Let go!" Ben cried, kicking back with his feet.

His sister struggled with the two boys who held her but it was no use. "What do you want?" she cried.

Danny swaggered up and sneered in her face. "Don't wet yer knickers," he jabbered, "us lads've only come a chumpin' fer firewood. We're gonna have a right blaze on the beach tomorrow." He pointed at the newly finished bonfire and called to Mark and the other boy. "Pull them matchsticks down, they'll do to light me ciggies wi'."

"No!" Ben protested as the yobs began kicking and smashing. "Stop it!"

Danny tittered and poked him in the ribs with a sharp piece of wood. "I'm sick of you, Cret!" he spat. "Yer always whingin' and whinin'. Well, here's summat to really skrike about!" Dragging Ben from the one called Terry, he threw him to the ground and kicked him savagely until the boy crumpled up with a pitiful wail.

"Leave him be!" screamed Jennet, but before she could call for help, a dirty hand was shoved over her mouth and it was all she could do to breathe properly. Then her head was pulled backwards so she could no longer see what was happening to Ben. The boys who held her were too strong and the more she struggled the more painfully they yanked on her arms.

Danny left Ben clutching at his stomach and gasping into the damp grass. "That's right, Glen," he sniggered, "keep her snotty ladyship quiet, can't have her bawlin' her head off can we?" He came swaggering up to her, "Not so tough now are yer?" he snarled. "Well, you was lucky the other day that's all." He kicked her shin but her cry was muffled by the dirty hand still smothering her. Danny hooted and pranced before her like a lunatic. "Look at the smelly Laurensons!" he laughed, waving his arms above his head. "One's barmy, the other's a stinking cow! And the only person who'll have them is nuts too – ha, ha!"

Jennet managed to tug her head forward, and the eyes that she turned on the Turner boy were filled with hatred. Using all her breath, she sucked at the hand that stifled her and bit down hard. Behind her Glen let out a shocked squeal.

"Ruddy Nora!" he howled, blowing on his palm. "She bit me – the cow bit me!"

Jennet seized her chance and squirmed round to free herself, pushing the other boy away as forcefully as she could. He went tumbling backwards like a skittle, and then she turned her blazing anger on the ringleader.

Danny stopped his capering, dismayed to see his mates so easily overcome. He stared at the girl and his nerve wavered for a moment as he saw a peculiar glint shine in her eyes. Was it his imagination or was that insane gleam really a fiery red? Then Danny rallied, remembering that he was not alone, Mark and the other boy were still with him. He signalled for them to stop destroying the bonfire and they sidled up, large sticks in each of their hands.

"Come on then, Laurenson," taunted Danny, "come an' get me – I dares yer."

Jennet was breathing strangely, for a while her mind had become so flooded with hatred that she had forgotten all else – even Ben. Her one intention was to rush at that hideous boy with her claws ready to tear his face off. Now she recoiled from that awful emotion – bewildered and appalled. Her face turned pale at the memory of the all-consuming rage that had taken hold of her, and at the evil thoughts that had come unbidden to her mind.

"Nathaniel," she whispered forlornly, "where are you? Help me please."

Now that all traces of fight had left her Danny jumped forward and raised his hand. "Yer as mad as yer brother!" he guffawed. "Go back to the funny farm!" And his hand whipped down to deliver a resounding *slap* across the girl's face.

Jennet staggered under the blow and had to clench her teeth to stop the inevitable cry.

Danny snorted and shot an expert missile of green phlegm into her hair. "Right," he called to the others," let's clear off. Don't take the wood – it's too crappy to bother wi'."

" 'Ere!" shouted Mark. "What about this?"

Danny giggled gleefully. "Yeah!" he snorted. "We'll have that!"

One by one, the gang leapt back over the fence and ran off up the grassy slope of the cliff. Held aloft, like a trophy of war, the boys carried the guy.

Ben lifted his head, his stomach felt cramped and bruised, but that was nothing when he discovered what they had stolen. He thought of all the hard work he and Mr Roper had put into making it, but no tears trickled down his face at its loss – for at the same time he remembered that there were other, more important concerns to worry about.

"Jen," he said croakily, "are you hurt?"

His sister was kneeling on the grass where she had fallen after that cruel smack. When she turned her face to him, Ben saw an ugly, livid mark burning across her cheek. She stared blankly up at him when he came over and, as he held her, he discovered that she was shaking.

"Don't worry, Jen," he tried to reassure her, "they've gone now."

The girl closed her eyes and shuddered, "It's not that," she mumbled, "but back then, something took hold of me – I lost control. I wanted to kill them all, and would have done too ..."

"I would have," Ben said, "if I were bigger. They're horrible bullies and deserve whatever they get."

Jennet was looking almost white. "No, it was more

than that," she told him, "it frightened me. I mean it."

Ben stared at her. He had never seen her so affected by anything before – except of course the accident. Frowning, a more sinister thought came to him; could this be another result of the third guardian's destruction? Were the evil forces already leaking out so strongly that they had infected his sister? Or was it another power that possessed her? "Well it's all over now," he said consolingly. "Come on, let's go inside."

Jennet slowly came out of her daze and unsteadily rose to her feet. "Oh," she said, "what about you? Did Danny hurt you?"

Ben shook his head. "I'll live," he replied, trying to sound cheerful.

She took his hand and her eyes stared out over the garden, falling on the wrecked bonfire. "Oh Ben," she said sadly, "how could they be so mean? And where's your guy – did they take that too? I'm sorry."

He shrugged. "It doesn't matter," he said simply, "it was only some old clothes stuffed with paper."

"But you spent so long making it," she sobbed, "it's just wicked, how could they?" Jennet took a deep, steadying breath then added in a determined voice, "Well I'm not going to let them get away with it, I'm going to tell Miss Wethers."

"You'll only cause more trouble!"

"I don't care," she said firmly, and with that they went into the cottage.

Miss Wethers was sitting quietly in the parlour, still avidly reading her romance when they disturbed her. She took one look at Jennet's face and covered her own with her hands.

"They did *what*?" she kept squeaking as they told her what had happened. "They did *what*?" The postmistress's mouth flapped open like a letter-box and she bristled with indignation. "The little brutes!" she exclaimed. "How beastly of them." Out came her tissue and it went dabbing about the girl's glowing face as she chirped her concern.

"Most distressing," Miss Wethers declared when the tale was complete. "That Turner hooligan is a danger to everybody." She wrung her hands together for a few moments as though she were screwing herself up for some brave action. Then, plunging her tissue back up her sleeve, she stepped back into the shoes she had discarded whilst reading and said in a tone that neither of the children had heard from her before, "I'm not standing for this! If Alice were here, she wouldn't stand for this kind of bullying, cowardly behaviour and nor will I. I'm going straight round to that young villain's house and have one or two sharp words with his parents. He needs keeping in order and if they won't do something about it I shall go to the police station – I don't care if they pack him off to a Borstal. I will not tolerate such disgusting behaviour!"

Into the hall she stormed and snatched her coat from the peg. "Jennet," she said, opening the front door, "you attend to your teas – I shan't be long!" The door slammed behind her and the normally meek postmistress went stomping off through the alleyway.

The children stared at one another in surprise. "Who would have thought that from her?" whistled Ben. "She wouldn't say boo to a goose."

"Must be made of stronger stuff than we thought," smiled Jennett. "But that doesn't mean you can keep frightening her like you have been doing. It makes you no better than Danny when you do that."

Before Ben could answer, there came a fierce hammering on the front door. Both children jumped and looked at each other fearfully.

MISCHIEF NIGHT

"Perhaps it's Danny again," murmured Ben.

"I don't think so, he wouldn't knock for one thing."

"He might, just to trick us."

"Well if we don't answer it we'll never find out," Jennet said, pulling the door open. She cast her eyes around the yard; it was dark and deserted. The November evening had fallen thickly, filling the place with silence and night shadows. "Strange," she murmured.

"Who is it?" asked Ben trying to peer over her shoulder.

Jennet moved back to close the door. "Weird," she said.

"What is?" cried Ben, ducking under her arm.

"There's nobody out here," she told him, "no one at all."

Ben said nothing, for his sister was wrong. Standing on the step, leaning on his staff and glowering impatiently, was Nelda's grandfather.

" 'Bout time an' all," the aufwader grumbled, "ah were gonna gi' up on thee."

The boy blinked in astonishment. Of all possible visitors Tarr was the last he had expected. "Hello," he began nervously, it was most unusual for any of the fisherfolk to call on a human and already he was wondering what this portended. "Is there something wrong?" he asked.

His sister looked down at him and pushed on the door. "Of course there isn't," she answered, thinking he was talking to her, for she was unable to see or hear the aufwader. "Shift out of the way, it's too draughty to leave it open."

But her brother did not budge and Tarr gave Jennet a curious stare. "Daft as owt!" he remarked. "Womenfolk are allus addle-pated. But aye, theer's summat wrong all right – very wrong."

Ben tugged at his sister's sleeve. "Jen," he hissed, "there is someone here, it's Nelda's grandfather."

"Oh," was all she could find to say. There were times when she completely forgot about her brother's "gift", as Aunt Alice put it. In fact, she would rather it was never mentioned, as it had only ever got them into trouble. She knew about the fisherfolk of course, but was never comfortable when Ben talked about them. "What does he want?" she asked.

"I don't know."

Tarr thumped his staff on the ground, rattling the terracotta flowerpots nearby. Jennet could not fail to see that. Then, the aufwader cleared his throat and coughed as though beginning a speech.

"Hark up, lad," he began, "ah's come to thee with a purpose – and trust you me, ah wouldna have come fer any other than her. It's been many years since I set foot in this town and that's just the way it would've stayed too." He paused to suck his teeth and gaze at the surrounding houses. "Lobster pots an' crates," he sourly commented, "ah dunna ken how tha can abide such hutches."

Ben stopped himself smiling. Tarr was extremely old and he didn't want to appear disrespectful. "So why have you come?" he asked.

The aufwader scratched his wiry white whiskers, clicking his tongue as though there was a bad taste in his mouth. "'Tis Nelda," he said, "she's the one what bid me come and sithee."

"Nelda!" exclaimed the boy. "But why didn't she come herself? And why come here at all? I tried to call her on the shore this morning but there was no reply."

Tarr held up his hand. "Aye," he nodded, "she heard thee, us all did ... shrikin' yer dunceful head off."

"Then why didn't she answer?"

The aufwader lowered his voice and shook his head sorrowfully. "Nelda were busy," he said. "Were tasks she had to see to …" He looked the boy steadily in the eyes and came to the point at last. "This night," he said, "the moon'll be full an' round and at such times do the Bridings take place. When the tide comes high up the cliff, my granddaughter'll wed."

"Married?" Ben whispered in disbelief. "But … who?"

But Tarr was staring into the sky and tutting at the lateness of the hour. "Enough," he barked, "we're a wastin' stood here. What ah wants to know … is tha comin' or not?"

"Me?"

"Tha's not deaf is thee? If'n tha's willin', best come along now. Bid thy sister goodnight for tha'll not be back afore dawn." And that was all he would say. The invitation had been made and that was what he had promised Nelda he would do. Leaning on his staff, Tarr hobbled down the step and walked slowly across the yard.

"Wait!" Ben called after him. The boy turned to Jennet and hurriedly tried to explain what was happening. "I've got to go," he told her, grabbing his coat, "tell Miss Wethers I'll be back later."

"Ben!" she shouted. "You can't go just like that! What am I supposed to tell her? She'll never believe me about those friends of yours."

"Then pretend I've gone to bed," he said, "she won't look in – and remember to leave the latch off the door, I don't have a key!"

Jennet stared helplessly after him. As Ben disappeared into the alley, she softly breathed, "Be careful," and closed the door.

In Church Street, few of the houses were lit and it seemed a forbidding, cramped place where the everlasting stream of night flowed through. When

Ben caught up with Tarr, the old aufwader was gazing fixedly at the ground, taking no notice of the buildings that reared up beside him. The boy was still struggling into his duffle-coat and when he eventually fastened the toggles he asked, "Why didn't Nelda mention it to me before? Who is she marrying? I thought she was still quite young."

Tarr ground his teeth together. "Aye," he bitterly agreed, "she'm a child still, but that has'na stopped *him*!" and he cursed under his breath. "An ill time this be, an theer ain't no one who can cure it. Hurry lad, theer's a might to get done this e'en – if'n my heart can bear the strain."

Pausing at the few steps which led to the shore, he pointed with his staff and muttered darkly, "The omens are bad for this. An icy wind gusts in over the waters and ah done seen fish floatin' dead on the waves. Foul critters of the black deeps what have no rights comin' to these shallows, an' each one had theer eyes pecked clean out. 'Tis a warnin', ah told 'em. *They* ain't pleased. Aye, an' all night long the souls were a-calling up from the Gibberin' Road – weren't no cave kippin' peaceably wi' that racket goin' on. Nah, us are bein' told – this Briding ain't proper, 'tain't decent and if'n it goes ahead … well, ah dursn't dwell on what may come about. Ah'll speak no more on it!"

Pulling the brim of his woollen hat down to meet his spiking brows, the aufwader pressed his chin into the neck of his gansey and pushed ahead. Beside him, Ben could only try and guess what was behind it all and, wrapped in this uneasy, grim silence, they vanished down the steps on to the sands, merging into the cloak of night.

* * *

Mr Taylor, the curator of the museum gave one last glance around; everything seemed in order, there was no one left, but he ducked his head just to make sure – he had once found a tramp hiding under a display case. There was nobody lurking there tonight however, and he had already checked the other rooms. Methodically he counted through the keys on his chain until he found the one he sought. With a jingle, the inner doors were locked and he strode across the art gallery to join the last visitor who was lingering by the main entrance.

"Takes a tidy while to see it all gets done," he explained, going through the keys once more. "Be getting a fancy alarm next month so that'll be another lot of keys I expect – put your pockets out something rotten they do. The wife's always complaining about the state of them, but you have to put up with these minor discomforts, don't you?"

The other man smiled with benign understanding. "An unsolvable problem," he said.

"Yes, but a necessary one. Can't be a curator without having keys, eh?" He turned the lock then tried the door to make certain. "Lovely," he beamed, "that'll keep the robbers out."

His brief acquaintance raised his eyebrows. "Do you have much trouble with burglars?" he inquired.

"Not usually," came the considered reply. "We did have a spot of bother a couple of months ago, mind. Some dirty thief broke in and filched one of our most interesting pieces."

"Really? What was that? You do have some wonderful treasures in there – that storm predictor for example, absolutely marvellous."

Mr Taylor glowed with pleasure at this compliment. "Yes," he admitted, "we're justly proud of our prognosticator, and that's what makes that theft so baffling. It wasn't anything really valuable that got nicked. Of course, when I say that I mean in money terms like the jet carvings and such, no this was something more uncanny you might say. It was the Hand of Glory that was nicked, a gruesome little exhibit but I was rather fond of it myself."

"I don't know what the world is coming to," remarked the other.

They walked slowly through the park and down towards the town which was now twinkling with electric light. At the foot of the hill Mr Taylor shook the man's hand and wished him well.

"I trust you did find out what you were after?" he asked.

"I did indeed."

"That's a thing I'd always like to get round to doing. Tracing the family tree is a rare challenge. I'm so glad to have been of assistance, I hope you were able to make head and tail of the abbot's book – I don't usually let anyone take it out of the case but you being a historian I thought, well, why not. You know – you've wheedled more out of that old library in the one afternoon than most of the people round here do in a year."

"Perhaps my researches were more important."

"Mebbe. Anyway, this is where I leave you, sir."

They shook one another by the hand once more and as the curator went his way Nathaniel said, "Thank you again – it's been a most enlightening day."

* * *

The warm buzz of the radio diffused through the darkened front room and the faint beat of the dance band was like the distant pulse of a dying man. In the fireplace the embers were a deep cherry colour and when they crumbled, the sound of the falling ash was like an expiring sigh. Mr Roper sat in his shabby armchair, his eyes closed and his head on his chest, but he was not asleep.

For hours he had sat there, watching as the light failed outside and listening to the fire dwindle and collapse. Slowly the shadows had mushroomed up around the chair, enclosing it in a gloomy canopy and still he had not moved. Mr Roper was lost in thought. There were so many things he still had not done, so many things left unsaid, now that it had come he found that he just wasn't ready.

Carefully, he unclasped the hands folded over his heart and a reflected light gleamed dully between his fingers. It was a small silver frame that the fading firelight had picked out – the one that contained a photograph of his late wife.

"Oh Margaret," he murmured, breaking the still calm, "a right mess I'm in." He pressed the glass to his lips and gave her a gentle kiss. "Won't be long now," he promised.

The smiling face of his wife gazed blindly out at him, but the visage was stained red by the fire's glow and Mr Roper laid it close to his breast once more. The evening drew on and the hands of the ticking clock on the mantel whirled around.

It was late when the doorbell rang. The severe noise seemed to hack away at the peace of the front room, utterly fragmenting it. The old man looked up from the chair, it was half-past eleven. Wearily he struggled to his feet, his legs stiff and aching after being seated for so long. Taking his time, he returned the silver frame to its rightful position next to the clock and shuffled out into the hallway. A tall figure was silhouetted against the glass of the door and the old man nodded as though he had been expecting this caller.

Opening the door, Mr Roper beheld for the first

time Nathaniel Crozier. The bearded stranger was standing on the path, his hands held solemnly in front of him, precisely the same stance as that of a vicar presiding over a burial.

"Yes?" Mr Roper began. "Can I help you?"

Nathaniel had been examining the nearby houses, all the curtains were closed – no one had seen him approach and ring the bell. He turned and considered the pensioner, a secretive smile forming on his face.

"Good evening to you," he purred, "would I be right in assuming you to be Arnold Roper?"

"Who wants to know?"

"My name is Crozier. I am a historian researching into local history ..."

The old man showed no outward sign of surprise that someone should come to see him at this late hour. But, before Nathaniel could elaborate, he shushed him. " 'Taint no use, whatever you're about," he said, "Arnold were my elder brother – died in the Great War, so you're wastin' yer time."

Nathaniel straightened, taken aback at this unexpected news. "Died," he repeated. "Did he leave an heir?"

"Arnold were only seventeen, weren't even courtin'. Now I'm sorry but there's a tin of cocoa waiting for me and it's too parky chatting on doorsteps."

The warlock smiled and showed all his regular teeth. "Then may I come in?" he asked. "Just for a moment."

Mr Roper rubbed his ear indecisively. It was no use putting this off, he thought – if it must be, then get it over with. "All right," he said, "come in."

Nathaniel stepped inside and let out a low, wicked chuckle as he closed the door behind him. "There are no lights on in this house," he observed. "Why were you sitting in the dark?"

" 'Taint always nice to see what yer talking to," his host replied pattering back down the hall.

Nathaniel's head reared. There was a touch of insolence in that voice and he wondered if Mr Roper knew his true purpose.

The kitchen light snapped on and the old man poured a quantity of milk into a pan. "Would you care for a cup?" he asked. "I always make it nice an' milky, guarantees a good night's sleep and keeps away the gremlins that'd otherwise disturb me. I don't like to be disturbed."

"No," answered the warlock, wandering from room to room switching on all the lights. "That's better, now we can see what we're about and just where we stand."

Mr Roper made no comment on this presumptuous action on the part of his guest, instead he turned the gas on and took a mug from the shelf.

"About your brother," Nathaniel continued. "What happened to his belongings after he died?"

The old man ignored him for the time being, occupied in spooning cocoa powder out of the tin. "Didn't have much on him," he eventually said, "only a watch my father left him, some letters and a photograph of us all."

"I didn't mean that!" the other snapped. "What about his estate here in Whitby? Where did his effects go?"

"Weren't rich enough to own an estate," came the stubborn and aggravating response. "Only these four walls and they passed to me after our Sammy and Harry went the same way, and after that our Mam passed on. Tough days they were, wouldn't go back to them. Memories cheat you know, there weren't never any good old days, not for the likes of ordinary folk. If I had the chance to nip back in time, I'd only do it to see my Margaret again. But then that's a pleasure I'll be having right enough one of these days, I reckon. I know when my time comes she'll be there waitin' fer me – Lord, how I loved her."

The milk started to boil but before he could turn off the gas Nathanial sprang forward and knocked the pan from the stove. Hot milk gushed everywhere and the pan was sent clattering over the linoleum.

"Don't play games with me!" he commanded, grabbing the old man and spinning him round to face him.

Throughout all this Mr Roper remained perfectly calm. He glanced at the mess on the floor and tutted. "Have to mop that up before it goes sour," he mumbled, "nothing worse than the smell of off milk."

Nathaniel screamed and pushed him against the sink. "Shut up!" he roared. "You know what I've come for! Tell me where it is, you old fool!"

Blinking mildly, Mr Roper's face held the expression one might show to a boasting child. "Are you so sure of yourself?" came his astonishingly cool reply.

The bearded man's eyes were filled with fury and his face was graven like stone. Seizing the pensioner by the arm, he dragged him from the kitchen and into the parlour. "It's only a matter of time!" he said. "Do we really need to undergo this charade? You will tell me. It just depends how much pain you're willing to suffer beforehand. I applaud your defiance, I wasn't expecting anything less, but enough is enough, you've made a stand, now tell me."

Mr Roper looked critically at his collection of salt-and-pepper pots, he was glad that he had dusted them today, for under the electric lights they were sparkling merrily. A gratified smile lit his face, yes all was in order.

Then he turned to Nathaniel and began talking of

something else. "After all this time," he sighed, "all these generations, the work of countless lifetimes ... a sacred treasure passed down the centuries – it takes yer breath away don't it?"

His eyes glazed over, staring beyond the confines of his cluttered parlour, his voice was filled with wonderment and awe, speaking softly and with reverence. "Can you imagine how ancient it is or how many of my ancestors have lived and died in its service? Through plague, plunder, war and disaster we have protected it, and in turn it has guarded us." Mr Roper lowered his misted eyes, a wan smile lighting up his face. "What a frightening responsibility it has been, and yet each of us, from the first to the last has never begrudged our duty." He laughed faintly, and shook his head. "It has been a sacred trust," he whispered, "and I'm not about to betray that merely for the likes of you."

A madness gripped Nathaniel, he released his grip on the old man and stared wildly round the room. "Well let's see," he said breathless with anger, "what shall we start with?" He grinned maliciously then cooed, "what a magnificent collection, you must be very proud of them." Snatching a cut-glass pepper-pot he examined it closely, handling it with extreme delicacy, then with a shout hurled it against the wall where it exploded in a shower of powdered crystal.

Mr Roper's heart quailed, this evil man could do anything he liked to him but not to his beautiful collection.

"Please don't," he begged.

"Didn't catch that," mocked Nathaniel, taking up another piece and smashing it the same way. "I really am most dreadfully sorry."

"No!" sobbed the old man.

Nathaniel then turned his attention to a glass cabinet in which at least a hundred cruet sets were displayed. With a laugh, he pulled it away from the wall and the contents went toppling down in a splintering crash.

"Stop!"

The warlock had lifted the set made in the shape of fireworks and was about to dash them against the fireplace but refrained from doing so. "You'll tell me?" he asked.

Mr Roper looked desperately at the chaos and destruction around him and thought with anguish of all those lovely pieces lost forever. Ever since Ben had left, he had been preparing himself for this encounter but he never thought it would be so cruel, he had been prepared to die to keep the family secret, but to have his life destroyed before his eyes was too bitter for him to stand.

"I'm waiting," said Nathaniel, the china rockets swinging precariously from his fingers.

"I ... I can't," the old man wept.

Shrieking with rage, Nathaniel flung them against the tiles of the hearth then rampaged from shelf to shelf destroying everything in sight. Mr Roper cried in despair as the horrendous clamour blared in his ears.

Nathaniel wiped the sweat from his brow and dragged his fingers through his unruly hair. The devastation was over and the parlour half-demolished.

"Damn you, Crozier," said the old man when he found his voice, "may you burn in the eternal fires."

"Thank you," he answered, not in the least out of breath, "I'm sure I would enjoy such a temperate climate. I do so prefer hot countries, they bring out the animal in one so much more easily I find."

"Do you think I'll tell you where it is now?" asked Mr Roper. "I'd rather die than help you."

Nathaniel burst out laughing. "Oh I know that!" he

chuckled. "That's the whole point you see – so much better to wound you first though. After all, I deserve a little enjoyment from this. I can't go around killing people just like that, where would the entertainment be in such a drab little exercise? No, I like to hurt them first, and I think I've succeeded here, wouldn't you agree?"

"You're insane."

"Now why is it everyone tells me that? Ever since I was small I've heard that over and over again." He made himself comfortable on the upturned display cabinet and rubbed his hands together. "Now then," he said brightly, "are you going to tell me where the second guardian is hidden?"

"Never."

"Well, at least you're consistent," he said but the smile had vanished from his face. "You do realize that I am going to force you to disclose its whereabouts? It will not be pleasant. Much better to tell me straight away."

"My family's kept that holy thing safe and secure for too long," replied Mr Roper. "I've sacrificed a lot to stay here and take care of it. What right have you got to take it now?"

"The right of conquest," answered Nathaniel coldly, "but you're wrong, you relinquished your stewardship of the guardian many years ago, when you married a barren woman. You should have had sons to take on this burden and look after you in your dotage. They would never have invited a warlock into their house. You've been a fool, Roper."

His dark eyes opened wide and the full might of his power came shooting out of them. "Now," he hissed, "tell me."

Mr Roper gasped and dropped to his knees. It was as though a tremendous weight was pinning him down, crushing and grinding him into the floor. Bolts

175

of searing pain lashed his body, stabbing, scalding, breaking, he uttered a feeble wail then hid his face in his hands. The torture intensified, his skin bubbled and his muscles wasted on the bone. When he next opened his mouth, no sound came from it, and he fell prostrated before his enemy, crippled with agony.

Nathaniel leaned forward, taking a sadistic delight in the pensioner's suffering. His baleful eyes continued to blast out their power and he wondered how much longer the man could last before surrendering.

A thousand daggers pierced Mr Roper's flesh and an army of stinging ants went creeping into the wounds. A stream of acid trickled from above, splashing on to his back, smouldering through the clothes and eating into his spine. That was it. The old man lifted a trembling hand and pointed to the open parlour door. "Kitchen ..." he whimpered, "under the floor." And he slumped on to the carpet, his torments over. "God forgive me," he blubbered, "forgive me."

"Congratulations," Nathaniel said admiringly, "you lasted longer than many half your age." Stepping over him, he strolled casually into the hall and entered the kitchen, where, kneeling, he tugged at one corner of the faded linoleum and ripped a great chunk out of it.

"Under here," he chanted ecstatically, "under here!"

The floor covering was old and brittle, already cracked in places, it was only the work of seconds to rip it to shreds. Nathaniel held his breath with excitement, revealed amongst the tatters were large flagstones and upon one of them ...

The warlock cleared the remaining scraps of lino away. Carved into the centre of the largest stone was a symbol of the crescent moon. Hastily he fished in

his pocket and brought out the plaster fragment. Sure enough, the mark corresponded to one of those inscribed there. Quickly, he took a knife from the drawer and levered the flagstone up an inch. Then he slid his fingers underneath and lifted it clear.

"What is this?" he bawled, staring into the space beneath. "It's empty!" His lip curled into a snarl and he whirled about. "Roper!" he shrieked. "Trick me would you?"

He was furious and charged back to the parlour, only to find that empty too. Even as he gazed incredulously round the wrecked room, a chill draught touched his cheek – the front door was open.

Down the dark ginnel, Mr Roper fled. He wasn't sure where he would go, he just had to escape. The memory of his agonies under Nathaniel still loomed large in his mind and, panting, he limped further into the echoing alley. Ribbons of grey mist swirled about his feet, whisking into turgid flurries as he staggered by, his frantic breathing steamed from his mouth and the blood sang in his ears. He must get free, away from that evil man, away to safety, away from pain – he had endured too much.

Suddenly a cold, hard voice rang out in the ginnel. It cut through the whirling mist, sounding hollow and dreadful.

"HALT!" it commanded.

Mr Roper cried out in alarm. Horrified, he swayed back and to but his feet refused to take another step forward. It was as if the mist had turned to glue and was holding him captive. Try as he might he could not wade through the clinging, foggy strands. His old heart quailed as the sharp sound of footsteps came to him out of the darkness and slowly he turned to face his fear.

The mist behind him billowed and curled, forming a spectral tunnel of smoke and framed at the far end of it, prowling slowly towards him, came Nathaniel.

"Old man," he sang, his voice bleak and sinister, "old man, I said I wouldn't play games, but I had forgotten what the night was. In these parts you call it Mischief Night don't you? A time of tricks and deception. Are you really this brave or merely senile? I shall ask you once more and this time you shall tell me the truth."

"Keep away," Mr Roper murmured, "keep away."

The mist eddied before the warlock as he strode closer, gathering thickly about his arms as he raised them and pointed at the trapped old man. This time it was different, there would be no entertainment, no lingering gloat over the physical pain. Just one, severe thrust with his mind, slashing through the flabby brain of his victim to extract the information he needed.

"Where is the second guardian?" he demanded.

Mr Roper howled as a black sword seemed to pierce his skull. He fell against the wall and his eyes grew large and wide. There was no resistance to that kind of mental power, he had lost.

As the darkness leaked into the old man's head, his teeth ground together and he slid to the wet ground. Nathaniel walked over to him, the mist wrapped around his shoulders like a great cape. Sneering, he thrust once more with the might of his mind and the broken figure below him groaned.

"B ... Ben," gurgled Mr Roper helplessly, "Ben has it."

Nathaniel scowled. "You entrusted one of the most precious artefacts in the world to an eight year old boy?" he rumbled in disbelief.

The old man convulsed as yet another intangible blade lanced his mind and searched for the truth. "Yes," he gibbered, "he's the one, I swear it."

"Then he must be made to give it up," said

Nathaniel coldly. "I must have a nice chat with him, like the one we're having now."

"Can't," wheezed Mr Roper, "you can't attack him. He's touched the moonkelp, the only ... the only living creature apart from the Deep Ones who has. Your spells would be ... be useless!"

Nathaniel gave a cruel little snort and the black sword twisted viciously in his victim's mind. "Don't be too sure, old man," he spat, "there are other methods at my disposal."

Mr Roper held his head in his hands, it felt as though it was going to explode. "Stop the pain," he grovelled, "make it stop."

A sickening smirk crept on to the warlock's face, "As you wish," he murmured, "I have learnt all I can here. You have my permission to die."

Mr Roper, kindly and mild, a gentleman always and keeper of the second guardian, perished in the cold mist.

10

THE BRIDING

The vast shape of the cliff reared massive and black above Ben's head. The moon was hidden by cloud so there was no light to guide him, and twice he slipped on the moss-covered rocks. Some way in front, Nelda's grandfather plodded on unerringly, making straight for the hidden entrance to the aufwader caves. Tarr was more sure-footed than any goat and could pick his way over boulders and between the pools of freezing water blindfold.

When Ben slipped for the third time, the old aufwader glanced over his shoulder and mumbled tetchily into the neck of his gansey, "Stop dawdlin' lad, we'm almost theer."

"Sorry," the boy replied. His hands were covered in green slime from the moss and he wished he had put his gloves on before they had set off. Wiping his palms on his coat he delved into his pockets to rectify the situation, but could only find one crumpled glove, the fingers of which were stuck together by an old boiled sweet. Ben grumbled to himself, he was always losing things.

Tarr called to him and they moved further round the black volume of the rock until the distant lamps of Whitby were hidden behind the spur. Gradually, Ben became aware of a pale radiance shining over the moss-covered ground and glimmering on the surface of the spreading pools. Looking up, he saw that the great stone doors of the aufwader caves were open wide and many of the fisherfolk were gathered at the entrance with lanterns in their hands. A low babble of talk began as they approached and Ben stopped a moment to hear what they were saying.

" 'Ere's Tarr now," a voice drifted down.

"Is the human with him?" asked another.

"Come an' see for thissen," replied the first.

"Uurrgh – nasty creature! Them's so ugly."

Ben's ears burned, and could feel their eyes boring into him. He had never seen the whole tribe together before, except from a distance at the funeral of Nelda's aunt. His nervousness at the prospect of meeting them steadily increased and this, mingled with his excitement made it impossible for him to concentrate on where to place his feet. For the fourth time he slithered and fell, grazing his hands on the wet shingle. High above derisive laughter broke out and the boy gazed ruefully at them.

Nelda's grandfather shook his head and retraced his steps back to Ben. "Now then," he said gruffly, "what ails thee? Tha's flappin' about like a crow wi' one wing."

Ben struggled to his feet, embarrassed to have looked so foolish. "I'm sorry," he said, "it's just so dark down here."

From the entrance, one of the aufwaders called, "Get brisk Tarr! The waters'll be over thy head afore long."

Tarr grunted disagreeably and waved his staff in the air. "Prawny Nusk, hold yer tongue and shine a light down 'ere. This poor tyke can't hardly see his hand in front of his face."

One of the figures held up its lantern and the silvery rays illuminated a small area of the shore. Tarr turned to Ben; the aufwader was outlined by the lamplight which shimmered along the edges of his large ears, glinted in his whiskers and formed a frosty halo all around him.

Holding out a knobbly hand, he said in a kindly voice, "Dunna pay no heed to them, folk'll hoot at owt if'n they's boggled enough. And mark me – us are all scared toneet."

So, helped by Tarr, Ben began to climb up the cliff face. Slowly, they ascended, finding footholds and scrambling on to small ledges until a number of weathered hands came grasping at the air above their heads. As the boy reached out for them he felt many fingers tighten about his arms and draw him upwards.

"Easy, easy," Nelda's grandfather shouted to them, " 'umans ain't strong, dunna break 'im."

Ben had seen it once before, but was still overawed by the size of the chamber. The main entrance to the aufwader caves was cluttered with small boats and kreels that leaned against the rough walls and festoons of weighted nets enirely curtained off one corner, making it look like the cocooned nest of some immense insect. Overhead hung the giant mechanism which operated the huge stone doors. This was a rusted jumble of enormous cogs, iron pulleys and long chains.

Evidently some effort had been made to try and decorate the chamber in honour of the occasion. Here and there, lamps had been hung from a piece of corroded metal and, strung between these were garlands of seaweed – laced with bright shells and smooth pebbles of iridescent, sea-polished glass. But the overall effect was a cheerless and disjointed hotch-potch. A dismal failure that was unpleasant to look on, and a more oppressive, funereal display would have been hard to imagine.

The fisherfolk who had hauled Ben inside, set him

on his feet then backed away nervously. Few of them had ever been so close to a human before, let alone actually touched one.

They eyed him warily, as though he might spring at them any moment and some even clasped fishing poles and boat hooks in readiness.

In turn, Ben stared at them. Most of the tribe were assembled there; with weathered faces, scored by deep wrinkles and burnt by the wind. All wore ganseys, patterned according to his or her family, though a few added to this thick woollen shawls or an oilskin found washed up on the shore. The womenfolk were generally smaller than their partners, and kept their hair long and loose down their backs, but some preferred to braid it with seaweed and tie it round with discarded seagull feathers.

One of the sea wives who had helped Ben up, brushed her hand against her cheek and murmured, "Its skin is so soft!" She gazed at the strange creature with wide eyes that were full of regret and sadness, and sobbed, "It's like … like a babe's."

Several of the other females went over and comforted her, throwing curious glances at the human child. A desperate emptiness showed in all their faces.

"What's the matter?" he asked. "Have I done something wrong?"

The sea wives shuffled forward, first circling the boy, then closing in on him. As they reached out their hands, Ben felt an overwhelming desire to turn back and jump out of the cave.

"A bairn!" they uttered sorrowfully.

"Let me touch it!"

A squat figure, with a necklace of shells and an eyepatch, pressed nearer to him and gently caressed his skin. A solitary tear sprang from her good eye and she hastened away to mourn in a dark corner.

A dozen other hands came stroking and patting, but

all were soft and tender, like the flutter of autumn leaves floating past his face. And then they fell back and he found himself in a ring of weeping women who rocked silently to and fro, their hearts broken and bleeding for what had never been.

Quietly, Tarr came up behind the boy and put his hand on his shoulder. "Nivver you mind them," he whispered in his ear, "remember, the curse of the Lords of the Deep lies heavy on us all. No bairn's bin born to us since Nelda – and her mother only did that for the great love she had for my son Abe." Silently he recalled the agonies Nelda's mother had suffered. The torture of the birth had been dreadful and it was a miracle his granddaughter had survived, no other baby ever had. "A lingering death it is," he lamented, "and the poor lass endured it for nearly two whole weeks afore she passed on – wasted and spent into the shadows."

Ben turned to look at him and found that Tarr, crotchety and bluff as he was, was crying.

"I'm sorry," said Ben.

" 'Tain't thy fault," muttered Tarr, wiping his eyes on his sleeve, "but the cruel hard hearts o' them what lives in the deep waters."

The boy fell silent and stared at the ground. It *was* his fault. If it wasn't for him, the mother's curse would have been lifted and hope would have returned to the tribe.

Tarr coughed and cleared the lump from his throat. "It's time," he said solemnly, "ah mun go t' fetch Nelda." He patted the boy on the back and limped from the entrance chamber.

Ben looked from one kippered old face to another. Now the initial shock had worn off, the male aufwaders were regarding him with resentment. Here was a member of the hated and untrustworthy human race, who had done them so much wrong in

185

the past. Their thoughts turned to all the legends in which "sighted" men had played a part. In those tales landfolk had always betrayed and done only harm to their people. It was mostly due to them that they were forced to live in secret and underground. Only one aufwader dared to smile benignly at the boy and Ben guessed this to be Tarr's friend, Prawny Nusk.

"Over here," he beckoned to the boy, "watch with me the tide a creepin' up the shore."

Ben turned gladly from those reproachful eyes and the chill sea breeze ruffled his hair. He smiled in gratitude at Tarr's friend and filled his lungs with the keen salt air.

The view looking out from the entrance was one vast stretch of water. The dark sea reached far into the invisible horizon, a mighty realm where wild things lived and bided their time. Deep and black was the night and the sky seemed to blend with the rim of the watery world, curving down into the distant waves, taking darkness into that cold, foam-topped world.

"She'm fillin' the pools now," remarked Prawny as he raised his lantern, "sithee down yonder, the tides racin' in. Won't be long, an then the poor lass'll be wed."

"I don't understand," said Ben. "Doesn't Nelda want to get married?"

Nusk only shook his head and the mane of sand-coloured hair shivered about his shoulders.

Only then did Ben understand Tarr's unhappiness. Appalled, he stared out at the expansive, rising waters, feeling sick and cold.

* * *

With a comb clamped between her teeth, Old Parry leaned back and squinted at what she had done. "Tha's lovely," she admitted after removing the comb, "a right, fair maid." The normally acid-tongued aufwader dabbed at her eyes and gulped back a cry. It was over three hundred years since she had wed her Joby and he had taken that final voyage on the black boat only fifty years after that.

Nelda stood still as stone near the entrance to her chamber. At that moment she was the most beautiful aufwader ever to have lived; her hair had been teasled and combed free of sand and now a coronet of rare, underwater flowers sat lightly upon her brow and more were woven into her long tresses. She was arrayed in a richly-embroidered dress which all the womenfolk had been at pains to complete in time, sitting up throughout the night to accomplish the delicate task. It was a glorious, blue-green colour that shimmered like the sea itself when she moved and, in the stitches, traced her lineage down many generations. About the neck tiny pearls had been sewn and around her waist was a belt of silver decorated with the three-pronged symbol of the Lords of the Deep.

It took three sea wives to fuss over and groom her in all her bridal finery. Old Parry was one of these, the other two were Maudlin Trowker and a toothless crone known only as Baccy because all she ever did was suck on a clay pipe and cackle to herself. If the truth be known, the latter did very little in helping Nelda to get ready, she only wanted to make sure she didn't miss out on anything interesting and sat nearby, hunched on a bunk sucking her gums and muttering battily to herself.

Maudlin fiddled with a stubborn bloom which refused to stay put in the young aufwader's hair, then she too stood back and heaved a great sigh. "Why," she said, "you'd outshine the moonkelp itself were it here."

Old Parry snorted. "Puh!" she exclaimed. "If it

were here the girl wouldn't have to wed at all."

At this, Baccy the crone gave a prolonged cackle and the pipe rattled between her blackened gums. Maudlin gave both of them an irritated glare then turned, smiling, back to the bride.

"Dinna fret yourself," she said, "it's a new life that's waitin' for you. At the close of the night you'll be Nelda Grendel. I know it ain't what you wanted ..."

"It's not what anyone would want," Parry chipped in.

Maudlin carried on as though she hadn't spoken. "But it may not be so bad. Aye, Esau was wrong to force this upon you but what's done is done. Look you to the future now – prepare for what lies ahead."

Old Parry stuck the comb into her tangled mass of grizzled hair where it wagged like the tail of a dog. "Bah," she grimaced, "dinna fill the maid's head wi' such claptrap! That Esau's an evil, covetous nazard who wants his face slappin' an' if'n he weren't the eldest of us all I'd do it missen. 'Tain't right any of this, why she's nowt but a lass, barely a babe and tricked into wedlock!"

Throughout all of this, Nelda remained silent. She had let them primp and preen her as was the custom, but that was all – she did not have to join in. Her eyes stared fixedly in front, a doll to be dressed and made ready – as though she was a sacrificial victim being prepared for the altar of some heathen and bloodthirsty god. Only this was to be a fate worse than death and the altar had a completely different function.

"You're ready," Maudlin told her. "Nelda?"

The bride-to-be blinked and stared round as if she had been asleep. Everything was strange to her, the dress felt unusual and her hair was soft as foam. "You've done well," she told them, "thank you."

"Yip!" yammered Baccy, momentarily removing her pipe. "Tha's all trussed up like a fish supper an' Esau's the one who'll be feastin'!" And she dissolved into a fit of squawking cackles.

Nelda stared dispassionately at the old hag, she was too numb inside to be angry at her idiotic and tactless remarks. Nothing seemed to matter any more.

"Dinna you listen to her!" advised Maudlin, but she leaned forward and pressed a small glass phial into Nelda's hand, whispering, "If'n you're nervy over tonight – you know what I mean – sprinkle a pinch of this powder into the old goat's drink – he'll be too full of drowse to think of aught else and kip for hours."

Parry was adept at listening to other people's conversations, especially whispered ones and let out a delighted squeal. "The maid won't need that!" she laughed. "Esau's too ancient! It's more than he can cope wi' just walkin' from one cave t'nother."

"Then why's he weddin' her?" retorted Maudlin and Baccy let loose again with her horrible cackling, only to cease suddenly as Tarr strode into the chamber.

Nelda lifted her head as he entered and rushed over, flinging her arms about his neck while he stood, rigid and immovable as a wooden post.

Maudlin took the hint at once. "Come along," she gabbled to Parry and the crone, "us'll be wanted at the entrance."

The other two gaped at her. Baccy had no intention of leaving, this looked far too interesting and Old Parry was dying to hear what Tarr had to say to his granddaughter on her wedding day.

But Tarr shot them both a dangerous glance and they hurried out of the chamber as fast as they could. Before she left, Baccy spat brown phlegm on the rushes to register her complaint then scuttled off.

"Oh grandfather!" Nelda cried, weeping for the first time. "I'm so unhappy!"

"Lass," he answered, relaxing and holding her close, "let me sithee. Why, tha's prettier 'an yer grandmither ever were." And for several minutes they clung desperately to one another.

Eventually, Tarr pulled away and dried the tears which had streaked down Nelda's cheeks. " 'Tis time, lass," he said in a wavering whisper, "that dreaded hour is upon us, is tha ready?"

She squeezed his hands tightly, drawing courage and strength from him. "That I am," she replied in a brave voice.

"Then let us get gone. Can't hide from it now – but you listen t'thy grandda when he says he's reet proud o' thee."

She linked her arm in his, and if she was aware that he was trembling, made no mention of it. Out of the cave they went, out to where Nelda's doom awaited her.

* * *

The tide had come in quickly, it lapped against the cliff face and still the waves rolled higher. Ben was very cold and his legs ached, for there was nowhere to sit down. He stared at the gurgling water below and watched it steadily rise. As the breakers crashed against the rock, the spray was caught in the light of the aufwader lanterns and showered a thousand sparkling mirrors back into the sea.

Prawny glanced back into the chamber, his face growing stern. "It begins," he muttered.

Ben followed his stare. Through the assembled fisherfolk came two wizened creatures and everyone stepped aside to let them pass; for here were Johab and Lorkon, the other members of the ruling Triad. Leaning upon their staffs they headed for the entrance, nodding to those who bowed before them.

The two aufwaders acknowledged Ben's presence with a brief twitch of their bushy brows. Then they parted and stood at either side of the great stone doors, their faces grim and troubled. Try as they might, they had failed to dissuade Esau from this ruinous path, and both shivered with fearful misgivings.

"Sound the horn," said Johab, motioning to the crowd.

Up to the threshold stepped the tallest of the tribe, yet even he was only a foot taller than Ben. In his arms he carried a large conch shell which he raised over his head for all to see. Then, putting it to his lips he blew with all his might.

Ben had never heard such a noise before, it was like a hundred trumpets blaring at once. It boomed around the cavern, bouncing off the rocky walls, deafening everyone and challenging them to withstand its roar. Then out, out over the sea it bellowed, shaking the waters and sounding the deeps, never was there such a voice to shout down the stars and make the moon herself tremble.

And then the aufwader with the conch was breathing rapidly, trying to fill his spent lungs. His face was almost purple and his knees knocked feebly together, his role in the ceremony was finished and he ambled back to the others – gasping and puffing.

The echo of the shell's blast was still resounding in the far distance, battering through the dark horizon until it faded altogether. Ben wondered what would happen next, everyone seemed to be waiting, holding their breaths in expectation – and then he heard it. At first he thought it was a delayed echo but no, this note was deeper than before. It was an answering call, and though it came from many miles away, it vibrated through the rocks and made the hairs on the boy's neck prickle and tingle.

A hushed murmur ran through the aufwaders, but before they had chance to discuss it, Esau entered the chamber and the whispers were silenced.

In came the eldest of the fisherfolk, shambling slowly forward, putting all his decrepit weight on two gnarled sticks which tapped out a harsh rhythm on the ground. His eyes darted everywhere, swivelling slyly from side to side. He glared at the tribe, his crabbed face twisted into a sneer.

Ben could not believe any living thing could be so old and asked Prawny in a low voice, "Who's that?"

"Esau," came the bitter reply, "the bridegroom."

The boy clutched at his stomach, so this was the one Nelda was to marry. Surely it was impossible! The leader of the Triad was vile and withered, his back was bent with age and Ben could feel nothing but revulsion at the sight of him.

Esau raised his shrunken head and, when his beady eyes lit upon the boy, a foul curse issued from his hideous lips. Malice boiled within him, he despised the landfolk and the urge to cast the child into the sea to drown nearly overwhelmed him. But this was part of the bargain with his future bride, the whelp had to remain and witness the union. Turning his back on him, Esau came to the threshold and waited.

Another rippling murmur bubbled through the gathering – Nelda had arrived. The womenfolk all sighed when they saw her, then wept, remembering what was in store for the unfortunate girl.

The young aufwader was holding tightly to her grandfather. Her face was set in an awful, grim expression but she held her head proudly and glided with a cold dignity smoothly through the chamber –

not flinching once from the shrivelled horror which leered at her by the entrance.

Passing Ben, Nelda's eyes wavered, flicking from her husband-to-be to the boy. But the occasion was too dreadful and solemn to allow for anything else. No welcoming smile crossed her small mouth, all she could do was nod once and continue on her way.

In the dark heavens, the moon appeared from behind a cloud and bathed the entrance in a cold, grey light. Nelda crossed into the pale glow, stopping at Esau's side, where Tarr reluctantly wrenched himself from her arm.

Kissing her forehead, he said, "May tha find joy lass – if'n tha can."

Nelda thanked him, then, choking back her misery, turned to face the groom.

Esau was regarding her with lustful eyes. Her hair was streaming in the sea breeze and the bridal dress fluttered closely about her. The moonlight picked out the small pearls at her throat and burned icily in the silver belt around her waist. She was beautiful, and the frozen dignity she wrapped herself in only made her more desirable and kindled the dark thoughts within him.

With his bearded chin resting on his claw-like hands he licked his lips and croaked, "Thou art indeed most fair, my love." The words went through her like hot knives but she steeled herself and he added, "Many gifts shall I shower upon thee, much wisdom shall I share – many secrets which I alone am privy to." The tiny eyes gleamed and a trickle of spittle dribbled from his mouth as he muttered, "Thou wouldst clap thy dainty hands with glee at the knowledge I possess," and he gave her a lascivious wink.

Nelda said nothing, but looked out to the shimmering waters. Esau grinned indulgently then pounded one of his sticks on the ground.

"Let the Briding commence!" he declared. Raising one hand he pointed to the black horizon. "Under cover of stars and moon," he called, although there were no stars and, almost as if he had frightened it away, the moon slid behind another cloud and did not reappear. A few of the other fisherfolk nudged each other and raised their eyebrows at this. A proper ceremony usually only took place on clear nights. As the darkness swallowed the sky once more, Esau continued, he was too impatient to be denied now.

"Under cover of stars and moon," he repeated defying the traditions of his people, "do I, Esau Grendel pledge mine intent – to take for mine own, Nelda Shrimp and bestow upon her such gifts that are in my power."

He looked over to her, smiling and showing his one, snaggled tooth. It was time for them to join hands. Nelda lifted hers and closed her eyes in disgust as Esau's deformed claw clasped itself around it.

"Now is the bond made," he cawed, "and I do call on the sea itself to bear witness." With some difficulty, he made a bow to the waves and bid Nelda do the same. When this was done, he raised his cracked voice and called out. "Now do I offer the prayer. Hear me, ye Lords of the Deep and Dark. Grant to thy loyal servants, Esau and Nelda, thine own blessing, that we may be sure of a merry life together hereafter."

This was merely a formality and, once the prayer had been given, a plump female came forward bearing a wooden dish. Upon it was a strange loaf-shaped cake and a length of string.

Esau took the cord and passed one end to Nelda, who received it as though it were a venomous snake. Then, slowly, she bound it around her wrist and Esau did the same.

"Now are we tethered," he gurgled, "and ever after shall it remain, with thee by my side, though there be no rope to bind thee."

"So shall it be," she said in a frail voice.

"Then let us eat and seal ourselves till the end of our days," he told her.

With her free hand, Nelda broke off a piece of the bridecake and bit into it. Without chewing she kept the morsel in her mouth and offered the rest to Esau whose lips snatched it greedily from her fingers. All they had to do now was kiss and the ceremony would be complete. With a quailing heart, Nelda bent down and the ancient creature upturned his face, both closed their eyes, one in repulsion, the other in ecstasy.

"Look!" cried Prawny suddenly. "Out yonder, a light is shining!"

Ben glanced out to sea. Sure enough, at the edge of the dark, watery world a faint glimmer had appeared. At once, everyone began to chatter in bewilderment and fear. Esau glared round and peered intently at the dim glow, scowling horribly. Confused, Nelda turned to her grandfather who narrowed his eyes, trying to discern what the eerie, pulsing speck could be.

"Hang on, lass," he told her in a frightened voice, "theer may be joy for thee after all."

" 'Tis comin' nearer!" someone cried.

Ben looked at Prawny. "What is it?" he asked. "Why is everyone so afraid?"

"Whatever that light be," Nusk replied, " 'tain't from no mortal lands. 'Tis a sign – from *them*."

Esau stamped his sticks on the ground and hissed. "We must not delay, let the Briding proceed!"

Grabbing hold of Nelda he pulled her towards his puckered, waiting lips but Tarr intervened, his strong hands restraining the ancient leader. "Us mun wait," he said gravely, "we dursn't carry on till us knows what *they* are wantin'."

The rest of the tribe agreed, and Esau mumbled irritably into his beard.

For a long time they remained motionless and silent, watching and waiting as the light drew closer. Presently, even Ben could see that it came from a small wooden boat, such as the fisherfolk used, and that a figure was seated in it.

The boat swiftly rode the waves, yet Ben could not tell how it moved, for the occupant was not rowing. It seemed rather that the sea itself was drawing it forward.

"Bless us," breathed Tarr in fear.

The craft had come to rest just before the entrance where the tide had risen level with the floor. But the vessel remained a constant three feet away from the rock, as if it had been forbidden to touch any part of the land.

Ben stared at the spectacle in wonder. The boat was filled with clear water, and it was this that glowed. The light was silvery blue and fell on everyone's face, coldly flickering over their features and reflecting in their eyes. Yet the vessel was damaged. A long, jagged hole gaped in the hull and should have made it impossible to remain afloat, but there it was, upheld by the hand of the sea. The boy was amazed and then the figure within commanded his complete attention.

Dressed in a loose robe of sea-green, it was a crouched shape whose lower half was submerged in the shining water. A large hood concealed the face and not even the shifting light could penetrate the black shadows beneath that cowl. Whatever was hidden under there, Ben thought, could stay out of sight, he had no wish to look on a face from the dark deeps.

The figure did not move, yet they all felt as though

it were studying them, gazing at each one in turn with invisible eyes and at some point everyone shivered.

As leader of the Triad it was Esau's duty to present himself. He managed a polite, if impatient bow then greeted the strange visitor. "I welcome thee, most noble guest," he said fawningly, "the Triad of the aufwader race is honoured at thy presence."

Then the figure began to speak. It was a chilling sound, full of despair, like the voice of the north wind. In a hard, ringing voice it cried, "Esau Grendel! I am a messenger from the Dark Realm. A herald am I, sent hither by the Three whom thy petty triad mirrors in dread."

The fisherfolk were dismayed at these words, for they were filled with scorn and they knew that the Deep Ones were angry with them. Only Esau remained undaunted, he leaned forward like a stubborn blade of grass that will not bend before the storm, and the messenger continued.

"In thy arrogance thou hast called upon my masters to bless this unholy union. Hearken to me Esau Grendel, know that this base lust of thine will be thy undoing. Turn aside from the folly of thy diseased heart – for thou hast asked and thou art denied. The Lords of the Deep and Dark withhold their blessing and dispatched me with this warning – continue in this and thou art doomed!"

Even Ben shivered at this, and he was aware of the terror that filled the rest of the cave.

"I await thine answer," the messenger said coldly.

Esau had been silent up till then, now he raised one of his sticks and pointed it accusingly at the herald of the Deep Ones. "Take this reply back to thy cruel masters!" he raged and behind him all the aufwaders recoiled in horror at the brazen insolence of his words. "They have lost the right to interfere in our affairs. 'Tis their curse which we have suffered under and I shall not be commanded by such bitter liege lords. Are they not content to see our race dwindle from this land? Must they refuse us a final happiness?"

"They deny thee nothing," rang the messenger angrily, "only a bride too young for thee. And I say again – beware!"

"Begone!" Esau demanded. "As a friend I welcomed thee but now do I turn thee away as mine enemy. Tell that to thy masters and may their thrones rot below the waves. I will have naught else to do with them!"

The herald said no more. Smoothly, the boat began to turn, but before it departed, the blank space beneath the hood turned to Ben. For an instant the boy thought he saw a cluster of many eyes staring out at him and from the folds at the bottom of the robe a livid green tentacle snaked out.

With an ominous rumble, the sea began to swell and, beneath the cold light, grew black and dark. As the boat sailed away, the waves crashed over the threshold of the entrance chamber, covering everyone in freezing salt water.

"What has tha done?" Tarr cried. "Esau, tha's angered *them* wi' thy haughty words! What possessed thee? Is tha mad?"

The waters crashed against the cliff and the rock shuddered at the violence of it.

"Close the doors!" Esau ordered. "They'll not fright me so easily. Let them rant all they can, they'll not batter the entrance down."

Another wave rampaged into the chamber, knocking several of the fisherfolk off their feet and dragging them towards the entrance.

Quickly, Prawny and another leapt at one of the chains and pulled down hard. With a slow grinding, the slabs of stone began to close. Everyone cowered back as a further wave hammered through the gap, tearing the nets from their hooks and throwing down the fishing boats.

Only Esau was unafraid, he stood amid the surging water, laughing madly while, still tied to his wrist, Nelda wept and struggled to free herself.

With a juddering slam, the doors closed and were sealed, but the fury of the Lords of the Deep continued to throw itself against them.

"Now!" Esau cried. " 'Tis time to finish what was started!" He dragged Nelda towards him and before any one could stop him, pressed his putrid lips against hers.

"Grendel!" shrieked Tarr furiously. "Dost tha know what tha's done?"

"Wed thy granddaughter!" he snapped back. "And there's not a thing thou canst do about it. The wench is mine for eternity!"

"But the Deep Ones!" muttered Johab in dismay. "They forbade you!"

"They no longer have dominion here!" he proclaimed. "Only the law of the Triad rules and I am its leader!" He swung Nelda before him and pushed her towards one of the tunnels. "Time for us to retire, my sweet," he told her.

Nelda untied the string from her wrist and backed away. "No," she protested.

"Thou canst not run from me now, my love," he laughed, "we are bound together for life." He cast a disgusted look at Ben then said, "I give thee a few moments with thy human friend. For it shall be the last time thou shalt ever see him. Remember the bargain, my pearl, the upper world is denied thee now." Shuffling off, he called over his shoulder, "Seek me in my chamber, there shall I be waiting."

Nelda watched her husband hobble down the

tunnel, then she ran into Tarr's arms and, after holding him tightly, turned to Ben, tears stinging her face.

"This is what I feared," she told him, "that day when I felt a dark fate was upon me and we would never meet again. Esau has forbidden me to leave the caves – I shall never see you, or the daylight until he dies." And sobbing, she told him how she had been forced into the marriage. Ben's heart sank, so this too was his fault.

"I'm sorry," he told her.

The aufwader shook her head. "It was my own rash promise that led me to this," she said, "the blame lies with me alone."

"But if I hadn't been got at by Rowena ..." Then he remembered Nathaniel, and knew this was his only chance to tell her about what had happened. Quickly he explained all that he knew and Nelda listened to his story with great interest, especially the part about Irl and the first guardian he had made.

"Never have I heard of such a thing," she murmured when he was done. "In all our legends none speak of this. He must have hid it well indeed. What of you, grandfather?"

Tarr frowned. "When I were a lad," he began, "I recall talk of summat girt and wicked sleepin' in the dark, but nowt of any guardian. Theer's only one in the tribe who might know of it."

Nelda knew who he meant. "Esau?" she breathed.

"Aye, he's the one. If'n any remember it'll be 'im."

She looked down into the tunnel where her husband had gone. "If this is as important as you say," she said to Ben, "then I will do what I can."

"Be careful," the boy told her.

Nelda managed a weak laugh. "I shall. A bride in name only will I be – have no fear there. Esau may yet rue this wedding day. Now I must go." She gave Ben a hug. "Goodbye, my friend," she said sorrowfully, "perhaps one day, when you are old and Esau is no more I shall venture from the caves and seek you out – remember me."

"Goodbye," sniffed Ben.

The aufwader waved farewell and disappeared into the tunnel.

Leaning on his staff, Tarr sucked his teeth thoughtfully. "Don't you go a-frettin'," he told the boy, "ah'll keep thee abreast of the news, an' bring you messages from my granddaughter. Come now, ah'll lead thee back to thy world," he smiled grimly at the boy's face – guessing what he was thinking, "theer's other ways into the caves apart from thissun. Ways that lead out on to the cliff top, tha'll not have to get so much as a toe wet."

And so he led Ben from the entrance chamber, taking him down secret passageways and up into the wild, stormy air above.

* * *

Esau sat on his bunk, stroking the bedclothes dreamily. Only the eldest of the tribe was ever allowed in this cavern, and for many years he had dwelt there alone, gnawing on his emptiness and slowly going mad with desire. But now he had a wife to share his life with and perhaps other things ...

It was a large place, lying beyond the throne room. Tapestries covered the walls, dating from earliest times and all the treasures of the tribe were stored in five large sea chests that he kept locked and the keys permanently about his person. The most unusual feature of the chamber however, was a circular pool set into the rocky floor. It was filled with black water, the surface of which was smooth as glass and Esau spent many long hours scrying into it.

THE BRIDING

The curtain which hung over the doorway was drawn aside and Nelda peered in.

"Welcome, my beauty," Esau said eagerly, "step into thy new home, what is mine shall be thine also." He shifted on the bunk so there was space enough for two but she pretended she hadn't noticed and wandered about the cave looking at everything with interest.

"No, my rosebud!" he cried warningly. "Don't touch that!"

Having seen the pool, she had knelt beside it – curious at the stillness of the water. Just as she was about to reach down and run her fingers through it, Esau had called out and leapt off the bunk to lead her away.

"Promise me, my bloom of the deep, that thou shalt never touch that pool." He stared down into the jet water and his voice faded to a whisper as he explained. "My Darkmirror, I call it," he breathed, "and a most hallowed thing. If I gaze long enough into its black heart a thousand sights can be seen. Places and peoples far off and days long gone – of the world that was and what the world may be. 'Tis the great secret of our tribe and only the leader of the Triad may use it, so leave well alone, my sweet wife."

"I shall," she answered.

Esau smiled, obviously relieved. "There's a comely, dutiful beloved," he cooed. Then, giving the pool one last glance asked, "Wilt thou swear unto me never to reveal to a soul the existence of my Darkmirror? 'Tis too dangerous a knowledge for the common folk to be aware of."

"I swear," she said, startled at the earnestness of the request.

"Nine times bless thee," sighed her husband.

"There is one thing I should like to ask," she began carefully.

Raising his hoary eyebrows he licked his single tooth. "And that would be?" he asked.

Nelda looked at him searchingly. "Have you ever heard tell of an old legend where Irl wrought a guardian to protect Whitby from a great evil?"

Esau's smile vanished for a moment and he said uncertainly, "There are many legends, and many concern Irl – where didst thou hear this one?"

"The human child told me," she replied.

Esau's face contorted into a hideous mask and he spat on the ground. "Forget about the landbreed!" he shouted at her. "He will be long dead before you set eyes on him again!"

"But of the guardian?" she insisted. "Does it exist?"

Esau refused to talk about it. "A hard and difficult day this has been," he muttered, "let us retire."

Limping over to the bunk, he patted the blankets expectantly and all thoughts of Irl flew out of Nelda's head.

"Oh no!" she cried defiantly. "A companion only shall I be! That was the bargain! Sleep well, my husband, for never will you delight in me! An empty marriage you have forced your way into!" Dragging the bedclothes from the bunk, she strode into a warm corner and made herself comfortable. "Goodnight," she said curtly.

Esau glowered and threw his sticks down in his temper. "Curse you!" he raged, but no matter how much he shrieked, the girl took no further notice of him and closed her eyes.

11

THE DEMON AND
THE DOG

The storm was raging savagely against the cliff.
Tremendous waves dashed themselves against the
rocks and the cobles in the harbour strained at their
moorings as the water came rushing in.

On the sands by Tate Hill Pier, Nathanial Crozier
regarded the unnatural tempest with keen interest.
"It would seem the Deep Ones have been stirred to
fury," he told himself. A brief doubt crossed his
mind. Could they be angry with him for killing Mr
Roper? Surely not, the death of one paltry human
would not interest them, unless of course it was one
who had their favour. Clutching the plastic bag he
resumed his work. It was imperative no one should
suspect his involvement in this night's gruesome
business. He must be above suspicion when the boy's
body was discovered.

Stooping, he looked into the carrier; it was bloated
with offal and gory shreds of liver which squelched
and wobbled like lumps of red jelly. "I hope this is
what it's partial to," he muttered distastefully.

By the pier wall, leading from beneath the houses
on the East Cliff, a wide outlet pipe opened on to the
sand. Nathaniel inspected it carefully. The grille
which had covered it had been torn away and

peculiar impressions had been left on the wet sand at the entrance.

Whistling softly and encouragingly, he dipped into the bag and threw a bloody piece of meat into the dark drain.

"Come on, my little beastie," he chuckled, "come to Nathaniel."

Another gruesome piece of flesh was thrown from his hands, followed by another, until a short trail had been made leading from the opening on to the shore.

Then he waited, patiently listening for the first signs.

There! Nathaniel put the squashy bag on the sand and held his breath. "Don't be afraid, my pet," he murmured, "I won't harm you."

A furtive snuffling echoed from the pipe, followed by noisy chewing.

"There's more out here, little one," the warlock promised.

Suddenly a scaly claw flashed from the shadows and snatched one of the bloody lumps. Instantly it disappeared back into the darkness and the loud chomping began again.

Nathaniel smirked, not long now, if he could only look into its eyes ...

He threw some more of the offal, letting it fall just short of the drain. There came an agitated scuffling, as though whatever it was could not decide whether to venture out or not. But the scent of the blood was too delicious – cats no longer satiated its hunger and it craved for sweeter, plumper meat. It stared out at the sandy world beyond the circle of the pipe, gazing at the tantalizing titbits lying there.

It was too much; the creature could bear it no longer and crept cautiously out, its luminous eyes blinking in the darkness and its nostrils questing for danger.

Nathaniel was fascinated. As the fish demon slowly emerged from the outlet he marvelled at its ugliness. The finned head appeared first, the eyes glowing like pale round lamps and the mouth gaped open to reveal the three rows of needle-sharp teeth. Then came the pot-belly and, with a rustle of its spiny fins, the hump-back followed. The last of the Mallykins crawled warily forward, then lunged ravenously at the slimy entrails which glistened on the sand.

"*Bon appetit*," the warlock said with some amusement.

The creature glared up at him. Hissing, it held the offal to its chest and scampered back to the mouth of the drain, lashing out with its other claw.

"Stop!" Nathaniel commanded. "You need not fear me – I shall not hurt you."

At once the fish demon froze, its primitive mind utterly dominated by the warlock's will. Letting the rancid guts splash around its clawed feet, it turned and trotted tamely over to the evil man, where it bowed in an almost comical manner – blood still staining its hideous jaws.

"Excellent," Nathaniel cooed, patting the foul monster on the side of its head, "if you serve me well you shall gorge on daintier meat than cats and butcher's left-overs." Crouching down, he looked into the Mallykin's dish-round eyes. "Be my instrument this night," he instructed, "perform one small task for me and I shall be forever grateful."

The creature flapped its stunted arms eagerly and hopped madly about the warlock's legs, like a dog keen to please its master.

Nathaniel scratched it beneath the chin, covering his fingers in blood from the offal as he did so. "Now my pet," he said lovingly, "follow this scent and devour what you find at the end of it." From his pocket he took a woollen glove and thrust it under the fish demon's snout. The glove belonged to Ben.

Gurgling, the Mallykin snorted the garment, memorizing the smell, then it sniffed the air and snuffled along the ground hunting for the trail.

"There's my fine animal," gushed Nathaniel, "go seek him out, find the boy and kill him. He must not stand between me and the second guardian." He paused, perhaps he should take the beast to Miss Boston's cottage and break a window for it to climb through. No, this way was better, he would be absolved from all blame.

The fish demon quivered as an electric shock passed through its misshapen form. The fins opened out along its head and back and it began to jabber excitedly.

"He's caught wind of something," said the warlock, vastly impressed, "go now, my destroyer, rend the child limb from limb and eat your fill of his puerile flesh."

Emitting a shrill squeal of delight, the Mallykin leaped into the air and bounded away, up the steps of the pier, then into the dark alleyways of the East Cliff, obeying its new master and pursuing its thirst for blood.

On the shore, Nathaniel threw back his head and laughed. Once the boy had been dealt with, the second guardian would be his.

* * *

Danny Turner inhaled deeply on the cigarette, letting the curling blue smoke issue from his mouth and nostrils.

"You look like a dragon," Mark told him. "Give me a go."

The cigarette was handed over and the other boy

puffed eagerly on it, but Mark was not as practised a smoker as his friend. Spluttering and coughing, he retched and passed it back.

Danny laughed at him. "Yer baby," he said scornfully, "y'ain't a man till yer can smoke, yer know. I've been doin' it fer nearly a year now." He took another great lungful of nicotine and offered it to Mark once more.

They were sitting beneath a lean-to on the grassy cliffside. It was a favourite hang-out of theirs; the sloping field was only used by grazing horses, so nobody ever bothered them. Danny would often slip out of doors late at night to sit under this sheet of corrugated iron and experiment with cigarettes. Tonight he had persuaded Mark Stribbet to do the same and the pair of them had spent a raucous hour sniggering at the day's events.

"Did you see that Cret's face when he saw us?" snorted Danny. "I bet he papped hisself!"

Mark was too engrossed in the cigarette to answer, he was trying to expel the smoke through his nose without swallowing it and was feeling rather queasy.

"Still," Danny continued, "I give that sister of his what fer didn't I?" He pulled a blade of grass from the ground and chewed the end of it reflectively. "She's a stuck-up dog she is, and did you catch the look she give me? Barmy as her kid brother. Just wait till tomorrow, first chance I get I'm gonna get her again. I might pinch me Mam's scissors and snip off some of Laurenson's hair – what do you think?"

"She's loony," commented Mark flicking ash on the ground, "I wouldn't touch her again if I was you. Nutters don't care what they do – she might grab them scissors off you and stab 'em in yer."

"Wouldn't give her the chance," protested Danny taking the cigarette back, "besides, I'm not scared of her."

"Never said you was."

"Good."

The next few minutes dragged by in silence as Danny sucked in the smoke and Mark stared at the glowing end of the smouldering tobacco. He had touched a nerve. Danny *was* afraid of Jennet, he hadn't forgotten the bloody nose she had given him. As a bully, he wasn't used to retaliation and the shock of it had taken him completely by surprise. He was only used to the frightened, smaller children who obeyed him out of fear and this obnoxious, defiant girl was becoming a problem. It had taken six of them today to get her. What were they to do if she came after them when they were on their own?

"At least we got this," Mark said to break the pondering silence. Holding up the guy, he shook it violently and threw it at Danny.

The Turner boy laughed. "If this were that Cret," he said, "I'd do this to 'im!" and he pounded the figure against the corrugated iron – the resulting sound was like peals of thunder rumbling over the cliff. "Then I'd break his arms like this," he crowed wrenching at the stuffed sleeves and tying them behind its back.

"You've split the head open!" remarked Mark in a mock scolding voice. "Mind you, there's prob'ly a lot more in there than there is in the real Cret's bonce!"

Danny guffawed and hurled the guy out of the lean-to. "We're gonna have an ace bommie tomorrow," he said. " 'Ere, what if we lob some bangers through the Laurensons' letter-box? We could even throw one at her if she opens the door."

Mark hooted, "Can you imagine her face?"

"An' if that old bat what works in the post office answers it so much the better. My old man give me a right what for after she'd been round. Me ear's still ringin' where he walloped me."

"That was Laurenson's fault. Looks like a snitcher she does."

"P'raps we could put a banger in her pocket," Danny mused in all seriousness.

Mark eyed him doubtfully. That was going too far, surely even he wouldn't do something so crazy? "She'd end up in hospital wouldn't she?" he ventured.

"Serve her right too," spat Danny, "she belongs in one – only wi' padded walls." He rubbed his nose muttering to himself, then he giggled and hunched over, pulling a Quasimodo face. "Who's this?" he cried, slurring his words and sticking his tongue out. "Nelda! Nelda!"

Mark tittered then hauled himself from under the lean-to. "Beggar!" he grumbled, staring over at the church clock. "It's quarter to one. If I don't get back soon I'll be knackered in the morning. You comin'?"

Danny sneered. "I can stay out a bit longer," he said loftily. "I ain't no baby, why I could be out all night and creep back first thing. I'd be fresh as a daisy an' me folks'd never catch on."

Mark shrugged, "Well mine would. See yer in the mornin' then – you callin' fer me or what?"

'S'pose," Danny replied.

Mark waded through the grass and headed for the hundred and ninety-nine steps.

Alone, Danny finished the cigarette and smiled to himself. He was pleased that the other boy had gone, he didn't want to share what he had brought out with him. Diving in his pocket he took out a can of lager. He tugged on the ring-pull and the froth spat over his shoes.

"Yer don't know what yer missin', Marky boy," he chuckled, sipping at the foam, "but then you'd most likely choke on this an' all. Too good to waste this is." The boy guzzled from the can and belched contentedly. "I think I will put a banger in her pocket," he decided, "an' mebbe a rocket too!"

Suddenly he became aware of a peculiar hissing coming from outside the lean-to. The boy scowled, if that was Mark back again, it was just too bad, he couldn't have any drink. The strange noise persisted and a knowing grin spread over Danny's face – his friend was trying to scare him.

"Pathetic," he breathed, "that's no way to do it. If he thinks I'm frightened he's loony as well!" Putting the can down, he crawled forward. "He should have crept up and banged really loud on the roof," he muttered, "that's what I would've done. But now – he's the one who'll be wettin' himself. I'll jump out an' bawl at him!"

Pausing for a moment, Danny listened. Mark was hopeless at this sort of thing – it sounded like he was gargling. Stifling a titter, Danny tensed himself, then leapt from cover and yelled at the top of his voice, "Gotcha!"

The cliffside was deserted.

"Mark?" Danny muttered. "You there?"

From somewhere nearby the noise began again. Danny whirled round – what was it?

"Stribbit if that's you ..."

But there was nothing, only the constant, seething hiss issued from the empty darkness followed by a series of snufflings.

Danny took a step backwards – this was weird.

Suddenly, a hideous, guttural shriek filled the air. Danny whimpered in dismay, before his eyes the discarded Guy Fawkes slithered across the ground as an invisible force pounced upon it.

The boy could only stare in disbelief whilst unseen claws ripped into the ragged jumper that covered the effigy, tearing wildly at the shirt and newspaper beneath.

THE DEMON AND THE DOG

A freezing terror washed over Danny, this was beyond him. He was petrified, his eyes bulged as the guy flew apart and the furious howls grew more impatient. With a final, disgusted squeal, what was left of the disembowelled figure was flung into the air.

The fish demon had been betrayed; its master had deceived it. Faithfully, it had followed the scent trail all the way up the cliff, only for it to end in a tasteless and undigestible victim. Spitting out bits of newspaper, it eyed the human child which stood motionless nearby – now there was a succulent feast. At that moment, the creature's mind was filled only by hunger and had worked itself into such a frenzy that it would not be denied. It wanted to sink its teeth on tender flesh that was ripe on the bone and guzzle honey-sweet blood that pumped round an urchin's heart.

With its long tongue slobbering over its chin, the Mallykin prowled closer, its eyes glowing greedily.

Danny shuffled backwards, still staring at the tattered remains of the Guy Fawkes which were now strewn over the cliffside. "Get out of here!" his brain told him. "Run you idiot!" But his legs were stiff and he could not turn away. Then, to his horror, he saw the grass part as footsteps stalked nearer.

"N ... no," he stammered.

The fish demon growled, its jaws dripping with saliva. Passing by the lean-to, it threw the structure down with one swipe of its claws and advanced, gibbering, with its black appetite driving it on – to death and slaughter.

Danny screamed and the power of his legs returned. Yelling, he charged over the grass but it was too late. The Mallykin could move swiftly when it needed – in seven bounding strides it had caught up with the boy and pounced on to his back.

Danny stumbled and went toppling into the grass – helpless against the invisible might of the fish demon.

Reaching the bottom of the one hundred and ninety-nine steps, Mark Stribbit heard his friend's screams. They were terrifying – awful shrieks and he instinctively knew they were for real.

"Danny!" he cried. "My God!"

But he was too afraid to run to the boy's aid. As the pitiful cries floated out over the sleeping town, all he could do was listen in dread. For the rest of his life Mark Stribbit never forgot those sounds. When they ceased, abruptly cut off and leaving the night quiet and peaceful once again, Mark let out a cry of his own and hurtled down the remaining steps.

"Let me in!" he yelled, hammering on the first door he came to. "Please! Wake up – it's Danny! Help me please!"

* * *

Miss Boston was annoyed. She had not been allowed to see Patricia Gunning since the day of her arrival in London. This morning, before breakfast, she had knocked at the sickroom door only to have the baritone voice of the nurse bark out that the patient was not up to seeing anyone. So, the old lady wandered downstairs to the dining-room and discovered that there was no breakfast ready for her.

When she found him, Rook, the butler, was still in his bed with a severe hangover. Drawing back the curtains of his small room she declared that he needn't bother cooking her any more meals – she would do it herself.

The man only groaned, shielding his eyes from the painfully bright light and pulling the pillows over his ears to shut out the sound of her voice.

"Really!" she clucked, looking at the stack of empty

bottles which lay about the place. "You must have been getting drunk every night for weeks!"

The kitchen, when she discovered it, was in a frightful state. The bin had not been emptied for goodness knows how long and had overflowed, spilling out over the floor tiles like decaying rivers of lava from a festering volcano. Old tins of beans littered everywhere and broken eggshells crunched beneath the old lady's feet as she gazed in disgust at the grimy squalor. Daring to peep into the fridge, she had found enough species of mould to write a book about and shuddered at the thought of what she had eaten the previous night.

Rolling up the sleeves of her blouse, she announced to the filthy kitchen that she was not going to stand for this any longer and promptly began hunting for disinfectant and a scrubbing brush.

By lunchtime, Miss Boston was sitting down at the spotless kitchen table eating her breakfast, having nipped to the local mini-market for provisions.

When Rook eventually stirred from his room, he staggered into the kitchen robed in a dishevelled silken dressing-gown, clutching his forehead.

Miss Boston tutted at his appearance and pointed to her watch meaningfully. "Dear, oh dear, Mr Rook," she said, "I find this very distressing."

"Madam," he burbled in a disrespectful tone and holding up his hand for her to speak more gently, "what I find distressing is your incessant carping and badgering. I would take it as a great kindness if you would keep your prattling trap well and truly shut! And another thing ..." he sniffed then turned a sickly shade of green. "What is that diabolical smell?" he asked.

"Merely my breakfast," she replied ignoring his rudeness, "some bacon, eggs and a tomato."

The butler recoiled from her as though she carried the plague. "Stop!" he begged.

"I beg your pardon," Miss Boston rattled on relentlessly, "I normally don't eat so much fried food – but I couldn't find any kippers ..."

"Kippers!" the man exclaimed and immediately dashed from the room with his hand over his mouth.

"Strange fellow," observed Miss Boston with a grin, "perhaps he has an aversion to fish."

When she had finished her meal and washed up the dishes, Miss Boston went upstairs once more to see if her friend was any better. Rook must have gone straight back to bed for he was nowhere to be seen.

On the landing, outside the sickroom, Miss Boston came to a halt. Judith Deacon was waiting with her feet planted firmly apart and her back squarely against the door, her dark eyebrows ploughed into a deep frown.

The old lady had to force a smile to her lips as she greeted the woman for she really did not like her one little bit. "Good afternoon," she began as brightly as she could, "may I slip in and see Patricia now?"

The nurse's face might have been carved from marble. "Out of the question, Miss Boston," she firmly refused, "Mrs Gunning is still too poorly at the present time."

"But surely just for a moment?"

"No!" the nurse snapped. "You cannot see her at all until I consider her to be strong enough."

"And when might that be?"

"Perhaps this evening, or perhaps tomorrow – I can't be certain."

Miss Boston sighed. "How disappointing," she muttered, staring past the large shoulders of the nurse to the closed door, "I was rather hoping to ... never mind – later will do."

"You should go out for the day," Judith Deacon

suggested coldly, "visit one of the museums perhaps? Much better than being stuck in here, it must be very boring for you."

"Yes," she replied, "maybe I will. I could buy some presents for the children and send them a postcard with a dinosaur on – Benjamin would love that."

And so Miss Boston spent the rest of the afternoon in the Natural History Museum, but her mind kept wandering off the exhibits and returning to the mysterious goings on in that house. Her anger was simmering. She felt sure that Patricia needed the help of a real doctor, but she had promised her that she wouldn't interfere.

"Confound it all!" she called loudly and her voice echoed throughout the high galleries, making every other visitor gaze at her in surprise.

When she returned, having bought a book for Ben and a bracelet for Jennet from the museum shop, the house was quiet and dark. It seemed that Rook had recovered enough to raid the cellar once more. Having been released from kitchen duties by that nuisance of a guest he had selected a rather good bottle of port this time and it was warming him very nicely.

Miss Boston slowly ate her dinner, it was only a thick vegetable stew, and listened to the butler's voice rising from the cellar. He was singing merrily to himself. "That man's nose will blow up like a balloon," she commented, "and, he'll only have himself to blame."

At eight o'clock she knocked on the sickroom door for the last time that night. The same deep voice told her to go away and Miss Boston stamped her foot in annoyance before trudging up to her own room, furious and irritated.

Now she was sitting up in bed; curlers in her woolly hair and a stern expression crinkling her wrinkled face until nearly all her features had disappeared. She was in a foul mood, her patience had been stretched to the very limit and her mind was ticking over everything that had happened. With her knees drawn up and the neck of her nightgown pulled high to keep out the chill which filtered through the entire house, she gazed into space – lost in thought.

"Alice Boston," she said, "there's something very wrong here, and I'm ashamed that you haven't done anything about it yet. That Deacon woman's up to some villainy and poor Patricia is at her mercy. What you ought to do is telephone a proper doctor straight away – hang all promises you made!"

Her mind made up, she quickly threw off the blankets and swung her legs from the bed. This was more like it, it was time for action – Alice Boston was not going to let that creepy nurse intimidate her any longer.

Just then a noise sounded outside the door. The old lady started, and stared at the handle as it turned slowly and deliberately.

Switching off the light, she reached for a brass candlestick and held it in readiness above her head whilst tip-toeing behind the door to wait.

Inch by inch it opened until a dark shape was visible beyond.

"Who's there?" Miss Boston demanded, her chins wobbling like never before.

"Alice?" came a weak voice.

Into the room came a frail, skeletal figure, its silver hair streaming behind, mingling with the fine material of the nightdress it was wearing. Limping towards the bed it wavered when it found it empty. "Oh nooo!" it wailed – stricken with fear.

Miss Boston was astonished, for a moment she thought a bewildered phantom had stumbled into her room but now she flicked the light back on. "Patricia!" she exclaimed. "What are you doing here?"

Mrs Gunning collapsed on the bed. She looked terrible, more emaciated than she had been yesterday, with dark hollows where her eyes had sunk into the sockets. Across the left side of her face was a disgusting, yellowish bruise which obviously gave her a great deal of pain. "Alice," she said hoarsely, "forgive me."

Miss Boston rushed over. "Patricia!" she cried, horrified at the condition of her friend.

"I couldn't stop her," Patricia explained with difficulty, "it was all her doing."

"The nurse?" asked Miss Boston, her temper boiling. "How dare she!" The old lady thumped the mattress in her temper and strode purposefully to the door. "I'm going to call the police!" she declared. "She must be a complete lunatic!"

"No," Patricia begged hastily, "there isn't time for that, please, Alice, come here."

Such was the urgency in the voice, that Miss Boston hurried back to her. "But she could have killed you!" she said.

Mrs Gunning shook her head in despair. "She already has, Alice," she whispered, "I won't last the night."

"Don't say that!"

"No listen to me," she implored. "Deacon has been poisoning me for weeks now, destroying me little by little each day. I was never seriously ill, that only happened when she arrived. She's evil Alice, you must get away from here!"

"I'm not leaving!" cried Miss Boston. "That nurse doesn't frighten me!"

"Then she ought to!" wept Mrs Gunning. "You don't know what she's capable of ... in all my life I never ... never came across a soul so black and empty ... completely malevolent – an evil force drives her ... she ... she is ... darkness itself ..." A fit of coughing made it impossible for her to continue and when it subsided there was blood on her lips.

"That's it!" stormed Miss Boston in outrage. "Where is the foul woman now?"

"Asleep in a chair in my room," Patricia wheezed, "it was difficult enough for me to escape without waking her. If she knew I had ..." she shuddered and clutched desperately at her friend. "You must go Alice!" she cried. "Back to Whitby where you belong!"

"I'm not going anywhere till I've telephoned the police!"

Patricia gave a sobbing laugh. "Why must you always be such a stubborn old fool?" she asked. "Do you still not understand? Has it not registered even yet?"

Miss Boston sat on the bed, her face blank, a sinister dreadful thought unfolded before her. "Patricia," she mumbled hesitantly, "you haven't told me why Miss Deacon has done this to you."

Grabbing the old lady's hand, Mrs Gunning held it tightly. "I was the lure Alice," she breathed desolately, "I am the bait which brought you here."

"But ..." the other murmured, "what for ...?"

Patricia's clouded blue eyes gazed steadily into her own. "Something is happening in Whitby," she said, "something horrendous and totally evil – they couldn't risk you being there to interfere with their plans."

"They?"

'I don't know who else is involved, only that you were to be kept away from Whitby at all costs."

Miss Boston slowly rose, her mind filled with apprehensions. "The children," she muttered, "what about them?"

Patricia pressed her hand to her chest, a creeping pain was eating through her. "You must go back to them Alice!" she urged.

"But what about you?"

"I don't matter any more!" Mrs Gunning shifted on the bed. Hidden beneath the folds of her nightdress was a squarish bundle and she brought it out thrusting it into Miss Boston's hands.

The old lady took it and a tear fell down her face.

"You know what it is?" asked Patricia in a rasping voice.

Miss Boston nodded. "Your Book of Shadows," she answered sorrowfully.

"A witch's most valuable possession," coughed Mrs Gunning, "all my knowledge, everything that I knew about the craft – even some secrets you never managed to worm out of me, Alice ..." She gasped for breath as the pain increased and Miss Boston knelt to hold her. "Deacon never found it!" she choked. "Always searched, though – beware her Alice! Take care of my book, take care of the children and ... forgive me ..."

The frail woman let out a long, agonized breath and collapsed in Miss Boston's arms.

"Patricia!" the old lady called. "Patricia!"

But Mrs Gunning was dead, troubled no longer by the wearisome world.

Miss Boston hung her head and kissed her dear friend goodbye. For some minutes she didn't move, too overcome by grief to do anything. Then, as she collected herself, she gently lifted the body and laid Patricia on the bed.

In death, the woman looked radiant; free of all care, her face seemed to regain the glow of youth and the savage bruising no longer marred her skin. With her silver hair flowing about her she looked like a warrior queen from some distant time, noble and proud, descended from saints and kings.

Miss Boston held the Book of Shadows to her breast and sorrowfully murmured, "Blessed be Patricia."

But there would be time to mourn later, for her heart was filled with fear – fear for the children and, if she would admit it, fear for herself.

"Come on, Alice," she said, "pull yourself together – you're a match for any malicious matron!" Still clasping Patricia's book, she scurried from the room.

In her bare feet, Miss Boston hurried down to the first floor landing. It was dark there. Ugly black shadows slashed across the carpet, forming ghastly shapes over the panelled walls – a dismal, fearful place. A chill draught blew up from the cold marble of the hall far below and she braced herself for the unexpected; anything could be hiding in those deep shadows.

Stepping carefully past the sickroom the old lady hastened for the alcove where the telephone stood upon a small table. It was horrible being there in the dark, she had never been afraid of it before, but here, in this house, it was different. Her shoulder blades itched as if someone was watching her but, although she kept looking round, Miss Boston failed to see anything. Gingerly she lifted the receiver, the buzz of the dialling tone seemed unbearably loud and she nearly replaced it to keep from disturbing the heavy silence.

With a trembling finger, she dialled the code for Whitby and then the number of the police station there. "Please answer," she whispered. "Hurry! poor Benjamin and Jennet – heaven knows what might be happening to them!"

The ringing stopped abruptly at the other end of the line and a voice answered, "Police, how can I help you?"

"Thank goodness," sighed Miss Boston gratefully – she had almost feared the town had disappeared. "Listen to me," she began in a hushed voice, "this is Alice Boston. I know it's late but you must go to my cottage – I have reason to believe something terrible is ... hello ... hello ..." They had been cut off.

She rattled the receiver cradle in panic. "Hello?" she cried, her voice rising in alarm. Not a sound came from the ear-piece – the line had gone dead.

Miss Boston slowly turned. "You," she muttered.

Standing on the dark landing was Judith Deacon. The large woman's face was a picture of anger and hatred. Dangling limply from her hands was the severed telephone cord.

"I couldn't permit that!" she growled. "We can't have you spoiling it all now can we, Miss Boston? Where is Mrs Gunning? She was very naughty, flitting off like that."

"Patricia's dead," the old lady told her accusingly, "and as soon as I get in touch with the constabulary I shall tell them exactly what you have done!"

The nurse laughed and took a menacing step closer. "Do you think I'd really let you out of here alive?" she cried. "You really are a stupid old hag!"

Miss Boston edged backwards "You're insane!" she shouted. "You'll never get away with it – all I have to do is call for Rook."

"The butler!" hooted Judith in derision. "He'll be well pickled by now. There'll be no help from him tonight!"

"But don't you realize what it is you've done?" asked Miss Boston, playing for time. "You're a murderess!"

"Mrs Gunning was old!" barked the nurse. "She'd had a good life, lived in luxury for years – what has she got to complain about? There's others in the world who never see such opulence."

"That's no reason to kill her!"

Miss Deacon prowled a little nearer, her masculine hands rising from her side. "I don't care," she rumbled, "I'm not sorry for what I've done – not sorry one tiny bit."

The rail of the landing banister pressed into Miss Boston's back and she knew she could not escape. "How can you say that?" she cried. "You poisoned and beat her – what sort of animal are you?"

Judith shrieked in rage and struck the old lady on the cheek. Miss Boston yelped, but even as she clenched her fists to retaliate the fight died in her and the anger curdled into terror.

"If I am an animal," the nurse seethed, "then I'm a proud one! Yes, I'm proud of what I've done! Now my beloved will be pleased with me – I have done all he asked and done it extremely well. Or rather I will have, after you've been dealt with. I see Mrs Gunning has given you her Book of Shadows – now where did she conceal that, I wonder? I never did manage to find it. You've saved me a great deal of trouble bringing it to me – how considerate."

"Your beloved?" stammered Miss Boston.

Judith closed her eyes and writhed with pleasure. "The most enthralling man I have ever known," she said huskily, "the only man I have ever known. There's no one in the entire world like him. Do you know what he does to me, Miss Boston? Can a dried-up old stick like you comprehend for one moment why the very mention of his name is exquisite torture to me?"

The woman took a further step up to her, with her eyelids drooping languidly and her tongue savouring each syllable. "Nathaniel – Nathaniel Crozier. He's the one who burns in my heart and scorches my blood – for him I would do anything, undergo any torment. He is why I breathe – without him I am

nothing. For the whole of my life no one so much as looked at me, but then *he* came along, with his charm and his power, he noticed this drab, unloved woman." Her lips peeled back, up to her pink gums and she bellowed, "I worship that man!"

As she spoke a change came over her, a mad light shone in her eyes and her voice became even deeper than before.

"Crozier," repeated Miss Boston, "but that's the man staying at the Gregsons', next door to my cottage!"

Miss Deacon tossed her head and a chilling, snarling gurgle issued from her throat. "That's right, you foul old crone!" she cried. "That's my darling Nathaniel – my beautiful, bearded god!"

Was it a trick of the dark, or were the nurse's eyebrows really growing thicker? Bristling over the bridge of her nose and spiking up to her temples.

"Crozier," Miss Boston said again, her mind confused and bewildered. Staring aghast at the increasingly nightmarish nurse, she grasped the banister for support then remembered at last where she had first heard that name.

"Oh, my Lord!" she cried.

Judith screeched with hellish laughter and the old lady cowered away, tipping dangerously back over the rail. The darkness of the hallway spiralled down below her, down to the cold marble floor. She felt her head spin, reeling from the unspeakable horror which was unfurling and from her grasp slipped the Book of Shadows Patricia had entrusted to her.

Down it fell, tumbling into the waiting dark, its leaves fluttering as it plummeted. Then with a thud, it crashed on to the marble and exploded – pages flying everywhere.

Judith Deacon's eyes blazed with a red light that burned with the unquenchable malice of Hades. Miss

Boston trembled, she had witnessed such a change once before.

"Soon Nathaniel and I will be together," Miss Deacon growled, and her teeth were visibly larger. "How I ache for him – how I yearn to feel his arms about me, squeezing until the breath is crushed from my body. I would die for him!"

She seized the old lady's throat with her hands and even as she grappled with her, the strong fingers mutated into claws and black fur crept down her fleshy arms.

"No!" gulped Miss Boston, as the grip tightened round her neck. "Can't you see he's using you? Nathaniel Crozier doesn't care one jot what happens to you – you're nothing to him!"

But Judith's frightening devotion to the evil man was overwhelming. She had no human voice left, and, with a cracking of bone, her square chin began to stretch and her nose tapered into a quivering snout.

Miss Boston felt her strength fail as the dreadful creature strangled the life from her. The glare from the blazing eyes lit her wrinkled face and her head was pushed back as the vicious teeth of the huge black dog came snapping down.

"Nooo!" she wailed. "Noooooo!"

The jaws bore down on her and Miss Boston felt the hound's hot breath beat against her exposed throat. This was the end, her ninety-two years had finally come to an abrupt halt. She who had saved the world from Rowena Cooper could not save herself.

A terrified scream rent the still calm of the night. It pierced the darkness for a brief instant – then was silenced forever.

12

BLOTMONATH

"Ben!" Jennet called, pulling the bedclothes off her brother. "Wake up!"

The boy yawned and gazed at her through one drowsy eye. "Mmm?" he mumbled. "Go away."

"It's terrible," she said, moving to the window and drawing the curtains back.

"What time is it?"Ben asked, reaching for the warm covers. "Oh, it's school today, isn't it?" Dozily he peered out of the window. Above the garden the gulls were riding the air and crying in morose voices to one another. Then the memories of last night came flooding back and his excitement banished all lingering traces of sleep.

"Oh, Jen!" he babbled. "It was amazing – Nelda got married, and to the most disgusting thing I ever saw. She didn't want to – he made her. Then a messenger came from ..." He faltered, his sister was hardly listening, and he noticed for the first time how pale she was. Ben frowned – what had she said a minute ago? "What's terrible?" he asked.

The girl hugged herself miserably. "It's Danny," she told him. "He's dead."

"You wish!" laughed Ben.

Jennet shuddered. "No," she cried, "I mean it! He's really dead – killed!"

The boy stopped laughing. "You're serious aren't

you?'' he gasped. "But how – when?''

"Last night, up on the cliff.''

Ben rubbed his head thoughtfully. "When I came back from the caves,'' he murmured, "there were lots of flashing lights up there – I didn't think, it must have been ambulances and police cars. I was too tired to take much notice.''

Jennet huddled into her school jumper. "It said on the radio they're looking for a wild animal,'' she intoned with macabre fascination, "some big cat, escaped from a circus or zoo. Danny must have been in a really bad way if they think that – I never liked him, but even so ...''

"A lion or tiger loose round here!'' Ben breathed. "Imagine.''

"Poor Miss Wethers,'' tutted his sister, "she was in a dreadful state before. Because she went round to the Turners' last night she thinks it's her fault Danny was out so late. She's gone off to open the post office now to keep herself busy, but you should have seen her, Ben – she's been through a whole box of tissues already.''

"I wish Aunt Alice was here,'' the boy murmured.

Jennet walked to the door. "I'll put your breakfast out for you,'' she said. "It's getting late, hurry up.''

Quickly the boy slipped on his uniform then opened the window. Leaning out he could just see a line of fluorescent tape cordoning off an area of the cliffside. Hastily he averted his eyes, he hadn't liked Danny but to be so interested in his death seemed morbid.

Presently he ran downstairs to the kitchen. Jennet had put a bowl of cereal out for him and, despite his growling stomach, the thought of his tormentor's demise squashed his appetite.

"I don't feel well,'' he said.

Jennet shrugged. "I know what you mean,'' she

admitted, "I couldn't face any either – hello, here's Miss Wethers again. She looks worse than before."

With a jangling of keys the front door was meekly opened and the postmistress entered, blowing her nose. Edith was wretched. Never had she known such a day, the effect on her nerves was horrendous. When she thought that only last night she had said such cruel things about that poor boy to his parents, she felt faint. How could she have been so wicked? It made her feel partly responsible for this distressing tragedy.

Her eyes were red raw and her spectacles splashed with tears. She had thought it would do her good to go to work and keep occupied but there she had heard even more terrible news. Snivelling into a sodden tissue, she groped into the kitchen and plumped down on a stool.

"Oh Jennet!" she whined. "I can't stand it! I'm all worn out – what a beastly day this is!"

"Have you closed the post office again?" the girl asked sympathetically. "Couldn't you face it?"

She received a series of vigorous nods as the woman's vocal cords were too choked to answer. Eventually she blubbered, "That lovely old gentleman, found outside his house – poor, dear thing. He was so polite." And she blew her nose so hard that the tissue was blasted to shreds.

Ben raised his head, an unpleasant thought stealing over him. "Who do you mean?" he asked.

Edith bit her lip. "Oh Benjamin!" she wept, floundering for a way to tell him. "It's Mr Roper – he's … he's gone to heaven dear."

The boy staggered from his seat, "NO!" he shouted. "NO!"

He pushed against the table and the cereal bowl went smashing to the floor.

"Ben!" Jennet cried as her brother dashed from the kitchen and fled upstairs.

"Let him go," Edith advised in between her sniffles, "poor boy – I think it would be best if you both stayed off school today. Oh I really don't know what to do. I tried to ring Alice but the London number she gave me is quite dead – I can't get any answer from it. What a harrowing morning!"

Ben yanked open the door to his room then hurled himself on to the bed and buried his face in the pillow.

"No," he wailed, "not him, not Mr Roper!"

For some time he wept, aching with grief and sorrow. He had loved that lonely old man. He was like a grandfather to him and now – like his parents – had been wrenched out of his life. It was as if he wasn't allowed to make friends or be part of a family – everyone he met was snatched away – first Mum and Dad, then the foster parents who didn't want him, now Nelda was forbidden to see him and finally this. Even Jennet was acting strangely these days.

"Why?" he howled, empty and isolated. "Why?"

Rolling over, the dejected boy stared in anguish at the ceiling – then he remembered the fireworks.

Hastily, he dragged the tin from under the chest of drawers where he had stashed it yesterday afternoon. They were extremely precious to him now, a parting gift from that kindly old man.

Reverently, he removed the lid and gazed within – a riot of colour met his eyes. "Thank you," he whispered, taking each of the brightly patterned fireworks out and examining them in turn. There were Roman candles, Vesuvii, a Catherine wheel, two golden fountains, a snowstorm, traffic lights and at the bottom, two packets of sparklers, one coloured – the other white.

They were a marvellous present, a celebration of their friendship in fiery bursts of stars and the tears that now rolled slowly down the boy's face were no longer bitter. They sprung from his memories of pleasant afternoons in the old man's front room and brimmed with the sad knowledge that such times were now over.

"I won't forget you," he said softly.

The peppery smell of gunpowder was strong on his fingers and Ben noticed that a quantity of black grains had leaked into the tin, collecting on a lining of brown paper that covered the bottom.

Curiously, the boy lifted the paper out and discovered that it was actually a flat parcel. Unwrapping it carefully he found inside a bag of faded crimson velvet. The material was musty, smelling of incense and a wild idea reared in his mind.

Holding his breath, he untied the neck of the bag and pulled out the treasure within.

At once he realized what Mr Roper had given to him – here was the second guardian of Whitby, and he gazed at the ancient thing in amazement.

It was a tablet of dark, stained wood and the design that had been carved into it was divided into three concentric sections. In the middle was a series of round images depicting the cycle of the moon, and all were inlaid with mother of pearl. Around this was a twisting border that had once been covered in gold leaf, but the ravaging ages had worn most of the gilt away.

Ben traced his finger over the flaking flourishes and curls, noticing that peculiar notches had been inscribed into the wood. These were part of a runic spell, calling upon the moon goddess for protection and strength. Around the outside of this, ran an elaborate sequence of magical symbols, to bind the power of the Deep Ones' enchantment. There were signs from the mystic east and some not seen since a great civilization sank into the sea. Great was the magic woven about this device and the boy could feel its power tingling through his fingers.

"The second guardian," he whispered. "Then it was his family who kept it all this time." And as he stared, an awful certainty gradually dawned – Nathaniel had killed the old man.

Hurriedly Ben shoved the wooden tablet back into the container and rapidly replaced the lid. What was he to do? Leaping from the bed as though fearing the tin might explode, he put his hand to his mouth. Nathaniel was bound to discover who had it now! The warlock would be coming for him next.

The boy had to tell someone – he had to make sure that evil man didn't get his hands on this guardian. It was time to tell his sister. Jennet must be made to understand what Mr Crozier was really like.

Ben ran down the stairs to the parlour where Jennet was sitting reading Edith's romantic novel.

"Jen," he said urgently, "you've got to listen to me. I know how Mr Roper died."

His sister put the book down. "Sshh!" she hissed. "Miss Wethers has gone to bed. Now, what are you talking about?"

"Mr Roper!" Ben repeated impatiently. "He was murdered!"

"Rubbish!" he girl snorted. "Look, she didn't tell you everything, but he had a heart attack. It was Doctor Adams who told her about it in the first place – Mr Roper was old, he had burglars last night, they wrecked his house and the shock must have finished him."

Ben shook his head violently. "That's not true!" he declared. "I know it isn't – listen to me, Jen, it's that man! That Crozier did it, Mr Roper was keeping something he wanted and he killed him for it."

Jennet's face assumed an ugly, angry look. "Shut up!" she demanded. "How dare you say that? You're just a child making up stupid stories. You've never liked Nathaniel – you're just jealous, that's it!"

The boy's mouth fell open in astonishment. He had never seen her quite so impassioned before. She was almost shaking with rage. "Jealous?" he mumbled. "What of?"

"Of him!" she cried gripping the arms of the chair and clawing at the material. "Of him and me – that's what! You don't like him because of what we mean to one another. You just can't stand the fact that I like someone else more than you!" There, she had said it, her breaths came in short little gulps of air and she glared at her brother for daring to criticize her beloved.

Ben felt as though she had slapped him. "You're mad," he told her, "if you could only hear yourself ..."

Jennet shifted on the chair but a brisk knock on the front door silenced whatever else she was going to say.

"Hello in there," came a voice, "is anybody at home?"

The girl's heart leapt and she sprang from the seat in delight. "Nathaniel!" she shouted joyfully. "Don't go. I'm coming!"

"No!" cried Ben, catching hold of her. "You mustn't let him in – he wants the second guardian. Jen don't!"

Roughly, his sister knocked him aside and hurried in a blind rush to the front door. "Good morning," she said coyly letting the man inside. "I wondered if you'd come round – I should have known you would."

Through the open parlour door, Ben saw the warlock stride into the hallway and kiss his sister on the cheek. But then his blood froze in his veins and his forehead was pricked out with sweat. A scream erupted in his throat and he had to clench his teeth to prevent it escaping. Into the house, close on the heels of Nathaniel, hopped the most detestable creature the boy had ever seen.

Helplessly, he watched as the fish demon waddled through the hall, its mouth stained with dried blood and its fins flexing in curiosity. It had never ventured inside a human dwelling before. Even in the old time, when only wooden shelters and stone huts nestled under the cliff, it had not dared to approach them. Now, however, its master's will pushed it forward, forcing it out in the daylight and driving it into the dens of the hated humans.

It gave the coat stand a cautious sniff, baring its razor teeth at the duffle hanging there, then it wheeled round and its eyes lit upon Ben.

With a bound, it flew into the parlour, claws ripping at the air. The boy wailed and stumbled towards the window in terror. Gurgling, the Mallykin pawed at him, tensing its scale-covered muscles and preparing to strike.

And then it wavered, its fins drooping as Nathaniel came into the room, shooting the creature a commanding glance. It tottered on its claws, uncertain and dazed. The warlock made a swift sign with his hand and the fish demon obediently scampered over to him. Crouching down on the carpet, it swayed from side to side, the pink tongue flicking in and out.

"Ah," Nathaniel said with feigned courtesy. "I see the amusingly bad-mannered Benjy is here also." For a moment he towered above him, then put a finger to his lips warning Ben to say nothing in front of his sister.

But the boy was unable to speak – so frightened was he by the fish demon.

Nathaniel smiled smugly and sat in the chair. He

was totally in control and savoured his authority. With a hollow purr, the Mallykin curled up round his feet.

"Say hello, Ben," said Jennet sitting on the sofa, "show Nathaniel you're not rude all the time."

Her brother dragged his wide eyes momentarily from the fish demon, just long enough to see the girl sitting calmly and utterly oblivious to what was really going on.

"Can't you see it?" he asked.

Jennet gave him a puzzled look. "Don't start that again," she warned him trying to sound superior and mature. "Honestly, Nathaniel, before you arrived, he was talking the most ridiculous, babyish drivel."

The warlock pretended to listen attentively to her, but his dark eyes were on Ben the whole time – malice flowing steadily from them.

Jennet cupped her chin demurely in her hand and lavished upon the man her warmest smile. "I'm so glad to see you. Isn't the news terrible?" Nathaniel seemed not to have heard her. "The dreadful news," she repeated.

"Yes, dreadful," he said distractedly before beaking the beam of smouldering hatred directed at Ben. "Oh, the boy on the cliff you mean? Yes, a singularly frightening incident." The warlock seemed to relish the words and he gave a knowing smirk, which only the boy saw, and his eyes wandered down to the fish demon.

"A veritable nightmare," Nathaniel resumed and Ben knew that his words were meant for him. "I fear that we all live in an uncertain world. Just when you think you are safe something – or someone – comes along and proves you wrong. The human body is very poorly designed, don't you think? We are all so very fragile, the slightest injury can defeat us, and it can happen so, so easily."

He tapped his fingers on the chair and at once the Mallykin lurched to its clawed feet and advanced towards the unwitting girl. Ben started forward but the creature hissed at him and began pacing around her threateningly.

"Stop making that silly noise," Jennet told her brother. "You know Nathaniel," she continued, "we were planning to have a bonfire tonight but it was knocked down yesterday. A shame, because I wanted to invite you to it – we could have had a lovely time. Still, the wood's all there. If you'd help we could build it up again. With your strong hands we'd do it in no time."

"Remember, remember," the warlock chanted, completely ignoring her request, "the fifth of November. Do you know why we light fires?"

"The gunpowder plot," Jennet enthused.

Nathaniel's eyebrows raised and he shook his head. "No," he said in a whisper, "that's what they teach you now but it's not true at all. It's merely an excuse, a decoy from the truth if you like and one cleverly masterminded by the oh-so-pious Christian church. People have always lit fires round about this time of year, long before sixteen hundred and five – and do you know why?"

Ben watched as the fish demon stood menacingly before Jennet's unsuspecting face, waving its claws dangerously close to her eyes.

"Bonfires," Nathaniel continued, revelling in taunting the boy, "the anwer is in the word itself, bonfire – bonefire. In almost every culture, this is traditionally a time of slaughter. The Anglo-Saxons called it Blotmonath – the month of blood."

The Mallykin spread its claws wide and twined them in Jennet's hair. The girl gave a flick of her hand, thinking a fly was tangled there.

"This was the time of great feasting," the warlock

muttered watching the boy intently, "when all the beasts who would not make it through the coming winter were butchered to conserve the stored feed for the rest."

"Ooh, it sounds spooky," cooed Jennet, enraptured by the man's melodic voice.

Nathaniel gave a slight, insidious chuckle and, turning to her, added, "But the carnage wasn't confined to cattle alone. Often the infirm, weaker members of tribes would be slaughtered – the sickly and the old, anyone who did not contribute to the community. An efficient policy, don't you agree? No wasters and idlers there "

He clicked his fingers and, at once, the fish demon clambered on to the back of the sofa, stretching its deformed arms out and bringing its gaping jaws down to the back of her skull, encircling Jennet in a ring of death.

"What great pyres there must have been in those forgotten times," Nathaniel persisted, "What splendid and unashamed barbarity."

"With all the deaths last night," Ben interrupted, "it looks like times haven't changed that much. Seems there are still a few barbarians left."

Nathaniel gave him a threatening stare, then he grinned horribly and said, "Jennet, be a good little love and make me a cup of tea."

"Of course," she said, only too willing to serve him. The girl left the room and the fish demon toddled fiendishly behind her.

As soon as she was gone, Nathaniel pressed the tips of his fingers together and asked in a harsh, teasing voice, "Well boy, what do you think of my pet?"

"It's just the sort I'd expect you to have," Ben replied, sounding braver than he actually felt. His heart was in his mouth. The thought of his sister alone in the kitchen with that foul abomination made his skin crawl and his palms were drenched in sweat. "If anything happens to Jen ..." he muttered.

"No need to be concerned," the warlock assured him, "the little fellow is entirely under my control, although I did make the mistake of allowing a measure of free will last night. That unfortunate boy on the cliff was meant to be you."

"Danny?" Ben gasped.

"Was that his name? It doesn't really matter, what does however is a certain device I believe your doddery friend gave to you. Be thankful that today I have decided to try a different tack to obtain it."

Ben sneered, his hatred for Mr Crozier distorting his features. "It was you who killed Mr Roper, wasn't it?" he accused.

Nathaniel beamed and said in a disgustingly casual way, "The old fool was too stubborn for his own good – I do hope you're not going to make the same mistake."

Ben had had enough, merely talking to the man made him feel dirty. "Call your monster in here!" he demanded. "Get it away from my sister."

"Tut, tut," remarked Nathaniel in disappointment, "now that isn't how it works is it? You give me what I want and I spare pretty little Janet."

"Jennet!" he corrected angrily.

"If you keep me waiting much longer, she won't need a name. Listen to me boy, all I have to do is relax my concentration and my cat will jump at the mouse. The Mallykin has a most voracious appetite."

There was nothing else Ben could do – it was either surrender to Nathaniel or let him murder his sister. Faced with this terrible dilemma, the boy had no option but to fetch the second guardian from his room. Leaving the parlour he glanced briefly into the kitchen, then dashed upstairs.

The fish demon was shadowing Jennet closely, pattering after her and mirroring her every move, always watching and gloating over her. Once it stood on her foot and she pulled away, staring at the empty air below in surprise. The vile creature hopped about madly, jumping on to the table where it gazed directly into the girl's face. The saucer-round eyes shone with a covetous, green light – how it would love to feast on her. Already last night's gorging was fading into a dim memory and its glistening pot-belly hungered for more.

When Ben came downstairs his sister was sitting back in the parlour and both she and the warlock were sipping at cups of tea.

Mr Crozier's eyes flickered over the boy as he entered and roved to the velvet bag he carried behind his back.

"Have you any biscuits to go with this?" Nathaniel asked the girl to get rid of her.

"Oh, I'm sorry," she apologized hastily, "I'll just get some." Jennet hurried into the kitchen, followed once more by the fish demon. As soon as she was out of sight, Ben handed the second guardian over and the man snatched it from him.

"At last," he breathed, thrusting it into his jacket pocket. "A wise decision boy. Now, if you wish to keep your sister out of danger I suggest you stay out of my way."

"What will you do?" Ben asked. "Will you destroy it like you did the one in the church?"

"You already know the answer to that. All the guardians must be dispensed with."

"There's only one more to find now, isn't there?" Ben said. "Well, you won't find it – even the fisherfolk don't know where it is. And they wouldn't give it to you if they did!"

"We'll see about that," Nathaniel spat in

annoyance. "A cat is a useful pet my lad. Set it amongst pigeons and any resistance is rapidly quashed."

"What do you mean?"

The warlock laughed wickedly, "How strong do you think the aufwaders are child? Are they prepared, do you think, for a confrontation with my little demon? He'll set them bolting down their filthy holes and it won't be long before the guardian made by Irl is uncovered."

Ben was horrified, "You can't let that thing loose down there!" he cried. "The fisherfolk would all be killed, they won't be able to defend themselves!"

"Ben?" said Jennet, coming in with a plate of biscuits. "What *are* you going on about now?"

Nathaniel twitched his fingers and the fish demon capered over to rest at his feet again. "What a delightful baby brother you have, dear Jennet," he told her, "we were just getting acquainted. He really does have the most intriguing imagination."

"I hope he hasn't been bothering you," she said, throwing Ben a moody glance.

Nathaniel helped himself to a digestive. "Not at all," he answered rising from the chair, "it's been most – rewarding, but now I really must get going." Giving Ben one last smile, he patted his jacket pocket and sang under his breath, "Remember, remember the fifth of November."

When they were in the hall, it amused Nathaniel to kiss Jennet lightly on the forehead. "Until next time," he said to her, "if you care to see me again that is."

"Of course I do," she said desperately. "Nathaniel I ... I ..."

"Yes?" the warlock asked, delighting in her torture.

"I love you!"

"Do you indeed?" he laughed mockingly. "How

sweet in one so young."

"I do," she insisted, "really."

In the parlour, the fish demon hesitated a moment, spitting hatefully at Ben, then scurried out after its master. With relief the boy heard the front door close and let out a great sigh.

"Thank God that's over!" he shuddered.

Jennet lingered for a while in the hall, pressing her fingers against her lips. Trance-like she wandered back to the room, a delirious smile traced over her mouth.

Ben couldn't believe it. "Are you *so* potty over that ... that awful man?" he cried. "Can't you see how blind you've been?"

The girl blinked as though stirring from a heavenly sleep. "What's up with you?" she asked.

"Crozier!" Ben stormed. "Didn't you hear what he was saying – or see how he treated you?"

Jennet regarded him with bemused astonishment. "Oh stop showing off," she said coldly, "it's not clever – you're only after attention. Well I won't stay here and listen, I'm going to finish my book in my room!"

"He's evil, Jen!" Ben cried, but the parlour door had already slammed behind her.

* * *

Joan Gregson knelt beside her husband and stirred the baby food around in the jar. She was haggard. All her life the woman had been a scourge and a scold but now Nathaniel had tamed her.

Timidly she obeyed his every word, cooked his meals and washed up after him. He was a terrifying guest to have under her roof and for the first time since the day of her wedding she longed to have her husband comfort her.

"Oh Norman," she said, her chin trembling, "what are we to do? Just what will become of us?"

Her husband made no reply. Ever since the warlock had forced him into his chair, he had been unable to move or speak. Staring fixedly into space, he was a shadow of his former self.

Mrs Gregson scooped up a spoonful of creamed banana and pushed it into his mouth. This laborious work was the only way to feed her husband – and, though most of the runny mixture dribbled obstinately out again, she felt that at least she was doing her best for him.

"If *he* ever lets us go," she promised, "I swear never to shout at you again. You can go to the pub any time you like and sit in your vegetable patch all day if you want."

The words fell on deaf ears – Norman Gregson could just as well have been a wax dummy.

"Please swallow some of this, dear," she implored and coaxed him. "You have to eat something!"

After several minutes, the distraught woman broke down and sobbed her heart out against her husband's shrinking stomach.

"Don't leave me on my own, Norman," she wept, "don't die on me."

"Really, Mrs Gregson," came a dissatisfied voice, "this house is a midden!"

Quickly, she jumped to attention – her guest had returned. "I'm sorry," she cried, "I haven't had time to do any tidying."

Nathaniel kicked over a pile of gardening magazines and they slithered over the floor. "Then I suggest you make time!" he scolded. "It's not fit to live in."

"Yes, sir," she agreed humbly. "I'm most awful sorry."

The warlock strode over to the fireplace. "At least

you keep a cheery hearth," he remarked, "that's something, I suppose. Mind you, I imagine that's for your dullard of a husband's benefit and not mine."

"Why no, Mr Crozier," she protested, "I wouldn't want you comin' back to a cold house."

He chuckled softly to himself and slipped his hand into his pocket. "Well I hope you're not neglecting your spouse," he said. "Remember what I said about bathing his eyes regularly, without the blink reflex they'll dry up."

"Oh no, sir," she answered, "I've been seein' to that all right. But what I was thinkin' ... well, you see, Mr Crozier, I was only wondering, if your stay was going to last much longer?" She shuffled away, expecting to be rebuked and made to suffer some terrible punishment, but to her surprise Nathaniel only nodded.

"Don't you worry," he said in a whisper, "I assure you I shall soon depart. My stay in Whitby is almost over, there remains but one thing more for me to accomplish and that is already in hand."

Mrs Gregson brightened at this news till a sudden doubt seized her. "You will set my Norman free when you go, won't you?" she asked.

"Dearest Joan," laughed Nathaniel, "believe me, when I get what I want, both you and your husband will be completely released from all your troubles." And he threw back his head to laugh at her.

"Now," he said, growing serious again, "would you like to see some fireworks, dear lady? It seems entirely appropriate for today."

"Whatever you wish," she murmured, fearing the cause of his horrible laughter.

The warlock took the second guardian from his jacket and turned it over in his hands.

"That's pretty," she ventured. "Looks expensive – antique is it?"

"Priceless," he informed her, "more ancient than your dull and flabby brain can imagine. See here? It says, 'STREONA MEC HEHT GEWYRCAN' – 'Streona had me made'. The craftsman who made this died over fifteen hundred years ago, perhaps more. What a truly beautiful marvel – it must have taken him ages to complete. A painstaking, lovely piece of art – so very, very exquisite and infinitely precious."

With that, he let the wooden tablet fall from his fingers and crash into the fire below.

"Sir!" warned Mrs Gregson, reaching for the poker.

"Let it be!" he told her. "Let it burn. Its time is over."

The flames crackled furiously over the guardian, rapidly consuming the ancient wood, spluttering and fizzing as it charred and turned to ash.

Nathaniel stared down with satisfaction as the magical device withered from the world. His face was illumined by a lurid, orange glow and he chuckled happily to himself.

Soon there was only a blackened piece left, a defiant chunk which refused to burn away completely. Nathaniel took the poker from his hostess and rammed it into the heart of the fire, splitting the stubborn fragment into many splinters which the flames then devoured.

A blinding light burst from the hearth, blowing soot and flames into the living-room. Mrs Gregson shrieked in fright but Nathaniel stood his ground and watched gleefully as a tremendous rush of golden sparks rushed violently from the grate and soared up the chimney.

"It is gone!" he cried. "The second guardian is no more!"

The woman stared dumbly at him, not understanding what he had done. Then the room grew dark.

"What's happening?" she whimpered.

In his hand, Nathaniel held the plaster fragment where the sign of the crescent moon glowed briefly and was gone. Beside the mark of Hilda only one other symbol remained. "Night has come early to Whitby," the warlock muttered.

Rushing to the window, Mrs Gregson cried, "The day is failing! It's as if the sun has died!"

Upon the mantelpiece, her ornaments began to tremble, then a china dog jerked and danced along a shelf until it fell off the edge and shattered on the floor. The window panes cracked and an ominous tremor rumbled beneath the cliff, shaking the very foundations.

Mrs Gregson leaped away from the window as the glass broke free of the frame and came crashing down in a million deadly splinters.

"It's an earthquake!" she screamed.

Outside, the yard rippled like the surface of turgid water and the length of Church Street buckled, spewing out its cobbles. The shrill clamour of windows exploding cut the air and great cracks zig-zagged through many buildings. Dislodged mortar rattled down and the door of the post office was torn from its hinges and fell with a crash out on to the pavement.

Mrs Gregson ran over to her husband and threw her protective arms about him. "You've done this!" she howled at Nathaniel. "Make it stop! Make it stop!"

But the warlock was too thrilled to hear her. It was starting already – *it* was waking. "I must see!" he cried. "I must get out there!"

"No," Joan panicked, "free Norman first. If we stay in here we'll die – the roof will collapse. You can't leave us!"

Nathaniel gave the woman a cruel smile. "Better to die quickly now," he scorned, "than shrivel before what I have awoken." And with that he left Mrs Gregson to scream alone, clinging on to the motionless body of her husband.

After an eternity of enchanted sleep and constraint, the hour of destruction had come at last.

13

THE WAKING OF MORGAWRUS

Ben staggered over the quaking shore where the threshing sand swirled in choking clouds. The tremor was already subsiding, and though it had left a trail of destruction in its wake, for the moment the danger was past.

The ground ceased its shivering, yet deep fissures had opened in the cliffside and jets of steam were hissing from the sea. The shock wave had been felt in every corner of Whitby and now the town was alive with the scream of alarm bells, sirens and the panic stricken cries of its inhabitants.

"Nelda!" shouted Ben as he clambered over boulders and leapt over gaping trenches. "Can you hear me? Anyone? You have to listen – it's Ben, Nelda's friend. I must talk to you!"

Reaching the massive concrete legs of the pier bridge, the boy scrabbled over the ledge and dropped on to the rocks on the far side. Already the tide was creeping in and he landed with a splash, the water filling his shoes and drenching his socks.

Ben paddled to the secret entrance of the aufwader caves and shouted up at the hidden doors. "Hello!" he called desperately. "You must listen."

If only he could warn them before it was too late,

they had to be ready when the fish demon came charging into their tunnels. A ghastly thought surfaced in his mind, what if that monstrous creature was already in there? Even now the fisherfolk could be fleeing before its terrible claws. Maybe that was why no one had answered him – perhaps the last tribe of aufwaders was already extinct.

"Nelda," the boy breathed miserably.

The growing gloom closed around him and the waters rose to his calves. A bitter wind blew in from the sea and Ben stumbled bleakly through the surging waves, back to the shore.

As he climbed over the concrete ledge once more, a stern voice called over to him.

"Is thee addled, lad? Tha's all wet!"

Standing upon a moss-covered boulder, with his staff in his hand and a scowl upon his face, was Nelda's grandfather.

"Tarr!" Ben cried, greatly relieved to see him. "I've got to talk to you – it's urgent!"

The aufwader ambled forward. "What's 'e bletherin' about now?" he grumbled. "Allus summat wi' these landfolk – allus mitherin' and goin' on about summat an nowt! As if ah didna have enough to worry at me."

"It's that Crozier!" the boy explained, hurrying towards him. "He's got a disgusting creature working for him now. It killed a boy last night and he says that he's going to let it loose in your caves!"

The aufwader listened to him gravely, "Nah!" he said. "Theer's nowt can get in our tunnels wi'out our lettin' it. 'Sides, it'll nivver find a way in – the gateways are all hid an' secret."

"I wouldn't bet on that!" Ben insisted. "You should have seen the thing. I think it could find anything – it was hideous!"

Tarr rubbed his chin. "Tha's wrong lad," he told

him, "ain't nowt in this world can worm its way down to us. We'll be safe – if'n the cliff don't fall about our ears that is. Did tha feel the land shiftin' afore? Ain't nivver done that in all me days!"

"But that was Crozier's fault!" Ben exclaimed. "He's got the second guardian – probably destroyed it by now. Goodness knows what'll happen if he gets hold of the last one!"

Glowering at the unnatural darkness around him, Tarr muttered, "Does tha truly reckon this Crozy feller is to blame fer this? We thought it were the Deep Ones still angry wi' us. But p'raps not. They'd have dragged the cliff into the sea, not shook it to bits." He turned a fearful face to the boy and added, "If'n that man can do this – ain't nowt he can't do!"

"You must warn the others!" Ben urged. "He'll send in his creature and, if they're not ready, the entire tribe will be killed!"

Tarr let out an angry and defiant shout, drove his staff into the soft moss and spun around. "Oh us'll be ready, lad!" he called. "Have no fear on that – we'll be a waitin' alreet! Yer man'll find we're a mite tougher than he's guessed."

"What should I do?" Ben shouted after him. "Shall I come with you?"

Without pausing, Tarr shook his head and yelled, "Nay, the tribe can see to itsen. Best if'n tha gets on home!"

The aufwader strode grimly away, along the slippery shale, across to where great clefts were channelled into the rock. Prodding the staff into the recesses and niches before him, Tarr searched for one of the secret entrances. With a faint rasping sound, a low doorway appeared in the cliff face and he quickly passed inside. Then the way was sealed again and invisible to prying eyes.

Ben kicked up a clump of wet sand. "No point me

going back to lovey-dovey Jen and dithery Edith," he glumly told himself.

The tunnel was a short one and Tarr soon found himself standing in one of the main passageways. "Fie!" he bellowed. "Bestir thisselves!"

The old aufwader marched down the caves, dragging aside the entrance curtains of the living quarters and shouting at those within. "Fetch the others!" he commanded. "Theer's trouble brewin'!"

"Hang on, hang on!" complained Prawny Nusk when Tarr looked in on him. "What's got thee in such a muck lather?"

"Plenty!" Nelda's grandfather snapped back. "So don't stand theer bogglin' – tha girt lummox! Move thissen."

Presently most of the tribe had been roused from their quarters, including Johab and Lorkon the two elders of the Triad beneath Esau, and all looked to Tarr for an explanation.

"Theer's mortal danger headed our way," he told them, "find what weapons tha can. Sticks, hooks, knives – owt. Then guard the entrances an' keep watch."

"What we watchin' fer?" asked Old Parry huffily.

"If'n tha finds it tha'll know," Tarr replied darkly, "it'll tear thee limb from limb."

A frightened babble broke out and Nelda's grandfather shouted at them crossly. "Tha's all wastin' time gibberin' 'ere!" he stormed. "Go cover every hole wi' net an' stand by them to be sure. If'n this divil does break through, theer won't be none o' us left!"

The severe look on his face and his angry words quelled them and some scurried away in fear to hunt out anything that could be used as a weapon.

"An' what'll you do, Tarr Shrimp?" Old Parry said archly. "Where'll you be when we're defendin' the gateways?"

Tarr glared at her, "Hold thy tongue, else ah throttle thee wi' it!" he warned. "It's the leader of the Triad ah've a mind to see – theer's summat he's got to hear."

"You do that!" she squealed. "Go traipse down to the deep caverns where you'll be safest, don't spare a thought fer us brave souls up here! So like your kin – Abe, Silas and Hesper, they all skedaddled, but mark what happened to them. Stone dead the lot!"

"Cork it!" Prawny told her. "Don't worry none, Tarr, I'll see t'it no ways are left untended, and I'll make sure idle, nasty minds have work t'divert 'em."

Nelda's grandfather clapped him on the shoulder. "Ah'll be back soon as ah can," he said gratefully.

"Shrimp," came the voice of Johab as the elder shuffled forward, "have a care when thou speakest to Esau – he listens to none but the counsel of his own black heart. Temper thine anger, else he will not hear thee."

"Oh he shall!" Tarr said firmly. "Ah'll make him!"

Johab glanced at Lorkon and the two looked uncomfortable. When they next spoke it was both together, covering up their distress with a rush of words. "Then we wish thee well," they said at once, "nine times bless thee."

Tarr nodded to them, then stomped off to find Esau.

"You should have warned him," said Lorkon quietly, "a wild animal is at its most deadly when witless. Who can foretell what Esau may do if Tarr corners him?"

"Have faith in Tarr Shrimp," Johab muttered. "I should rather beard the leader of the Triad – deranged and perilous though he is – than that one in his present humour."

"Yet Tarr is ignorant of Esau's strengths. Even we who have sat beside him these many years, know not the boundaries of his power."

"Nor indeed the source of it," Johab breathed,

staring down the black tunnel in concern and listening as Tarr's footsteps grew faint. "May the Three watch over him," he murmured.

Down the steep Ozul Stair went Tarr. The earth tremor had loosened some of the steps and now they rocked perilously under his weight. Grimly he reflected that they would not withstand a second violent quake, and made his way as speedily and as carefully as his age allowed.

Through the high caverns and dripping chambers he passed. The way was no longer safe, wide cracks had opened in the shale floor and plumes of scalding steam gushed from the deeps below. In the gallery of fossils, Tarr gazed warily about him. Several of the huge, blackened skeletons had been shaken free of the stone and were hanging precariously over the path, the primeval bones creaked threateningly as he walked beneath. Hurriedly the aufwader ducked under a low, protruding rib cage and came finally to the Gibbering Road.

The slender bridge was wreathed in mist, shimmering behind towering columns of dense cloud. It was an ethereal arch that linked one world to another but was present in neither. Tarr took a cautious step closer, the steam blinded him and it was impossible to tell where the ground stopped and the precipitous chasm fell sharply away.

Holding his staff before him, he tapped it against the rock and slowly groped forward. The bridge drew nearer, appearing briefly through gaps in the fog, before a sudden rush of steam snatched the vision away again. Only the constant, boiling hiss of the infernal vapours filled the aufwader's ears, and for that he was thankful – if the lamenting dead had been shrieking he was sure to lose his footing and fall headlong into the yawning gulf.

The staff touched the empty air and Tarr drew

quickly back, searching for the beginning of the bridge – a little to the right, there it was.

Nervously, he stretched out a foot and tested the strength of the stone. There was no telling what the earthquake had done to the Gibbering Road – in fact, he had been surprised to find it still in one piece.

"Shrimp!" called a cold, cracked voice.

Tarr faltered and his foot slipped on the wet rock, for a second he teetered on the brink, the vast, immeasurable drop seeming to drag him down. But striking out with his staff he regained his balance and leapt back from the deadly bridge in fright.

With the firm ground beneath him once more, the aufwader glared about him but the suffocating steam enshrouded the far side of the bridge and all he could do was wait and listen.

"Return to the upper caves," demanded the voice, "the tribe have need of thee! Wouldst thou prove Parry's words to be true? Art thou indeed escaping the danger by bolting hither?"

Tarr thrashed his staff through the thick vapour, slicing and tearing at it for all he was worth. "Ah know thee!" he cried. "Come out of the smoke, Esau – where ah can sithee!"

At that moment, the columns of steam subsided and the aufwader caught a glimpse of the far side of the chasm. Standing by the bridge, leaning on two sticks and bent almost double, was the leader of the Triad. His beady, black eyes were gleaming fixedly at Tarr, as though he had been able to pierce the blanketing mists all the time. At his side stood Nelda, her face was pale and she called to her grandfather in dismay.

"Be careful!" she cried. "He'll kill you if you try to cross!"

Esau whipped round and slapped her. "Silence!" he roared. "I did not give thee leave to speak!"

"Hoy!" bellowed Tarr furiously. "Keep thy hands off her!"

Esau turned back to him and cackled. "Begone," he wailed, "the upper world is thine now, Shrimp, I do relinquish my sovereignty there. Go back to the woes and strife above – let my bride and me be at peace from it all. The years of the tribe are numbered, only hours remain to you now. A beast is coming, a demon from the dawn of days and you shall wither before it like ice in flame!"

"How dost tha know?" yelled Tarr. "Who told thee of it and of Old Parry's words to me?"

Esau's derisive laughter boomed through the smoke like the howls of Death itself.

"Never shalt thou learn the answer to that!" he shrieked. "Such wisdom is for the leader of the Triad alone and to the chill grave will I take that secret. Flee whilst thou may, Tarr Shrimp! For even now the Mallykin pries and pokes upon the cliff, it may be squirming into the caves as we speak."

"Then tha must help us!" Tarr shouted. "Theer is a way, the human boy told me. Where is the guardian made by Irl? Where were it hid all that time ago?"

Esau sucked his gums peevishly. "Thou ought not to listen to the tongues of the landbreed!" he spat. "For they were ever a fount of lies and deceit. There never was any guardian – Irl wrought nothing with the moonkelp he stole!"

Dragging himself away from the edge of the precipice, he called out. "Now shall my wife and me withdraw into this small realm. Never to set foot outside its borders, our eyes have gazed the last upon the stars and moon and the great waters are denied us. The Lords of the Deep no longer hold sway over our lives. Here in the dark stomach of the earth we shall die together."

"Grendel!" bawled Tarr furiously. "Listen to me, if

the guardian does exist and this fiend takes it, it'll not be just the tribe who are doomed!"

But Esau had spoken his last word and, casting a malevolent glance at Nelda signalling her to follow, he hobbled away.

The aufwader girl took a wretched step after him, but she faltered and turned back towards the curtain of mist.

"Grandfather," she called, "did you really see Ben?"

"Aye, lass," came the reply, "but greatly troubled he was."

"This guardian is important, isn't it?"

When Tarr answered, his voice was filled with dread and horror. "Oh Nelda!" he cried. "Tha should be here, on this side of the abyss. We might not see each other again. Ah can feel the fate of the world pressing down, an' we're caught like crabs in a pot. It's all endin', the dark is closin' round and soon theer'll be nowt but night."

She stood graven like stone as his sobs came floating through the steam to her and at last Nelda knew what must be done. The lives of everyone she held dear were in her hands – only she could save them. At that moment, standing on the brink of the terrifying gulf, the girl came to a horrendous decision.

"Goodbye, Grandfather," she said, but her voice was thin and weak and he did not hear her.

Abruptly, a deep rumbling moan issued from the chasm – "The souls of the dead are stirring,"murmured Nelda as unbearable shrieks echoed out of the mist in fearful blasts.

Upon the other side, Tarr strained his eyes trying to peer through the fog, his patience was finally rewarded as the clouds dispersed for a moment. But the sight which he beheld made him tremble more than ever.

"Nelda!" he shouted. "What is it?"

His granddaughter looked awful; her face was ghastly, like one who has heard the pronouncement of some terrible, condemning sentence. Her grey eyes were as two embers that smouldered with horror and she turned away, without seeming to see him and walked after Esau with leaden steps.

Tarr called out to her, it was as if she was going to her death. But Nelda made no sign that she had heard him and vanished into the caverns beyond, back to the chamber of the Triad and was lost as the mist surged in once again.

With the shrill, banshee wails gibbering insanely about him, Tarr whispered, "No, Nelda – dunna go to him." And a great tear rolled down his craggy face.

Nelda moved as though she were in a dream. She was aware of all that was going on around her, but it was as if she were viewing it from some far distance. Her feet led her to the hallowed cavern where the waterfalls splashed around the gurgling springs. But all was dim and vague, a realm of shadow shapes and hazy glimmerings. Were they voices she could hear amid the babbling water? Why were they urging her to turn back? Slowly she drew aside the tapestry curtain and made her way into the Triad chamber.

The light from the lamp above the central throne flickered sharply over her small form. The rock crystal about the silver boat shone like the moon on the waves but the radiance was cold, colder than the dark deeps – where the moonkelp bloomed.

Nelda raised her eyes to it and found herself wondering who had created the cunning lamp. Could Irl's hands have wielded the hammer which formed the silver timbers and could he have hewn the crystal from the cliff? Was it more than a natural flame which shone there? The idea grew large in her mind and she strode quickly to her husband's chamber to confirm it.

Esau was hunched over the pool, his bow-legs tucked under his trailing, forked beard. Staring down, he gazed intently into the Darkmirror, searching for answers to appease his gnawing doubts.

The still water remained black and calm and he knotted his brows, projecting his will out into the liquid seeking for a sign.

"Show me," he grunted, his eyes bulging from their wrinkled sockets, "yield up thy secrets." His temples throbbed under the strain of his concentration and he did not see his bride enter the chamber. "Hah!" he snarled. "The darkness clears – there! I see it!"

Below him, the pool pulsed with a dismal glow and strands of gloom twisted and whirled in its depths. Esau clasped his gnarled claws as faint images swam into view; some were there only for an instant, hardly long enough for him to discern what they were, whilst others lingered and he gabbled excitedly as he recognized them.

There was Tarr trudging back through the tunnels, to his death, Esau hoped – then the vision changed and another scene enfolded before his eyes. At the main entrance to the aufwader caves many of the tribe were collecting boat hooks and fishing nets and seemed to be in great distress, then he saw others guarding the lesser ways, a flash of scales leaped through the dark and for a moment the pool was blank.

Esau's lips parted and his gums squeezed together impatiently. "More," he jabbered, "I must see more!"

In the inky pool, an image of the cliff top formed, and there, standing tall and arrogant amid the gravestones was Nathaniel Crozier. At once he looked up, his eyes glaring from the surface of the water. It was as though he could see the ancient aufwader, for he raised his hand and pointed threateningly – then he dissolved. Now the Darkmirror showed the ocean bed, where sinister shapes lurked in the flowing weed and coral reefs. Ruined pillars and crumbling statues rested against mountains of broken stone and emerald fish darted to and fro between barnacled masonry. Then a silvery-blue light shone up to Esau's shrivelled face as the outline of three gigantic thrones drew near. Next, he found himself looking on the open sea, where an island of black rock rose from the waves and the mists wove densely about it. The pool sank into blackness once more.

Esau let out a rattling breath, tired and weary from his mental exertions. Then, his tongue licked his withered lips and he stared longingly at the still, black water. Lowering his head, like an animal at a pond, he crouched further down and lapped the surface, making a disgusting sucking noise.

"What are you doing?" asked Nelda, repulsed by his base display.

Startled, her husband flew backwards, his mouth dripping with oily liquid. He stared at her in alarm, then rage took him. "Spying on me?" he squawked lumbering to his feet. "I'll teach thee, bride of mine!"

But Nelda pretended to be sorry for surprising him. "Forgive me," she apologized, "I did not mean to creep up on you – I thought you heard me come in!"

So humble and complete was her contrition that Esau's temper cooled, yet he glanced at the Darkmirror shamefully. " 'Twas merely a fancy of mine – nothing more," he hurriedly explained, "I did think I saw a fish swimming there and wished to make certain, that is all."

Nelda said that she understood; if Esau was mad enough to drink stagnant water that was up to him. She looked at the elder uncertainly, then prepared herself for the task that lay ahead.

"Husband," she began, "my grandfather's words have frightened me. Are we all to die? Is a great evil really to be awoken by the actions of one human? What will become of us?"

Esau chortled and wiped the slime from his lips. "Save thy sorrow," he told her.

"But I cannot," she wept and the tears which brimmed in her eyes were genuine.

The elder crept forward, reaching out a deformed claw to her cheek. "Poor, sweet wife," he muttered, "thou art indeed afraid. Have no fear – Whitby is safe, I promise you that."

Nelda stared at him, "How can you be sure?"

Esau sniggered and tapped his brow with a twig-like finger. "Trust in my wisdom," he cackled. "For nigh on four hundred years I have led the Triad, learned in all lore am I – none save the Three beneath the waves know more. I am master of the rhymes that charm the tides and raise the winds, versed in the mournful speech of sea birds, of the tales carried from forgotten lands in the morning of the world. Have faith in me, my wife – Esau Grendel knows and sees all. When I tell thee no hurt shall befall Whitby, believe it. I am certain because the last protector is safe – no harm will come if it remains where it resides."

"Then you lied to my grandfather!" she cried. "The guardian does exist!"

His sharp eyes danced over her and his toothless grin widened unpleasantly. "That is correct, my sweet," he murmured.

"Tell me where it is!" Nelda begged. "Please."

But Esau would not be persuaded, he gave her a covetous glance then turned his back and ambled over to the bed.

Nelda ran after him. "If I guess," she said, "would you tell me if I was right?"

The elder hauled himself on to the bunk and watched her from beneath hooded lids. "I might," he muttered.

"Then the lamp!" Nelda declared. "The one above your throne – Irl made it didn't he?"

Esau chuckled wickedly, and fingered his beard, enjoying the sight of her pleading for his help. "Indeed," he mumbled, "it was Irl's hands that wrought the silver boat and mined the gleaming crystal."

Nelda made to run from the chamber. She had to take the guardian away from danger, the Mallykin would soon be here to seize it and deliver it to its master.

As she hurried to the entrance, Esau's cracked voice called out, "But that is not the device Irl made to keep Morgawrus at bay!"

The girl froze. "Morgawrus?" she repeated.

Her husband rolled on to the bed and nuzzled his head into the blankets. "The dreaded one," he softly chanted. "That which spreads disease and anguish, that which the Deep Ones overthrew in the beginnings of time and who sleeps beneath us even now – whose slumbering groans rise up from the deep chasm under the bridge of stone."

"The Gibbering Road," said Nelda. "Then it is not the souls of the dead who cry out?"

Esau shook his head and sprawled his shrunken body over the bunk. "No, my love," he told her, "the shrieks are but proof of the weakening enchantment. For many years now I have heard the moans grow stronger as the terror begins to stir. But have no fear, the spells will hold whilst Irl's guardian remains in place."

Nelda edged towards him. "Where is it?" she asked again.

Her husband only laughed back at her. "Now thou

art in my power!" he declared. "Hearken to thyself, where is thy pride now?" He giggled insanely and his face twisted with bitterness and longing. "Did I not see thy scorn and sense the loathing thou felt for me?" he cried. "The strength of thy hatred was mighty. To what distant corner has it slinked, to leave thee begging for my wisdom now?"

"But the tribe!" she exclaimed. "Do you want everyone to perish?"

Esau thumped the bed with his fists. "Sacrifices must be made!" he squealed. "Our noble friends do buy us time with their lives. The Mallykin will never venture to this deep realm and who knows – perhaps it will be slain?" He scrutinized her closely, then asked, "What sacrifice wouldst thou make, my bride?"

"I would do anything to save the tribe," she sobbed, giving up any hope of finding the guardian in time.

Her husband gave a low, guttural chortle. "Then I have decided to tell thee," he said, rubbing his hands together as a cunning glint shone in his eyes. "On one condition ..." he added slyly.

*　*　*

At the East Gate, three aufwaders hammered fishing nets into position, resting only when the entrance was completely covered.

"That's reet," Prawny told them, "now guard it wi' yer lives – at the first sound of owt moving inside, give a shout and stand on guard."

He dashed along the passage and found Old Parry and Baccy the crone peering suspiciously into a narrow crevice. In their hands they held long knitting needles and a rusting harpoon that had belonged to Parry's late husband.

When they heard him coming, they whisked round and raised their weapons. "Scupper it!" trilled Baccy, slashing the air with her needles. "Cut the brute's head off – rip his legs out!"

"Crikes!" shouted Prawny, springing backwards to avoid their fierce onslaught.

Old Parry uncovered a lantern and grumbled to herself, disappointed to find that it was only him.

"Well done," he praised them, "if this critter's got any sense it'll keep away from both of 'ee."

"I tell you it won't dare show its ears," chuntered Parry, "if it's got any that is. Tarr's finally gone feeble in the head; he were allus barmy but now he's real cracked. We're all wastin' our time."

Baccy jabbed the air with her knitting needles, anxious to stab something. "Spike and stick," she crooned. "By gow, I'll plunge 'em in and wiggle 'em round. Gut the animal – make a broth from its gizzards and patties from its brains, hee, hee!"

"Foolishness," remarked Old Parry tersely. "We'll be stood about fer days – theer's nowt gonna happen, except maybe she'll get one of her addled notions and try to stab me instead. I've a mind to get meself off home and put my feet up."

Leaving them to it, one complaining, the other poised for action, Prawny hurried further down the tunnel to check on the rest of the defences. He thought of those two terrible old sea wives awaiting the enemy and grimaced – they had nearly frightened him out of his skin. When the creature itself finally appeared he hoped he would meet it more courageously.

"Steel yerself, Nusk," he said, keeping a firm hold of the cudgel in his hand. "You don't want to be found lackin' when the time comes."

He thought sadly of his poor wife. She had been dead for many years now, but he could still picture her in his mind when he was lonely or needed to feel close to her. Valdi could always be relied on to cheer him up, or tactfully dispense sound advice. Prawny wished she was there now, to goad him on, and tell him how brave he would be against the unknown enemy.

"Don't let me bring shame on my line," he implored. "You've faith in yer old spouse, aintcha Valdi?" But she, like so many others, had fallen prey to the curse of the Deep Ones and had vanished from this world long ago. Only the echoing dark heard him and Prawny felt his courage dwindle like a sputtering candle, trickling down his spine and oozing out of his boots.

Ducking beneath a low archway, he stepped on to a narrow path that steadily climbed. This led to the high pass, which opened out on to the abbey plain. It was the only entrance he hadn't yet visited to oversee the defences, but knew that four of the tribe had gone to make sure the gate was closed.

The way was nearly pitch black. In this section of the caves the lamps were few and far between and, as he passed one, his shadow would fly before him, blotting everything out in a nightmarishly distorted shape.

"Keep yer wits," he sternly reminded himself, "ain't nowt but a shadow. Are yer afraid of that, yer big daisy?" As if in answer his pace increased until he was fairly jogging along – to reach the high pass before the imagined fears that lurked in the darkness reached out and grabbed him.

At a fork in the passage, he stopped and listened – something was wrong. Holding his breath, Prawny glanced round the rough rocky walls, puzzling over the strange noise.

A muffled scraping was coming from above his head. As yet it was faint and indistinct, but with every beating second it grew nearer.

"Rabbits?" he mumbled curiously. "Sometimes their warrens do burrow deep." With a wry smile he remembered the year that the upper chambers had been overrun with them. "Mebbe Baccy'll get her broth after all," he chuckled.

But the sounds were too frantic and harsh to be the work of rabbits. Something with immense strength and unswerving intent was digging and tearing its way through the ground.

Prawny stared up at the dark ceiling. It was very low at this point in the tunnel and, standing on tiptoe he pressed his ear against the earthen roof.

The sounds were much clearer now, he could hear the creature's breath wheezing and gasping as it ripped up the soil and dived further down.

The aufwader stepped away, his heart thumping violently in his chest. This was it! They had been wrong to assume the enemy would enter by one of the main gates – it was making its own way in!

With a dull clatter of dry clay and small stones, a fistful of soil showered down upon his head.

"Bless us!" Prawny choked, gripping the cudgel in his hand and dredging up whatever valour he had left.

"Well, it'll not get by me!" he said, hoping his voice sounded confident and brave.

A further cascade of earth poured over the path and the aufwader uttered a curse in fear. Suddenly, a large clod of soil was kicked from above and a mouth-shaped hole gaped down at him from the ceiling.

Prawny trembled. "No," he breathed in horror.

Out of the darkness came a squat, misshapen head and a pair of luminous eyes gazed balefully at him.

"Parry were right," warbled Prawny in a terrified voice, "it don't have no ears." Pressing himself against the wall, he whimpered, "Get you gone! You'll not come down here – I ... I won't let 'ee!"

Silently, the foul creature began to squirm from the

hole. Keeping its grim stare fixed steadily upon him, the fish demon crawled out – its gills twitching expectantly.

"No you don't!" Prawny shouted, swinging his cudgel round in his panic.

Hissing in dismay, the fish demon snaked back into the ceiling, clawing hastily at the loose earth which rained down in a frenzied stream.

"That's right!" roared Prawny, greatly encouraged by the creature's apparent cowardice. "There's plenty more where that came from. Come back and I'll give 'ee such a clout, yer'll be flung into next year!"

But only silence flowed from the hole – the creature had escaped.

Prawny chuckled to himself, relieved that he had not brought disgrace to the Nusk name. Raising his cudgel, he warily prodded at the opening with it.

At once the scaly claws flashed out, seized the weapon from his grasp and hurled it far from reach.

"Help!" Prawny screamed. "It's here! Help me ..."

Before he could run, the ferocious talons bit into his shoulders and, yelling for his life, the aufwader was dragged off his feet.

"Aaaiiiyeee!" he shrieked, kicking his legs furiously and thrashing wildly with his arms. "Heeeeelp!" Up into the dark hole the Mallykin hauled him – up to where his screams ended abruptly and all his struggles were over.

On to the tunnel floor, the fiend dropped. Flicking its ugly head from side to side, it sought the subterranean air currents and searched the scents that drifted upon them. The delightful fragrance of fear filled the caves – that was good, its prey would be the tenderer for it. Emitting a horrible screech, it gave a lurching hop, then bounded down the passage – Prawny Nusk's blood still dripping from its jaws.

Nelda struggled back into her gansey, shivering with a cold sickness in her stomach. Esau was lying asleep on the bed beside her, his contented, grunting snores wafting a wisp of his beard that had strayed across his face.

The girl's flesh crawled, she couldn't bear to look at the vile creature any more and she jumped from the bunk as though it had stung her.

A grim and desolate expression was carved into her features. For the sake of all, she had sacrificed and suffered much, but now that was over – only the future mattered.

Stealthily, she approached the still pool and, kneeling on the ground, slipped her hand into the black water. The liquid was horribly cold and set her teeth on edge as she fumbled on the slimy bottom, seeking for what Esau had said was there.

A putrid smell issued up from the disturbed sediment and she balked when she remembered that her husband had drunk this poisonous filth.

Esau grumbled in his sleep and turned over, his mangled claws groping at the empty space beside him.

"Where is it?" Nelda murmured fretfully, Esau might awaken at any moment. Had he lied to her? Was this another of his tricks? Just when she thought despair would overwhelm her, her fingertips touched something amid the freezing ooze.

Trembling, the aufwader drew her hand from the stagnant water and there was the guardian Irl had made.

Quickly she washed away the clinging foulness and gazed at the wondrous device in her grasp.

It was made of jet – but the carving was a monstrous, twisting shape, fashioned in the form of a hideous serpent. Nelda shuddered at the sight of it, never had she beheld anything so frightening, a ghastly representation of evil and darkness. The eyes of the serpent were closed, but beneath the lids something golden glimmered and sparkled.

"Moonkelp," she breathed.

The coils of the jet beast were twined about the three pronged symbol of the Lords of the Deep and, behind the gruesome head, Irl had inscribed these words: "By the powers of the greater Triad do I commit this guardian. May the bonds of enchantment bind the enemy ever more and keep Morgawrus tethered in the dark."

Nelda mouthed the inscription with trembling lips, and as she did so, the nape of her neck prickled and a wave of cold seeped down her spine. It was as if an unearthly presence was watching her – was the ghost of Irl standing at her shoulder? A soft breath lightly touched her cheek and Nelda jumped up in alarm, but there was no one there.

Upon the bed Esau moaned. There was no time left, she had to leave. With a last, contemptuous look at her husband, Nelda fled from the chamber hugging the guardian to her breast.

* * *

The upper levels of the caves were in uproar. The fish demon had breached the defences and was scampering unchallenged down the tunnels. It was a mad, ravaging nightmare that stormed through the caves like a whirlwind of death and slaughter. Already seven fisherfolk had fallen before its vicious claws and the heat of their blood maddened it even more – driving it insanely on.

Any who heard its shrieking cries were chilled to the marrow and many cast down their weapons when the first of those curdling calls came echoing down the dim passages. Heedless of all else, they flew blindly through the caverns to escape the oncoming terror, crashing into those still at their posts and struggling with them to get by. One aufwader blundered headlong into a disused chamber and tumbled down a deep mine shaft, smashing into the sheer sides as he fell and hitting the bottom with an awful, bone-shattering crunch.

The few who kept their heads and remained on guard were met with savage fury as the pet of Nathaniel Crozier tore into them. Spears and boat hooks were thrown aside as the iron jaws snapped at throats and when the hump-backed fiend had slain them it would throw back its fin-crowned head and give a yodelling gurgle of victory.

"On!" thundered Tarr, leading a small band through the dim halls to the upper levels. "It must be killed!"

The others were horribly afraid, but he drove them on by the force of his voice and his commanding will. The creature had to be stopped. If it cost the lives of them all it would be better than running cowardly away and eking out a miserably shameful existence elsewhere.

"Remember the tribal wars!" he bellowed. "The battles of them days make this seem a reet picnic! This is nowt to the perils our kin endured back then. Draw thy knives and think no fear!"

"I canna recall that far back," muttered one of the group mutinously, "an' neither can he! 'Sides, them wars were a disaster and cost the lives of most of our folk. Are we to squander our lifeblood as they did?"

Marching beside this dissenter was Johab. He dug the grumbling aufwader in the ribs and said, "My grandsire did battle in them wars – and so did Tarr's.

Hush yer yellow chelpin afore I squander thy blood mesself!"

But the others were inspired by Tarr's words. They thought of the noble houses of the three tribes that had once been and drew their strength from it. Theirs was a princely lineage, the present tribe was but a gleaning of all that remained of those doughty aufwaders. This coast was theirs by right and only the Lords of the Deep could take it from them – certainly no base fiend from the ancient world.

In all, there were eight in the company and Tarr herded them up the tunnels, swinging his staff over his head, crying out challenges and defying the fearsome shrieks which sped to meet them. All braced themselves for a brutal encounter, anger kindled their hearts and soon they too were shouting war cries – eager for the combat to begin.

"The Three will guide us!" they boomed. "They will watch over our fate! Bless the tribe! Save the tribe!"

Raging through a wide cavern, they tore into an adjoining tunnel and suddenly all was chaos and confusion.

"Eeeeee!" screeched a panicky voice. "Out of my way! Eeeee!"

A squat shape barged straight into the middle of the aufwaders. Sticks clattered over the ground and startled wails filled the cramped passage.

"It's got me!" someone squawked.

"Kill it!" called another.

"Let me go!" howled the shrill voice. "Tarr Shrimp call them off!"

Nelda's grandfather strode angrily up to the tangle of wriggling bodies and dragged the bewildered fisherfolk away.

"Parry!" he snarled. "What are yer doin'? Stand up, woman!"

Old Parry struggled to her feet, bawling at the top of her discordant voice. As soon as she had heard Prawny's death screams she had run for her life, leaving Baccy to face the terror alone. Down the caves she had scuttled, wailing and knocking aside those foolish enough to stand in her way.

"Move!" she yammered, spinning round and hurtling into the recovering group once more. "It's after me! Get away, let me through! Eeeeee!"

"Parry!" Tarr shouted, striding up to her and shaking the sea wife by the shoulders. "Get a grip on thissen! What's all this about?"

She quivered like a cornered mouse and her glance darted over Tarr's shoulder to the shadowy passage. "You ain't got no right to keep me!" she protested. "It's all in vain. I heard Nusk when the monster got him."

"Prawny ..." muttered Tarr sadly.

"Aye," she squealed, "and many more since – their voices have followed me down the caves and always at my heels it came galloping, chasin' me – I even heard it chatter to itsen." Parry wriggled free of Tarr's grip, "Well it'll not feast on me!" she cried and trampled by those still in her way.

"Come back!" Johab called. "Stand and fight."

"Let her go," said Tarr, "she'd only hinder ..."

"Aaaaiiiyeeee!"

A bright silver arc sliced through the gloom and an aufwader fell dead to the ground. The enemy had found them and due to Old Parry's demented interruption they were caught unawares. The creature flew at them through the darkness, its eyes burning with hate and malice. A second furious sweep of its claws threw two others to the floor and it immediately leapt upon their bodies to launch itself at the rest.

"That's fer Prawny!" Tarr roared, striking out with

his staff and catching the Mallykin across the neck. It squealed in pain and whirled around, raking its claws at him. The aufwader dodged the attack and brought his staff down once more. This time the blow glanced off the creature's back. A splintered knitting needle was embedded in the shoulder; Baccy had evidently stood her ground and had managed to strike before the creature killed her. Tarr's staff drove the needle deeper into the scaly sinew.

Maddened and yowling in agony, the fish demon pounced, flattening him against the wall, where it snatched the staff from his hands and bit it in two. Then its bloody jaws lunged for his throat.

From the shadows, a blade shone brightly and Johab plunged a knife into the creature's side. Screaming, it released its victim and whirled viciously round. Johab quailed, his action had saved Nelda's grandfather – but he was done for.

"Noo!" he howled, as the full might and fury of the enemy sprang at him. The cruel claws slit his throat and the elder was dashed against the rock, slumping to the ground like a discarded ragdoll.

The Mallykin was furious now, baited into a terrible rage that nothing could withstand. All it craved was to drink its bloated fill of their hot blood. The luminous eyes became narrow slivers of green and it took a menacing pace closer to the three fisherfolk that remained.

The aufwaders were utterly petrified, and the weapons drooped from their hands. A string of saliva oozed from the open jaws and a joyous gurgle bubbled from its flapping stomach.

"Leave them!" rang the commanding voice of Nathaniel suddenly. The fish demon whipped about and sniffed warily – where was he?

"Seek out the leader," the warlock demanded, "Your appetite can be satiated later."

The fish demon let out a confused whine; the voice was inside its head. "Down to the lower caves," the voice declared, cutting through the creature's primitive mind, "you shall find him there – now go!"

With a final hiss of consuming hatred, it rushed between the remaining fisherfolk and disappeared into the blackness of the caverns beyond.

Tarr groaned and coughed, his neck was clawed and bleeding. "Where is it?" he choked, stumbling to his feet. "Don't let it get away!"

But the others had had enough. They stared helplessly at the corpses of Johab and the others and silently lay their weapons on the blood-drenched ground.

"It's over," said one, "we canna fight against that."

"We must," spluttered Tarr.

The aufwaders shook their heads. "The tribe is finished," they declared, "the Deep Ones have deserted us."

Tarr shook his fist at them. "Theer's no escape," he shouted, but they would not listen.

"Our time is over now," they said. "The caverns are no longer ours – we have lost."

Their spirits were completely quashed and their faces betrayed the sickness in their hearts. They were tired of everything, weary of the world and all its troubles, appalled at the loss of their friends and stricken by the fiend that had attacked them. Their grief was immeasurable and, dragging their feet in the crimson-stained dust they trailed despondently up the tunnel.

"Deeps take 'em," cursed Tarr, "all is lost now."

Stooping over the bodies of his fallen comrades, he said a quiet prayer. "I canna gi' up hope," he murmured dismally. Then he found the two splintered shards of his staff and he covered his face with his hands. The others were right, there was no point in going on, the time of the aufwaders was over. Tarr's keen spirit sank within him.

"Grandfather!" came a voice. "Grandfather, where are you?"

At once Tarr leaped to his feet. "Nelda!" he shouted and the flame of hope burned brightly in his breast once more.

Running from the shadows of the far passageway, the girl raced towards him and flung her arms about his neck.

"Oh Grandfather!" she cried. "You're hurt."

She stared at the clawmarks at his throat, then saw for the first time the fallen tribe members.

"I'm too late!" she wept. "Is everyone dead? Did the creature kill them all?"

Tarr's eyes narrowed. "Has tha seen it?" he asked.

"I was hurrying up the Ozul Stair," she nodded, "when I heard something pattering down towards me. So I hid in a cleft in the rock and the beast ran by – it was a loathsome thing!"

"Aye," he agreed, "but what's it doing down theer?"

"Esau," Nelda whispered, "it's gone for him! That's where the guardian was – that's what it wants!"

Tarr searched Johab's body for his knife and said gravely, "It canna have that! Ah mun get after it!"

"No!" cried Nelda clinging to him. "The creature won't find the guardian down there – look, I've got it here." She showed him the jet carving and her grandfather gazed at her sorrowfully.

"Oh lass," he whispered, "how did tha get the old goat to gi' it up?"

Nelda said nothing, but she lowered her eyes and he held her more tightly than before.

"Well, you mun get it out of here!" he told her quickly. "Won't take long fer that beastie to come back."

"But what shall I do with it?" she asked. "I never thought about that."

Tarr glanced up the tunnel. "Take it to thy human friend," he instructed, "anythin' to get it out of the caves. Go now – while theer's a chance."

"But what about you?" she demanded.

"Ah'll stay here," he said solemnly, "theer's still a few of our folk loose in the caves. They're all of a panic and'll need to be found. Even the likes of Old Parry can't be left for that divil's pleasure."

Nelda hugged him. "I'll be waiting for you, Grandfather," she said, "promise me you'll leave as soon as everyone's been found."

"Ah swear, lass," he told her.

The two of them hugged one another desperately. Then, clenching the guardian closely to her, Nelda darted up the passage.

"Now," Tarr muttered, brandishing the knife fiercely, "ah'm gonna make that beastie squeal if it's the last thing ah do!"

* * *

Esau gave a complaining groan as his blissful sleep became increasingly troubled. "Nelda," he burbled, "my dearest beloved ..." The elder rolled on to his side and a wide yawn divided his wizened face.

With a jolt, he awoke. Esau rubbed the sleep from his eyes and gazed about the chamber. Where was his bride? He pulled a sullen frown and scratched himself lazily.

"Nelda!" he called. "Nelda?" There was no reply, but outside the cavern he heard the rumour of unpleasant screeches far, far away.

"Where is she?" he mumbled irritably. "A wife ought to wait upon her husband. I must be sure she learns what else is expected of her."

276

He dragged himself from the bed and reached for his sticks. "What is that clamour?" he shouted, as a terrible crashing resounded from the Triad chamber. "Be that you wife?" he cried. "Get in here and tend to my wants. I would eat some vittles now ..."

Esau's voice dried in his throat, for at that moment the curtain was wrenched from its hooks and went sprawling across the chamber.

"Noooooo!" he wailed.

Framed within the low doorway was the hideously deformed figure, whose fins ruffled and shook with odious glee.

"The Mallykin!" Esau croaked. "How did the wight find me? How did it reach the lower realm?"

Snarling, the creature took a prowling step closer, its round eyes glowing malevolently at the ancient aufwader.

Esau shrieked in dismay and flung one of his sticks at it. The hobgoblin of the waters sprang aside, raised its deadly talons and burbled wickedly.

Nelda's husband staggered across the chamber, he had to escape it – but the toad-like apparition hopped nimbly towards him. Then Esau noticed the pool and his legs collapsed under him.

"What madness is this?" he screamed.

His Darkmirror was swirling, the filthy water bubbled and spat as the bottom of the pool began to tremble.

"Curse thee, Nelda!" he screeched. "Thou hast betrayed us and sealed all our fates! The guardian of Irl ought not to have been moved – couldst thou not guess the reason – didst thou not see what the Darkmirror is? What hast thou done?"

Even as he watched, a great split appeared beneath the water.

"Morgawrus!" he yelled. "He stirs! The end is come!"

The crack gaped wider and gradually a pale yellow radiance welled up, filling the entire chamber with an awful light and a blistering heat. The pool churned and the fish demon yammered in dismay as a huge eye blinked open in the chamber floor.

Esau tore at his beard; the dark slit of the pupil glared up at the insignificant aufwader.

The terrible glance rooted him to the spot, and the hellish light shone angrily through the stagnant tears – tears which he in his folly had drunk. He had only done it in order to gain wisdom and indeed Esau had learnt much from sipping daily at the stinking brine, but it was this that had driven him insane. The still pool had been a distillation of pure evil and, once he had dared to taste it, Esau had been lost.

"Morgawrus," he gabbled, his gnarled hands scalding in the heat of that dreadful gaze, "spare me, return to thy slumber. Have mercy!"

The cavern trembled as the gigantic enemy of the world twisted its buried head. Esau fell on his face, grovelling before the eye of the dark god as it shifted beneath the rock. This was where the Deep Ones had imprisoned it many thousands of years ago, trapped beneath the cliffs of Whitby, to sleep out eternity under their enchantments. But once more its cold black blood pulsed through its endless veins and up above, the town juddered as the vast heart began to pound and beat.

Prostrated on the ground, Esau felt his skin bake under the scorching blast of the eye. His forked beard singed and steamed, shrivelling upon his chin and his scalp smouldered sending up a reek of brown smoke.

"Nelda," he murmured in his agony, "forgive me …!"

Into the sizzling heats of the eye crept the fish demon. The bright light had frightened it at first but

the irresistible sight of Esau prone on the floor, helpless and unarmed was too much and it swiftly overcame its fear. Gurgling with delight, it flew at Esau, who threw back his head and let out one final mad laugh before the Mallykin slew him gleefully.

Now surely its master would be pleased, it thought, as the eldest of the fisherfolk gasped and croaked his way to the unknown shores.

And then the cavern shook suddenly and the livid green slit of the pupil swivelled round at the bottom of the pool. Morgawrus was awake, the sleep of aeons was past.

Revelling in the aufwader's blood, the fish demon looked up, startled at the quaking world. The lid of the eye snapped shut once more and sank into a black void, leaving an empty well in the ground. The nightmare serpent was moving.

At once the rocks shuddered with cataclysmic violence. A massive part of the floor ruptured and cracked asunder as Morgawrus seethed below. Yelping in fear, the Mallykin scurried to its feet as the unsupported ground crumbled and fell completely away, crashing down into a gaping abyss.

"Get out of there!" commanded the voice of Nathaniel in its head. "Return to me!"

Shrieking, the fish demon bounded from the cavern as the ornately decorated roof buckled and quivered ominously. Then, with a horrendous shattering of shale and rock, the entire structure collapsed. Thousands of tons of rubble came crushing down and the broken body of Esau was buried beneath the full weight of the cliff.

Out through the Triad chamber the Mallykin fled and the three thrones topped in ruins at its heels. The silver lamp was smashed and the crystal waves it rode upon shivered into glittering dust.

To the fish demon it seemed that the whole world

was ending and it tore out of the hallowed hall bleating shrilly. Behind it the stalactites splintered and broke from the ceiling, thrusting into the ground like stone spears – stabbing at the very heart of the aufwader realm. And as the serpent rumbled and snaked in the depths, the sacred springs of the blessed shrine boiled away to nothing.

Still the Mallykin hurtled on, leaping over the fissures that yawned suddenly beneath it and veering between towering columns of rock that burst from the floor and drove ever upwards, smashing into the high galleries. Finally the Gibbering Road reared up before the squealing creature. The slender bridge stretched out before it and the fish demon threw itself on to the treacherously narrow way and began pattering hastily across.

In the black gorge far below, Morgawrus slithered. At last its loathsome head was free and a tremendous roar blasted up from the invisible deeps. The dreadful noise reverberated underground, booming throughout the earth and shaking its molten heart.

Upon the bridge the fish demon screamed, for the voice of the serpent shook the stone and to its shrieking horror it saw jagged cracks suddenly appear. The Gibbering Road flew apart and the fragments plummeted down into the chasm.

Emitting a terrified squeal, the last of the Mallykins toppled, and as it went spinning through the darkness to its death, the creature felt Nathaniel wrench himself from its mind.

A monstrous black fin stretched up from the abyss as Morgawrus started to uncoil and the sides of the precipice were demolished as it thrashed and writhed. In claps of deafening thunder the sheer walls were destroyed and amid clouds of engulfing dust they slid into the evil darkness. The end had indeed come.

14

SHADOW OVER WHITBY

A grotesque, unnatural night covered Whitby, and the folds of its vast, black shroud pressed heavily down. In the harbour, the water boiled and steam mingled with the dark, forming putrid clouds that rolled over the quayside and poured sluggishly into the town. Down the narrow streets the terrible shadows flowed, filling the doorways and stealing into the cosy homes beyond. It was a blinding, impenetrable gloom that entered the hearts of the inhabitants, instilling each one with dread and despair.

On the West Cliff, a gas main had fractured and the inhabitants of the nearby houses were hurriedly evacuated. On the East side, the power cables were down and all the windows looked blank and dark. The telephone lines were also severed and the panic of the people rose to fever pitch. Cars careered into one another, skidding into shops and spinning off the quay. Chaos reigned everywhere and harsh sirens blared across the seething harbour.

Upon the shore, Ben watched as the two halves of Whitby were gradually eclipsed by the creeping shade. Behind him, the sea was still, broken only by occasional jets of white smoke. The tide had ceased, no waves came lapping up the beach and the air itself seemed to hold its breath.

"Jen," the boy murmured as the dense black fog swallowed Church Street and the red roofs were lost from sight. He knew he had to get back, he should be with his sister.

Quickly, Ben began to run over the sand, the clinging darkness swirling about his knees – but then he froze.

Frightened voices were on the air. Terrified gabbles and dismal wailings were issuing from the cliffside. Out of the many secret entrances, poured the surviving members of the aufwader tribe. Into the choking gloom they staggered, relieved to escape the ferocity of the fish demon's attack, yet dismayed at the bewildering midnight world that greeted them.

Ben hurried over to the cliff face and shouted to them. "What's happened?" he called. "Where's Tarr? Is Nelda safe?"

A bedraggled company stumbled out on to the rocks. Three of their number were horribly wounded – slashed and gored by the Mallykin's claws – and they leaned heavily on their comrades. Only one of them turned to look at the boy and he glared down, consumed with hatred.

"The tribe is finished," he spat. "This is the fault of your kind!"

Even as he spoke, a distraught clamour rose amongst the others – one of the wounded they had carried from the tunnels was dead and, wailing, they gathered around him.

"I'm sorry," Ben spluttered.

"Get gone, landbreed!" an aufwader screeched, stooping to pick up a large stone.

The boy hastened away, leaving them to mourn in private. They would not have much time to grieve, he told himself – *something* was waking.

* * *

In the main entrance chamber, Nelda stood alone. Everything she had known was destroyed. The great stone doors lay sprawled over the rocks below and the black mist flowed keenly in, engulfing the broken fishing boats, creeping between the tangled nets and strangling the flame of the single lamp which had miraculously remained lit.

Nelda stepped carefully over the snaking chains and shattered timbers. Then, directly above, the rusted mechanism gave a juddering creak and the girl fled from the cavern as immense cogs and pulleys fell, crushing the wreckage behind her.

Out into the cloying dark she ran, climbing swiftly down the slippery wall of rock and landing soundlessly in the rippling mist.

Pausing only to look back and pray that her grandfather was safe, she splashed through the sea and made for the shore behind the pier bridge.

The rest of the tribe were still there. None of them knew what to do; they had nowhere to go – the caves had been their home for so long that nobody wanted to leave them, yet it was too dangerous to stay.

Nelda saw them huddled in forlorn groups, shaking their heads and muttering grievously to themselves. They had endured much that day and she knew what intense emotions were wringing their hearts – yet she had suffered the deepest hurt. Pushing such thoughts to the back of her mind, the girl forced herself onward, there was still much to do.

"Ben!" she shouted. "Wait!"

The boy was walking over the sands, trudging wretchedly home. Quickly, he glanced round and saw the aufwader girl tearing towards him.

"I have it!" she cried, brandishing the last guardian over her head for him to see.

"How ... how did you find it?" he asked when she pressed it into his hands.

Nelda shivered and said quickly, "What matters now is we make certain the guardian is safe."

Slipping the carving into his coat pocket, the boy glanced back at the darkened town where shrieks of panic came echoing from the fog. "I wish Aunt Alice was here," he said anxiously. "She'd know what to do next. And what about Jen and Miss Wethers? What if something's happened to them?"

"Then that shall be our first action," the aufwader told him. "Let us be certain they are safe, but we must make haste."

The two of them hared over the shore and plunged into the blanketing mirk that smothered Whitby.

High upon the cliff top, amid the tombstones and towering over the shore, a solitary figure stood, his coal-black eyes penetrating the mounting gloom.

"So," Nathaniel softly uttered, "the cave maiden stole it, did she?" And a cruel smile flickered over his bearded face. "Then all is not lost, there may still be a chance for glory. The force that is stirring may yet be mine. But this time, I leave nothing to chance. If I have to risk the fury of the Deep Ones then so be it – the boy must die. I'll snap his neck myself." Hurrying through the graveyard, he leapt down the steps.

*　*　*

"Jen! Jen!" Ben called, hammering on the front door. "Let me in!"

"Hurry," Nelda said beside him. She pulled the neck of her gansey over her chin and shivered. The yard was almost pitch black, completely drowned by the eerie mist which, even as they waited, grew steadily thicker.

"Jen!" the boy shouted again.

The door rattled and was swiftly yanked open. "Benjamin!" cried the voice of Miss Wethers. "Where have you been? I'm at my wits' end!" The spinster's hand reached out and, catching hold of his coat, she hauled him inside.

With a lurch, Ben tumbled into the cottage and Nelda nipped in behind – just as the postmistress slammed the door again. Miss Wethers fell to her knees where she proceeded to block up the gaps with a draught-excluder and a heap of cushions and pillows.

"We've got to keep it out," she squeaked, "whatever it is! Goodness me, Benjamin, have you been wandering in these fumes all this time? What have you done to your lungs, child? As soon as this filth blows over we must rush you to the hospital." She stuffed the last of the pillows in place and flapped to her feet, eyeing the barricade doubtfully.

"I've been going out of my mind with worry," she scolded him. "You should have come back as soon as the tanker exploded."

"What tanker?" Ben asked.

Miss Wethers fluttered her hands in consternation and her voice rose hysterically. "Well something exploded!" she declared, seeking a rational explanation for the chaos that had engulfed the town. "The whole house shook – I suppose this nasty smoke is the oil burning. Oh dear, it must be a gargantuan spillage, and there'll be all those poor birds clogged with oil."

"It isn't anything like that!" the boy tried to tell her. "This is Nathaniel's doing! He's destroyed two of the ..."

But the postmistress was not listening to him. "Come into the parlour, Benjamin," she said. "The windows are all intact there, thank heavens – you should see the kitchen and the front room! We must

286

wait until the fire brigade come to rescue us, I've heard the sirens. Oh if only we were at my house – there's a gas mask in one of Mother's cupboards."

She fluttered into the parlour and Ben threw Nelda an exasperated glance. "We must not tarry here," she told him, "the guardian must be taken to a place of safety."

He nodded grimly and ran after Miss Wethers.

In the parlour the curtains had been drawn and several candles burned brightly. On the armchair sat Jennet; the girl's face was sullen and she looked up briefly when her brother entered.

"I heard what you said," she muttered coldly. "Haven't you stopped playing your childish games yet? Leave Nathaniel alone – he's out there too."

"Oh Jennet," tutted Edith distractedly, "do stop thinking on it. Really, Ben, your sister's done nothing but talk about that Mr Crozier – she even wanted to go out and find him but I wouldn't let her."

"Good," Ben cried, "he's evil, Miss Wethers."

Edith lit another candle and bemoaned the lack of electricity. "Cut off when the tanker exploded," she told herself for the umpteenth time, "although I can't see how. I wonder if we should drink lots of milk – would it line our stomachs and protect us from the noxious stuff? Maybe we should sit under the stairs ..."

"Why won't she listen?" Ben hissed to Nelda.

"Because she's frightened," the aufwader replied. "Deep down she knows there is more to this than she pretends, but she cannot face the horror. Perhaps if they could see me I could make them understand."

"Jennet," Ben said, "Nelda's here, the tribe's been driven from the caves and most of the tunnels have collapsed."

"Benjamin!" squeaked Miss Wethers in alarm as she taped the edges of the curtains to the wall just to make certain the room was securely sealed. "What are you talking about?"

"The fisherfolk!" he told her, running out of patience and wanting to scream in frustration. "They live under the cliffs – or they used to, but I'm the only one who can see them. There's one here now."

Edith stared at him, "Oh dear," she whined, "it's the pollution, it's affected his brain. Lie on the couch and be a good boy – the authorities will be coming soon, I'm sure they will." But the wailing engines were in the far distance and she gripped the chair arm distractedly.

"We waste our time," Nelda said. "We must leave this place – show her the guardian, she will have to believe you then."

"Look!" Ben cried desperately, taking the carving from his pocket. "This is the last protector of Whitby, made by one of the fisherfolk thousands of years ago."

Edith gazed at the jet serpent and fiddled with her collar uncomfortably. Even Jennet leaned forward and she gave her brother a curious glance.

"My," muttered Miss Wethers fearfully, "wherever did you find such a gruesome object?"

"I didn't," he told her, looking across at Jennet. "Nelda did."

Edith covered her eyes, confused and bewildered by his insane ramblings.

"Crozier wants it," Ben continued. "He's already destroyed the other two. That's why all this is happening, don't you see? Something is waking and it's all that man's fault – it'll destroy everything if it gets free. Crozier is totally insane!"

That was too much for Jennet. She let out an outraged howl and pounced at her brother, knocking the guardian from his hand and shoving him to the floor.

"How dare you!" she screeched, her face contorting into a ghastly mask. "Shut your stupid mouth! Nathaniel wouldn't hurt a fly – he's mine – I love him – he loves me!"

"JENNET!" shouted Miss Wethers in horror. "What are you saying? Leave Benjamin alone at once. Just listen to you, child, what has that man been telling you?"

The girl tossed her head and laughed. "You're only jealous," she barked, "jealous because he loves me and not a wrinkled old prune like you! Did you honestly think he would fancy a dried-up spinster who spends her days licking stamps and sorting postcards? Why should he even look at you when nobody else ever did?"

Ben recoiled from his sister; that was not her voice speaking – it was more like Rowena Cooper's, even her face had changed and her mouth was drawn wide and ugly.

Miss Wethers strode forward to give the girl a sharp slap, but her hand quivered impotently and she ran sobbing to her chair. "How could you?" she wept. "How could you say such foul and hurtful things?"

Nelda stared at Jennet with understanding and took a deep breath. "She cannot help it," she told Ben gravely. "Your sister is consumed by a powerful enchantment. The Crozier man controls her now – she is his creature."

"No," the boy whimpered, "she can't be."

Nelda hurried to the door. "Now we must truly leave," she urged, "this place is not safe for your sister will betray us to him. She has no will of her own."

Ben squirmed away from Jennet, then seized hold of the jet carving and hurried from the parlour.

"Benjamin!" Edith called. "Where are you going? Come back."

Jennet snarled and leapt after him, dragging the boy back by the hair.

"Oh no, little brother!" she yelled. "You're not going anywhere with that. If my Nathaniel wants your piece of junk then I'll see he gets it."

"Jen!" he shrieked as the girl pushed him into the wall and snatched the guardian from his grasp.

At this, Nelda let out an angry shout and flew at her. With a surprised wail, Jennet felt an invisible fist punch her stomach and she doubled over – winded and shocked.

Miss Wethers screamed in fright when the jet serpent seemed to fly from the girl's hands of its own accord as the aufwader wrenched it away.

"EEEKK!" she squawked. "The girl's possessed! Benjamin, run for the vicar!"

The boy was more frightened for his sister's safety than anything else. "Are you hurt, Jen?' he asked.

The girl only growled at him.

"We must go!" Nelda pleaded. "We must …"

Her voice faltered as her keen ears heard something. Then they all heard it. Outside, ringing over the concrete of the yard, came the sound of quick footsteps.

"We're too late," breathed Nelda.

"It's him!" Ben cried. "He's come for the final guardian – he'll destroy everything!"

The postmistress gave a small, terrified whimper and rose from her chair.

Only Jennet was pleased; she laughed and fires danced brightly in her eyes. Running into the hall, she rushed at the front door and started to drag away the pillows and cushions.

"No!" Ben yelled, as he and Nelda darted after her. "You mustn't let him in! He'll kill us all!"

"Nathaniel!" Jennet called excitedly as she fought with the latch. "Nathaniel, they won't let me come to you. I'm in here!''

"Miss Wethers!" Ben shouted. "We can't hold her."

Dithering in the parlour, Edith threw up her hands and scurried to help them.

"Let me go!" the girl screamed. "I must see him, I must hold him!"

"No, Jen!" her brother bawled. "He's bad! Come away from the door. Miss Wethers – do something!"

Edith grabbed the girl's waist and together the three of them dragged Jennet out of the hall.

"You'll be sorry!" she snapped. "He'll hurt you for this!"

Nelda picked up a cushion and threw it at the girl's head. "Tell her to pipe down," she said to Ben. "Sshh! The footsteps have stopped – he's right outside."

"Is the door locked?" Ben whispered to Miss Wethers.

The postmistress nodded hurriedly.

"That signifies nothing," Nelda told him, searching the room for a weapon. "Once a man of power has been invited over a threshold there is no lock that can bar his entry, the way is always open thereafter. Crozier will come – he will reach us."

"Then what can we do?" Ben cried. "We're done for!"

"Close that door," Nelda instructed, picking up a china vase and testing the weight of it. "We must attack as soon as he enters."

Ben did as she said, and from the hallway, they heard the latch rattling.

"He's trying to get in," breathed Miss Wethers in terror.

The lock clicked and the footsteps strode into the hall.

"Nathaniel," mouthed Jennet feverishly, her eyes

blazing and her teeth glinting long and sharp in the candle-light.

The others huddled into the corner of the room; Nathaniel Crozier, high priest of the Black Sceptre, whose very name was a curse and whose own hands had butchered many, had come for them.

Nelda raised the vase above her head and Ben gripped the last guardian to his chest. Miss Wethers crammed her mouth with tissue and the parlour door swung open.

Edith screamed as a black shadow flew into the room and Nelda flung the vase with all her strength. It hit the wall by the door and shattered with a great crash. Quickly the aufwader reached for something else to throw but was stopped by a commanding voice which cut through the air like a razor.

"What on earth have we here?" it demanded.

The anxious face of Alice Boston peered round the door in bemused astonishment and she gave the shattered vase a quizzical look. "I was rather fond of that," she clucked, then the old lady grinned at them all. "I don't suppose there's any tea in the pot?" she asked.

The others gazed at her dumbfounded, then they relaxed and rushed over, wrapping their arms tightly about her plump body.

"Goodness!" she woefully exclaimed. "I leave Whitby for a few days and all hell breaks loose. The town is in uproar, what with buildings on fire, people running about like headless chickens and this horrid, clammy fog." She squinted down at Nelda who, to her eyes, was slightly blurred. "You needn't tell me who's behind it all either," she added, "that I already know."

Only Jennet had hung back from the heartfelt greetings. It was Nathaniel she wanted – nothing and nobody else was important to her now. Where was he

– why had he not come? Brushing past the others, she ran to the hall and rushed into the billowing mist.

"Where are you?" she called.

"Jennet?" Miss Boston's voice came to her.

The girl whirled round and saw Aunt Alice staring at her curiously. "What have you done with him, you old witch?" she screamed.

Miss Boston flinched as though she had been hit. "Come in out of the cold, dear," she managed to say. "You're upset. Come back inside, there are those who love you more in here."

But the girl turned to flee and the old lady hurried down the step after her. Raising her hand, she made a curious sign in the air. "Jennet!" she shouted. "Stop! In the name of all that is holy, listen to me!"

"No," Jennet whined, but she wavered as her mind cleared a little and her legs buckled beneath her. Then the girl fell senseless to the ground.

"Benjamin!" Miss Boston called. "Nelda! Come and help me! Oh, I hope it isn't too late. Please Lord, don't let her be lost to him."

Presently Jennet was lying on the sofa and the old lady tutted in annoyance.

"I should have foreseen this," she reprimanded herself.

"Will Jen be okay?" Ben asked. "What did you do?"

"Merely called for help," replied Aunt Alice mysteriously. "Don't worry, she's just fainted. If only I had come back sooner. Still I should be thankful I'm here at all. Praise be for drunken butlers is all I can say." The others stared at her, not understanding a word and the old lady shook herself. The dreadful memory of Judith Deacon's body lying broken on the marble floor and surrounded by the fragments of a port bottle reared before her again.

Standing by the door, Nelda was impatient to

leave. "The guardian must be taken from here," she insisted. "Crozier may still come."

Miss Boston stroked Jennet's hair, then turned to the aufwader and held out her hand. "May I see it?" she asked.

The aufwader showed her the jet serpent and the old lady studied it with a scowl. "I cannot allow this to continue!" she stormed, her fierce spirit raging within her. "This appalling man must be stopped – it's time I confronted him!"

"But you can't!" Ben protested. "He's too powerful!"

"Have faith," she told him, tucking the guardian into her blouse. "He must have some weakness or he wouldn't have sent me all the way to London. Besides, I have one or two little surprises left. I'm not totally defenceless."

Suddenly the entire cliff shuddered and in the yard outside a chimney stack came crashing down.

"Morgawrus," Nelda murmured. "He wakes."

Miss Boston swept a tweed cloak about her shoulders. "The time has come," she declared. "Edith, you stay with Jennet. Ben and Nelda, come with me." And the three of them hurried from the cottage.

"Take care, Alice," Miss Wethers called as they disappeared into the mist. The postmistress wiped her forehead then buried her face in her hands, failing to notice that Jennet was beginning to stir. A hellish light welled up behind the girl's eyelids and they snapped open – glaring at the oblivious Edith.

* * *

Tarr gazed about him. It had been a difficult task rounding up those who had fled from the fish demon, and they had barely escaped with their lives.

Now he stood awkwardly on the sand, missing his staff, and surveying the grim scene before him.

Whitby was completely covered by dense layers of mist that muffled the frantic clamour of shrill alarms. Occasionally, through a break in the smothering screen, tongues of flame shone out and the buildings that burned blazed furiously. The townsfolk were crowding the streets, trying to escape the black fog by hurrying as far inland as they could. Only the church and the abbey remained unsullied by the creeping dark and they reared over the town like proud beacons surrounded by a sea of night.

"'Tis finished," he muttered. "Everything is ended."

"Shrimp," cried Old Parry waddling up to him. "Look there, your granddaughter approaches, and with two of the landfolk – has she no shame?"

Tarr ignored her. Obviously she wasn't going to let the fact that he had rescued her change her cantankerous ways.

Over the sands charged Miss Boston, her cloak flapping and flying. At her side were Ben and Nelda and the young aufwader ran ahead to hug her grandfather.

"Oh, lass," Tarr cried in delight, swinging her round and holding her tightly. "Ah feared ah wouldna' sithee again."

"Mr Shrimp!" Aunt Alice cried sombrely. "Take your people away from here, lead them into the town – the shore is too dangerous."

Tarr gaped at her. "They'll not set foot in yon stinkin' place," he said flatly. "If'n we're to die we mun do it here, where we have allus lived."

"Then they are sure to perish," Miss Boston rapped back. "Look!"

She pointed out to sea and there, on the outermost spur of the East Pier, stood a solitary figure.

Nathaniel Crozier was silhouetted against the dismal horizon and his arms were raised in exultation as the water bubbled and thrashed wildly.

"A storm is coming," warned the old lady, "the worst there has ever been."

"Deeps take me!" muttered Tarr, realizing what was about to happen. Calling to the rest of the tribe, he cried, "Follow me, we mun clear out from here and seek shelter in the town of the landfolk."

There was surprisingly little resistance from the others. The tribe now looked to him for guidance and even Lorkon, the only surviving member of the Triad, accepted his decision without rancour. Only Old Parry objected, but they were all too weary and afraid to listen to her. Tarr was their leader now and he started shepherding them along the shore towards the town.

"And you go with them, Benjamin," Aunt Alice told him.

"No," the boy cried, "I won't leave you – you don't know what Crozier's capable of."

"On the contrary," she said bitterly, "I am only too well aware of his deceit and cunning. Now, please, do as I ask."

Nelda took hold of Ben's hand. "Come," she said, "your aunt is right. We have done our part."

The old lady smiled at her gratefully. "You see," she murmured, "it's up to me now – this is my battle, not yours. From here I go on alone."

Ben gazed at her anxiously. "But ... but," he spluttered.

Miss Boston bent down and kissed him. "Goodbye, Benjamin," she said. "Take him away from here, Nelda dear."

"I shall," the aufwader replied. "Farewell."

Aunt Alice pulled the brim of her hat over her eyes and the tweed cloak swirled madly about her as she marched towards the stone pier and ascended the steps.

"She has great courage," commented Nelda, "I could not face what she must. Hurry, we have to catch up with the others. The tide is already racing in." And she pulled him gently towards the town.

Ben twisted round and saw for the last time the old lady's indomitable figure as it hurried along the pier. Then the mist closed and he saw no more.

*　*　*

The sea was angry now and violent waves crashed against the square stones of the pier, lashing the full might of its rage upon them in a frenzy of destruction.

Through battering walls of stinging spray, Miss Boston struggled. The brutal strength of the breaking waves almost knocked her off her feet, but she steadied herself and pressed on.

The salt rain hammered down and the old lady shielded her eyes from its merciless onslaught. Not far now; she could see the small lighthouse at the end of the pier and before it – Nathaniel.

The warlock crowed triumphantly, leaning into the growing storm, revelling in its savagery and defying it with his laughter. The waves smashed into his legs, but his fists were locked about the railing and though the sea plucked and tore at him he resisted and clung on tenaciously.

Turning his head, his dark gaze fell upon Miss Boston as she tottered towards him and he hooted. "The end has come!" he cried. "Even though one guardian still remains, the enchanted sleep is over. No need to murder that detestable child after all."

Aunt Alice grasped the rail as the sea burst over the side. "You revolting creature!" she shouted, her mouth filling with brine. "You killed Patricia."

"Don't forget that old fool Roper," he interrupted with a vile chuckle.

"Ernest?" she cried. "Him too?"

But the warlock had turned back to the sea, where the water had turned a disgusting, inky green.

"Spare me your tiresome grief," he snapped, "there's nothing you can do now, old hag. You're too late, it's too late for everyone. Only *I* understood, only *I* realized what my stupid and greedy wife failed to comprehend."

"Aren't you a trifle too sure of yourself?" Miss Boston scorned, raising her voice to be heard against the roaring waters.

Nathaniel grinned. "No one knew except me," he bragged. "Who would have guessed it? Not a dabbling amateur like you, you with your precious tea parties, wart curing and furtive seances." He stretched out his hand and in an arrogant sweep of his arm, encompassed the darkness that was Whitby. "The whole town," he grandly announced, "was founded and built on the back of Morgawrus, a serpent so huge that it can swallow the contents of the entire harbour in one vast gulp. The enemy of all living things it was called in the beginning of days and the coast was laid waste for miles around, choked by its poison and blackened with its fires."

"And you've woken this unclean spirit!"

"How else could I dominate and control it?" he cried.

"Benjamin was right," Miss Boston declared, "you are insane!"

The warlock laughed at her. "We'll see," he exulted, "for the head of Morgawrus is already free."

Miss Boston stared at the boiling surface of the waves. "But, surely," she cried, "if it leaves the underground caverns, Whitby will be utterly destroyed!"

Nathaniel did not answer, for at that moment the sea exploded, mountainous spouts of water soared into the heavens and putrid brown froth erupted from the depths as a hideous shape slowly rose.

Miss Boston opened her mouth and called out in fear, but her voice was drowned by the roar of the waves and the monstrous head of Morgawrus burst from the raven deep.

The pier shivered, dwarfed by the ghastly nightmare which reared up beside it, and Aunt Alice dropped to her knees in horror.

"The enemy of all living things," Nathaniel rejoiced. "Was there ever such a diseased, malignant vision of disaster?" he screamed with joy.

Two golden eyes blasted upwards, searing the night like great furnaces and plumes of steam screeched into the sky around them. The head was massive, encrusted by barnacles and the reeking scum of millennia. It was a repulsive aberration that shamed nature and mocked the symmetry of creation. An endless torrent of stagnant water gushed from the immeasurable jaws and stained the pier black.

A deafening screech issued from three huge nostrils as Morgawrus breathed, and the row of gills that gaped below the eyes yawned wide – like a hideous range of grinning wounds.

High the fetid apparition reared, towering far into the sky, the five, tortured horns that crowned its head raking the clouds and tearing the canopy of the world.

Miss Boston balked at the stench that beat from this perilous nightmare. She was soaked to the skin and wept in bleak despair as the warlock raised his arms to begin his evil work.

"Now!" he cried. "While the drowse still lies heavy on it – I seize my chance!" He clenched his teeth and summoned the dark forces at his command. "Aid me!" he ordered. "Give me the strength to conquer and control!"

The air about his fingertips shimmered and a livid green flame flickered into existence. For a moment it crackled feebly, then snaked across his palms and swiftly grew brighter. Down the warlock's outstretched arms the energy twisted, entwining him in a glowing spiral of magical force.

High above, the vast head opened its ravening maw and a hollow cry bellowed from the dark throat. The noise rent the heavens, buildings toppled and huge chunks of the cliffs crumbled into the sea.

Minuscule in the serpent's shadow, tears streamed from Nathaniel's eyes as he quaked under the strain of his exertions. The power which channelled through him was treacherous, almost impossible to control and he shrieked in agony as the pressures intensified.

"Concentrate," he howled. "Hold on until the forces reach their peak."

The flames that weaved about him were dazzling now, flashing and sparking with jags of lightning.

Miss Boston turned from the harsh green glare and frantically babbled words of protection and challenge under her breath. She had been wrong to come – just being near the serpent filled her with uncontrollable despair and Nathaniel's powers were far beyond anything she had ever encountered.

"Now!" yelled Nathaniel and he threw back his hands. At once, the spitting flames leapt from his fingers and bolted upwards. The jagged stream of energy burst through the air, striking the ghastly head, which roared more fiercely than before. This time the pier rocked and the stones cracked, the railings buckled and the wooden extension broke away, collapsing thunderously into the sea. The breath of Morgawrus howled like a gale and tore inland – creating a whirlwind which sucked up the sand and fell viciously upon the town.

Huddling at the bottom of the abbey steps, the remains of the aufwader tribe vainly tried to shield themselves from the deadly storm. It was as though the whole shore was screaming about them and the grit scored their faces and cut into their hands. Ben hid his face whilst Tarr grimly held on to his granddaughter as the tempest raged ferociously.

On the pier, Miss Boston let go of her hat and it was snatched from her head as she clung for dear life to the twisted rail.

The warlock's spells crackled furiously over the serpent and, though the beast tried to pull away, the dazzling flames held it securely.

"Creature of the primeval dawn," Nathaniel proclaimed, "hear me!"

The fires surged and the head shuddered, trying one last time to escape the terrible forces which gripped it. Down it plunged, sinking into the waves, churning the water and screeching in protest.

"You will be mine," the warlock commanded. "You have no will of your own – obey my words, obey me!"

The serpent froze, the enchantments scalded and blistered and Nathaniel's voice finally cut through – biting savagely into its mind.

A triumphant smile flashed across the man's face as their two wills strove with one another. The brain of the creature was vast, yet the countless years of sleep had made it sluggish and his quick mind sliced in, jabbing through the defences like a keen blade. The contest was his; he was a master of domination and, as the serpent's mind peeled away before his razor-like senses, he knew he had won.

Deep into Morgawrus the warlock delved.

Projecting the essence of his warped being out into the dark labyrinth of the monster's drowsy memory, where fleeting images of swamps and desolation pulsed and glowed. But Nathaniel was ruler there now, and he enslaved the serpent – binding it to his service.

Miss Boston watched the silent combat in disbelief – the awful man actually seemed to be succeeding. The eyes of the apparition dimmed, gradually glazing over and, in a trance-like stupor, the head swayed from side to side. In a steady, continuous stream, Nathaniel's power flowed across to the beast, quenching, conquering and controlling it.

Her white hair plastered down by slime and frightful ooze, Miss Boston finally took a grip on herself. "What's the matter with you, Alice?" she cried amid the storm. "Get up there and stop that foul man!"

Lumbering to her feet, the old lady rushed forward. "Stop!" she yelled, grabbing the man's arm and dragging him away.

Nathaniel shrieked, his concentration was broken and the mental link between him and the monster snapped momentarily, sending him reeling backwards.

"You imbecile!" he bawled. "You could have killed me!"

"This has gone on long enough!" she shouted. "You must stop!"

"Get out of my sight, you odious hag!" he cried. "Morgawrus is mine to command – and nothing on this earth will be able to stand against us."

Turning his back on her in contempt, Nathaniel looked on his terrifying slave. "All will be ours," he laughed, "now and forever more. Heave out the rest of your coils my beautiful horror. Show the world how easily you can destroy. Let the town of Whitby crumble into the bottomless pit."

"No!" screamed Miss Boston. "You mustn't." And she threw herself at him, pummelling the man with her fists and kicking him with her feet.

Nathaniel staggered under the ferocity of the old lady's attack. One of her punches caught him on the chin and another went straight into the ribs. Miss Boston was like a mad thing and he blundered against the railing in surprise. But the advantage was not hers for long. Swiftly the man recovered and he shoved her roughly away, his face black with wrath.

"Whitby can wait!" he growled. "It's you who'll die first – but it's a pleasure I'll undertake myself."

Never had Nathaniel Crozier been so incensed; like a tiger he sprang and the old lady fell beneath him.

"No," she wailed, as her head hit the ground and his strong fingers closed about her neck. The warlock squeezed his hands together and the breath choked in her throat.

"Look your last on this world, old woman!" he snarled.

Miss Boston tried to pull his hands away but it was no use, he was far too strong. With a strangled cry, she turned her eyes from his evil face and fixed her gaze on the ruins of the abbey which rose majestically in the distance.

A darkness greater than that which had already engulfed Whitby closed about her and the old lady's hands fell limply to her sides.

"Nathaniel!" came an urgent voice. "Nathaniel!"

The warlock looked up uncertainly. Running towards them along the pier was the small figure of a girl.

Miss Wethers had proven to be a poor guard and Jennet had escaped from her without difficulty, hurrying instinctively to the shore. She knew he would be there, she could sense his delicious presence. Now he would take her away and they could be together always.

She hurtled to greet him, but her stride faltered. The head of Morgawrus loomed monstrously up out of the mist and the girl cried out. Staring at the grotesque spectacle in fear, she felt faint again and stepped back apprehensively.

But the creature still seemed to be in the grip of Crozier's influence and made no sign that it had seen her. Jennet cautiously edged into the beast's great shadow, her obsession with the man driving her through the danger.

"Nathaniel," she called, "what ... what are you doing?"

The warlock was crouching over the body of Aunt Alice, his hands tight about her throat. Jennet was bewildered. What was happening?

The warlock rose, his fingers twitching. "What do you want?" he sneered.

The girl wavered, unsure of herself. Miss Boston looked so pale, what had her beloved done? She stared incredulously at him. His face seemed cruel and less handsome than she remembered – how harsh his voice sounded, and the horrible dark eyes cut right through her.

"Will you never stop pestering me – you boring child?" he spat. "Your constant simpering grates on me. What does it take to be rid of your pathetic attentions – shall I throttle you as well?"

It was as if a veil were torn from Jennet's eyes. Finally she saw the man's true nature and she gasped at her own foolishness as the last vestiges of his control left her.

"Aunt Alice!" she screamed, rushing to the old lady's side. "You've killed her!"

Nathaniel sniggered and his fingers fidgeted for another victim. "Come here, little one," he sang, "let

me embrace you too."

"Stay away from me!" Jennet cried.

The warlock closed in on her. "Come to Nathaniel," he chuckled, "let him hold you, it won't take long – I promise."

"Keep back!" Jennet warned.

"What's this?" he murmured. "Would you deny what has been burning in your heart since the day we met?"

"Don't you touch me!" she screamed.

"How fickle is woman," Nathaniel growled, stealing closer.

The girl fell back and the warlock reached out for her.

"Don't you dare!" came a croaking voice.

Nathaniel turned and Jennet grinned with joy. "Aunt Alice," she gasped, "I thought you were dead!"

"For a minute back there so did I," muttered the old lady, gingerly touching the red marks at her throat. Then she glared angrily at Nathaniel and shook her head at him. "I suppose I should be grateful for your slipshod incompetence," she shouted, "it seems you can't do anything right – look behind you."

The warlock stared at her, what was the old bag jabbering about now? And then a doubt crossed his mind and he spun round. The eyes of the massive head were bright again, and glowed down at them as though it understood everything they said.

Nathaniel frowned, disconcerted for a moment and then his mouth fell open and his hands flew to his temples as a fearful voice boomed inside his mind.

"Tiny insects," Morgawrus spoke, the forbidding sound echoing inside each of their heads, "what paltry webs do they spin? What petty plots do they nurture in their fleeting existence?"

The warlock threw his arms open. "Remember," he roared, "you are mine to command! My will is yours!"

Terrible laughter cut deeply into the three small figures on the pier as the serpent reared up. "Too long have I been tethered in sleep," it shrieked. "Thou mayst have wakened me, little man, but thou canst not make me thy thrall. I shall not trade one set of bonds for another."

"I demand it!" the warlock cried, running to the buckled railing and pointing up at the creature.

"Enough!" screamed the serpent. "Cast thy feeble sorceries elsewhere. Now are my wits restored and thy powers are as nothing compared to mine."

Nathaniel was incensed; he had dared much to come here and he was not prepared to simply stand by and let all that he had strived for slip away.

Screeching, he put forth his powers. Terrible lightning rent the sky and the surrounding waters flashed as the lethal energies discharged down into the deep. Yet every furious volley of enchantment broke against the unassailable might of the gigantic serpent and fierce green stars went spinning, out of control, into the night.

Miss Boston clung to Jennet as the warlock wrangled and strove. The air was alive with his evil magic and they pressed themselves against the floor as spectral flames screamed over their heads.

Every black art Nathaniel ever knew, every bewitching charm, every incantation and devilish wizardry to confound and subjugate, he directed at Morgawrus. But the counter-strokes were dreadful and anguish mounted in the warlock's breast as he struggled to maintain the force of his attack. Then it happened. Nathaniel flung one last, desperate enchantment at the nightmarish head and the battle was over.

"A futile display," Morgawrus mocked. "In truth is that the best thou canst do? You have lost, little man."

Thanks to the delay Miss Boston had caused, the creature had been given enough time to shake off the lingering traces of sleep. It could not be caught off guard a second time. All Crozier's glorious dreams were in ruins and his life was forfeit.

The great golden eyes blazed down at him, flowing over with menace and evil joy – now it was the serpent's turn to attack.

"Spare me!" grovelled Nathaniel shrilly as the head swooped vengefully down. "I can help you!" Consumed with panic, he screamed a spell of defence but it shattered as Morgawrus came for him. The tremendous jaws of his nemesis gaped open and a gale of putrid breath screeched all around the terrified man.

"Aaaaaarrrrggggghhhh!" howled Nathaniel as the poisonous fumes blasted into him. He tried to cover his face with his hands but his arms were rigid and he could not move his legs to run. All over his body the skin crackled and solidified – turning a dull chalky grey. Throwing back his head, he screamed once more, but the cry dwindled to nothing and his mouth was frozen wide, his face locked in an expression of absolute terror.

The hideous sight of Morgawrus towered over him, its vast bulk filling his eyes – before they too calcified. Wracked in torturous agony that devoured his petrified soul, the warlock perished, and only a solid figure of stone now stood where he had been.

Jennet and Miss Boston could only stare in horror at what they had just witnessed, and the girl buried her face into the old lady's cloak – screaming for her dead parents.

Then the victorious serpent shook its head and, at

the sound of its laughter, the statue of Nathaniel trembled and shattered. A thousand ammonites smashed to the ground, rolling into the sea and the waves came rushing over the side to eagerly wash the rest away.

Aunt Alice tried to comfort the child at her side. "Hush dear," she cried, but the shadow fell upon her and the baleful eyes glowered down at their stricken figures. Slowly and threateningly, the disgusting head swung round to them.

"More of the human kind," the frightful voice echoed in their heads. "Hath that loathsome breed over run my realm? I shall not rest again till all traces of their infestation have been swept into the waters or scorched from the land. This place is mine – I am Lord, I shall vanquish the light and blight the things that grow in the field and ripen on the bough. Nought shall survive the despair I shall bring. A new age of death is come!"

The three nostrils trumpeted and the open maw dripped a river of deadly juices.

"Aunt Alice!" the girl yelled in terror.

Miss Boston staggered to her feet and pushed Jennet behind her.

"Return to your slumbers!" she demanded. "The world has moved on, there is no need of you any more – you are an anachronism here. Begone to the tunnels of your gaol and sleep for another thousand centuries till man's time is over and you can roam the oceans free of hindrance."

The terrible gale blasted from the serpent's mouth once more and Miss Boston boldly leaned into it, not a trace of fear betraying her stern countenance.

Jennet cried out as the dark forces screeched around them, and she trembled, waiting for her flesh to petrify as Nathaniel's had done.

"I defy you, Morgawrus," Aunt Alice proclaimed,

"leave now before you anger me." She folded her arms and her hair streamed wildly in the ferocious tempest.

Her insolence enraged the terrible creature. "Thou art lice!" it roared. "And I shall crush thee!"

The eyes blazed with searing heat and a stream of white hot flame shot from the narrow slits – streaking towards the frail woman below.

Miss Boston reached anxiously for Jennet's hand and held it tight as the deadly fire rained down. A cloud of black smoke and ashes exploded where she stood and the huge head of the monster descended through the choking fumes as they slowly cleared.

There, amid a smoking ring of cinders and charred stone, Miss Boston cautiously opened one eye and sighed in relief – both she and Jennet were unharmed.

"How can this be?" Morgawrus bellowed in fury and the waves crashed about its long, scaly neck. But Aunt Alice continued to stand her ground. Though battered with stinking spray, she glared at the abomination above and would not be daunted.

"Return," she said again, "or must I compel you?"

Morgawrus reared back and his horns rammed into the pier, gouging into the stone as if it were soft clay. "What protection hast thou to resist and withstand my power!" he demanded. "What guards thee against the might of mine wrath?"

"Enough to keep me safe and force you back under the cliffs," she retorted, "that which Irl began long ago but which he never completed!"

With her left hand, she clutched at her breast and raised the other high into the air. "Prepare yourself, oh misbegotten creature of the dismal dark," she solemnly announced. "You have had your taste of freedom but the chains are forging anew and you must sleep once more."

The serpent opened its massive jaws and the dark void of its cavernous mouth sailed down to swallow her.

Miss Boston took from her blouse the last guardian. It was warm to the touch, having absorbed all the lethal forces that Morgawrus had hurled at them. As the jaws approached, she called beseechingly into the night and held the guardian out before her.

"Hear me, oh Lords of the Deep and Dark," she cried, "renew the strength of the enchantment you laid upon the enemy many ages ago. I plead to you, goddess of the moon, Great Mother of us all – instill this device with your strength."

The cruel pinnacles of Morgawrus's fangs came ravaging for her. Scraping across the pier to where she stood, and Miss Boston called out for the last time.

"Lord God in heaven," she prayed, "defend us from this foulness and deliver us from the fear of it ever after!"

Jennet screamed. A black tongue, like a colossal slug, slithered over the stone, which hissed and dissolved beneath its glistening bulk.

Miss Boston lifted the carving above her head. "All three powers work as one at last," she shouted. "Separate no longer!"

A deep rumble resounded through the night. On the horizon, beneath the line of the sea a golden radiance welled, through a tear in the clouds the disc of the moon shone and, upon the cliff, the abbey gleamed white and cold.

In her hands, the eyelids of the jet carving sprang open and a brilliant light shone from the crystals behind them. High into the shadow of Morgawrus the waxing power flew and the head recoiled before it.

"No!" the serpent screamed. "The light – it blinds."

Miss Boston's arms trembled. The forces that were pouring from the carving were staggering and she felt them jolt through her body as they were unleashed upon the fearful enemy.

"I warned you!" she cried, wincing as the guardian grew hot in her grasp. "The powers of this world and beyond are united in this device now – as they should have been from the beginning. So long as the earth lasts, so shall you, but in a deathless sleep from which there is no waking."

The glittering light raged about the monster's head and it screeched deafeningly. A terrible fatigue set into the sinews of its coils, creeping slowly through its veins, numbing the nerves and turning the black blood to ice. Shaking its horns, the serpent fought to dispel the numbness which ate into its putrid flesh, but the manacles of sleep tightened all the more.

"Return to the stinking pits beneath the cliffs!" Miss Boston commanded in a quaking voice.

From the churning waves, a host of white sparks shot into the air and Morgawrus shrieked as titanic forces began to drag it under.

"Let the guardian of Irl finally undertake its true work," the old lady shouted.

"I shall escape," the serpent cried. "Enchantments fail, the guardian may be broken."

Aunt Alice sobbed as the carving burned into her palms. "Into oblivion I consign you!" she called. "Into the long dark of eter ... eternity!"

Down sank the huge neck, drawn back into the dank caves from which it had escaped. The sea crashed over the battered pier with horrendous violence and Jennet clung desperately to the old lady as the world seemed to tip and tidal waves pounded them out of existence.

A malignant and ghastly glare shone from the serpent's eyes, but it was no match for the light which blazed from the guardian. The narrow slits roved desperately round – all hope was destroyed and the glowing eyes were extinguished.

The water churned tempestuously as the repulsive head fell. Down into the mad sea it descended, a vast wave crashed against the head and drowned the beast's howling cries.

Miss Boston shook uncontrollably as the great dark eyes slid beneath the sea. Still the guardian poured out its banishing rays, reaching into the murky deeps, lighting up the sea for miles around. Under the cliffs Morgawrus was compelled to return and the earth rumbled as the immense head pushed back through the caverns of its ancient prison.

"Trouble the ... trouble the world ... no ... no more," the old lady commanded. 'Be for ... forever at its roots, till the ... the end of ti ... time.'

Smoke streamed from her hands as the guardian scorched her skin – no longer was it a carving of jet, but a divine thing of purity and might that shone with the combined force of the sun, the moon and the stars.

Jennet shielded her eyes from the cone of light around her. She could feel Aunt Alice shuddering under the strain of the guardian's immense power and the old lady whimpered piteously.

The girl pulled at Miss Boston's cloak. "Make it stop," she cried, "the creature's gone!"

But the old lady couldn't; the carving continued to shine and the splendour of its glory was destroying her. A dazzling halo engulfed Aunt Alice's trembling form and, squinting through the glare, Jennet beheld Miss Boston's face.

The wrinkled skin was shrivelling, withering before the almighty light like a moth in a flame. The girl wept in horror and tore at the old lady's arms.

"Let it go!" she screamed. "It's killing you!"

Aunt Alice was too weak to answer, her strength was failing and the relentless brilliance drained the life from her body.

Jennet looked around helplessly, then leaped up and snatched the guardian from the old lady's grasp. Miss Boston wailed and fell back – her palms smoking hideously.

The carving fell to the ground, where it continued to throb and blaze and Jennet threw herself to the old lady's side. "Aunt Alice!" she sobbed. "Aunt Alice!"

Miss Boston feebly moved her head. One side of her face seemed stiff and lifeless and the whole of her left side was drawn awkwardly into her body. A great tear rolled down her shrivelled cheek as she struggled to speak. "Jennet," she uttered thickly, "is … is it over?"

The girl tenderly raised the white woolly head and rested it on her lap. "Yes," she replied, her own tears splashing on the old lady's face, "it's all over now."

A faint smile flickered about Miss Boston's mouth. "Be … be a good gir … girl dear," she murmured, "take care of … of Benjamin …" And her eyes slowly closed.

"No!" howled Jennet. "Please, don't leave us – *please.*"

A pale glimmer rose about them; the unnatural night was lifting and the day stole over the town once more. But the sun was bleak comfort to the figures on the wrecked pier. As the daystar sparkled over the waves, the light of Irl's guardian dimmed and the eyelids closed over the crystals. The work was done and the device became jet once more. The invocations that Irl had never been able to utter had finally been completed by Miss Boston and now she too drifted close to the dark shores of death. The danger was over but she had paid dearly for the safety of all.

As the soft daylight spread over Whitby, three small shapes ran along the pier. Ben, Nelda and Tarr hurried to reach the two figures at the far end.

When he saw what had happened, the old aufwader halted and took hold of his granddaughter. "Nay, lass," he muttered, "leave tha friend be, let him alone wi' his kin."

Jennet cradled the old lady in her arms as the peaceful afternoon began afresh. There was much work to do in the town, many buildings had been devastated and the roads were in chaos. But for Alice Boston her labours were over.

"Jen!" the boy cried. "What happened? What's wrong with Aunt Alice?"

His sister lifted her raw eyes to him and he felt a cold pain close round his heart. "I think she's dying," the girl wept.

On a cold, January morning, an ambulance trundled over the repaired cobbles of the East Cliff and drew up at the end of Church Street.

"'Ere we go!" called the driver, jumping from the cab and opening the rear doors.

Inside another man helped him with the patient and together they lifted her down.

A tragic change had altered Miss Boston. A severe stroke the doctors had called it, yet it was more than that. To save the world from Morgawrus she had sacrificed herself – but fate had decreed that she should not die. Instead the old lady was a pale reflection of who she had been. Her ninety-two years had descended heavily upon her: arthritis crippled her hands and her legs were brittle stalks. Although the doctors assured her that she would regain her voice given time, at present she could only mumble unintelligibly.

Muffled and swathed like a babe, they wheeled her through the alleyway and into the yard beyond.

All her friends were there to welcome her home. Standing by the door of the cottage were Jennet and Ben and they rushed to greet the old lady, putting Eurydice on her lap, and behind the children scurried Edith. Even Mrs Gregson and her husband were there to see their neighbour return, and Norman stepped forward, giving her a bunch of snowdrops, which he pressed into her useless fingers.

"It's lovely to see you back again," whispered Jennet into Aunt Alice's ear.

The ambulance men hauled the wheelchair over the steps and pushed Miss Boston into the parlour. The old lady gazed around at the altered room. Her

316

bed had been brought downstairs and was now next to the window. The men muttered a few hushed words to Miss Wethers then smiled kindly at her and left.

Edith had retired from the post office at Christmas and was now living permanently at the cottage. "Well, Alice," she said, "What do you think? We've all worked so hard getting it ready for you. Mr Gregson helped us bring the bed down – I can't get over how he and his wife have changed. They're really rather pleasant nowadays. She even helped me sew these new curtains so they'd be ready in time."

She placed her hands in front of her and bent down, talking slowly and deliberately to be sure the invalid understood. "Now," she chirped, "how about a cup of warm milk – do you think you could manage that?"

The figure in the wheelchair glared truculently at the well-meaning but patronizing ditherer, then gave the slightest of nods. Miss Wethers clapped her hands together in delight and fluttered into the kitchen.

Alone with the children, Miss Boston looked at them with happiness in her eyes. After months in hospital it was marvellous to be home.

"Mmmm," she mumbled, struggling to speak to them, but her voice was trapped inside her paralysed body and her heart bled in despair.

Ben took the snowdrops from her hand and kissed it gently. "Don't worry," he told her, "it'll be fine. Me and Jen won't let Miss Wethers treat you like a baby." Giving her a warm grin he then added, "And tonight, I've got a surprise for you."

* * *

The last of the fireworks shot into the sky, bursting with flowers of red and orange fire.

On Tate Hill Pier, the small group who had been watching applauded; it had been a splendid display.

"Lovely," twittered Miss Wethers, "but I still think you should have lit them, Jennet."

The girl gazed down at her brother on the shore. "No," she replied, "they were Ben's way of celebrating Aunt Alice's return, and I think they had a special, private meaning for him as well."

On the sands, Ben stared into the dark heavens. "Goodbye, Mr Roper," he said, "and thank you."

"Well it's high time we got back indoors," Edith clucked, "you must be frozen, Alice. Perhaps two hot water bottles weren't enough. I'll have Doctor Adams complaining if you catch a chill." Taking hold of the wheelchair's handles, she turned it and pushed homewards.

Miss Boston gazed a moment longer at the boy on the shore, aching to thank him.

"Ben!" Jennet called. "We're going in now."

"Coming," he answered, running over the beach to join her.

Leaving the dark shore behind, they followed the two old ladies back to the cottage where the fire crackled cosily in the grate and Miss Wethers made hot chocolate for them all.

The cold sea lapped silently over the sand, the night was filled with shadow, and from a dark well of gloom, stepped a small figure.

Nelda stared after the children until they disappeared into the narrow streets. She had been watching them for some time, the flashes of the fireworks dancing in her large grey eyes. She had desperately wanted to talk with Ben but something had prevented her calling to him.

The surviving fisherfolk had moved back into the few dismal caves that had not been destroyed and now they lived a hard life, in cramped and wretched conditions. The great stone doors had, after many attempts, been lifted back into place – but without the opening mechanism they remained firmly shut and the tribe found other ways to enter their tiny realm. The guardian of Irl was entrusted to Nelda's grandfather and he had been elected as the new leader of them all, dispensing with the old ways of the Triad.

Now Nelda stared at the icy stars that glinted over the sea. The time was coming when she must tell; she could not keep her terrible secret, she needed to confide in somebody.

Rubbing tears from her eyes, the aufwader wandered sorrowfully along the shore. The curse of the Deep Ones would now claim her, as surely as it had her mother. Gazing into the black distance, Nelda wept, her doom was certain, for inside the young aufwader – a child was growing.

ROBIN JARVIS

Look out for more exciting titles by
Robin Jarvis:

THE DEPTFORD MICE SERIES
The Dark Portal
The Crystal Prison
The Final Reckoning

THE DEPTFORD HISTORIES
The Alchymist's Cat
The Oaken Throne

THE WHITBY SERIES
The Whitby Witches
A Warlock in Whitby
The Whitby Child
 (*available in October 1994*)

All these titles can be bought from your
local bookseller, or can be ordered direct
from the publishers. For more information
about Robin Jarvis books, write to *The Sales
Department, Campus 400, Maylands Avenue,
Hemel Hempstead HP2 7EZ.*